A Place to HIDE

by

ROBERT FLESHNER

O & W PUBLISHING COMPANY, INC.

Washington, DC 20006

This book is a work of fiction. Names, characters, places and incidents either are products of the author's imagination or are used fictitiously. Any resemblance to actual events or locales or persons, living or dead, is coincidental.

Published by Orville & Wilbur Publishing
750 Seventeenth Street, NW, Suite 1000
Washington, DC 20006

Copyright © 1995 by Robert Fleshner

All rights reserved, including the right to reproduce this book or portions thereof in any form whatsoever. For information contact Orville & Wilbur Publishing, 750 Seventeenth Street, NW, Suite 1000, Washington, DC 20006

Library of Congress Catalog Card Number: 95-069287
ISBN: 0-9646496-0-8

Orville & Wilbur Publishing is a division
of O&W Publishing Company, Inc.

Cover art by Victor Pakhomkin.
Book design by Arista Advertising, Inc.

Printed in the U.S.A.

For Phyllis, Michelle and Daniel

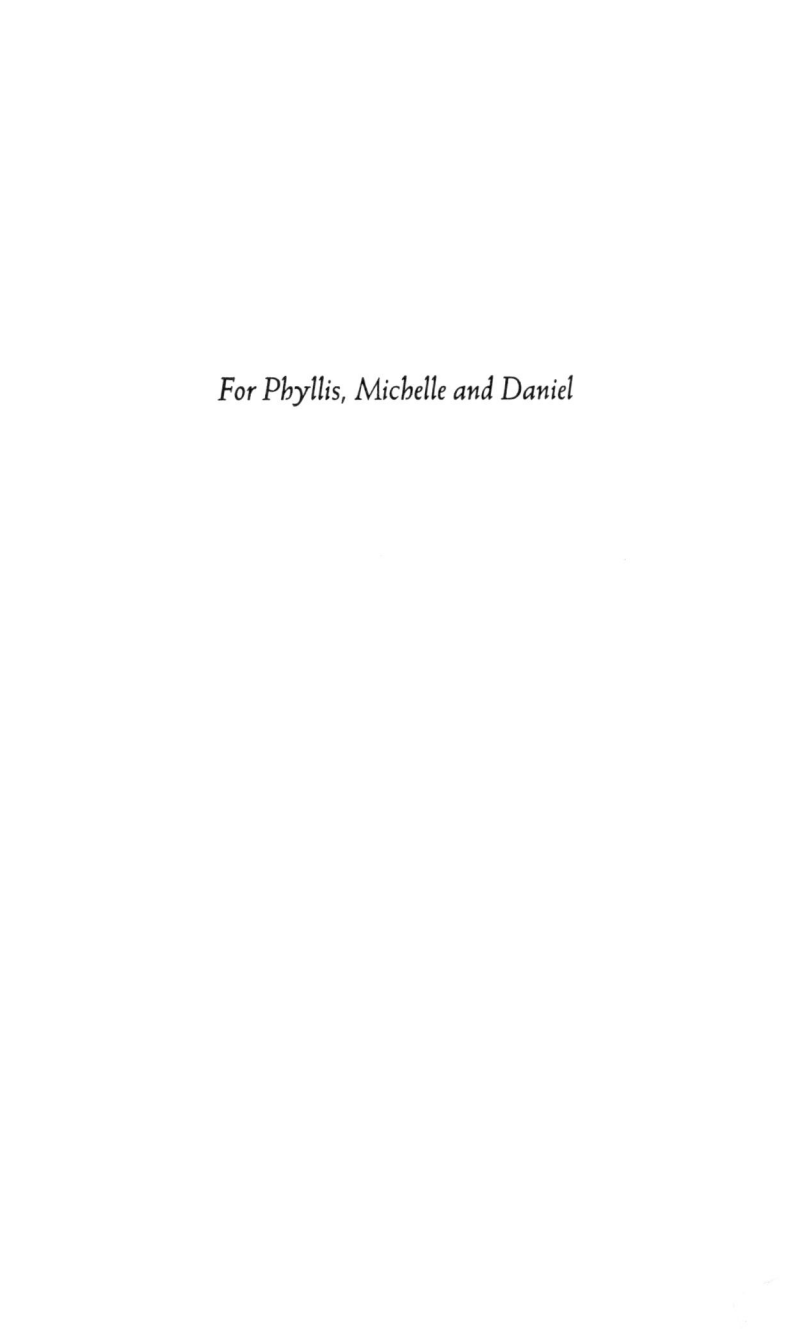

A Place to Hide was truly a group effort. Undoubtedly, I have forgotten individuals who provided assistance along the way. My failure to mention them below in no way diminishes the value of the assistance they provided.

With apologies for the lack of specificity in acknowledging those who helped, I am delighted to thank Fanny Chakedis, Stacia Cropper, David Cutler, Jeremy Dott, Don Epstein, Orin Heend, Marcy Heidish, Leslie LaPlace, John Marcus, Natasha Mokina, Neysa Narena, Gemma Nocon, Mike Olshonsky, Victor Pakhomkin, Joyce Renwick, Lynn Wehrenberg, and M.L., who, although he doesn't know it, made this book possible.

Chapter One

The first thing Donald Lubins noticed was the dust. He had been working as a roustabout for Stone's Big Top Circus for only three weeks, yet every last one of his possessions was coated with a light brown silt that somehow made him feel cheap and dirty.

Lubins actually didn't mind the dust, and the people at The Big Show seemed okay. After all, they had given him another chance when virtually everyone else was unwilling to be so forgiving. But he wasn't used to the lifestyle. He shared a ten-by-twelve-foot room on the last traveling circus train with two other guys. One guy had been with the show for five weeks, the other guy for twenty-five years.

Being the least senior of the three, Lubins was given the least desirable accommodations. Not that there was much difference between the three beds, but Lubins had to climb over the others' belongings to get to his bed. And he had to climb back over their belongings if he needed to take a leak or a dump in the middle of the night. Plus, his bed was the lumpiest of the three. But it was a bed, and the train was heated. Things could always be worse. He had come that close to homelessness. If anything, things were looking up.

Lubins' story was different. At least he liked to think it was. He was once a successful college professor, teaching comparative literature and creative writing at a number of different institutions in the New England area. In the mid-eighties life wasn't half bad for the man who hated to be called "professor."

The teacher seemed to be leading an idyllic life, with a sweet wife and two children, and a tenure track at Dartmouth College in New Hampshire. The key word here is "seemed" for things really weren't going all that well in the Lubins' household. For reasons which were never quite clear, there was always an undercurrent of distrust running from Lubins to his wife, Julie. In fact, Julie hadn't done a damn thing to deserve her husband's constant harping, and lurking behind corners. Yet there he was always expecting something to go wrong, always suspecting.

It probably wasn't all that unexpected that in the end, Lubins was the one who broke the trust. He got sexually greedy, and decided to taste the nectar of a particularly precocious nineteen-year-old student. Then, when he gave the clearly inferior little sweetheart an "A" in his Comparative Lit. course, it caused a minor uproar among the close-knit college community. The administration became privy to all of the sordid little details of Lubins' tryst, and it wasn't long before Julie wised-up as well.

In one black month, Julie left and took the kids, and Donald Lubins was denied tenure. His little sweetie went home for the summer, then transferred to an obscure Midwestern college the following year, never to be heard from again.

For Lubins, it seemed like a fitting end to what once had been a promising career, a promising marriage, and a promising life. Always the smartest child of Richard and Rita Lubins, Donald had lived a fairy-tale childhood for seventeen years, until one day it all went "poof."

God, he remembered it like it was yesterday. Sitting in Mrs. Graff's history class, junior year in high school.

"Excuse me, Mrs. Graff." It was Jenny, the pert little blonde girl with the enormous boobs, who worked in the office at Glenwood High. "Principal Thorndyke would like to see Donald Lubins."

"Me?" Donald had replied pointing to himself.

"Yes," Jenny had said shyly, shrugging her shoulders, her oversized breasts being pulled up for the ride, and causing her to self-consciously cross her arms in front of her.

Donald got up and walked out of the room, and began heading down the hall with Jenny.

"What does the Dyker want?"

"I don't know. There's some lady in his office."

Her name turned out to be Mrs. Lynn. She asked Donald to have a seat in that obsequious way that seems to take a lifetime of training. Donald sat, and gave Mrs. Lynn a quizzical look.

"Donald, your birth mother has asked to see you. I'm not sure how she tracked you down, but she's here in town."

"My what?"

"Your birth mother. The woman who gave birth to you. You do know you were adopted?"

Mrs. Lynn rambled on, but Donald didn't hear a word out of the prissy old woman's mouth. He just stared at the floor, terrified that he would explode into tears if he so much as glanced up, or that he might do or say something awful if he opened his mouth.

Birth mother. Adopted. Now, it all began to make sense. His hair, which was so much darker than his brothers'. His innate intelligence, which neither of them shared. His total lack of grace on the ball field which was in complete contrast to both Ian and Scott. Not to mention the fact that he was almost a head shorter than each of them.

Memories of the confrontation with his family still pained Lubins. The yelling. Ian and Scott cowering under Lubins' unending glare and constant disapproval for days, weeks.

Looking back on it, yeah, he probably had overreacted. But everything seems that way. Passion fades with time.

Eventually, Lubins buried it, repressed the fact in some back alley of his mind, and resumed a cordial, though thoroughly ungratifying relationship with his family.

One thing, one big piece of baggage he took with him was the inability to trust. Anyone.

College wasn't what it should have been, that was for sure. Hurt by his parents' deception, however well-intended, Lubins never relaxed. He never played, always fearful and overly sensitive when it came to other people's feelings.

Lubins worked through some of the hurt in the years immediately following graduate school. For a while, in fact, it seemed like he was doing well. His marriage seemed to indicate that he was flourishing, as did his unblemished professional record at Dartmouth. On the surface, his affair seemed unfortunate, but nothing about it indicated where he was headed.

Lubins had an impressive resume, and was able, for a time, to hide the fact that he had been canned by Dartmouth for philandering with a student. He was able to pick up work at some lesser-known institutions, and when he was terminated from those jobs—once because the administration learned about his past, and once due to a battle with the head of the department about some asinine policy or another—he caught on at the junior college level. Eventually though, his past, or his inability to maintain a low profile, caught up with him wherever he went.

For a time he worked at a high school in California under an assumed name, and that seemed to go pretty well. But a former student, who obviously didn't like his grade, and who was now an investigative reporter for *The Manchester Union*, tracked him down and burst his bubble. Vindictive little shit, working for that bastion of liberal journalism.

As the recession took hold in 1990, Lubins found himself out of work more often than not. For a time he waited tables and when he couldn't even hold on to that job, he took to cleaning those very same tables. But Julie's parasitic lawyers always seemed to be lurking around the corner. They kept sending him notices about child support and alimony. And they kept trying to garnish his wages.

Lubins didn't blame Julie. In fact, he wanted to make the payments, wanted the kids to be well cared for. But he hated the lawyers. They were so damned cold about it. And employers who are paying the minimum wage generally don't take too kindly to the paperwork and administrative crap involved in garnishing wages. So Lubins soon realized he needed to get away from the low-life bastards who made their living off other people's misery. That's when he decided to run away with the circus.

He was living in a YMCA in Lakeland, Florida, the winter home of Stone's Big Top Circus, when articles began appearing in the local papers about the impending return to Lakeland of The Big Show. Soon after Thanksgiving the show would return to Lakeland for a six-week overhaul before it set out again on its forty-four city tour.

Articles detailing the glamour and grandeur of The Big Show appeared on a daily basis. Lubins sat in the Y at the breakfast table and smiled. He pictured himself clad in a silly little outfit, floating through the air and grabbing the trapeze with aplomb until he realized that the circus would be a marvelous place to gain some breathing room. He needed to hide from Julie's lawyers while he figured out what to do with his life.

Julie's lawyers might be shrewd, but Lubins doubted that they were creative enough to track him down on the road, so he signed on as a roustabout the day the circus came to town. And he did it with just the hint of a tiny little grin curling the edges of his tiny lips.

There were only two times per year when the circus stayed in one place for more than a couple of weeks: between Thanksgiving and New Year's when the show underwent its semi-annual refurbishment, and during the Easter holiday when New York played host to the tour's longest engagement. Other than that, the show traveled constantly. As Lubins soon realized, the people who comprised The Big Show were uncomfortable staying in one place for too long. Each had his or her own reasons for wanting to move. For many it was just wanderlust, but for others, it was the escape they felt, the relief of knowing that nothing was permanent.

Each week, the huge cocoon that enveloped the circus inched its way along another set of train tracks headed for another faceless arena. For each city it was an annual event, but for those who worked for Stone's Big Top Circus it was a way of life.

The first week in Lakeland was different from anything Lubins had ever experienced. That first group meeting was nothing short of astounding. Eighty, maybe a hundred, people cramped into a little room in the back of the Lakeland Civic Center. Something was going on that night in the arena so they couldn't use the main area.

Lubins scanned the room, transfixed by the wild outfits the circus people wore. Flashy, exotic-looking wardrobes for the performers. Gold and silver like Lubins had never seen people wear before, not so much as jewelry, but as ornaments attached to clothing. Studded shirts, loud buttons, braces attached to shoes.

"Hello, and welcome to The Big Show." It was Phil Stone, the flamboyant, yet elegant and highly respected owner of the last great circus in America. Stone leaned forward on the back of a small desk chair, his long arms dangling, and his tie, which he wore loosely knotted, brushing against the top of the chair. Lubins couldn't believe the shock of silver hair the tall thin owner sported.

There were performers from South America, Europe, Asia and the Middle East. Lubins looked around and smiled, but said nothing, his mind totally boggled by the panoply of colors and sounds.

Stone paused, his hands in the air for effect, as his words were translated. And translated again. And again. Five times in all. It was like being at the United Nations, for chrissakes.

Lubins was placed with the Flying Ortiz Brothers' trapeze act. The general manager, Mike McGee, explained that he needed good, sober workers to do the rigging for the high-flying acts. He accentuated the word *sober* in a way that gave Donald pause.

One small mistake, McGee explained, could mean the

difference as to whether one of the Ortiz Brothers would be able to walk, or rather fly, another day.

"For some of you," Stone continued, "this is the pinnacle of your career. As a performer in the circus arts, you have reached the ultimate career achievement. Congratulations. For others of you, this represents a chance to travel. Or a chance at some kind of personal redemption. Whatever the reason, welcome. Welcome to our circus family."

Lubins grimaced at the sound of the word "family." He had left two behind. It was eighteen months since he had seen his children Robbie and Laurie. And Julie, whoever *she* was to him now. It was even longer since he had seen his adoptive parents and his stepbrothers, Ian and Scott.

"Family," continued Phil Stone, "is what everyone of you is to me. I will treat you as such, and I expect the same in return. It's a reciprocal concept, family."

Lubins looked around. The Ortiz brothers were wearing clogs. He shook his head and grinned. I mean who the hell still wears clogs? And Mora the Great, the female animal trainer, boy was she a piece of work, sitting in the front row with a little tiger cub curled up in her lap.

After Stone finished, McGee stood up to continue addressing the group, which immediately became noticeably less attentive.

"For those of you who are new, the pie car, where we serve gourmet meals—" McGee said with a smile, pausing to wait for the hissing and jeering to stop. He held up his hand and asked for quiet before resuming. "The pie car doesn't take cash."

"That's 'cause the food ain't worth cash," someone screamed from the back to a smattering of applause.

McGee tried to hold it together. "If any of you need dukie books to use at the pie car," he continued, "we've got 'em in the trailer. You know, you need those little coupons to eat! Now, let's keep our noses clean, steer clear of the townies, work hard, and have a good year. Thanks."

Chapter Two

Connie Parker was late. She hopped out of the shower, and glanced at the little pink alarm clock she kept near the sink. Stuart would be over to get her in less than twenty minutes, and she still had to get dressed and dry her hair, not to mention put on her makeup.

Connie truly wasn't looking forward to the Tobacco Institute's annual holiday party, but she most certainly was excited to be going with Stuart. Stuart was the best thing to happen to her since she left home.

Searching through her messy bathroom drawers did little to unearth Connie's suddenly missing hair dryer. Biting her lip, she headed for the bedroom and her closet. As she sped past her bed, the flowery quilt lying crumpled on the floor, she glanced over and saw *"Truman"* lying open on her bed stand. Stuart had purchased the biography for her the previous week after the two had engaged in a lengthy and passionate discussion about the years immediately following World War II. It was the first time a guy had bought a book for her. Ever.

Connie fished out a short, black cocktail dress and slipped it over her head. Her auburn hair, the wispy bangs covering the top two-thirds of her minuscule forehead, was the perfect color to offset a black outfit. At least that's what she always was told.

The little pink clock which announced that Stuart would be knocking on her door in exactly seven minutes, was getting irritating. It wasn't so much that she minded keeping her boyfriend waiting. Rather, it was the thought that her perceived tardiness might create in Stuart an illusion of male superiority, a haughtiness about things petty at which men seemed to excel.

But Stuart never seemed to mind when she was late. He'd just fix himself a drink, snap open a magazine or one of the five newspapers to which Connie subscribed, and kick back and wait.

Stuart was the lead lobbyist for the Tobacco Institute, a job that Connie couldn't understand. She rubbed her chin ruefully while dabbing on some rouge. Stuart was successful—extraordinarily so—and undoubtedly was paid quite handsomely for selling his soul. Still, it never ceased to amaze Connie how men could put their ethics aside so easily.

The doorbell rang. Connie still hadn't found the hair dryer, but was otherwise ready. She wrapped a bright red towel around her hair and answered the door.

"I love it, Ms. Parker," Stuart cooed, "is it new? The latest in hair wear? Wherever did you find it?"

"Shut up," Connie laughed as she took a swipe at Stuart who caught her arm, pulled her close and twirled his tongue inside of hers. "I'll just be a couple of minutes if I can ever find my hair dryer," Connie gasped as she pulled herself away. Stuart was a bit over six feet tall, and every bit of 200 pounds, and when he hugged her demure, small-boned frame, Connie felt crushed.

"You left it at my place last night," Stuart informed her, his pale blue eyes twinkling noticeably against his permanently tanned skin.

"Darn," Connie shot back, "that's right. I wish you would buy one already, or I should just leave it there and get a new one. Hey," she continued with a snap of her fingers, "I've got a travel dryer. Five minutes, I promise."

Stuart just smiled.

Connie was brushing her mostly dry hair, and applying a light coating of styling mousse, when the phone rang. Her immediate inclination was to ignore it, but Mother hadn't been feeling well, so she headed for the bedroom and picked up the receiver.

"Constance, how are you?" It was Dad. "Surprised I finally got you instead of that annoying telephone answering appliance."

Connie took a deep breath, and glanced down the short hall to see if Stuart, ensconced in her modern, black-leather-adorned living room, could hear her. No way of knowing.

"Hi, Dad, how are you?" she asked, only partially trying to conceal her distaste for the man whom she had spent so much of her life trying to please.

"Not bad. That big-shot lobbying life of yours got you out till all hours, or did you just ignore the phone when I called after eleven last night?"

Connie rested her hands on her hips. The phone was tucked under her ear and jaw, and rested firmly on her shoulder. "I unplugged it," she lied.

"Ah, tired from too much of that high call-girl living, Constance? Well," he continued, not allowing his daughter to interject, "I spoke with your mother last night and she seems to have rallied a bit. Have you called her?"

"Actually I have, two nights ago."

"Well, maybe your 'better late than never' call helped her spirits, my dear. Always good to hear your voice. She is, after all, your only mother, and you, her only child. You sound in a rush, bye now."

12

Connie slammed down the phone and gave it the finger. Then she shook her head, mumbling, "Men, men, men."

Carlisle Parker ran the Farmers and Merchants Bank in Kirk, the small southern Illinois town where Connie grew up. The old man simply was not happy about Connie's chosen lifestyle. But that was nothing new. Hell, he wasn't even amused when Connie cut high school one day and tried to meet him for lunch. Said it was dishonest, and he wouldn't write her a note. And she had expected a hug.

Connie had a heap of trouble when she refused her father's entreaties to apply to law school a decade ago, therefore she was in no mood to fight with him now. Although, at thirty-one, Connie felt less and less constrained to live by her father's rules. Anyway, it didn't much matter because Connie's career as a lobbyist was flourishing. There was even a recent article about her in the local rag. *The Washington Gazette*, which ranked the nation's top lobbyists, had described Connie as beautiful, devastatingly beautiful. Connie certainly wasn't about to take issue with a magazine of such obvious impartial judgment and good taste.

There were a number of years, mostly in high school, which the reporter obviously didn't know about. During this time, Connie, charitably could have been described as awkward. In retrospect, that period of her life probably helped Connie, for she hadn't jumped to the upper levels of Washington's lobbying community through her looks alone. A graduate of Wellesley College, Connie was beguiling and shrewd. Of course, *The Gazette* article, which ranked Connie second only to Stuart among the top lobbyists in the country, didn't make mention of those facts. About the closest the reporter came was to mention that she was addicted to *Jeopardy*. Like virtually everyone else, the reporter seemed to be fascinated by her looks.

Toward the end of her senior year in high school, shortly after she had been accepted to Wellesley, when life should have been nothing but graduation gowns and beach parties, Connie's parents separated. The marriage between Carlisle and Annie Parker had about as much warmth as the Illinois winters which the family suffered through each year. Carlisle really hadn't wanted children. On more than one drunken occasion he had reminded Annie of that fact in a voice that carried clearly to Connie's room, despite the fact that her door was closed to protect her from her father's railing.

Despite the occasional fury brought about by Carlisle's drinking binges, the Parkers had stayed together and lived their lie for almost twenty years, just so Connie wouldn't be scarred by a divorce early in life. But the frigid air that blew through the perfectly decorated home, and the icy stares, more than compensated. Despite the Parkers' best intentions, their daughter quite clearly was affected by their stony relationship.

The Washington Gazette knew nothing about all that, however. According to their oh, so knowledgeable reporter, Connie's devastating beauty was something that some men feared, while others found it all-consuming. She used it judiciously, the magazine said. And ethically.

Connie Parker never, ever offered sex in return for a favor, according to this month's much-ballyhooed cover story. In fact, her dealings with the men from whom she needed favors were quite to the contrary. But the more Connie explained what she needed done and why, and the more she steered clear of the issue of sex, the more most of them wanted her.

It made for good titillating journalism. Connie was happy to see it in print. At least the part about her ethics. If dear old Dad was going to see the article, he might as well have the pleasure of knowing that his eighteen thousand lectures about honesty had made an impact.

Because of her success, Connie didn't need anyone else's money to make her feel comfortable, and that was just as well. Connie saw all too clearly what dependence on a man's income had done to her mother, for Connie was convinced that it was her mother's inability to work out a suitable financial arrangement, and not any concern for Connie, that had kept the Parkers together all those years.

Connie glanced around the corner to where Stuart sat in the living room. Men, she thought, what a breed. Then she lightened up a bit. This guy seemed a bit different, at least on the surface.

Oh, Stuart acknowledged her beauty, and most certainly was drawn to it. But he acknowledged her brain too, and he challenged her every belief. He could sometimes out-argue her on the topic of the ethics of tobacco lobbying, and Connie felt damn strongly about that issue.

Stuart was the scion of a wealthy Rhode Island family. He had lived in Washington for the last twenty years, having stayed, like so many before him, after attending Georgetown University.

Stuart donated substantial portions of his mid-six-figure salary to the American Cancer Society, in an all-too-obvious attempt to assuage his guilt. Nonetheless, he continued in his life's work, and argued with anyone who brought up the subject of tobacco, often until well into the night, in various stages of inebriation.

Stuart didn't carry an ounce of fat. He had a strong, chiseled chin, and narrow, little lips which never had carried a cigarette between them, despite his lobbying efforts.

If Stuart had any failing, it was that he liked to party a bit too much. That was the life of a Washington lobbyist, he would say, with a shrug. As far as Connie could tell, for Stuart Katcavage life was good.

The only stress Stuart ever seemed to mention came from his parents, who decidedly were disappointed that he hadn't settled down. The Rhode Island Katcavages wanted grandchildren. Stuart had two substantially younger sisters and a gay brother, so, for the time being, it was up to him.

Connie met Stuart at an intimate gathering in a Georgetown mansion in mid-October. Fifteen people attended, and Connie immediately had no use for ten of them. She had angled over to the corner where Stuart was holding court, and tried to horn in on the conversation, but was unable to do so. Finally, just as the evening was ending, she had been introduced to Stuart. The two went out for a cup of coffee afterwards, and ended up back in Connie's apartment after closing down the diner with a raucous discussion about Martin Luther King's assassination. It had proved so much fun that Stuart hadn't left. For two months.

Now that it was December, Stuart's parents were coming to town the following week to celebrate Christmas and meet Ms. Connie Parker, the woman who apparently had captured their son's fancy.

Connie, though certainly more interested in Stuart than any of her previous lovers, hadn't particularly been forthcoming with details about him when speaking to either of her parents. Oh, sure, she had mentioned him, she didn't want any histrionics if she had to tell them that she and Stuart were getting married, but there was no need for details just yet.

Connie took a deep breath and headed for the living room. Stuart had his feet up on the couch, had a vodka and tonic in one hand, and the latest issue of *The New Republic* in the other.

The radio was blasting. "This is the Best of Buell," the announcer screamed. "Bits from past Mo Buell shows, spliced together for your enjoyment until Washington's favorite jock gets back from his fun in the sun."

"Everyone's on vacation, even that little shit, Buell," Stuart lamented as he looked up at Connie. "Hey what's wrong?"

Connie felt a wave of nausea from the mention of Mo Buell, which combined with the pounding pressure in her temples brought on by the phone call from dear old Dad to cause a sensation of true misery. Somehow, Connie managed a wan smile.

"Nothing," she said, trying to sound offhanded, but failing horribly.

"You sure you're okay? You seem awfully pale."

"Too much makeup?" Connie recovered.

"No, I don't think that's it," Stuart said softly. "You wanna do something else, blow off this party?"

"No, no, no," Connie replied with a wave. "I'm okay, really. It was just dear old Dad, laying on the guilt trip, you know, about my mother being sick and all."

"Should you go see her?"

"I don't know, I don't know." Connie ran her slender fingers through her bangs and looked off toward the kitchen, avoiding Stuart's eyes. She pursed her lips and began to respond, then thought better of it.

"What?" Stuart asked expectantly.

"I don't know. It's just that every time the phone rings I cringe."

"You know I've been getting those weird calls lately."

"I know, but you don't let stuff like that get to you. You just blow it off." Connie curled her lip and bit and shrugged. "Let's go," she changed the subject. "We can talk about it another time."

Stuart edged his BMW through the downtown traffic and headed for Georgetown. The Tobacco Institute party was being held in a private club on 31st Street, tucked between two yuppie-style restaurants.

Connie thought about Buell each time there was a lull in the conversation. It hadn't ended well with the pesky little deejay. The fight at the Blue Moon was tacky, not to mention embarrassing. Connie was shocked there hadn't been more fallout from it, given Buell's generally high profile, but apparently he wasn't all that proud of clearing all the dishes from the table and into the lap of the society woman sitting nearby. Connie never mentioned the episode to anyone either. Semi-public spectacles just weren't all that becoming.

Connie held her counsel about her mother, deflecting Stuart's well-intentioned, gentle prodding. The conversation soon drifted off to less taxing topics, the party being chief among them.

"Is there anyone you really want me to meet?" Connie inquired.

Stuart snorted. "Nah. I mean these aren't the most scintillating conversationalists."

"Okay, turn it around. Is there anyone you really don't want me to meet?"

Stuart took a deep breath and considered the question. The light was turning red so he slowed the car and stopped to look at Connie.

"Actually, one guy who might be at the party that I'm not particularly thrilled about is my old barber, that guy Giavonni. You remember? He's the guy that got me into that real estate deal. You know, the one where I lost the hundred grand."

"Yeah, I do remember. But, what would he be doing there?"

Stuart grunted. "The guy cuts literally every man's hair in this town."

"Except yours," Connie smiled, running her fingers through Stuart's thick, wavy blonde hair.

"Well, hell, you know, it's not even the money," Stuart snapped. "I mean it didn't break me. But those guys who were supposedly doing the investing took everybody's money and headed off for Bermuda. The damn thing was a scam from word one."

"Well, I know you well enough to know that you're not going to let him get away with it," Connie said, tensing ever so slightly as she waited for the reply.

"You're right. I asked an old friend of mine, Jim Evans, for some help. Jim's the U.S. Attorney for D.C."

"To do what, an investigation of some sort?"

"Yeah. I mean, it seems to me that those guys were all in cahoots, Giavonni and the supposed real estate guys. It's just too cute otherwise."

The party given by the Tobacco Institute was like most of the other Christmas parties that year, only more so. It was a stiff, formal affair with too many people and mediocre food. But the liquor was good and it flowed freely. For that, Connie knew, her date was thankful. Stuart liked his liquor, and that was actually one of the few areas of disagreement between the two lobbyists. Connie simply wasn't a big drinker.

Connie left Stuart's side early during the party and mingled easily with the other friends of the purveyors of cancer. She watched Stuart from a distance and admired his strong, broad shoulders, and muscular, athletic build.

As the evening wore on Connie began to get antsy to leave. But this was Stuart's crowd, and she didn't want to push it. She began to inch her way over towards Stuart when she noticed that he was raising a toast with a graying, but distinguished-looking, man who had a decidedly foreign appearance. As she made her way through the crowd toward Stuart and his drinking buddy, Stuart spoke.

"Sweetheart, I'd like you to meet Joseppe Giavonni. Joseppe, this is Connie Parker."

"Nice to meet you, Joseppe."

"You are even more beautiful up close than from far away. It is a pleasure to meet you, Connie. I was just telling Stuart that he and I should bury the hatchet, as you say, at least for the Christmas season. There will be plenty of time for fighting later. I just brought Stuart a drink. Can I get you one?"

"No thanks, mine's fresh," Connie replied with a smile as she held up her club soda.

Shortly before midnight, Connie was able to drag Stuart away from the party.

"What was that scene with Joseppe? I thought you were trying to get the guy indicted?"

"I was," Stuart said, obviously drunk. "But he came over earlier and we raised our voices," he continued, as he stumbled and fought to regain his balance. "So when he came back with a drink, and said we should bury it, I figgered what the hell! You know, holiday cheer, and all that."

As they made their way home, Stuart didn't seem any more drunk to Connie than he had after any of the previous Christmas season parties. Too drunk to drive, to be sure, but no drunker than usual.

Connie was a bit surprised to see Stuart begin to nod off as she inched his BMW through the Georgetown traffic. She stopped at a light and glanced over at him. It was dark and Connie was having difficulty focusing, but something about Stuart's features seemed a bit different. His skin seemed, what, maybe a bit pallid? Who could tell in the darkness?

Besides really needing a bathroom, Connie felt fine. She headed for Stuart's apartment in the Watergate. By the time they reached the luxury penthouse, Stuart was barely awake. Connie lugged him in, and with a tremendous effort was able to remove his shoes and clothes, prop his head on a pillow, and arrange him comfortably so he could sleep it off.

Connie took a bit more care with herself. She went to the bathroom, brushed her teeth and washed her face. Next, she applied an ample amount of skin cream to her smooth, pale complexion. She brushed her auburn hair vigorously, except for the delicate, wispy bangs which she gently massaged with her fingers.

Once finished with her pampering, Connie slipped into one of Stuart's oxford shirts, crawled into bed, and leaned across Stuart to turn off the light. Out of the corner of her eye, she caught Stuart's face. It looked older, less vibrant than her mind told her he really was. She shook her head, cursing the alcohol, and flicked off the light.

Connie woke up with a start early the next morning.

What was that gurgling sound, that smell which reminded her of almonds? She jerked her head in the darkness but she couldn't see. Without her contacts she was lost.

Still not that familiar with Stuart's apartment, Connie fumbled in the dark for her glasses. Finally finding them, she placed them on her nose and groped for the light. As she snapped the switch on the antique, porcelain-based lamp which washed the room in light, she gasped, horrified by what she saw. Stuart's mouth was open slightly, his entire face was covered with vomit, and his skin had taken on a deathly tone of grey.

Connie ran to the bathroom. She snatched a towel from next to the sink and ran back into the bedroom. She gently began trying to wipe away the grotesque, multi-colored glop which Stuart apparently had been ejecting throughout the night.

When she finally was able to clear the vomit from around Stuart's face and neck, Connie gently placed her hand on Stuart's forehead. It felt cool and lifeless. She placed her finger on his neck. There was a weak pulse at best, maybe none at all, Connie wasn't sure. She shrieked as she grabbed for the phone.

"Hello, yes, it's an emergency! Yes, I would like an ambulance to be sent immediately. Yes, the address is . . ."

Chapter Three

Mark Clifton awoke earlier than usual the day before the night before Christmas. December 23rd was cold, but sunny, without a hint of precipitation. Carol had left to visit her ailing father in Sarasota, Florida, where Mark had agreed to join her for a semitropical Christmas celebration the next day.

So he was up early. It felt strange, waking up without Carol. He hadn't done it for over a year except for a three-day period in November when he was trying a tax evasion case in New Jersey, and one day before that when she was away on business.

With the holiday sneaking up, almost catching the busy lawyer by surprise, an early morning had become a necessity. There was banking to be done, a haircut to be gotten, and perhaps most important, presents to be bought. Not to mention that Crisfield had to be taken to the kennel, where he would spend his Christmas. Mark tried not to think about that. After all, Crisfield was only a dog, he wouldn't know they were gone for Christmas. Or would he?

Mark quickly rolled over. He popped up, his wiry body coming alive like he had received a prod from something unspeakably hot or sharp. Mark looked at the emptiness beside him, and quickly flipped on the radio. Carol hated Mo Buell, the famous D.C. morning radio personality, but Mark kind of liked him. It was a guy thing. At least there was one good thing about Carol's absence.

"Yeah it's good to be back in the saddle, D.C.! Keep those cards and letters coming. Hey that's what I'd like to be doin'! Uh oh, what's the FCC gonna do now, I just said something vaguely sexual. Dumb bureaucrats! Dumb, dumb, and dumber. I mean, who are we kiddin' here?

"Hey I'm almost finished with my book. It's a tell all. You are gonna love it. Tells all about the women I've had. Tells all about the crazy stuff women want from me. Man, and it's all true too, that's what is so great, folks. All true."

Mark smiled. Mo had a touch of an ego. Mark reached the shower door and pulled it open. He turned on the water and hopped in. He had become accustomed to showering with Carol, so the stall seem unusually large this morning. Despite Carol's absence, or maybe because of it, Mark followed his usual pattern and used Carol's shampoo. His dark brown hair was wildly curly and unruly, and he luxuriated in the process of sudsing it and massaging his scalp. Once finished in the shower, Mark shaved and dressed for work while Mo ranted on.

"I gotta tell ya, this vacation did me some good. I mean, when I left, I have to admit, I was kind of bumming you know, 'cause this piece of tush I was seein' dumped me. I mean can you believe it? Anyway, I just needed to get away, know what I'm sayin'?"

Mark left his Beatles' tie unknotted and shirt collar unbuttoned, since he was stopping for a haircut on his way to work. He skipped the overcoat and walked briskly out the door, with a designer's dream of *"Paperback Writer"* displayed on the tie which flew over his shoulder.

Mark could tell that Joseppe Giavonni, barber extraordinaire, was in a holiday mood. "Happy Anniversary, Markie," Joseppe cried out, as Mark walked through the door of the old-fashioned barber shop.

"That's right," Mark replied. "It's been twelve years now since I first came here."

"You know the rules, Markie," Joseppe replied. "Anniversary haircuts are for free!"

"I'm not going to argue, Josep."

"So, Markie, how has your holiday season been?"

"Good, Josep, and yours?"

"Couldn't be nicer, Markie, couldn't be nicer!"

Joseppe snipped and cut and shaped, and the two shared small talk about the season, like they had shared for the last twelve years. Mark had been coming to Joseppe for twelve years not only because Joseppe gave a good haircut, but because Mark loved Joseppe Giavonni.

Joseppe was an Italian immigrant who had worked hard for everything he earned. When he came to America during the 1960s, he was penniless. First, he changed the spelling of his name from "Giuseppe" to "Joseppe," thinking it would help him pass more easily. Then he obtained a work visa. Okay, he used a little sleight of hand, but he immediately became a productive member of society.

Joseppe's business slowly grew, and word of his engaging, European personality and good work with a scissor spread. During the early 1970s it became fashionable for all the post-Watergate-era breed of politicians to get their hair cut at Joey's Barber Shoppe, and Joseppe Giavonni was usually the barber of choice. It was the anti-snob thing to do.

Many of Joseppe's customers dated back to those

days, and Joseppe dispensed a healthy dose of political commentary along with his razor cuts.

Joseppe hated Republicans. Always had. Oh, he'd cut their hair all right. You know, politics should never get in the way of making a buck.

As more and more politicians got their hair cut by Joseppe, high-powered lobbyists began to come too. In the beginning, they were looking for a leg up on their opponents in the political wars. They thought, perhaps, Joseppe would give them some gossip or insight. After a while, they realized Joseppe was getting information from them, not giving it to them. But they loved him just the same, and they all kept coming back every four to six weeks, even the mostly bald ones.

The middle-aged Italian man was the most popular barber in Washington, DC, without question, although, there was an increasing minority that didn't particularly care for Joseppe. After the fawning feature story in the "Style" section of *The Washington Post*, many people felt that Joseppe had gotten a bit too big for his britches. Mark thought they were just jealous.

"By the way, Josep," Mark broke the sudden silence, "wasn't Stuart Katcavage one of your customers?"

"Oh, Markie, wasn't that about the saddest thing you ever heard?" Joseppe shook his head as if he still couldn't believe his high-powered customer had met his demise.

"The papers made it sound like he drank himself to death. Seems kinda bizarre to me, Josep."

"You know, Markie, I was at the party where Stuart was the night he died," Joseppe countered. "I was only with him for a short while, but he certainly didn't seem to be drinking that much, if you ask me. I mean, I've seen him drink more at a summertime picnic. You know," the barber continued, "in the Old Country, I saw men drink ten times as much as Stuart did that night. Hell, I did it myself. No, Markie, he couldn't have drunk himself to death. I don't buy it, not for a second."

Joseppe shook his head again, and refocused his attention on Mark's half-cut hair. "Hey, Markie, how about if I just send you out on the streets like this?" Joseppe laughed, changing the subject.

"I don't think my clients would be too impressed," Mark retorted.

Joseppe finished giving Mark the same haircut he had given him for the past twelve years, and Mark gave Joseppe the same Christmas present he had given him for twelve years—a double payment. Mark wondered if he would have to give Joseppe the cost of three haircuts if the barber stopped dispensing the free anniversary cut.

Mark shook his barber's hand warmly, wished him a happy holiday, knotted his Beatles' tie and headed off for the rest of his errands in preparation for his trip to see Carol's dad, the elder Mr. Keegan. Mark had never met the man, but he felt like he knew him. Carol had an extensive photo collection, and she loved going through it, pointing out various scenes of familial bliss to Mark. She loved her dad, and it was time for Mark to meet him.

Mark strode quickly toward the bank, caught in the crush of holiday shoppers. He found himself humming, and began singing under his breath. "Old man, take a look at my life, I'm a lot like you were. . . ."

The streets were teeming, and people were smiling. Mark patted his jacket pocket to make certain his plane tickets were still there. It was almost Christmas.

Chapter Four

Donald Lubins, you're not homeless yet. Lubins could not believe his eyes. He had finished rigging the netting for the Flying Ortiz Brothers, and taken a seat in the front row of the empty arena when Mora the Great strutted into the center ring in full performance regalia. The circus' most famous performer was wearing royal blue and gold skin-tight pants studded with rhinestones. Lubins stared in amazement. It must take three people to get her into those pants. Minimum.

The animal handler extraordinaire did not wear a shirt or blouse as such. Instead, she wore a cape draped around her neck which flowed down her back and barely covered what it needed to in front. It was of the same ostentatious colors, and, if possible, was even more rhinestone-studded than the painted-on pants.

Lubins' eyes were glued to the most famous circus performer of all time as she made her way into the center ring. Seven of the fiercest looking cats that Lubins had ever seen were brought into the center ring inside a cage of steel. Each was individually let out of its cage and allowed into the center ring. As each cat came in, Mora cracked her whip and screamed out a command in Italian. Each of the graceful beasts immediately took its place in the ring. There were three lions, three tigers, and a liger, a crossbreed of a lion and a tiger of which Mora seemed the most fond.

Lubins maintained his childlike trance as Mora calmly put the animals through their paces. They walked on two legs, rolled over in unison, and leapt through hoops of fire.

The circus' most highly educated roustabout was impressed. He hadn't seen Mora perform her entire routine before. But it was now only two days before opening night and one day before the first dress rehearsal, and even Mora the Great had to prepare.

As Mora finished her routine, she hugged each of the cats with a love so clear that it nearly brought a tear to Lubins' eye. Mora trotted out of the center ring and began to slow just as she approached Lubins. Lubins tensed, not knowing what to expect.

Mora reached out her hand and gave Lubins a high five. "Good session, eh?"

"Very impressive, Mora," Lubins called out with a quick smile. The encounter was the first between Lubins and the circus great. You see, Lubins was assigned to the Flying Ortiz Brothers, the second most popular act performing with Stone's Big Top Circus. And there was an unwritten rule: The Ortiz were the Ortiz and Mora was Mora. Period.

Lubins had found the entire rivalry amusing when he first arrived at the circus three weeks earlier, but it hadn't taken him long to realize how seriously the circus professionals took the situation. Lubins knew it was no time to get cute. He was already a lot closer to the end of the road as far as employment was concerned than he cared to think about, and he couldn't blow it. So far, he had succeeded in keeping an extremely low profile. He had discovered real quickly that that was the best way to survive on The Big Show.

"So, smart guy, what d'ya think?"

Lubins looked up to see the smiling countenance of Manuel Ortiz, the head of the Flying Ortiz Brothers. Had Manuel seen the exchange with Mora? Lubins doubted it, but he couldn't be sure.

"Well, it is the first time I've ever seen Mora perform. The cats are really gorgeous creatures, aren't they?"

Manuel broke into a wide grin and placed his tightly muscled arms at his sides, his hands firmly on his hips. The short, stocky, and powerful leader of the second most popular circus troupe in the world appeared to like Lubins' answer. "They are absolutely beautiful, my friend, absolutely beautiful. Especially that liger. Have you ever heard it purr? Make your heart go soft. Now," Manuel said as he jumped up, "it is time for our act."

Lubins double-checked the rigging which he had helped to configure a bit earlier. The last thing he needed was for the king of the high fliers to have a problem. In the short time he had rigged for Manuel, Lubins had learned quickly that the young flier was a perfectionist. And a ball buster. And any problem he might encounter, he undoubtedly would blame on the lowest level employee he could find. Manuel was a great guy.

As Lubins rechecked the final hook and tied the last knot, the ring boss nodded his approval. Accompanied by the raucous sound of the theme song from *Rocky*, the Flying Ortiz Brothers came prancing into the center ring, which moments earlier had been occupied by Mora the Great.

They, too, were scantily clad, only they wore leopard-skin pants which reached from the hips to midcalf and left little to the imagination. Their tops, though separate pieces, gave the appearance that the Flying Ortiz Brothers were wearing overalls. Each wore clogs, which they kicked off as they reached the net.

First Manuel, and then his brothers, pulled themselves up by the side of the net until they were sitting on the net itself. Then they hoisted themselves up, one at a time, on a rope which hung next to the platform on the left side of the ring. In seconds the three Ortiz brothers, Manuel, Arguello, and Hector, were at the top of the hippodrome track on a small, silver platform.

Hector grabbed the flying trapeze and swung himself into a position that few mere mortals could equal. He hooked each of his legs over the bar and hung from the trapeze facing downwards with his knees wrapped around the shiny metal rod and his arms extended into the air awaiting one of his flying brothers.

Arguello was the first to take the leap. He grabbed the second trapeze and hung from it by his arms. He began swinging and swaying gently to and fro. When he built up enough momentum, he thrust himself forward, somersaulting through the air twice and grabbing Hector's hands at the last possible second. On the back swing he quickly twirled around and grabbed the trapeze bar which he had just released, and swung back to the silver platform.

Manuel was slightly more daring. He did two and a half somersaults before allowing Hector to catch him by the ankles. Arguello followed with a triple somersault, Hector snatching him out of the air by his hands a split second before the flying gymnast would have headed straight for the net.

Then came the fun. Manuel swung on his trapeze extended in the air but facing away from Hector. When he built up sufficient speed, he thrust himself away from his trapeze bar and sailed backwards through the air turning three somersaults before finally coming to roost in his brother's hands with a jolt.

It wasn't pretty, and Manuel was disgusted with himself. He wriggled free from Hector's grasp and allowed himself to drop onto the net below. The net propelled him back up and he was able to grab hold of his trapeze bar. He swung back to the silver platform and called out to his brother that he was going to try the reverse triple again.

Try though he might, Manuel could not perform the routine to his own high standards. After trying about fifteen times, he called it a session. He screamed at Lubins to take down the rigging so the next inconsequential act could have some time in the ring. Smiling, Lubins complied with the wishes of Manuel Ortiz, frustrated flying trapeze artist.

Mora the Great threw a huge Christmas party that night. She had commandeered a party room at the Lakeland Civic Center, and invited most of the cast and crew of The Big Show, although she quite conspicuously neglected to mention the party to the Flying Ortiz or any of their crew.

The party started fast and got wild early. Mora the Great's sexual proclivities were a matter of much conversation on the circus train and in the dressing rooms. While her appetite was huge, no one was quite sure if it was boys or girls, little or otherwise, that Mora preferred. From what Lubins could glean, the superstar seemed to be more than willing to go with the flow, and she regularly accepted favors from whoever was available.

On this particular evening, Mora was holding court with two sixteen-year-old boys from Bulgaria. They performed in a tumbling act and had spent their whole lives around the Bulgarian State Circus. They had heard of the legendary Mora the Great when they first began performing, and they were thrilled to be in her presence.

Mora undoubtedly was imagining the mathematical possibilities as she sipped her gin and tonic. The mood was upbeat.

Shortly before midnight, with the party heating up nicely, the booze flowing freely, and both sixteen-year-olds ensconced in Mora's lap, Manuel led a contingent of the Ortiz brothers into no-man's land. Lubins quickly digested the situation, and he could see Mora's dream of a teenage-boy sandwich evaporating before her very eyes. Everyone knew this was Mora's function, and the Latin community definitely was not welcome.

Lubins watched uneasily as Mora gently pushed her young friends aside and sprung from the couch where she had been holding forth. The self-proclaimed "Queen of the Ring" meant to confront Manuel, but it was evident to Lubins from the moment Mora stood that the great goddess of the beasts was none too sober.

Mora lurched her way towards her rival and demanded an explanation for her competitor's presence.

"I do not need an invitation, Ms. Mora," Manuel replied sarcastically. "You do not own this building and it is not your right to tell me I cannot come here. You have slapped me in the face. You have tried to do my family dishonor. I will not soon forget it."

Lubins watched with surprised relief as Manuel, his face flushed with anger, turned on his heels to leave.

"Hey Ortiz," Mora called after him. "Screw you, your honor, and your whole goddamn family!"

"This time, Ms. Big Shot, you've gone too far," Manuel screamed while shaking his fists and storming out the door.

It was nearly one a.m. when the Ortiz family returned with their crew, including a very reluctant Lubins. Manuel burst through the door, and his comrades-in-arms immediately closed ranks. Before Mora could remove her sweet little boys from the positions they had resumed on her thighs, she was engulfed by the Ortiz warriors, though the Latinos seemed unsure of themselves in the face of a female competitor.

As the first punches were thrown, Lubins avoided contact, milling about in the middle of the floor. Just when it seemed as though he might escape all the bedlam, Lubins was knocked forward, and found himself face-to-face with one of Mora's goons. Lubins smiled wanly then quickly tried to duck as the oversized, hairy workingman swung wildly. Lubins was stung as the huge fist glanced off his cheek. Before he could regain his balance he was hit again, and he felt himself tumbling to the ground.

Two workingmen were kicking mercilessly at Lubins as he curled into the fetal position. He peeked out from behind his hands—which he was using to try to protect his face—to see what was happening. Matters did not appear to be going all that well for the Ortiz brothers. Arguello was down, and so was Hector. Manuel was nowhere in sight.

Lubins was about to cover his face again when he felt the boot wallop him on the right side of his face. Pain seared throughout his jaw, neck, and shoulders. He felt his whole body spasming as he tensed for the next blow. Just as he sensed another boot headed his way, Lubins heard Mora call off the troops.

Lubins rolled over and slowly rose to a sitting position. He certainly hadn't acquitted himself spectacularly, but at least he hadn't run away.

The Ortiz contingent quickly exited the party room, many of them bleeding, others severely bruised. With opening night two days away, circus management was sure to be thrilled.

Shortly after the circus' answer to gang warfare ended, Lubins was in the men's room staring into the mirror. His left cheek was a blotchy red, and so swollen that it threatened to burst right through his skin. The right side of his jawbone was no better, having expanded to at least three times its normal size. His eyes were bloodshot; his hair sticky, matted, and raunchy. Lubins winced as he looked into the mirror, as much from what he saw as from what he felt. Ah, he thought, if only Julie could see me now!

Finally, as he dabbed at the reddest and puffiest parts of his face, Lubins thought about his brothers. His stepbrothers, that is. "Ian and Scott would've come in handy tonight," he mumbled. "They would've kicked some butt tonight. Nice kids. Not too bright, but nice," he said to himself.

A big-time prize fighter, Lubins was not. He had gotten the shit kicked out of him. And he wasn't even sure why. He knew he had no choice. If he hadn't followed Manuel Ortiz's call-to-arms, Manuel certainly would have seen to it that Lubins' days under the big top would have come to an unceremonious end. This way, at least he had some chance of retaining a method of feeding himself, however difficult a task that might prove to be in his current condition.

Lubins stumbled back to the tiny berth he shared on the train with the two other workingmen whom he barely knew, and was pleased to see that they were still out partying. He put his throbbing head on the sandpaper pillowcase, and within seconds he was dreaming about better days.

Chapter Five

Connie Parker trembled as she tried to answer the police sergeant's questions. He was big, in fact, very big. Looking at him, Connie guessed six-five, two-fifty. And he was black, very black, even against his navy uniform. The sergeant appeared to be gentle and kind. And, he was a' patient man.

Connie sniffled and dabbed at her nose with a handkerchief as she repeated the facts surrounding Stuart Katcavage's death to Sergeant David Moore.

"Sergeant, I mean no disrespect," she sniffed, "but it doesn't take a genius to figure out that someone must've killed Stuart. He didn't have that much to drink, and, like I said, his skin, it was so grey. This wasn't your ordinary, run-of-the-mill drunk aspirating his own vomit."

"No," Moore said, in a deep, gravelly voice, as he held up his huge hand. "If all that is true, it wouldn't take a genius to figure that out. Course that don't mean it's right."

The pencil looked tiny in Moore's hand as he completed the mound of paperwork required by the D.C. police. He looked up from his writing, and smiled gently, his dark brown eyes looking light against his jet black skin. He scratched his short, wiry, slightly graying hair, looked up at Connie with sadness, and then continued. "Mr. Katcavage was a popular man. Well-liked. We've already had a lot of people snoopin' around here, including a lot of reporters. They're gonna be bugging you as soon as you leave here. Now if you want, I can arrange to have a squad car drop you off wherever it is you're going."

"That's really kind of you, Sergeant Moore," Connie said, her eyes still trained on the floor. "I'm not sure if it will be necessary." Connie paused, then glanced up and met the Sergeant's eye. "Before I go, I'd like to speak with the medical examiner or the coroner or whomever it is that I need to talk to about getting an autopsy done."

"Yes, ma'am, you've made your wishes in that regard extremely well known. I've dealt with many people before, Ms. Parker, but none as insistent as you," the sergeant continued with a broad smile which revealed a missing tooth on the lower left-hand side of his mouth. "I'll go and get the examiner to come down here. You just wait a minute and we'll be right back."

With that, the sergeant pushed his way out of his tiny wooden chair and headed for the door.

Connie nodded and smiled. "Thanks," she said, "I appreciate it."

Connie sat quietly in the sparsely furnished interrogation room. She glanced at the ancient grey metal table which looked like a thousand scared witnesses had dug their fingernails into its surface thereby sending a chill down the spines of their interrogators. There were three equally abused wooden chairs with deep gash marks in them, apparently from those being held in custody grinding handcuffs against them.

Connie squinted up and noticed a fluorescent light bulb partially covered by a yellowing, broken plastic fixture. The walls were painted bright white, and in stark contrast to the few furnishings, looked fresh and clean.

When Moore hadn't returned for ten minutes, Connie stood up and began pacing. She gnawed on her fingernails, something she hadn't done in years. She caught herself doing it, thought about stopping, but continued anyway. She figured she was entitled.

Finally, Moore returned with Ken Yamaguchi in tow. The District's medical examiner was a string bean of a thing, standing at least six four, but hardly weighing more than 150 lbs. He looked like he was right out of school, and Connie was shocked when he said he'd been the coroner for almost fifteen years. He appeared to be a mixed breed, one-half Oriental, one-half something else, probably Caucasian.

Connie found herself answering yet another avalanche of questions. Yamaguchi wasn't thrilled at the idea of conducting an autopsy, not because of anything intrinsic having to do with the work itself, but because of the parties involved. Stuart was extremely well-known, and Yamaguchi's findings would be closely scrutinized. No one likes to have half the world looking over his shoulder while he works.

Connie tried to calm Yamaguchi's fears, assuring him that she wanted to know how Stuart had died for her own reasons, and she had no intention of bringing his findings to the press or anyone else with ulterior motives.

Finally: "Okay, Ms. Parker. You are very convincing. I will conduct an autopsy. But you need to be patient. These things take time."

"How much time?"

"A week, maybe a bit more."

"Thank you both," Connie said as she rose, composed herself, and offered a handshake first to one of the skinniest men she had ever seen, and then to one of the largest. Moore gently took her hand and walked her to the door of the police station.

"Ms. Parker, I want you to know, if the autopsy shows anything, we'll hop on it right away. We're here to help you. And rest assured, Ms. Parker, as of now, no one suspects you."

Connie looked at him with surprise and a touch of anger. "Sergeant," she said reprovingly, "I can honestly say that thought never crossed my mind."

Chapter Six

The telephone is an inconsiderate device at best. At 6:30 New Year's Day morning, the phone's ringing was more than obnoxious, it was downright outrageous.

Mark Clifton's mouth tasted as if it was filled with cotton balls. The kind that are way too big, and just a bit too coarse. And from what he could feel of his teeth, he imagined they wore little green mohair sweaters, each individually knitted. His head was pounding. God, it was pounding. As he fumbled in the darkness, trying to grasp the receiver and yank it off its base, he struggled to pull himself together.

Mark had spent New Year's Eve with Carol at two different parties. Since he wasn't a particularly big drinker, the three beers and one glass of champagne he had consumed, had taken their toll. Mark was finding it awfully difficult to locate the phone. Finally he succeeded.

"This better be good," Mark sputtered into the receiver as he picked it up.

"I, I am very sorry to wake you Markie. This is Joseppe. Joseppe Giavonni. It is not good. In fact, Markie, it is very, very bad. Have you seen today's paper yet?"

"Joseppe, I didn't even know it was today yet!"

"Yes, Markie, like I said, I am very sorry. But, if you look in today's paper, the business section, you will see that I've been indicted!"

"What for?" Mark said, scrambling to an upright position.

"I'd rather not get into it on the telephone. Is it possible for us to meet? Obviously, I need a lawyer."

"It's going to take me a few minutes to get my act together, Josep, How 'bout, say, my office at eight o'clock? You know where it is don't you?"

"Yes, Markie, I'll be there. And, Markie, thank you."

Mark gently placed the phone receiver back into its cradle. Carol stared at him in disbelief. "What do you mean 'your office'?"

Mark started to explain, then thought better of it. He didn't really know what the hell was going on himself. He forced his way out of bed and squinted into the mirror. His eyes, caked shut from sleep, valiantly fought off the light. He looked almost as bad as he felt. Did anyone get the license plate of that truck?

Mark grabbed his transistor radio and headed for the can. He turned on the radio, and almost fell over it was so loud. He quickly lowered the volume, plopped down on the toilet, and rubbed his eyes.

"Yeah," the voice on the radio screeched, "us guys don't have it as glamorous as you might think. Us morning deejays have to get up at four-thirty to get in by six. It sucks, but, hey, the dough is pretty good so who's complaining?

"Hey, normally I'd get New Year's Day off, but I just got back from vacation, so what the hell. Damn program manager thought I'd had enough mornings to sleep in.

"Anyway, anybody see this morning's paper yet? First thing you do this morning has got to be to look at the business section. That Katcavage case just gets weirder all the time. Hey, who knows? I've made my feelings clear on this show before. Connie Parker dumped me, and I don't think any other man should have her if I can't, so I wasn't upset in the least to see Katcavage buy the farm. I mean after all, as far as I'm concerned, he was doin' my girl. But the barber? What has he got to do with this whole thing? Some kinda fraud or conspiracy thing. Next thing you know, somebody will say he was doing her too. I mean who does this chick think she is?

"Say, anyone know the difference between a slut and a bitch? That's right. A slut will give it to anybody. A bitch will give it to anybody but you! And let me tell you, I think that joke is apropos this morning."

Mark got up off the toilet, turned off the radio, and shaking his head, made his way over to the shower. The hot water began to take effect, and Mark rubbed both eyes, and gently massaged his temples. Joseppe Giavonni indicted?! For what? Fraud and conspiracy if that lunatic Buell was right. Geez, what a week! First meeting old man Keegan, the first parent of a girlfriend Mark had met since Tina, and she had been dead for almost six years. Now this.

Mark quickly dressed. "Woke up, got out of bed, dragged the comb across my head. . . ." he hummed as he headed out front for the newspaper. He sat down with a cup of coffee and opened to the tiny New Year's Day business section. At first he didn't see anything of interest. But then, towards the bottom of the second page of the business section he saw an article entitled "Barber to the Rich and Powerful Indicted." The piece was short, and Mark finished it in under a minute.

Joseppe had been indicted for allegedly participating in a real estate scam. Mark remembered Joseppe asking him to invest in a real estate limited partnership, oh maybe, six, eight months ago. But when Mark said no,

Joseppe hadn't pressed. Apparently, Joseppe had gotten some of his other customers to invest, and the partnership had turned out to be a scam. Man, this one hurts, Mark thought, as he read the article a second time. Joseppe Giavonni. The living embodiment of the American dream. Grew up poor in a tiny town in southern Italy. First came to the United States as an illegal alien but soon was able to overcome that distinction, albeit through lies.

Joseppe's story was that of Everyman the Immigrant. He started in America penniless, knowing not a soul. And he built a business and a reputation in the community based upon hard work, dedication, and integrity. True, there were some who didn't like Josep, but Mark chalked that up to jealousy. Joseppe Giavonni was a bit of a controversial character, though as far as Mark could tell, he was far more beloved than anything else.

When Mark got to his office at ten minutes before eight, Joseppe was standing in the cold, waiting. "I would say Happy New Year, Josep, but I guess it isn't, so far."

"I can't believe what is happening, Markie. I did a favor for a couple of my customers, they paid me something in return for doing it, and now I'm going to jail." Joseppe was on the verge of tears.

"Nobody's going to jail so fast, Josep. Let's go into my office and look through the indictment and see what you're charged with. Then I want to hear your side of the story. Remember, in this country you're innocent until proven guilty. And the government, in a criminal case, has an extremely difficult burden of proof.

"It's very important that we maintain a positive outlook about the situation. Otherwise, it will take an even greater toll on you and your family." Mark had this speech down pat.

Mark found his sleek, black key card, inserted it into the slot by the front door, waited for the click and opened the door to let Joseppe in. They both smiled. The heat was working.

Mark led the way through the Williamsburg style design in the spacious reception area into his cluttered, simply furnished office. He removed case files from the black cloth embroidered guest chairs so he and Joseppe could each sit in one. Then Mark disappeared into the coffee room. He put up a large pot of very strong coffee.

As they settled in, each with his hands wrapped around a big mug which emitted the steamy aroma of fresh brewed coffee that somehow took a bit of the sting out of being awake so early on such a cold morning, Joseppe began to speak. "Do you remember when I asked you if you wanted to invest in units in a real estate limited partnership?"

"Yep. I sure do."

"Well, that's why I've been indicted. For helping a couple of my customers sell limited partnership units in a real estate trust."

"Well, Josep, it's no crime to simply help someone sell limited partnership units. There's more to it, isn't there?"

"Yes, Markie, there is," Joseppe said, sounding resigned. "The guys who asked me to do the selling, George Moran and Jackson Caulfield, raised something like about $15,000,000. Then they took it and started a company in Bermuda. They sent out one letter to the investors talking about some potential property they were going to buy. Only problem, no one heard from them again.

"Ya' see, Markie," Joseppe opened his arms wide and stood up, placing his mug of coffee on the edge of Mark's desk, "these guys were real estate professionals, or so I thought. They were both deal makers in the mid-'80s and, I think, made a fortune. But then everything went south.

"You remember, I asked you a number of times when I was cutting your hair what you thought about some of their deals. They always wore the most expensive clothes, they always gave the biggest tips and they always drove the most fanciest cars.

"Anyway, they told me about this idea to get back into real estate. They said everything had reached the bottom. All they needed was some cash and they could make some great profits by buying up property at a very low value, and then selling it later when the market swung back.

"So they asked me if some of my customers might be interested. They tell me they gonna pay me $5,000 for each of my customers who buys a unit. Each unit was $50,000. They tell me that's a good commission.

"To me, Markie, it was real. Markie, I swear to you. These guys raised, I don't know, about $15,000,000 and I helped them. Lots of my customers bought units. They trusted me. But you know, George and Jackson, I guess they never planned to do the right thing. I haven't spoken to either of them in over two months. I think they're in Bermuda," Joseppe said as he picked up the mug, looked into it, and sat down.

"Hey, Josep," Mark said lightly, but he was interrupted before he could continue.

"Do you know Moran and Caulfield, Markie?"

"No. No, I don't think so," Mark replied cautiously.

"George—that's Moran—is an immigrant like me. His family was very colorful. His mother was in the Antonio Circus back in Italy. She was always getting into some kind of trouble, you know. Little stuff, but always physical. I remember once," Joseppe said with a smile, "when she was out in a little bar in Milan, and some guy tried to come on to her. She was pretty good-looking. Anyway, she beat the crap out of him, and all hell broke loose. It was always something like that.

"Caulfield, I guess I cut his hair for, like, ten years. He was a real estate guy, very professional. I don't exactly know how they hooked up."

"Did you say you cut Moran's hair too?"

"Yeah, on and off. He would disappear for weeks or months at a time, then he would show up again. Usually without an appointment. I'd tell him, 'George I'm sorry, but I have nothing available today.' And he'd say, 'that's okay, Joseppe, take your time. I'll wait.' Sometimes he'd wait for hours. I thought that was weird."

Mark nodded. "Ya' know, Josep," he finally replied, "I'm gonna need every last shred of physical evidence you have on this case. Papers, advertisements, if there are any, a record of whom you spoke to and when, whom you sold the units to, if you can remember, offering documents, if there are any, and anything else you can think of.

"One more thing, Joseppe. I hate to bring up money, especially at a time like this. But I'm gonna need a $10,000 retainer to open a case on this. My partners insist upon it."

"That's okay, Markie. One thing I do have right now is some extra cash," Joseppe laughed.

"Did you bring the indictment papers with you?"

"Yes, here they are," Joseppe handed an envelope to Mark.

"Thanks, Josep. Listen, we're gonna take care of this, I promise, okay?"

"Thanks, Markie. Thanks for everything." Joseppe

stood, and Mark extended his hand. The barber shook it firmly, and began heading out of Mark's office. Mark followed him through the vacant office toward the front door.

"I'll call you very soon," Mark promised, as he released the security lock.

Mark slid behind the wheel of his rust-infested RX-7 and headed home. He easily navigated the empty New Year's Day downtown streets. As he drove he twirled the back of his hair. *"A Day in the Life"* had given way to *"Yesterday."* His mind wandered back to his conversation some months earlier with senior partner, Jack Christian.

"Mark," the old patrician had said, "We can't have you working with Carol, it's as simple as that. Too many opportunities for conflicts of interest and bad judgment. That'll be all."

Mark never had a chance to answer the old tight-ass. As he neared his block, Mark realized he was no longer twirling his hair, he was tugging on it. He shook his head as he pulled his hand away, and he gave out an abbreviated snort.

"Jack," he said, as if the senior partner was sitting next to him. "Jack, Jack, Jack."

Chapter Seven

It had been over a week since the death of Stuart Katcavage. Still, Connie Parker had heard nothing from the medical examiner's office. Her repeated calls had gone unanswered, and her frustration was building.

Connie bit her upper lip as she put on a simple black dress and flat black shoes. It was an outfit she actually hadn't worn much while she was dating Stuart, so it was still on the "okay to wear, doesn't remind me of Stuart" list.

Connie approached the medical examiner's office confidently, and made her way to the receptionist's desk. The dull, graying woman sitting there stared blankly at Connie.

Connie shifted from one foot to the other. "Hi, is, um, is Mr. Yamaguchi available?"

The woman picked up the telephone on her desk without acknowledging Connie or giving any indication that she had registered Connie's question. Momentarily, she informed Connie that Mr. Yamaguchi would be right with her.

"Hi, Mr. Yamaguchi, I hope I'm not taking you from something urgent," Connie extended her hand with a smile.

"No, Ms. Parker, what I am doing at the moment can be put aside for you. How may I help you?"

"Well, Mr. Yamaguchi," Connie continued formally, "it has been some time since you began conducting the autopsy on Stuart. I was just wondering if you had learned anything yet?"

"Why don't we go into my office, Ms. Parker?"

Yamaguchi led Connie down a narrow, dingy hallway. Connie had never seen such a scuffed wall. The linoleum floor hadn't been waxed in years, and little bits and pieces of it were chipping off. The hallway was poorly lit and windowless. It gave Connie the willies. She wondered how many stiffs were lying around, toes tagged.

Yamaguchi's office was pretty much what Connie expected. It contained the same putrid, off-yellow walls and the same chipped, yellowing linoleum floor. And it was clear from the dust piled up in the corners and on top of files that he locked his door long before the cleaning crew arrived, if it ever did.

Yamaguchi's office had one single light fixture, if you could call it that, in the center of the ceiling. It also had a fluorescent desk lamp on top of the slate grey, government issue, metal desk.

The medical examiner offered Connie a chair. As she sat, she sneaked a look at him. His eyes betrayed little.

"I really do appreciate the fact that you're willing to take time from your obviously very busy schedule to see me, Mr. Yamaguchi. Can you please tell me what you've learned now?"

"I concluded the autopsy on Mr. Katcavage this morning," Yamaguchi began. "The findings confirmed your fears. Mr. Katcavage did not die from an overdose of alcohol, aspiration, or any other type of intoxication. He was poisoned," the medical examiner said.

Connie stared at the little man impassively, waiting for him to continue.

"I found significant levels of cyanide in his blood. It appeared, from what I could tell, that the cyanide entered his body somewhere in the few hours prior to his death. I will be formalizing my findings and filing my report within the next week."

Connie really wasn't surprised. She stood from the ridiculously uncomfortable metal chair in which she had been sitting for less than two minutes. "Thank you for your time and for that information, Mr. Yamaguchi. Will I be able to get a copy of the formal report?"

"I'll see what I can do, Ms. Parker. I truly am sorry for your loss and if there's anything else I can do to help you, please let me know.

"You know," he continued quickly, "I really wasn't supposed to give you the results of the autopsy until I filed my formal report. I would appreciate it if you would keep it to yourself until next week when my report will finalized."

"You can count on it, Mr. Yamaguchi. And thanks again," Connie extended her hand in the same businesslike fashion that she had earlier.

Yamaguchi took Connie's hand in both of his and held it longer than appropriate. Then he sighed and said, "Again, Ms. Parker, if there's anything I can do . . ."

As Connie hurried out the front door of the building, eyes firmly focused on the ground, she nearly walked head first into Sergeant Dave Moore.

"Ms. Parker, how's everything?"

"Oh," Connie replied blushing, "coming along I guess."

"Actually," Sergeant Moore continued, "I was planning to call you. We're stepping up our investigation, and we'll be needing to talk to you. Will you be around?"

"Yes, Mr. Moore," Connie replied curtly, "I have no immediate travel plans."

Connie headed straight for the U.S. Attorney's office. She walked into the plush, but fraying, reception area outside of Jim Evans' office, and introduced herself to the elderly woman behind the desk. The primly dressed receptionist gave Connie a faint smile of recognition from behind her large teak desk as she buzzed Jim Evans. The prosecutor immediately bolted out of his office with a big smile on his face. Connie looked away as she registered his look of pure delight at seeing her.

"Can we talk privately somewhere, Jim?" Connie began.

"Is my office okay, or were you thinking of somewhere a bit more intimate?"

"Your office is fine."

Connie shook her head, complaining to herself about the utter predictability and despicable nature of the male gender.

Evans' office was a far sight better than the one in which she had just left Yamaguchi. The tall, middle-aged prosecutor had a large oak desk which was neatly piled with papers. His deep brown carpeting was worn and slightly tattered, but it was clean and there wasn't the slightest hint of linoleum. The office was four times the size of the hole-in-the-wall inhabited by the medical examiner.

Connie accepted Evans' offer of a seat and made herself comfortable. At least these chairs had firm backs and cushions. Evans took the seat next to her, crossing his long legs and smoothing the crease in his pants as he did so. His desk chair remained unoccupied.

"So, Connie, how have you been?"

"Oh, getting by, I guess."

"I'm sure you're still shocked and appalled at what happened. I haven't heard anything from the medical examiner's office, so I guess they haven't completed their report yet."

Connie smiled just slightly. "I just came from Yamaguchi's office. He wasn't supposed to tell me, so don't come down on him too hard, but he found cyanide in Stuart's blood. Stuart was killed, but that's no big shock. We damn sure didn't need a coroner's report to figure that out."

"I guess that gives me what I need to go ahead. Technically, of course, I'll need to receive a formal report from Yamaguchi before I can begin conducting an investigation. I know you're gonna want me to move on this thing quickly," the prosecutor said, holding his perfectly manicured hands in front of him, palms facing down. "But rules are rules."

Connie stood from her chair. She leaned over towards Evans. "I understand the system, Jim," she said. "Nevertheless, it would make me very happy if you would start the investigation now."

Evans cleared his throat. He stood up, then quickly sat back down again. "Okay, Connie, I will begin an informal investigation immediately. But you'll need to keep that under your hat, so to speak. I wouldn't do this for just anyone, you know."

Connie stood erect. "Thanks, Jim," she smiled, "I appreciate your flexibility."

Connie left Jim Evans' office feeling, for the first time since the awful, unspeakable event, in a slightly upbeat frame of mind. She walked along Constitution Avenue, and decided to head back towards her office on Capitol Hill. It was a sunny and warm day for January and it felt good to be outside.

Connie let her ankle-length black, lambs' wool coat hang open. The cool air felt refreshing around her neck and legs. She squinted to see through the sunshine and purposefully walked down the impressive, monument-laden boulevard which graced the southern tip of the nation's capital.

Abruptly, she stopped and sat down on a bench along the side of the road. She pulled her wallet out of her pocketbook, unsnapped the compartment which held pictures, and slid out one of her favorite pictures. They were in Georgetown, walking along the towpath. Stuart had stopped a stranger and asked him to take a picture of the two of them. For posterity, he'd said at the time. For posterity.

As she stood to head back toward her office, Connie let the tears run freely down her cheek. They were far gentler, and more easily controlled than the tears of recent days. Who knows, thought Connie, maybe I'm getting more in control.

The phone was ringing as Connie walked through the door to her apartment. She dropped her bag and trotted over to it. She answered and waited. Nothing.

After saying "hello" twice, Connie stopped speaking. She gently hung up the receiver, and sighed deeply, before slumping into a chair. She sat, her coat still on, waiting, half expecting the phone to ring again.

After an hour, Connie dragged herself out of her chair and headed for the bedroom. She flung her coat on the bed and quickly replaced her dress with a pair of sweatpants.

Connie was heading back toward the kitchen to fix a bowl of clam chowder when she spontaneously grabbed the phone and called her mother.

"Hi, Mom, how are you feeling?" she began, trying to sound upbeat.

"Okay, Connie. Coming along. How 'bout you dear? Still upset about your friend?"

Connie held her tongue. To Mom, Stuart was a "friend."

"I'm fine, Mom, really, coming along just fine."

"Oh, that's good, Connie, really good. Say, is it any warmer there than it is back here in the old Midwest?"

"Almost always is, Mom. You still have a nurse with you?"

"Helen is here now. She only works about six hours a day. You know I'm up and about again, cooking, sewing, the usual, just a touch slower than normal is all."

"Hey, that's great, Mom. Really great."

A couple more minutes of banality was all Connie could stomach, so she excused herself and hung up. It was always so difficult to get Mom off the phone, although Connie couldn't understand why, since the older woman never had anything of substance to say.

Connie headed for the bathroom. She fixed her makeup, and made a beeline out of the apartment. The place was beginning to seem awfully small.

She hopped in a cab and directed the driver, who spoke absolutely no English, to drive through the early evening traffic to the Ritz Carlton at 16th and K.

Hopping out of the cab, Connie took a deep breath and bulled her way past the doorman to the hotel bar. She slowed as she approached the bartender, a man who looked familiar, but whom Connie did not know.

She took a seat in the dimly lit, highly polished brass bar, and ordered a gin and tonic. She wanted to make this quick. Leaning back a touch on the tall, but sturdy, wooden bar stool, Connie swiveled her neck from side-to-side, craning it in every direction possible to see if there was anyone she knew in the sparse crowd.

After satisfying herself that she was at least momentarily anonymous, Connie did a second neck-revolution, this time straining to see if there was a man worth meeting tonight. She spotted at least three candidates, and she knew it wouldn't be long before one of them made sure that she wasn't alone any longer. She took bets with herself as to which one would approach first, and what his opening line would be.

"Can I buy you a drink?"

It was the guy she had picked as least likely. So much for instincts. And his opening line was straightforward, and not the least bit awkward. Maybe this wouldn't be all that difficult after all.

"Gin and tonic. Please. Or should I say thanks?"

"You can save the thanks for the bartender. I'm Bill Owens," he said extending his hand. He was probably six two, maybe an inch shorter, with broad shoulders, and not even the hint of an expanding waistline. Connie pegged him as early forties, his dark hair graying ever so slightly around the temples.

Connie shook his hand gently. "Victoria Pebbles," she smiled. Friends call me 'Vic'."

"Nice to meet you Vic. You in town for a convention?"

"No, business trip. I'm a consultant in the P.R. field. Working with some lobbyists. You?"

"Lawyer. Here for a round of meetings with the S.E.C. Client got in a bit of hot water over some securities it issued last year."

"Sounds interesting."

"Not really."

It didn't take but one more drink before Connie headed upstairs with Bill Owens. The sex wasn't bad, but it was what followed that gave Connie her kicks.

"So, was that as good for you as it was for me, Bill?" she cooed.

"It was excellent! I assure you I had no idea Washington could be this much fun."

"What's your wife gonna say, Bill?"

"Excuse, me," Owens stammered as he reached for the covers.

"Listen," Connie began with a beguiling smile, as she wagged her finger toward the man who an hour earlier was a stranger. "She doesn't have to find out, okay?"

Owens looked stunned. "Okay. But?"

"Two hundred bucks."

"What?" The still naked man screamed. "What are you, a call girl?"

Connie smiled. This was the best part. "That remark will cost you, Bill," she sneered. "Make it two fifty."

"This is an outrage!"

"Uh, uh, uh," she cut him off, still wagging her finger. "I strongly recommend that you shut your mouth, as in *now*," she said, snapping her fingers for effect.

Connie found her way over to the side of the bed where just moments earlier Owens had flung his pants in an absolute fit of passion. She retrieved them, and removed his wallet. As the man who only moments earlier had climaxed in bliss watched, paralyzed, she removed two fifty dollar bills and seven twenties.

"Ten dollars off for good behavior," she smiled as she quickly pulled on her panties and dress. "It has been a real pleasure doing business with you, Mr. Owens. It's a crying shame you can't share your little tryst with anyone, it was so much fun. One day, when I'm a contestant on *Jeopardy* I'll wink to you!"

Chapter Eight

Donald Lubins awoke to a pounding headache. He gingerly crawled out of his lumpy bed trying not to awaken his roommates. He made his way through the narrow corridor on the train and into the men's bathroom. He flicked on the light switch and was horrified by what he saw. His cheeks and eyes had turned a ghoulish purple/yellow. His left eye was swollen nearly shut. His right eye was bloodshot and angry.

He gently touched his jaw and quickly realized it was brutally sore. He wondered idly if it was broken, and whether he would need to have it wired shut. He tried to remember exactly how it had happened, but it was all a blur.

Well, at least the Ortiz brothers would know he was a loyal kinda guy. They would know he wouldn't let them down. If nothing else, he would still have a job, and could still feed himself. 'Course, if they had to wire his jaw shut he wouldn't be needing too much in the way of solid food!

He walked quietly back through the train wondering what time it was. He knew it was early, and virtually everyone had partied hard the night before. The last thing he wanted to do was to wake any of the previous night's irritable combatants.

He slipped off the train and began walking across the

dusty back lot of The Big Show. He made his way into the empty arena and sat down in the first row. Every time he tried to touch his face, he grimaced with pain. He wondered aloud if he should go to the hospital.

The Florida sun was beginning to rise, and it shone through the doors of the small arena. It was going to be an unseasonably warm winter day in Lakeland. As he focused the best he could on the sun, Lubins suddenly realized he was devastatingly thirsty. His hangover, combined with his body's need to heal itself, was robbing him of fluids. He was well past dehydrated; he was downright parched.

Lubins stood up and woozily made his way to the water fountain on the far side of the arena. He drank deeply and felt somewhat replenished. He suddenly craved something more substantial. A cup of coffee, or better yet, some iced coffee. Or a coke. He made his way over to the pie car, but the place that housed the main form of sustenance for circus employees during their travels didn't seem open.

As he approached the pie car, Lubins felt a small ray of hope. There was a sliver of light coming from the side. Lubins walked around to the front of the car. There was a single individual in the car, just opening the front.

"Didn't think you'd be open this early," Lubins said with a smile, or at least the best he could muster.

"I'm not really. Another ten minutes till openin' time," the swarthy tattooed man replied.

"Anyway, can I get a cup of coffee, or a Coke now?"

"Nope. Ten minutes."

Lubins snorted to himself, and dragged his excruciatingly sore body over to the stands and sat in the first row. He ran through the performances of Mora the Great and The Flying Ortiz Brothers in his mind, as he waited for the pie car to officially open. After fifteen minutes, Lubins headed back to the pie car.

"Hi, can I get a coke now?"

The man behind the counter just glared at him. Then he pointed to his watch. "Two more minutes," he sneered.

Lubins stared in disbelief, but quickly realized the jerk behind the counter was holding all the cards. Lubins stood his ground, waited for four minutes, then repeated the question.

The pie car operator took a can of coke from a bucket of ice. Lubins smiled, savoring the pleasure which was about to be bestowed upon him.

"That'll be three dukies," the clerk said coldly.

Lubins mouth momentarily dropped open. He'd forgotten all about the dukie system.

"Sorry, I, uh, I left my dukies back in the train. I got some cash, though, can I buy some dukies?"

"Gotta get 'em from the general manager, and he don't sell 'em this time of the morning."

Lubins stood helplessly in front of the pie car, staring at the Coke. "Can I pay you some cash, just this once, I, uh, I'm really thirsty."

"Nope. Not allowed."

"Can I buy some dukies from you?"

"Nope. You're gonna have to go get 'em from the train."

Lubins shuffled away from the pie car. He had no dukies back on the train and he knew it. He'd spent his few remaining ones the night before on dinner.

Lubins knew the food at the pie car was barely edible, but they couldn't ruin a Coke, and the coffee wasn't bad. The beaten up teacher-cum-roustabout looked longingly over his shoulder as he trudged away.

He decided to head out towards the town of Lakeland. He had five dollars with him, and although he knew how entirely unpresentable he must look, he doubted McDonald's or Wendy's would turn him away.

As Lubins padded along the empty streets of the sleeping town he saw a clock on a bank. It was 6:52. One of the fast food joints would probably open by seven o'clock at the latest. With renewed vigor, he picked up the pace and continued stumbling along on his journey towards town.

After an eternity of swaying to and fro, using as much energy to stand as to actually move forward, Lubins spotted a flashing neon sign. His eyes were so blurred that he could not read it. He forged ahead dizzily trying to keep a steady course. He was bummed when he realized the gaudy neon was merely for someone hawking insurance. What the hell was an insurance salesman doing with a neon sign?

He trudged on. His thirst was overwhelming. He now knew he needed something cold, and he needed it fast. Sugar or caffeine would help a damn sight too. Finally, like an oasis in the distance, Lubins saw the golden arches.

He reached the front door an eternity later and pulled it open. The air conditioning climbed all over him like a welcome cold blanket. He stumbled through the doorway and into the promised land. As he approached the counter to place his order, Lubins could feel the clerk, who couldn't have been more than sixteen, and had the pimples to prove it, recoil in horror. She gasped, but then caught herself. "May, uh, I, uh, help you, sir?" she stammered.

"Yes ma'am," Lubins managed a wry half-grin with his response. "I'd like an extra large Coke and an extra large iced tea."

"Anything you say, sir," the clerk replied as she gagged at the damage to Lubins' face. As the young curly-headed blonde girl waited for the Coke to fill the cup she looked back up. "You with the circus?" she asked with a hint of suspicion in her voice.

"Yeah," Lubins said haltingly. "Yeah, I am."

With a look of utter disgust, she held up the drinks. Lubins grabbed the Coke from her hand and downed the entire thirty-two ounces in one motion as she stared in disbelief. Then he took the iced tea. Before he could begin drinking, she interrupted him. "That'll be $2.60 for the drinks."

"Oh, yeah, I almost forgot, I was so thirsty," Lubins replied, as he lifted the five-dollar bill from his pocket. He placed it on the counter and waited.

As the clerk gave Lubins his change he smiled. "I don't always look like this, I promise," he said as he turned and walked away.

Lubins felt a bit better as he made his way back towards Stone's winter quarters. He actually began to laugh a little. He had never gotten the shit kicked out of him, even when he was a little kid. His big, athletic half-brothers, Ian and Scott, had always materialized as if from thin air, just when he was in the most precarious of spots. But now it somehow almost felt like a rite of passage.

When he got back to the train, Lubins saw signs of life. As he was about to step onto the platform nearest his room he saw John Ricketts, the purchasing manager, motioning towards him. Lubins walked over to Ricketts to see what he wanted.

"McGee was looking for you a couple minutes ago, Donald," the purchasing manager indicated, without commenting on Lubins' appearance.

Lubins tried to act nonchalant. "Thanks, do you know where he is?" the fallen warrior asked.

"Yeah, he's already in his trailer," Ricketts said, referring to the general manager's mobile work place.

Lubins made his way over to McGee's trailer. He knocked on the door. Almost immediately the show's general manager asked him to come inside.

McGee's trailer was an eight foot by ten foot cubicle which traveled as part of the train from city to city. It had wooden floors and two metal desks, one of which had a computer and a printer on it, while the other was cluttered with paper. There were two metal desk chairs with ancient, misshapen wheels. The trailer's ceiling was exactly five feet ten inches from the floor. Anyone taller than that had to stoop.

Lubins' hair barely grazed the ceiling as he let himself in. "Good morning, Mike, I heard you were looking for me," Lubins began.

"Yes, Donald, why don't you sit down," McGee offered as he avoided Lubins' eyes and motioned to the one empty chair in the trailer.

Lubins took a seat, and tried to roll it over closer to the short, stocky redheaded general manager, but it was no use. Lubins stood and moved the chair closer. The prehistoric wheels were obviously not going to do it for him. He looked at his employer and waited.

"Donald, I heard there was quite a ruckus last night and I can see from your face that you were in the middle of it," McGee began. "Mora is really flipped out. I gotta do something, you know, make it look like I'm taking action. I'm gonna have to let you go."

"Mike, I can't believe it," Lubins began. "Manuel dragged me into it. I was in my room sleeping when he and his brothers came and got me. I know I haven't been here very long but can't you tell I'm not a fighter?"

"Look, Donald," the general manager began soothingly, "I think I believe what you're tellin' me. In fact, I like you. You're one of the few workingmen who seems trustworthy. But there's a hierarchy at the circus, and you're at the bottom. I'm afraid I need a scapegoat.

"Look, if things don't work out for you wherever you end up, try and come back in three or four or five months. Maybe I'll be able to use you then. Who knows?"

Lubins could see he wasn't going to get anywhere with the GM. His employment of last resort had unceremoniously come to an end. Lubins accepted the envelope with his remaining pay and left McGee's office downcast.

Lubins pawed at the dirt as he slowly made his way across the desolate open lot between the general manager's trailer and the train. He had been with the show for seven weeks.

Lubins quietly opened the door to what was most certainly his humble abode—make that former abode—and began quietly packing. His soon-to-be former roommates snored, oblivious to the turmoil around them. In minutes, Lubins was gone.

It was bad enough that he was suddenly unemployed. But his face, God his face! He knew no one, but no one, not Mother Theresa herself, would give him a job in his current state. He also knew he was pretty badly beaten up and it was going to take days, if not weeks, for his face to heal sufficiently to be presentable. He checked his wallet, his pants, and the little pouch he kept in his suitcase. He was in better shape than he thought. He had $179.88.

The Y cost fourteen dollars a night, and he could bum some food at a soup kitchen. He had almost two weeks' worth of shelter and food if he didn't blow it on anything extravagant.

Lubins swung his duffle bag over his shoulder. He walked down the platform of the train and began making his way across the wide, open field back towards downtown Lakeland. He retraced the steps he had taken a few hours earlier and plopped himself down in McDonalds. He found a newspaper sitting on a chair, bought a cup of coffee, and began idly thumbing through the classifieds.

The paper open, he ignored it. With a terrific distaste in his mouth, Lubins began to think about people he could call, people he could lean on. People don't generally help you out, Lubins knew that, and unfortunately, he had used up most of his chits when he dropped the glass tray on his foot while waiting tables, what was it, a year ago now? His foot was a mess then and he could barely walk for weeks. So he had called his half-brother Scott who took him in for two weeks. God how Lubins had hated that. Letting Scott know that his help was needed. Letting anyone know for that matter. It was anathema to Lubins.

Scott was an auto mechanic. Wife. Two kids. Little split level in the 'burbs. Coupla beers at night after work. A regular Joe. Scott put up with him then, but there was no going back, Lubins knew that. What's more, Lubins didn't want to go back. Ever.

Ian wasn't an option. He had sustained a serious knee injury working in a factory and lived alone collecting disability. Ian was an unhappy soul, even less trusting than Lubins, if that was possible. Ian was barely able to dress himself and face the day. The last thing he needed was to see his older, supposedly successful, half-brother in this condition. Actually it might help Ian to feel a tad less sorry for himself, but Lubins quickly dismissed the possibility.

Ex-wife Julie wasn't a realistic possibility because Lubins couldn't let the kids see him like this. Ditto for the parents. No way.

Lubins wondered how long it would take to heal, and whether there would be any permanent impairment. It was just like the foot injury which left him unable to run without his left foot splaying out wildly, but with no other problems worth discussing.

He glanced back down at the paper. He knew he was unemployable, but he told himself it was important to look anyway. He placed his elbow on the table and tried to rest his jaw in the palm of his hand, but it was too painful. He jerked back violently at the mere touch, and attracted looks from the middle-class clientele of America's favorite fast-food place.

The tables surrounding Lubins remained empty despite the fact that the restaurant was getting crowded. Lubins knew he was a pariah, and it was already beginning to get to him. Suddenly he sat up. If these damn southern crackers couldn't accept him for what he was he was going to head back north. Maybe he could track down his cousin, Josh, in D.C. Yeah, maybe he could.

He slung his duffle back over his shoulder and headed out the door. The interstate was less than a mile from the restaurant. Lubins set out slowly, but with determination. It took him nearly a half hour, schlepping his duffle bag and shuffling along on physically hungover, exhausted, achy, heavy feet. Eventually he made his way to the entrance to Interstate 4. He put down his duffle bag, and defiantly thrust his thumb out directly in front of the sign which prohibited walking, cycling, and hitchhiking. He stood, barely lucid, hoping that some gentle soul would see him for what he was and pick him up.

But it was not to be. After two hours of standing in the radiating heat, Lubins again began to feel dehydrated. Suddenly, he noticed he was hungry too. That he wasn't going to get a ride had become quite evident. That he needed some form of sustenance was equally as evident. Lubins grimaced, turned around, and began the long trek back into town. He passed the McDonalds for a third time that day, but this time he couldn't bear to go in.

Two store fronts down was a Wendy's. Lubins bought himself another large Coke, a hamburger, and fries. Within seconds he had inhaled it, and though he was still starving, he decided to leave. He knew he had taken in enough fuel to keep him going for a few hours, and money was too precious to spend topping off the tank.

Ten years earlier Lubins would not have had any idea where the Greyhound bus station was in Lakeland, Florida, or any other city for that matter. Now he knew exactly how to find it. Just head for the seamiest part of town.

Shuffling along, carrying his worn and tattered duffle, the bruised and battered former circus roustabout made his way right to that very station. There, he asked how much it would be for a bus ticket to Washington, D.C.

"That will be seventy-eight dollars, sir," the plump, friendly, middle-aged clerk said with a kindly smile.

Lubins grimaced. "That, that's a bit more than I was expecting."

The clerk kept right on smiling. "I have an idea, sir," she said. "How 'bout if we get you a ticket to Alexandria, Virginia. That ticket costs fifty-eight bucks. Then you can take the metrorail into the District of Columbia for a few bucks more."

Stunned, Lubins looked up. She was still smiling, like she had the greatest job in the world, and her whole life was just too damn good to be true.

"Okay," he said. "And thanks."

Lubins bit his lip, parted with some of his hard-earned pay, and sat down to wait for the bus which wouldn't be leaving for nearly three hours. He clutched his ticket against his chest, his eyes wide open.

As he sat in the deserted Greyhound terminal, Lubins finally began to relax. Slowly, he drifted off to sleep. The next thing Lubins realized, the middle-aged, polyester-clad clerk was shaking his shoulder gently. "You're gonna miss your bus unless you hurry, sir," he heard her say.

Lubins smiled, nodded his thanks, and boarded the bus for the thirty-two hour trip to Alexandria via every podunk town in the entire southeastern United States.

Lubins had managed to find some old newspapers next to the garbage in the terminal, and he began thumbing idly through them. But he was soon nauseated by his attempt to read during the bumpy bus ride. He leaned against the window and closed his eyes. Suddenly he smiled. It was extremely unlikely that anyone would take the seat next to him in his current condition. Every cloud has its silver lining.

Stretching across the two seats, Lubins slept on and off throughout the night, his mind drifting from childhood memories of games with Ian and Scott, to his marriage, to the fight with Mora the Great's henchman and back again. By the time he awoke for good the sun was rising. He was nearly delirious with hunger and thirst.

He stumbled his way forward to the front of the bus. The driver glanced up at him expectantly, but didn't say a word.

"Excuse me, sir," Lubins began. "I was wondering if you could tell me where we are, and when we might be stopping."

"Well, wonder no more, my man," the driver, who was almost all stomach, bellowed. "We are in the great state of South Carolina, and we'll be in Greenville in under an hour. We'll stop there."

"Thanks," Lubins said, managing a small grin as he turned and headed back to his seat.

Once back in his seat, Lubins gently touched his jaw. He was thrilled when he realized it had dropped from the size of a grapefruit to, perhaps, a peach. Every little bit counts.

As promised, the bus pulled into Greenville in just under an hour. Lubins, still trying to conserve money, purchased three bags of potato chips. He knew they contained little, if any, nutrition, and yet he couldn't help himself. He craved the salt. He found an empty cup which he filled with water at the fountain, and he was in business.

Before long, they were underway again. The bus zigzagged through the Carolinas and by nightfall was rapidly approaching southeastern Virginia. Lubins was feeling stiff and anxious. He wasn't far from Northern Virginia. By tomorrow night at this time he would need a place to stay. The $58 bus ride suddenly didn't seem so expensive when Lubins realized it had provided him with two night's lodging. Since the Y in Lakeland costs $14 a night, quick math told him he was only paying $30 to travel to Alexandria.

As the bus arrived in Alexandria, the sun was just beginning to peak over the horizon. It was glowing a sensational reddish-yellow, and Lubins, tucked inside the cocoon of the Greyhound bus, didn't have a notion as to what the temperature was.

He soon found out. He shivered uncontrollably as he stepped from the bus and quickly made his way into the small station. He put down his duffle bag and purchased a cup of coffee. He found a newspaper lying on the floor and picked it up. Finally, he gathered himself and went to the men's room. He glanced in the mirror and was no longer disgusted by what he saw. Perhaps that wasn't such a good sign. He was getting used to seeing himself beaten up. The swelling had gone down noticeably around his eyes and along his jaw. Pretty much all that remained were the deep bruises and a few scrapes and cuts.

For the first time, Lubins noticed how badly he needed a shave. But he wasn't sure if his jaw could stand having a razor dragged across it. He decided to try.

He lathered his face with hot soapy water, and pulled out a Bic disposable, the same one he had already used ten times too many. He gently began grazing the razor against his cheeks. The blade was dull from overuse, and he nicked and caught his skin more times than he cared to think about. He quickly drenched a paper towel with cold water and dabbed at the eruptions on his face. After an eternity, he was done shaving, and done bleeding.

Lubins took a deep breath and went to the clerk in the station seeking directions. He was pleasantly surprised to learn that there was a Metro stop within walking distance. He slung his duffle bag over his shoulder and set out.

The Metro ride into Washington set back the cost-conscious Lubins an additional $1.65. He now had slightly over $100 to his name, no place to stay, no job, and as far as he could tell, no future. On the bright side, he had little to lose by taking a risk at this point.

Lubins took the Metro into the District and got out at Metro Center. It seemed as good a place as any. He pulled out the little pad upon which he kept phone numbers and addresses for the few people whom he still knew. He hadn't spoken to his cousin Josh for nearly two years, but he was his best hope. For a moment he panicked. He cursed himself for not having called Josh ahead of time from Lakeland. After all, they do have phones in Florida. Dumb. Very dumb.

Scraping his foot on the gum-infested pavement, he popped a quarter into the pay phone, dialed the number, and then listened as the odd, computerized voice whined, "the number you have reached is not a working number. Please check the listing and dial again."

Lubins gently placed the telephone receiver back in the cradle. He pulled out another quarter and called information and gave the operator his cousin's name. There was no listing in Washington, D.C.

Lubins thanked the operator and requested the number of the YMCA closest to Metro Center. Then he called the Y and asked for directions. It was four blocks away. He picked up his duffle bag for the thousandth time in a week, pulled the shoulder strap on, and set out. He shivered. It damn well better be a short four blocks.

Chapter Nine

Jackson Caulfield came to the phony real estate office in khakis and a T-shirt, the same way he had been dressed for the last four months. He intended to do the same thing he had done for the past four months. Nothing.

He and George Moran had scammed the unsuspecting citizens of Washington out of $15,000,000. The money was sitting comfortably in a secret bank account protected by the good folks of Bermuda. For a fee, of course. Moran had insisted on opening a separate account for himself and Caulfield didn't protest. They had split the money sixty:forty with Moran taking the majority although Caulfield had never quite figured out why. It was easier to accept Moran for what he was than to argue with him.

Caulfield had been living the good life for four months. But he missed some of his friends back in Washington, and he knew it was likely he would never see them again. And while he didn't miss his bitchy ex-wife, he did miss his grown children. They were both in college and neither had spent too much time questioning why their father sent their monthly allowance in the form of money orders. It paid the bills and bought them books and CDs so Caulfield knew they didn't care what form it took.

Every so often, someone would come in off the street or call M & C Real Estate. But no transactions were ever consummated. That wasn't the idea. The very thought of working for a living! Caulfield wasn't quite sure why M & C even existed, but Moran had insisted upon it, and Caulfield knew better than to fight with his partner. So they kept the office running and even paid a secretary to answer the phones. Caulfield wondered about Belinda. She never inquired as to why there was no correspondence, or how the bills were being paid. She sat, polished her nails, went out to lunch, and went home.

Caulfield bopped into the office on January 4th and picked up the mail. He began leafing through the back issue of *The Washington Post* which the office received sporadically, at best. When he got to the business section he saw the article about Joseppe. He did a double-take and screamed out for his partner.

"Hey, Jack, what are you worried about?" the slimy Moran retorted, cracking all ten of his huge knuckles in under five seconds. "I think it's great news. Those fuckin' morons will never find us down here. And now that they have someone to frame for the whole damn thing they won't even bother to look. And you know what's best? That barber, Mr. 'I'm an immigrant who made it big in the new country' gets what he deserves. I mean c'mon, you don't actually feel sorry for him do you?"

"I don't know, George," Caulfield began. "I can't see Joseppe just rolling over for this thing. He's got some pretty high-powered customers, some of whom he didn't bilk, and if he gets one of them to represent him, we could find ourselves in a bit of hot water. I don't know, George, I just don't like it," Caulfield said as he shuffled from one foot to the other.

"Well, Jack, you didn't think this thing was just going to blow over with no investigation, did you?" Moran said, with a bit more edge in his voice. "I mean, hell, have you ever done anything outside the Four Corners before?"

"Huh?"

Moran quickly jumped up from the chair where he had sat down only seconds before. For a man of his girth, he moved quickly. He stood on tiptoes, cracking both ankles as he did so. He tried to run a hand through his slicked-back, thinning, jet-black hair, but it didn't budge.

"C'mon, Jackson," Moran said sarcastically, "what did you think, none of Joseppe's customers would get angry at being duped?"

"I don't know what I thought, but, you know, the more days that passed, the more I thought that maybe, just maybe, nothing would happen."

"Don't worry. You worry too damn much. You worry too much about rules and shit. We can make up our own rules as we go along, that's what I keep telling you."

Caulfield looked at his partner. He seemed somehow to be even more out of touch than Caulfield remembered. While they talked, Moran's shirttail, which had taken on a life of its own, began crawling out of his shorts.

There were two Georges, Caulfield knew that. There was the one who tried to show some semblance of caring about social mores and rules and regulations. And then there was the one who made it up as he went along.

Caulfield shook his head, and followed Moran as he headed into Caulfield's office. Moran walked over to Caulfield's desk and picked up his coffee mug.

"Where'd you get this thing?" Moran asked, as he inspected the mug.

"Actually, it's one of the few things I brought with me from the mainland," Caulfield explained. "My son, John, gave it to me about fifteen years ago."

Moran smiled. "It's old," he said. "Think it'll break if I drop it?"

Caulfield tried to look nonchalant. "Don't think so," he said in a clipped voice.

Smiling, Moran held the mug high over his head, and then released it from his grip allowing it to crash to the ground where it shattered into a dozen pieces.

Chapter Ten

Connie Parker rolled over in her bed. It was cold on the side where she hadn't been sleeping, and the covers were totally unrumpled. It had been two weeks since Stuart Katcavage was killed. That's the way Connie was referring to it now. Killed. Not died. Killed.

Connie showered and dressed in a suit which was a medium shade of grey with a powder pink blouse. She wore a thin, fine, gold necklace and no other jewelry. She gave absolutely no thought to Bill Owen until she spotted the two hundred and forty dollars sitting on her kitchen table. Grimacing, she snatched the money off the table, placed it in an envelope, and addressed it to The Pediatric AIDS Society, a charity in which she was quite active. They would put it to good use.

As she was about to leave, Connie was momentarily startled by the ringing of the telephone. She walked over and answered the phone in the kitchen.

The music on the other end was sharp and clear, the theme song to *Jeopardy*, ending just before Alex Trebeck kicks in.

"Whoever you are," Connie snapped, "cut it out!" She slammed down the receiver.

Connie walked the short distance to her office despite the bitter cold. Halfway there she finally buttoned her coat against the wind.

She walked through the door of the lobbying firm where she was employed, saying hello to the receptionist, but not waiting for an answer. She took off her lamb's wool coat, and hung it on the hook behind the door. She helped herself to a cup of coffee, and settled into her office.

The work was piling up. She began leafing through some of the papers on her desk to see which powerful companies wanted to influence which weak-kneed senators. It was mostly routine stuff. Connie dug through most of it, discarding more than she saved. She took a few personal calls and refused a number of business calls, asking her secretary to say she was in a meeting.

One message from her secretary was a bit troubling. Sergeant Moore of the D.C. police had called twice. Connie picked up the phone and tried to reach Moore, but the cop who answered the phone indicated that the Sergeant was unavailable. It was not his shift. Connie left a message.

Just before lunch, she dialed the U.S. Attorney's office.

"What a pleasant surprise," Jim Evans answered the phone.

"Why should you be surprised to hear from me?" Connie snapped, "I told you I would be following up."

Evans paused, then responded haltingly. "Connie, we've done a lot of investigating." He cleared his throat. "And I believe we're making substantial progress. In fact, I believe we'll have a murder indictment within the next few days."

"Can you tell me who your suspect is?"

"I'd rather not. Besides which, I would definitely rather not do so on the telephone."

"If it's the telephone you're worried about, I'd be happy to come to your office to meet with you," Connie offered.

"How 'bout dinner tonight?"

Connie paused before answering. She made a point of sighing deeply into the phone. "I don't think so, Jim," she finally said. "How about lunch instead?"

"Okay," Evans relented.

Plans were made for one o'clock with Evans choosing Club Nouvelle. Connie shook her head as the prosecutor made his choice. It seemed like an awfully inappropriate place to be discussing a murder indictment, but then, Connie was used to inappropriateness.

As Connie hopped in the cab which she hailed to take her to lunch, her coat got caught in the door. She had to ask the driver to pull over so she could open the door and pull it out. She smiled with resignation. The first time she and Stuart had actually gone out together the same thing had happened. Stuart had asked the driver to pull over, then insisted that Connie sit still as he got out of the cab, walked to the other side, opened her door and rescued the bottom of her coat.

―

Connie arrived at Club Nouvelle close to ten after one. She saw Evans pacing nervously near the maitre'd's stand. Connie smiled. Should've come even later.

Club Nouvelle was dark and romantic. The food was so-so, but the atmosphere was incredible, if you were in love or trying to be. At the moment, Connie was neither.

They were seated at the most private table in the place. Either Evans had a running account at Club Nouvelle, or he had paid off somebody handsomely to get this table. You don't just luck into the corner table that's four feet away from its nearest neighbor.

As they were seated, Evans tried to make small talk, but Connie was having none of it.

"Please tell me what you've found, Jim," Connie said firmly.

Evans looked slightly hurt. Nevertheless, he shifted gears smoothly like the consummate courtroom lawyer he was. "We've done some background checks on a number of people, and we've talked to almost everybody at that party. We've also done toxicology checks and spoken with a number of experts about Stuart's death. We are going to the grand jury on Wednesday to present our evidence."

Connie leaned over the table. "And what, Jim, is your evidence."

"I told you already, Connie, I really shouldn't be discussing the case until we go to the grand jury. It's probably unethical to do so."

"Look, Jim, I'm happy to sit and talk with you and I'm happy to have lunch with you, but what I really want is to know who you are going to ask the grand jury to indict." Connie said firmly as she held Evans' gaze. "It means a lot to me, Jim," she continued. "And, unless I'm mistaken, you're in no danger unless I speak to someone about it."

Connie continued to gaze into the prosecutor's eyes. Finally Evans could stand it no longer.

"Okay, look, I'll tell you if you promise not to tell another soul until the indictment is returned next week."

"You're assuming the grand jury will return an indictment," Connie said with more than a hint of question in her voice.

"They will," the brash lawyer replied confidently.

"Okay, then, tell me, is it someone I know?"

"It's as you suspect, I believe." Evans leaned closer. "It's the haircut man."

"That's what I figured you'd say," Connie sighed and

leaned back. "On the one hand, it doesn't take a real genius to have come up with that answer. So I'm not bowled over with enthusiasm. On the other hand, if that's who you really think did it, then he should be indicted and we should go after him full force. I want Stuart's killer brought to justice and I want it done now." Connie thumped the table with her fist.

Connie wished the meal was over. She had gotten the information she came for, but now Evans wanted to shmooze, to be social. She wasn't in the mood.

Connie didn't lose her grace. She sat through the rest of the lunch and put up with Evans' leering all the while counseling herself to be cautious. She didn't want to do anything to burn a bridge with anyone. Especially the man who might be prosecuting the murderer of Stuart Katcavage.

Lunch mercifully ended and Evans picked up the tab. Connie doubted the U.S. attorney's office budget included lunches at Club Nouvelle, but she also knew there was no way the macho Jim Evans was going to permit her to pay for lunch. Maybe he would put in for reimbursement and maybe he wouldn't. Who cared.

Connie hopped a cab back to her office. She breezed past the receptionist, snatching her messages and unbuttoning her long coat as she walked.

She quickly looked through the messages as she sat down behind her desk and decided none of them needed to be returned. There was no return call from Moore. She got up as quickly as she had sat down, put her coat back on, trotted past the receptionist again, only this time going in the opposite direction. "I'm outta here," she called over her shoulder as she pushed through the door.

Her office, which in previous stressful situations had

provided solace, now seemed claustrophobic and suffocating. She headed for home. She still had a hundred or so pages to go in *"Truman."* She needed to finish it. One day, Stuart would want to discuss it.

Chapter Eleven

Mark Clifton got to his office early on the first working day of the new year. He reread the indictment against his newest client, and called Peter Long into his office. He briefly explained the case to Peter and asked him to begin putting together some research on securities fraud in particular, and common law fraud in general.

Mark watched the young associate as he furiously took notes about the latest criminal case to come into the firm of Christian & Lane. Peter seemed only too happy to be working with Mark again.

When Mark finished explaining the indictment and the research he wanted Peter to undertake, he asked the young lawyer if he had any questions.

"I'm happy to be working with you again, and I hope it works out," said Peter. "It would be a shame if it didn't, for a lot of reasons."

Mark glanced up from his desk when Peter had finished. Something about the young man was disturbing. His manner and tone seemed perhaps somewhere between unfriendly and menacing. But was Long to be taken seriously? Who was he?

"It's nice to be working with you as well, Peter," Mark managed to say, in a voice that was both unenthusiastic and dismissive.

Mark watched the gawky, aptly named associate sidle

from the office, and wondered just exactly what Long had meant to convey. It was meant as a threat all right, about that there could be no mistake. But a threat of what? Mark snickered. The kid was inept, unable to even make a convincing statement of intimidation. Mark pursed his lips and shook his head. He decided to call Carol for a consultation.

After not finding Carol in her office, Mark decided to head out and run a couple of errands. He walked briskly. It was cold. Bitter cold. He had his collar turned up and a scarf wrapped tightly around his neck. But he couldn't see taking a cab. He was only walking four short blocks, and he was feeling pretty good even though he had forgotten to wear gloves. His hands were firmly thrust into his pockets. Even still, they were a bit cold. Mark couldn't remember the last day in Washington when the temperature had barely broken zero.

As he made his way along Pennsylvania Avenue, Mark spotted a homeless person he had never seen before. He grimaced in anguish. How the hell are you supposed to tell the really needy from the sham artists? Better to give to charities, he thought, and let them decide.

Many of the homeless who inhabited the streets near Mark's office had become familiar figures. Mark knew virtually all of them by sight. He even knew some of them by name. But he tried not to learn their names. Because to learn their names only humanized them.

As he walked towards the unfamiliar face, the man looked up at Mark. Mark happened to be fondling a quarter in his pocket at the moment their eyes met. Instinctively, Mark took the quarter from his pocket and flipped it towards the cup the man was holding.

Through sheer luck it landed right in the middle of the cup, and coffee splashed out of it onto the startled street person.

"Another superstar is born!" the man called out in a distinctive baritone.

Mark stopped dead in his tracks. "Professor Lubins?" he asked.

"Who wants to know?"

"Mark, Mark Clifton. I had you for Comparative Lit. at Wesleyan about fifteen years ago."

"Yeah, that sounds about right. I taught there around then. Yeah, maybe in the mid-to-late-seventies, before I headed off to Dartmouth. What did you say your name was again?"

"Mark Clifton."

"What kind of grade did I give you?"

Mark blushed. "You gave me an 'A,' Professor Lubins."

"I tell you Mark, your name sounds a bit familiar, but I can't place your face at all."

"I had really long hair and a full beard in those days, so I probably look a little bit different. Especially with these clothes on," Mark said, as he gestured towards his classic grey tweed overcoat and Brooks Brothers' suit.

Mark could feel his arm hairs standing on end, and his ears suddenly felt like they could hear the tiniest sound as he stood a couple of feet away from the bedraggled character who had once held a position of trust, power, and respect. Mark looked first down at his feet and then to the horizon beyond. "Can I buy you a cup of coffee, considering I just ruined the one you were drinking?"

"Yeah, now that's an offer," Lubins said. "That's an offer I won't refuse."

The unlikely duo walked to the next block, and Mark

deposited the professor at a table in the local Kentucky Fried Chicken and headed toward the counter for some coffee.

Lubins seemed positively gregarious when Mark returned. "So, Mark, what kind of work are you in? You look damn prosperous!"

"I'm a lawyer, Professor Lubins. After Wesleyan I took a year off, and then I went to Boston College Law School. When I graduated I worked for a small firm for a little while, but I hated it. So I joined the Justice Department and worked as a prosecutor in the White Collar Crimes Division. Last year I went back into private practice doing defense work." The words tumbled out of Mark's mouth.

"Hey, when I was growing up, you know what we called this place? Come Fuck Me Fried Chicken," Lubins said, with a sudden staccato burst of laughter. "Look, Mark," Lubins continued, turning serious, "I know that you're probably wondering how I ended up on the streets. But, you know what? It's not a pretty picture, and I don't feel like painting it."

"It's really none of my business, Professor Lubins."

"Yeah, well that's true. People, Mark, I warn you. They'll only let you down. Never, I mean never, put yourself in a position like this, where you've got to look for someone to help you through, help you get a cup of coffee. People always used to let me down, Mark, but they don't anymore, know why? Cause I don't let them, that's why. I stopped expecting anything, so now I'm not let down, if you follow me."

They were done with their coffee, and Mark could feel the awkwardness, which had never really lifted, growing heavier, like a mist forming in the distance and closing in.

Mark knew he had to get back to work. He had a meeting scheduled in ten minutes. But what was he going to do? Gee, Professor, nice to see you again. Take care, and, hey, if you wind up in these parts again, let me know, okay?

"You staying anywhere or are you trying to tough it out on the street?" Mark finally managed.

"I was staying at the YMCA up until a couple of days ago. Then my money ran out. I still get over there to take a shower and try and shave and stuff like that. But I really don't have a place to stay," Lubins said, studying his feet.

"Listen, Dr. Lubins, I have a small apartment in upper Georgetown. It's no great shakes, but its a roof over my head and it's warm. I'd like it if you would stay with me until you get your feet back on the ground. My girlfriend, Carol, stays with me a lot, and I've got a golden retriever named Crisfield. I doubt Carol would mind, and if you like dogs, Crisfield is great fun."

"The Good Lord must be looking down on me," Lubins said, but Mark couldn't tell if it was sarcasm or gratitude which colored the statement.

Once he had convinced his former professor to accept the offer of shelter, Mark had another problem on his hands. He had to be back in the office momentarily for a meeting. Liberal though he might be, he had difficulty with the idea of bringing Lubins into his office, at least in Lubins' current condition.

Mark pulled ten dollars from his wallet. "Get yourself something to eat, and pick up whatever else you'd like. I've got to go to a meeting back in my office which starts in five minutes. I'll meet you right here at 5:30."

"Okay," said Lubins. "Thanks, Mark, you're okay."

Mark narrowed his eyes as he said goodbye. Again, that tone of voice. It was the kind of intonation that separated itself from the crowd, and you would know exactly how to take it if you knew the person using it even marginally well. Given the circumstances, Mark could only guess.

Mark walked rapidly out of the fast food restaurant with the smell of grease keeping him company on the way out the door. What the hell was that last half hour? Some kind of a surrealistic dream? He could hear Paul McCartney's voice rattling around in his head as he headed back upstairs. *"Yesterday. All my troubles seemed so far away...."*

Mark sat through the compensation review meeting with less interest than usual. He wondered to himself how Lubins could have fallen so far. But he worried too that the former teacher was nuts or a drug addict. I mean this guy is going to be living in my apartment in about two hours, Mark thought.

When the meeting ended, Mark bolted for Carol's office. He told his virtual live-in girlfriend that they were going to be having company for the evening. Then he told her who.

"Well, hon, you know, I certainly have no problem with him staying with us. But I do think it's kinda wild the way the whole thing happened," Carol, said with a shrug, as she caressed the silver teddy bear pin which she wore on the lapel of her teal suit.

"It really is. Look, I gotta tell ya," Mark said, speaking quickly, and in a more high-pitched tone than he could ever remember using, "I'm having second thoughts about the whole thing myself. If you feel uncomfortable, I'll understand if you want to stay at your place for a couple of nights."

"Is that what you want?"

"Shit, no!"

"As long as you're there, I'm sure I'll be safe. Who knows, if it's too weird then I'll go back to my place, okay?"

"Sounds good," Mark said, as he looked at his watch. "I guess I'd better get going so I can meet him when I told him I would. I don't know if he's got a watch or what but I'd hate to stand him up. I'm sure he's feeling shaky enough as it is."

"Yeah, I'm sure that's probably true. "I guess I'll see you later."

"Thanks, sweetie."

Mark gave Carol a quick, almost furtive kiss. Then he slipped on his coat and headed for the door. He didn't want to keep the professor waiting.

As Mark walked through the door of the fast food restaurant for the second time that day, he quickly spotted Lubins in a corner booth with the remains of a huge bucket of fried chicken and a drink. Mark's former teacher also had a copy of *The Washington Post* which he was poring over in close detail.

"Hey, Dr. Lubins, I'm back!"

Lubins looked up. "Oh, hey, Mark. Is it time to go?"

"Sure."

Despite the bitter cold, Mark had actually walked the three miles to the office that morning. He doubted Lubins was in any physical condition to make it on foot back to the apartment. Mark also noticed that Lubins now had with him a terribly weathered duffle bag. Lubins certainly wouldn't want to lug that thing all the way back to the apartment.

As they stepped outside Kentucky Fried Chicken, leaving behind the remains of what Mark figured was probably the best meal Donald Lubins had eaten in some time, Mark hailed a cab. In ten minutes they were dropped off in front of Mark's apartment house.

It was an unassuming brownstone with twelve units. Mark lived in the largest of these units on the top floor. The building had an elevator despite having only three floors. Mark had only ridden in the elevator while carrying grocery bags or other heavy items, but he didn't want Lubins to schlep the grungy looking duffle, which probably housed the better part of his life, up the steps.

Mark felt the silence as the two rode the elevator to the third floor. When the doors opened Mark announced that his apartment was the first one on the left, and he headed off in that direction with Lubins in tow.

"Like I was saying," Mark turned to Lubins, "you'll be staying in the den. It has a pull-out sofa, and it'll give you some privacy."

"You mean you don't even have a bedroom for me?" Lubins laughed.

"Sorry. That's the best I can do," Mark said with a smile. Mark showed Donald Lubins where he would be staying. Mark knew it was probably the tenth different bed Lubins had slept in that week. Then Mark shuddered. It was more likely to be the first bed in which Lubins had slept in that week.

Lubins appeared thrilled. He showered and put on a filthy, rumpled T-shirt with a pair of oily, slightly loose-fitting jeans. Mark tried not to stare as Lubins made his way back to the living room where Mark was sitting, watching the evening news, and glancing through *The Wall Street Journal.*

Finally, Mark made a point of looking up. "Would you like to throw some clothes in the laundry?"

"Nah," Lubins replied. "I really appreciate everything

you're doing for me, but I don't want to put you out any further."

"Don't be ridiculous," Mark replied. "Throwing in a load of clothes is hardly a bother."

Mark jumped up from the couch, and motioned for Lubins to follow him into the kitchen. There he pointed out the compact washer/dryer combination in the far corner. He demonstrated its use, showed Lubins some detergent and told him not to be shy.

Lubins thanked Mark, shrugged his shoulders and padded back to the den. He picked up the omnipresent duffle bag which looked like it could use a good scrubbing itself, walked back through the living room and dragged it into the kitchen.

Again, Mark found himself staring. He watched as Lubins opened the washing machine and turned the duffle bag over on top of it emptying the entire contents of the decrepit, old bag into the washing machine. Though Lubins' belongings were meager, the apartment's washer was compactly built. His clothes came right to the top.

Mark was amused by Lubins' attempt to force his clothes into the machine, an attempt which eventually proved successful. Mark could tell that Lubins hadn't used a washing machine in some time, and was having trouble remembering how hard he could push down on the clothes without causing a problem. Lubins poured in some detergent, twisted the knob, and pulled it out. He appeared slightly stunned when he heard the water begin cascading into the well of the machine. He picked the cover back up quickly in an apparent attempt to assure himself that the water wasn't flooding the kitchen. Then he let the top drop, clanging it noisily. He traipsed back into the living room.

Mark watched as Lubins in his filthy jeans sat on

Mark's new, white, living room chair. Grimacing, Mark said nothing.

"I know you just had a late lunch," Mark began, "but I was wondering if there's anything in particular you might like for dinner?"

"I'm fine, Mark, really I am. I don't even need dinner, really I don't."

"How 'bout a pizza?"

"I haven't had one in a while, but it sure sounds good, real good," Lubins said as he licked his lips. "But, hey," he continued, holding his hand up in the air, "only if that's what you want."

"I love pizza, Professor Lubins. I'll go order one."

"Hey, Mark, can you do me a favor?"

"I'll try."

"Stop calling me 'Professor' or 'Doctor,' okay?"

"Ya' know," Mark said, his cheeks flushing a bit, "when you're used to calling someone a certain name it's hard to change. When I was growing up, I used to always call my parents' friends Mr. this or Mrs. that. Now, whenever I see any of them, I still call them that even though it drives them nuts. I don't do it for that reason, it's just that that's what I'm used to. Anyway, I'll try not to call you that anymore."

"Thanks, Mark," Lubins said with a slight snicker.

Mark slipped into the kitchen where he placed the pizza order. He followed that with a telephone call to the office to Carol. Her briefcase was already packed, she informed Mark, and she was on her way to the apartment. And yes, pizza would be just fine.

Carol and the pizza both arrived at the same time. Mark introduced her to the now clean, though still shabbily dressed, Lubins. As he opened the pizza box,

Mark decided not to offer his guest a beer. Who the hell knows what role alcohol played in the man's demise, Mark thought. Sure he was being paternalistic, but, hey, the guy was living with them, it was his prerogative.

"I've got Coke, Diet Coke, and a bunch of different kinds of juice, Donald. What can I get you?"

"A Coke, please. I need to keep pumping caffeine right about now."

Carol, who had gone into the bedroom to change, returned wearing sweatpants and one of Mark's huge Boston College sweatshirts. Mark saw Lubins smile as she returned. The professor hadn't lost his sex drive, that was certain.

For someone who claimed not to be hungry, Lubins monopolized the pizza. He ate half of it himself, and from the looks of things, easily could have eaten the entire pie without much trouble.

Mark suppressed an urge to crack a joke about Lubins' appetite. He just wasn't sure how Lubins would react to that type of humor.

When they finished eating, Mark broke out the ice cream. Lubins' appetite continued unabated. At a moment when Lubins was seriously preoccupied with the two scoops in his bowl, Mark glanced over at Carol and the two shared a wink.

As he downed the last of his ice cream, Lubins offered to clean up.

"That would be great, Donald," Mark said, and he ushered Carol into the living room.

Once the dishes were cleared, Lubins transferred his laundry to the dryer. Then he joined Mark and Carol in the living room.

Mark turned on the tube. It was time for the Mo Buell

show. Hard to believe that yokel had his own cable T.V. show. Harder to believe that Mark watched it. Carol popped up as Mo began screeching.

"Honestly," she said, with mock disdain. Then she smiled. "I'm gonna make some calls," she followed up, her smile broadening. "Hope you learn something."

Lubins looked nonplussed. Mark explained who Mo Buell was, and why Carol was leaving the room.

"He's considered more of a man's kind of jock. You know, he's kind of vulgar. I don't particularly care for his politics, but the guy is really funny, and he'll say just about anything."

Mo ranted on about high-powered lobbyists for a while as Mark and Lubins looked on. Mark laughed self-consciously a few times, not sure if he should try to explain to the impassive Lubins what was so amusing, or if he was better off just leaving well enough alone.

Mercifully, the dryer kicked off. Mark glanced at Lubins who didn't seem to notice.

"Hey, Don," he said, "clothes are dry."

Lubins popped up. "Thanks," he said, as he retrieved his clothes and stuffed them back in the duffle bag. Lubins then excused himself and returned moments later in clean clothes. Although they were paper thin from wear and were fraying tragically at the edges, the flannel shirt and jeans had cleaned up reasonably well. Lubins looked respectable. And from the smile on his face, he apparently felt like a million bucks.

An hour later, Lubins said it was time to call it a day. Mark left Lubins in the den, and headed back into the dining room where he picked up his recently made cup of coffee and made his way into the bedroom. Carol was lying in bed, reading a murder mystery. She looked up from her book and smiled.

"Well, whaddya' think?" Mark asked.

"He certainly seems nice enough," Carol said, though her voice betrayed a touch of uncertainty.

"He's edgy. But wouldn't you be if you were in his situation? I mean the guy has come down a long, long way. So how would you feel if you were him?"

"Hey no need to attack, sugar bear," Carol said coolly. "I'm sure I'd feel real shaky too. He's probably felt shaky for a while now. Do we have any idea how long it's been since he held a job?"

"When we were coming back here in the cab he told me he'd only been on the streets for a few days. Only since his money ran out. So if he's had money as recently as a few days ago then either he's panhandling or he had a job. I mean I doubt the guy was collectin' unemployment."

"So you figure he may have had a job, what, maybe a month ago?"

"I don't know exactly when, but it couldn't have been too long ago."

"Aren't you dying to know what happened to this guy?"

"Damn right," Mark snorted. "But I can't see asking him point blank, 'hey Donald, how is it that you became homeless?' "

"No, of course not," Carol smiled. "But there are other ways to find out than hitting him over the head with it. Did he give you any hints?"

"Not really. Talked kind of bitterly about people, you know. He told me not to rely on people 'cause they'll only let me down in the end."

"Sounds like he's feeling a little sorry for himself."

"Not unusual for someone in his situation, don't you think?"

"Yeah, no, you're right about that, though he didn't seem all that bitter to me."

"A little hard to tell. Jury's still out, don't you think?"

"I guess," Carol sighed gently.

"Let's go to bed," Mark said with a sudden finality. "This has been a weird day. A real weird day."

Chapter Twelve

Donald Lubins, ex-professor, ex-waiter, ex-busboy, ex-circus roustabout and ex-homeless person, woke up after a long, restful night's sleep. Although time had become somewhat meaningless for him in the last few weeks, Lubins nevertheless glanced at the clock on the desk in Mark Clifton's den. It was shortly after ten o'clock. Lubins had slept for over eleven hours. He yawned, stretched his arms out over his head and pulled himself into a sitting position. He pulled his jeans back on and smoothed out the flannel shirt in which he had slept. Then he popped out of bed. He walked over to the window and looked out. It was sunny and bright, but judging by the fact that there were very few people outside, it was probably still damn cold.

Lubins opened the door that led from the den back into the living room. The apartment was silent. He tiptoed towards Mark's bedroom and gave a listen. He heard footsteps and he tensed, but it was only Crisfield. He petted the dog's soft golden fur gently and began making his way back towards the kitchen. He noticed a piece of paper on the kitchen table. He walked over towards it and saw that it was a note from Mark. He read the note which indicated simply that Mark and Carol had gone to work and that he, Donald Lubins, twenty-four hours removed from homelessness, should make himself completely at home. The note further indicated that Mark would try to call him in the late morning, and he should answer the phone when it rang.

What is this, Lubins thought, an ex-student's idea of a sociological experiment, or some do-good liberal on a self-righteous power trip? Or was it finally just, what, good luck?

Lubins gently placed the note back on the kitchen table, and began smiling broadly. He began shadow boxing, and then broke out into a full-blown, disco fever dance complete with pirouettes and high leg kicks. He pranced around the apartment in this hyper-aerobic state until his left foot began to ache, and he noticed he was panting.

He plopped down in the easy chair in the living room. He picked up the remote control and flipped on the television set. He cycled through the channels quickly, not caring what was on. All of a sudden he jumped out of the easy chair, and ran towards the kitchen. He quickly filled the kettle with some water and put it up to boil. Then he began frantically looking first through the cabinets, and then the refrigerator.

He found a loaf of rye bread. He quickly stuffed two pieces into his mouth, barely wasting the time to chew. Then he took two more pieces out of the package and rammed them into the toaster. He found some jam and butter in the refrigerator. He took the cover off the jar of jam and dipped his hand into the sticky substance. He licked his fingers while he waited impatiently for the bread to become toast.

As he was looking around the kitchen he saw a couple of pieces of fruit in a basket on top of the counter. He picked up the pear and bit into it. In seconds he was finished eating it. Just then, the toast popped out of the toaster. He grabbed both pieces, burning his jam-coated fingers slightly, and dropped them onto the counter top. He swabbed on mountains of jam and butter then folded both pieces in half and quickly wolfed them down.

Lubins looked around the kitchen as he gently patted his stomach. He opened the refrigerator for the fourth time in the last ten minutes. He took out a box of leftover Chinese food. He found a fork in the drawer to the left of the refrigerator, and he began digging into the kung pao chicken. It was extraordinarily spicy, and Lubins savored the taste. He quickly knocked off the remainder of the box and flung it into the garbage pail. Then he opened the refrigerator yet again. He was looking for something to drink. He saw beer, wine, orange juice, apple juice, and lemonade. He had long since gulped down his coffee, and he longed for something cold. He picked up a bottle of beer and rolled it around in his hands. It was some fancy brand he didn't recognize. He put it back in the fridge and pulled out the container of lemonade, drinking directly from it, and savoring every last ounce.

With Crisfield curled up on the living room couch, Lubins set out to do some exploring in the other rooms of Mark's apartment. First he made his way towards the successful lawyer's bedroom. Lubins smiled. His former student was getting it right there in that bed from an unreasonably attractive young woman.

Lubins walked over to the large, walk-in closet on the right side of the bedroom. He opened the door and turned on the light. On the left side were a bunch of boring men's suits and a number of Beatles' ties. On the right were the clothes worn by the woman upon whom Lubins' eyes had gloriously danced the previous night. He removed one of the hangers containing a particularly slinky, teal-colored dress from its spot in the closet. He held it up to the light. He shook his head as he smiled and imagined Carol wearing it, and then removing it. Then he quickly placed the hanger back in its appointed place amidst its sisters in the closet.

Lubins glanced across the room towards the bed. He imagined Carol lying there, and again he shook his head. Damn, she was better looking than any woman had a right to be. He put his hand down his pants and quickly rearranged his suddenly bulging crotch. Pesky thing, that crotch!

As Lubins stared at the bed, with both hands firmly down his pants, massaging gently, he was startled by the ringing of the telephone. He ran over to the night table next to the bed and answered it.

"Hey, Donald, how's it goin'? How'd you sleep?"

"Uh, hi, Mark," Lubins stammered, before regaining his footing. "I slept fine, really good in fact. Thanks."

"Well, make yourself at home and help yourself to anything that's in the refrigerator."

Lubins laughed. "I kinda already did," he said.

"Good," came Mark's reply.

"Listen, Mark, I'm getting a little antsy being cooped up in here. Is there any way I can go out for a while and maybe get a newspaper or something?"

"Of course. If you look in the first cabinet in the kitchen against the far left wall there's a hook with a key on it. That's the key for the dead bolt. Take it with you and make sure you leave the regular lock unlocked but lock the dead bolt.

"Carol and I should be home around seven and you're welcome to join us for dinner. I'm not sure what we'll do yet but you're definitely invited."

"Thanks. I'll see you later."

Lubins hung up the phone. He walked back into the

kitchen and quickly found the key. He snatched it off the hook and deposited it in his pocket after first checking to make sure that the hole in his pocket wasn't big enough for the key to fall through.

He made his way back into the den where he folded up the sleeper sofa and replaced the pillows. He did the best he possibly could to lace up his boots considering that the decrepit laces were constantly tearing. He took what passed for his winter coat out of his bag and let himself out of Mark's apartment. In seconds, he was on the streets again.

The biting air cut right through his shopworn denim jacket that was better suited to use as a coverup for a teenager wanting to affect a devil-may-care attitude on a cool spring day. The day felt both depressingly cold and not so cold at all. Lubins had a place to return to at least until Mark came up with an excuse to kick him out.

During his short week on the streets, Lubins had made exactly one friend. Her name was Mary. He had no idea what her last name was, and he was quite certain she had no idea what his last name was either.

Mary had told Lubins that she had been living on the streets on and off for four years. She freely admitted to being an alcoholic. What little money she was able to gather from panhandling she immediately spent on cheap booze.

Mary carried her life around in a Bloomingdale's shopping bag which had torn at the seam innumerable times, only to be taped back together again. She liked to joke about the bag's former owners, and how it had certainly dropped more than a station or two.

A few nights ago, during a bitter cold spell, Lubins had tried to talk Mary into coming into a shelter. Of course, there was no convincing the middle-aged alcoholic that she was in danger. Either she was unaware of the problems which the cold could cause her, or she didn't care.

So Lubins had spent the night with Mary on a grate not far from the White House. Oh, he had taken a few nips from the cheap vodka she was drinking, but just to keep himself warm. He knew he could suffer from exposure if he wasn't careful, but in the short time he had gotten to know Mary, a strong bond had formed.

Now a few days later he went looking for her. He still had a little over $5 left from the money Mark had given him yesterday. He wanted Mary to have it.

Although he had been cold and a bit bewildered during the cab ride of the day before, Lubins was still in possession of his faculties. He oriented himself quickly once outside of Mark's apartment, and he began heading down through Georgetown back towards downtown Washington.

He was walking for nearly an hour when he finally began to recognize some of the scenery. He recognized the corner where the truck from Martha's Table gave out soup at six o'clock every night. He knew he was close to Mary's home. He trudged on.

When he got to the grate where Mary lived, Lubins quickly realized that his friend was nowhere to be seen. Lubins assumed that Mary had panhandled some money and was off buying booze or, better yet, he hoped, some coffee. He walked around the corner and found the man that Mary referred to as "Tiny" half-asleep on his own personal grate. Donald shook Tiny until he came around.

"Where's Mary?"

"Ambulance came and took her away las' night," came Tiny's reply. "She near on froze to death. They said they wuz takin' her to the hospital."

Unable to speak, Lubins stared straight at Tiny. He pawed at the pavement for a minute and rubbed his forehead. Suddenly, viciously, he kicked the wall next to Tiny. "Shit, man, shit. Why didn't you get her inside somewhere?"

"Hey, man," Tiny responded. "Where the fuck were you, at the Taj fuckin' Mahal?"

"Where'd they take her, Tiny?" Lubins demanded.

"Got me," the enormous, disgusting old man replied.

Lubins shook his fist at Tiny, kicked the grate he was lying on and stormed away. He skulked around the block, hands thrust deeply in his pockets. Shortly, he came back to the grate which Mary called home. He saw her belongings packed neatly in the Bloomingdale's shopping bag. Had they been there ten minutes earlier? Lubins couldn't remember.

Lubins sat down on the grate. He gnawed at the inside of his cheek, vapor escaping with each short breath. The warm air from below, though steamy and gritty, felt good. As the sun began setting behind the high rises, Lubins forced his stiff and creaky bones into a standing position. His legs had already begun to numb from the cold, despite the steam from below.

He began walking, unsteadily at first, then a bit more confidently, back towards Georgetown. He thought momentarily about blowing his remaining money on a cab ride, and depending upon Mark to give him more. He quickly dismissed that thought. Mark was undoubtedly going to figure out a way to assuage his guilt shortly and then the lawyer was going to dump Lubins real quick. Better to save every cent possible.

As Lubins walked along Pennsylvania Avenue, heading for the warmth, if not the solace, of Mark's apartment, he paused in front of the emergency room at

George Washington University Hospital. After a moment's hesitation, Lubins strode into the hospital, and walked directly up to the admission's desk where he engaged the young black woman behind the desk. "I'm interested in finding out if you brought in a patient last night who was homeless."

"Unfortunately, sir," the woman responded, in a lilting island dialect, "there are lots of homeless people in this city and lots of them come through these doors. Unless you have more information to go on other than the fact that this person was homeless, I'm afraid I can't be of much help. Now if you'll excuse me. . ."

"Hey," Lubins called out, "her name is Mary. She's oh, I don't know, I'd say about fiftyish. She's got thick, matted grey hair and she's about five feet six inches tall. She's not what you'd call pretty, but she has a sorta, I don't know, sweet look to her. And she's a drunk."

"Well that's not much of a shock," the clerk said with a crooked grin. "Seems like most all homeless people are drunks."

"Whatever you say, ma'am," Lubins replied with a devilish grin. "Isn't there somebody who can tell me if Mary was brought in last night? I know she was picked up by an ambulance."

"Who are you, anyway?" the clerk asked, her singsong abruptly taking a suspicious turn. "Are you a relative?"

"No," Lubins admitted, "just a friend."

"I'm really not supposed to give out information to friends concerning who may or may not be in the hospital. And I wasn't on duty last night," the clerk continued, softening again. Then she sighed. "Let me take a look in the admission charts from yesterday, and see if there's anything that might help you."

"Thank you," Lubins replied. "I appreciate it."

"I don't see anything on the admissions chart, sir," the clerk said, earnest now. "It doesn't sound like your friend was brought here."

"Unless she was brought in dead. Then she wouldn't be on the admissions chart, would she?"

"No, we've been accused of being pretty liberal with who we admit, but as far as I know we've never admitted a dead person before!"

"How would I go about finding out if she was brought here but turned out to be dead?"

"She'd be at the city morgue. We wouldn't keep a corpse here for long. Here's the number. You can try there. Good luck," the woman behind the counter said, suddenly acting curt again.

"Yeah, thanks, although I'm not sure what that means. I really don't hope to find her there," Lubins said ruefully. "I really don't."

"No, I'm sure you don't."

Lubins fished out a quarter and placed the call.

"Yes," Lubins said when the phone was answered. "I'm interested in learning if you brought in my friend Mary last night. Kinda beaten up. Fiftyish, grey, matted hair."

"Actually, sir, there was someone brought in who meets that description. Don't know her name though. She didn't have any ID."

"Do you know where she was picked up?" Lubins asked nervously.

"No. I wasn't on duty."

"Isn't there a file or something?"

"Who are you, sir," the voice at the other end demanded.

"A concerned friend."

"Look, sir . . ."

Lubins gently hung up the phone. He trudged out of

the hospital's emergency room. It was dark and excruciatingly cold outside. Before leaving Mark's apartment, Lubins had written down the lawyer's address. He began to hail a cab, but as soon as one approached, he turned quickly away and began walking towards Georgetown all the while waving contemptuously at the driver. He thrust his hands as deeply as they would go into his pockets and turned towards the apartment. Damn it was cold.

Chapter Thirteen

Connie Parker had a cocktail party to attend in a few hours. Not a big deal. She knew it was going to be just like all of the others, and she just couldn't muster the energy.

Despite her benign neglect, Connie's lobbying practice was thriving. A friend or playmate wasn't in the cards, at least not yet, not in the midst of all these people she knew. So there was no purpose for her to attend the cocktail party except that it was being given by Michael Cohen, a powerful ally, and sometimes business associate.

Connie sat with Michael on the board of directors of the Pediatric Aids Society. They had worked together closely on many matters of great importance to the charity, and Michael was one of the first to call after word of Stuart's death had circulated. Connie hadn't really felt like attending to any of the Society's business since Stuart's death. She thought that perhaps this would be a good way to ease herself back into the picture without having to see a whole office full of well-wishers at a board meeting.

Connie dragged herself home from the office and changed into a party dress. It was longer than most of her wardrobe, falling only about an inch above the knee. She flung a scarf around her shoulders, adjusted her makeup and put on the coat she had just taken off. She shook her head slowly as she slipped her arms into the sleeves. She shivered at the thought of going out again, took a deep breath, and fished her keys out of her pocketbook.

Just as Connie was about to head out, the phone rang. She reached for the receiver, then changed her mind. The answering machine clicked on. Her father was "checking in." Connie made a tentative move toward the phone, hesitated, then picked it up.

"Dad," she said, with a start, but she was too late. Carlisle Parker was not one to rattle on to an answering machine.

Connie stepped outside of her apartment and made a last-second decision to take a cab. Not in the mood to drive, especially not alone.

She arrived at the party about thirty minutes after it had started. Connie felt downright naked walking in alone. As she handed her coat to the woman checking such items, she caught a catty sneer being directed her way by a frumpy looking old maid who was standing ten feet away. Connie recognized the look, had seen it—the exact sneer—once before, only it hadn't been directed at her, but rather, at her mother.

Connie remembered all too well the day she had gone to her cousin Virginia's confirmation with her mother. Dad had begged off, saying he didn't feel well. God, how Connie remembered, although she had only been seven at the time. Her parents had fought in their passionless way about Carlisle's refusal to go, and how it would look. Connie had listened intently, but not really understood. All she knew was that she and her mother were going to the confirmation and her father was not.

Connie remembered distinctly walking into the party—they had missed the ceremony—late, tugging at her mother's dress. Just as Mom was about to say hello to Virginia, Connie had looked up and seen the most incredible look of utter disdain on the face of one of the older women attending the party. It was the same look she had just seen repeated tonight.

Looking away, Connie composed herself as she momentarily thought about verbally attacking the woman. But she thought better of it and headed for the bar. She started to order a vodka tonic, but thought better of that too. She asked for a club soda. With lemon.

Connie looked around at the various groupings of people carrying on their self-important conversations. She finally chose the people whom her instincts told her would be least offensive and headed towards them.

For the next half hour, Connie exchanged banalities with the group trying her best to disguise her disinterest. Her drink was quickly replenished before she even finished it by an overly attentive, servant-like man. She didn't bother to protest. Unlikely she would overdo it on club soda. And lemon.

Connie spotted Michael Cohen and spent a few minutes catching up. She accepted condolences from a number of other board members as well, so the party, in fact, did serve a useful purpose.

As the party began breaking up, Connie spotted an old friend, Jayne Proctor. Jayne looked a bit chunkier than Connie remembered, but her smile was just as winning. Connie and Jayne had worked together when Connie first graduated from college and they had remained in touch, on and off, throughout the ensuing decade. Jayne was a very strong lobbyist in a very narrow niche. She represented a number of nonprofit organizations seeking legislative initiatives pertaining to mental health. And she was very good at her chosen profession.

Jayne had been married five years earlier, but it soon ended in divorce.

Connie had lost touch with Jayne when Jayne was going through her divorce. As she recollected this, Connie felt both embarrassed and uneasy. She thought about walking past Jayne as she had on a couple of previous occasions, but decided against it.

If Connie's failure to be supportive had bothered Jayne, she never let on. She was always cordial and warm when she saw Connie. This time was no exception. Jayne immediately disengaged from a conversation when she spotted Connie.

"Connie, it's so nice to see you," Jayne began. "I'm so sorry about what happened to Stuart. You, you guys looked so happy at the Tobacco Institute party. It's a great loss to all of us, and especially to you," Jayne said as she took both of Connie's hands in her own.

"Thanks," Connie replied, as she looked down at the floor. Then she looked back up at Jayne. "How's everything with you?" Connie asked. Suddenly it was important.

Jayne shrugged. "Oh, you know, still gettin' loot for loonies as they say," Jayne laughed.

"How 'bout socially?" Connie asked with such earnestness that she surprised herself.

It was still rather loud in Michael Cohen's house. Jayne looked quizzically at Connie. "Did you say 'sexually'?" she asked, narrowing her eyes.

"No," Connie snickered. "I said 'socially'. But if you want to tell me how things are going sexually, that's okay too!"

Connie laughed again and this time, Jayne joined in. "Hey, we should get together for dinner or drinks some time," Jayne blurted out.

"No time is better than the present," Connie smiled.

Before she knew it, Connie found herself putting her coat on for the umpteenth time that day, and hailing a cab headed downtown for Ricardo's. Italian food sounded just about right for a cold, lonely, winter's night.

"How 'bout a bottle of Chianti while we wait to order?" Connie suggested.

"Fine," Jayne responded with an easy-going smile.

The night of her little tryst with Bill Owens notwithstanding, Connie hadn't had much to drink since Stuart's death. The wine went straight to her head. She felt almost as though she was watching herself in a home movie. Oh, she knew she was going on like a babbling brook, but she couldn't stop. She just couldn't stop.

Despite her feeling of otherworldliness, Connie was aware that Jayne was listening attentively. Everything else was out of Connie's temporarily limited capacity for observation. Connie tried to cleanse herself, to rid herself of all the demons which had been building up since Stuart's death. She told Jayne about Jim Evans and Ken Yamaguchi and everyone else she had gotten to do things they probably weren't supposed to. And she talked long and hard about Joseppe Giavonni. Or however you pronounced it. Jayne interrupted occasionally to ask a question or offer some insight.

The one thing Connie never mentioned was the little deal with Owens. In the long run what did it matter anyway? A woman has a right to a little no-strings pleasure just the same as a man, right? The money, well that was just a little game she liked to play. Sort of like Robin Hood.

Towards the end of the conversation, Jayne expressed some reservations about the U.S. Attorney's theory that Joseppe had killed Stuart. "Look, Connie, you know as well as I do, that Joseppe was an extremely highly respected man before he was indicted. Think about it. Every damn guy," this she said with an air of disdain, "in all of Washington seems to get his hair cut by Joseppe. It's like a damn men's club in that place. It's almost like they did away with all these other guy things so Joseppe is the replacement. Anyway, what was my point? Oh, yeah, lots of people really respected him, at least before all this." Jayne sighed. "Anyhow, you've got your hands full. I just hope you're sure, that's all. I mean, I guess I can understand how he might have gotten greedy, so the fraud indictment I can buy. But murder?"

"Evans' theory is that he felt threatened. He knew Stuart was on to him and he knew he was going to have to give up all of the funny money he got from Moran. So he killed Stuart."

"Wait a minute," Jayne replied. "Who's Moran?"

"Oh, George Moran, do you remember him?"

"I was afraid that's who you meant. Didn't you date him for a bit?"

"Yeah, I did. Until he wouldn't listen anymore."

"What do you mean?"

"He was kinda kinky, you know? He wanted to do some, oh, let's just call it unusual stuff. He wanted to go beyond the 'usual' unusual and I told him he was out of bounds. And he says something like, 'You don't make the rules. All you people think you make the rules, but you don't. I make the rules.' So I had to drop him."

Jayne blushed ever so slightly. "Tell me again, how was he involved?"

"The barber was duping people on George's behalf. George had Joseppe offering his customers a real estate deal. When the customers put up the bucks, Joseppe got a percentage. Then George split."

"So Evans thinks Joseppe did it?"

"Yeah. Stuart was trying to get Evans to indict all of them. Joseppe, Moran, and the other guy, I forget his name, George's partner, for fraud. So Evans figures that Joseppe figured if there was no complainant then there'd be no case against him."

"Wouldn't Moran have the same motive?"

"Sure, but he's in Bermuda, and has been ever since Stuart and the rest gave Joseppe their money."

Jayne took a deep breath, and let it out slowly. "You know Joseppe at all?" she finally asked.

"Just from having met him the night Stuart was killed, and that was like for three minutes."

"But you know George."

"Sure."

"Could George have put him up to it?"

"Sure I guess anything's possible, why do you ask?"

"I don't know, just thinking how I'd react if I was on the jury that's all."

"You'd want to do justice," Connie said emphatically, "and find Stuart's killer!"

"That's exactly right," Jayne replied softly. "That's exactly right."

Chapter Fourteen

"So, I'm gettin' a drink when all of a sudden this guy stumbles in," Gary Schofield explained as Mark rolled his eyes. "And I look over and it's the fuckin' judge! I mean the case is still with the jury and who knows what kinda questions they might have and here's this pompous ass who's been sittin' on the bench for three days with his fuckin' self-righteous attitude and he's drunk as shit!"

"That's great," Mark replied. "Did anyone else see him?" It was a question Mark always asked Gary. Funny how there were never any witnesses to Gary's stories.

"Nah, there was no one else around. I mean we were in this little rinky-dink Sheraton in god-forsaken Tallahassee, Florida. Who the fuck is gonna be in a place like that at four o'clock in the afternoon?" Gary asked as he tugged at the tight little knot of a ponytail on the back of his head.

Plenty of people, Mark thought. But he knew better than to argue with Gary or try to burst the private investigator's bubble. Besides which, the stories were fun, however apocryphal.

"So, anyway, I say to the guy, I say, 'Judge Lafton, is that you?' and he says, 'Who is that?' I mean he's totally stunned that someone recognized him. But he's still drunk as shit. So I say, 'Whaddya think is gonna happen in the Lopez case, your Honor?' and he says 'Oh, that fuckin' bitch! She deserves to lose hands down. But you never know once the case goes to the jury.' I mean, can you believe the judge said that to me?"

Mark laughed. "Why is it that these things always happen to you?" he asked his favorite private investigator.

"Hey, I don't know, I guess I just have the kinda face that makes people want to talk to me. Either that or I'm just in the right place at the right time. But it happened just like that, I swear it did!"

"Anyway, Gary," Mark interjected, "the reason I wanted to have lunch with you today is to tell you about a case I'm working on. You stopped in last week to see if I might have some work for you. Well, this might fit the bill. It's the barber case."

Gary nodded his head and asked Mark to describe the case. Mark began at the beginning. The very beginning. He could see Gary getting fidgety, as the investigator tugged repeatedly at his ponytail, but detail was important. Mark filled Gary's ears with the kind of minutiae that only premier defense lawyers remember. The story took nearly a half hour. Mark patiently ignored Gary's occasional cracks which punctuated nearly any conversation the lawyer had ever had with him. Somehow, Gary always felt that other people's troubles were hilarious.

Once, when Mark chastised Gary, the investigator became very serious and explained that he couldn't get too close to his clients. Otherwise, he would get too involved in their cases and that wouldn't be healthy. Mark had accepted this explanation at face value until Gary burst into peals of uproarious laughter.

Mark finished briefing Gary and the latter immediately jumped on the bandwagon. Mark wasn't exactly surprised. In the first place, it was a chance to make some fairly easy money, and none of Mark's clients had ever failed to pay a bill when due. In the second place, Mark knew it probably sounded like a fun case. Of course, there were two other reasons why Gary was sure to accept, in fact, jump at the assignment. A substantial part of the investigation would need to take place in Bermuda. And talk show host Mo Buell would need to be interviewed, and possibly tailed. Two plum assignments.

Gary and Mark shared a cab back to Mark's office where Mark provided Gary with a complete copy of the file. Gary promised to review it and begin working the case immediately.

Mark watched as Gary headed out the door. Gary was tough. And he was solid. At just under six feet tall and 190 pounds, he had gone just a tad soft around the edges. But physically, he was still a match for any man. And he was afraid of no one.

Mark had hired Gary for many cases, most recently on the Southeast Airlines case during which Gary had almost lost his life. Southeast had hired common thugs whose sole purpose was to find and dispose of Gary Schofield. The hired guns came close, beating Gary mercilessly, and leaving him for dead.

Gary recovered fully from his injuries and later became a key witness in the case. Although Gary had helped Mark tremendously on the Southeast Airlines case, Mark knew Gary considered the case a personal failure. Gary had told Mark more than once that he believed he had let Mark down. In the first place, he hadn't obtained as much information about Southeast as he would have liked. Furthermore, to hear the P.I. tell it, his beating was somehow his own fault.

Mark had no such thoughts. Gary had performed admirably against a difficult adversary, and Mark did not begrudge him a thing. To the contrary, Mark felt a certain sense of responsibility for the physical injuries Gary had suffered.

When he got back to his office, Gary immediately began reviewing all of the documents in the file and jotting down notes. When he was done reading the file for the first time, the private investigator called Mark. He only had a few questions, and Mark was able to answer most of them. Then Gary called Joseppe Giavonni, and the investigator wasn't looking for a haircut.

Gary met with Joseppe the following day for over an hour. The barber seemed honest, forthcoming, and a bit, how you say, nervous, although not overly so considering the circumstances. On the whole, Gary liked him. That was good. It always made it easier to work the case when you liked the client.

Gary stopped by Mark's office on his way back from seeing Joseppe. Before Gary could strike up a conversation about the hotshot haircutter, Mark blurted out, "Hey, did I tell you about this guy who's staying at my apartment?"

"No," Gary answered sharply, "and either Carol is gonna be very disappointed to learn you're a faggot or else she's thrilled cuz she's having a menage a trois!"

"Sorry to disappoint you, Gary, but it's neither," Mark came back, a bit more calmly. "Actually it's kinda bizarre. I was walking down 17th street when I saw this homeless guy. Now, I don't usually give any money to the homeless—"

"Yeah, fuck' em!"

"No, it's not that. It's just that I could never tell which ones to trust and which ones were full of shit. Anyway, I flipped this particular guy a quarter—"

"As opposed to flipping him the bird!" Gary interrupted again.

"Are you gonna let me finish?" Mark said, the exasperation building in his voice. Gary waved his arms expansively and motioned to Mark to continue. The investigator could tell this was going to be good.

"Anyway, like I was saying, I flipped this guy a quarter, and it lands in his cup. Only the cup has coffee in it!"

At this point, Gary could stand it no longer. What began as, oh, a medium-pitched laugh, soon sped into uncontrollable, tear-inducing staccato bursts of laughter. Finally he gathered himself. "You mean you threw a quarter which landed in this guy's cup only he wasn't even panhandling?"

"That's right," Mark responded. "But he screamed out, 'another superstar is born,' and that is what an old college professor of mine used to say all the time. So I did a double-take, and sure enough, it's my old teacher from Wesleyan."

"You gotta be shittin' me man," Gary replied, unsure whether to laugh or act dumbfounded. "I mean you find some of my stories hard to believe? What are the fuckin' chances that you would flip some bum a quarter, it would land in his coffee cup, and the fuckin' guy would be your old teach?" Gary was having a whale of a time.

"Anyway, I couldn't leave the guy on the street. I mean he was one of my favorite teachers. Granted, it was like fifteen or sixteen years ago, but still. So he's been staying with us for almost a week now. I tell you, he's got quite a story."

Gary bit the inside of his mouth. Suppressing a smile, he replied, "I can hardly wait to hear."

"No, really, it's like one of the most ridiculous stories you ever heard. He was teaching Comparative Lit., first at Wesleyan, then at Dartmouth. Anyway, he was up for tenure in like about two years. But he ends up having an affair with one of his nineteen-year-old students. An absolute knockout, to hear him tell it. This must have been, oh, I don't know, maybe ten or twelve years after I had him. Anyway, his wife catches on and boots him outta the house. Then the university finds out, and they decide to deny him tenure saying he's unfit to teach college students, particularly girls."

"I don't know, sounds to me like he probably taught her a thing or two," Gary laughed.

"Yeah, but I doubt any of it was in the curriculum! Anyway, his whole life begins to unravel. He gets a job teaching at a junior college first and then ends up at some podunk high school. He bounces around some and next thing you know parents at one of his high schools are making wild accusations. According to him he never touched any of his high school students. But one of the parents found out about what happened at Dartmouth and went nuts. Said she didn't want her precious little angel in this guy's class. So he loses that job too.

"So, he does a little lying and gets another job. Then he loses that one too. I can't remember how many times it happened but before long it's 1990 and the economy goes south. And he can't find another decent job. He waits tables for a while and even ends up doing some roustabout work for the circus. Can you believe it?"

"Geez, I think I'm gonna have to keep that one for my repertoire. I mean, if I told you that story, you woulda thought I was making it up, huh?"

"Didn't you actually work for the circus?"

"Yeah, for about three years, but I wasn't a workingman, I was in the purchasing department."

"Were you undercover?"

"Not at first, but I did a little later on. They thought the General Manager was stealing from them."

"And?"

"Wasn't him, it was the veterinarian who used to come to the show a coupla times a week. He'd steal all sorts of stuff. Turned out he was just a kleptomaniac. No drug problem or drinking. Just liked to steal. Anyway, how long did you say this guy's been living with you?"

"About a week."

"And, uh, you just gonna let him stay forever?"

"No, obviously we can't do that. If you wanna know the truth, I already feel like it's a bit of an intrusion into my life. But I really can't figure out what else to do."

"Did this guy have a family?"

"Oh, yeah, I forgot to tell you about that. That's the really heartbreaking part."

"I can hardly wait."

"No, really, it's sad. When his wife kicked him out he had two kids, a daughter who was six and a son who was four. He saw them for a coupla years while he was paying child support. But when his life fell apart, he stopped paying child support so, obviously, he hasn't been able to see them for a while."

"If he hasn't been paying child support, there's probably a warrant out for his arrest."

"True. But I don't feel like telling him that."

"He sounds like he's reasonably bright. I'm sure he already knows," Gary replied with a worldly glance.

"Look, I know I'm not the damn head of social services, but I'd like to see this thing through. I'd like to try to get him a job, doing just about anything, so he can at least afford a roof over his head. Even if it's the Y. I just don't want to see him sleeping on a grate."

"I always knew you were soft, Mark, but this is a bit too much. I mean I'm sure he's fine and all that, but you got a million things on your mind and the last thing you need is this guy hangin' around."

"What do you suggest Mahatma Ghandi?" Mark said pointedly.

Gary could tell his friend was getting pissed off. "I don't know, do you think he has any desire to go back and see his wife and kids?" Gary asked, this time a bit more sensitively.

"Yeah, I'm sure he does. In fact, he told me he does. But he has no idea where they live and he says he can't find them and he's afraid if he does his wife is liable to hit him up for all sorts of back child support and all that stuff."

Try thought he might, Gary couldn't resist. "Ah, true love, isn't it wonderful!"

"Hey, I've got an idea, Gary," Mark said, with an enthusiasm that concerned the investigator.

"I don't think I like the sounds of this one," Gary replied, narrowing his eyes.

"Since you're such a big-hearted, liberal kinda guy, I thought you might be willing to track down this guy's wife on a *pro bono* basis. You know, I think all investigators should do some *pro bono* work. It would do you some good, just like us lawyers."

"Oh yeah, you guys are just the pillars of society, you lawyers!"

"Well," Mark continued, "what do you think?"

"Tell you the truth, I thought you were gonna suggest that your dirtball friend should come and live with me for a while. So this sounds like a break. Have him give me a call, so I can ask him some questions and I'll see if I can help."

"Thanks, Gary, I appreciate it," Mark replied, pursing his lips.

"No problem, Sidney white shoes. Always happy to help out a loser!" Gary snickered. "I'm outta here."

Chapter Fifteen

Donald Lubins was almost finished packing when Mark walked into the apartment. The lawyer looked at him in an odd way, as though he couldn't quite figure out exactly what was happening, though he knew he should be able to.

"What's up, Donald," Mark finally mustered.

"Just getting my things together," Lubins muttered.

"Going somewhere?" the lawyer smiled.

Lubins sighed deeply and turned away from Mark. He squashed his clothes into the duffle bag and turned back to face Mark.

"Yes. Yes I am, Mark, although where I couldn't say."

"Why? You're welcome to stay here, I already told you that."

"That's very nice, Mark. It's a big feather in your liberal cap, really it is. Buys you lots of points in your world, but I can't stay." Lubins looked down at his feet and kicked the inside of his right heel with the toes on his damaged left foot as though he was trying to knock some dirt from his shoe. He looked back up at Mark who stood silently by the doorway. "Sorry," Lubins said with a tinge of despair in his voice and a barely discernible raised left eyebrow.

"Donald," Mark began and then grabbed for his chin with his left forefinger and thumb. He rubbed thoughtfully looking for all the world like he might scrape off the top layer of skin in the process. Abruptly, he stopped and dropped his hand to his side. He stared straight at Lubins. "So, this is the thanks I get? Some bitter bullshit about my motivations for taking you in?"

Lubins appeared momentarily shocked, the courtroom lawyer getting the best of him for a split second. But the former Comparative Lit. professor wasn't exactly ill at ease with the spoken word either.

"Look, Mark, you were very kind to me, really you were, and I don't ascribe ill motives to you, okay? It's just that people don't do things for other people, they do things for themselves. My parents didn't adopt me for me, they adopted me for them. They had a need, convoluted though it may have been, and I satisfied it.

"You're no different. What you're doing for me is really for you. Makes you feel good about yourself, your, your humanity."

"C'mon, Donald, you mean no one, not anyone, does anything for altruistic reasons in your view? What about people who volunteer in homeless shelters or who take in AIDS babies?"

Lubins shrugged. "They do it for themselves, Mark. Believe me, I've been there. People will only let you down if you let them. If you protect yourself, then they can't let you down."

"My God, you're a psychiatrist's dream! You put up a wall around yourself and pull away because of your fear of being hurt, I mean, shit, I could diagnose you."

"Now I'm a house guest of Sigmund Freud! Thanks, Mark. Thanks for everything. I hope to get on my feet again real soon, and I'll call you when I do, okay?"

With that, Lubins zipped his duffle and headed for the door. He thrust out his hand, gave Mark's a cursory grip, and forced his way past the bigger and healthier man. Stepping aside slowly, Mark let him pass.

Mark didn't do much of anything for the few minutes immediately following Lubins' abrupt departure. As he was about to head for the bedroom, and remove his suit and tie, there was a knock on the door. Opening it, Mark found himself confronted by Lubins whose face was contorted, and whose cheeks had tears sliding down them like drizzle on the side window of a car.

"Don't you get it, Mark?" he sobbed. "A woman died on the streets last night and no one gave a damn. Not her family, not the social services people who are paid to supposedly care, not any of her so-called friends. You know who had spent the most time with her during the previous twenty-four hours, the last day of her life, do you know, damn it?"

Mark shook his head.

"I did!" Lubins screamed. "And then where the hell was I the night she needed me, the night she died? I'll tell you where I was! Right here in the lap of luxury!" Lubins dropped his duffle, his shoulders pumping up and down as he sobbed uncontrollably.

Mark made a tentative move toward Lubins and lightly touched the distraught man's shoulder. When Lubins didn't resist, Mark gently put his arm around the still crying soul, and slowly reeled him in until they were embracing in a huge bear hug. Mark held the hug only for a moment, and then released Lubins, whose tears were slowing.

"Donald, please, please listen to me for one second," Mark begged.

Lubins looked up, his eyes narrowing, and Mark continued. "I don't think you should head out tonight. It, it's supposed to be bitterly cold. It's supposed to warm up by the weekend. If you want to leave then, no argument. But please stay tonight."

Lubins bit his lower lip. "I don't know, Mark," he began in a halting voice. Then he brightened. "I've got an idea. How about a cup of nice hot tea. It'll give me a second to think, and it'll help me if I decide to head out. What do you say?"

Mark smiled. "You got it, Donald, but I got a real slow electric burner. Could take a while to brew."

Chapter Sixteen

Before Jackson Caulfield even had his morning coffee, his partner jumped down his throat.

"Are you really gonna send those stupid letters?" George Moran screamed, first cracking all of the humongous knuckles on his left hand three times, and then following that with a double cracking of those on his right hand.

"Look, George," Caulfield began without making eye contact, "you know my position. I think to protect ourselves we need to try and make this look like a legitimate operation. That's why we set up the office down here, and that's why we're gonna send letters to each of the investors."

When he wasn't met with a response, Caulfield continued. "Now I don't suggest for a minute that we're gonna put a return address or a telephone number on it. But let's at least try to give this some attempt at legitimacy."

"Why, Jackson?" Moran said as he leered at his partner-cum-foe. "What's it going to prove?"

"Look, George, when we first met on that Waterside deal in '87, you remember the conversation we had?"

Moran glared into Caulfield's eyes for so long that Caulfield looked away.

"Ancient damn history Jackson. You were fifty pounds lighter, and I had a lot more hair and a beard when that deal went down."

"Yeah, but—"

"But what!" Moran screeched, his voice heading up at least two octaves.

Caulfield tried to locate his backbone. "When that deal went down, we were successful 'cause none of the investors could ever prove anything. We weren't so blatant, that's all."

"Jackson, you really are a moron, aren't you? In the Waterside deal," Moran began sarcastically, as he cracked his left ankle back and forth in front of him, "the investors made their money back and even got a small return."

"Yeah, but we made a small fortune."

"But they didn't outright know they were being had, and they couldn't prove anything anyway!"

"Exactly my point, George," Caulfield shot back, his confidence increasing.

"Jackson, you keep forgetting, we're not playing by the conventional rules of engagement anymore. I told you, I make the rules, so let's get on with the business of having some fun."

Caulfield looked out his lone window, and saw the oleander and hibiscus hedges being buffeted by a stiff breeze. He glanced up, but there wasn't a cloud in the sky.

Just then, Belinda, the lone employee of M & C Realty buzzed Caulfield.

"Yes," Caulfield said into the phone, happy for the momentary respite.

"Mind if I go to lunch now?" Belinda asked. She asked every day, though the time varied. And every day Caulfield told her that he didn't mind.

Paget Parish didn't have much other than residences and a botanical garden, so Belinda had to cycle over to

Hamilton for lunch. Caulfield never kept track of the time she was gone, and he never questioned when she left. Today, though, he lingered over the answer a bit longer than usual, before approving the request. It was the only piece of office business that M & C Realty ever transacted.

"Bitch wanna go to lunch?" Moran asked when Caulfield replaced the receiver. Caulfield nodded.

"When are you gonna go on a diet?" Moran suddenly asked.

Caulfield rubbed his chin and looked away. "You know," he said softly, I've really only gained about thirty-five pounds since the Waterside deal, and my wife used to think I was way too thin, so I don't know that a diet is called for yet."

Moran gave a wicked snort. "I believe that's 'ex-wife' you're talking about, pal, and she's not here to protect you. I think you need a diet, and remember, I make the rules."

With that, Moran spun on one foot, and began to head for the door.

Caulfield followed the big man's departure with disdain. What a fat pig, Caulfield thought. Talk about a mega-case of projection!

Moran spun back around, almost as if he could feel Caulfield's eyes fixed upon his back.

"What?" Moran demanded.

"Nothing," Caulfield replied, lifting his eyebrows.

"I could learn to hate you, Jackson, you know that? And people I hate don't usually fare too well. You know why, Jackson?"

"Tell me, George. I'm dyin' to know."

"'Cause I make the rules," Moran replied with a look in his eye that was somewhere between a twinkle and a fire.

Chapter Seventeen

Connie Parker's voice was steady, but expressionless, as she answered the phone. "Hi," prosecutor Jim Evans began. "How are you, Connie. Not working today? This is Jim Evans, in case you didn't recognize the voice."

"I did. What can I do for you?"

"I'm sorry to bother you at home, but I thought you might not mind me calling to tell you that the grand jury indicted Joseppe Giavonni today."

"Congratulations," Connie replied without intonation.

"Are you okay?" Evans asked, apparently disappointed at the lack of reaction.

"Yes, I'm fine, Jim. Thanks for calling with the information, if you need me, you know where to reach me."

"Connie?"

"Yes?"

"One other thing. I told Dave Moore about the indictment. He won't be needing to talk to you anymore."

"What does that mean?" Connie demanded.

Evans hesitated. "It, uh, it means that you're no longer under investigation by the police," he replied softly.

"What a crock," Connie snorted as she slammed down the receiver.

Connie inhaled deeply, and ever so slowly released the oxygen she had taken in. She put her head back down on the pillow and gazed to her left, to the empty expanse of bed lying next to her. She reached back over towards the phone and started to unplug it, then changed her mind.

Connie sat up. She swung her legs off the bed and made her way into the living room. She opened the liquor cabinet and pulled out the bottle of Stolichnaya which had collected dust in the weeks since Stuart's death. The Russian vodka had been Stuart's favorite drink.

Connie hated vodka before she met Stuart. It was her father's favorite drink. Actually, it wasn't the vodka she hated, since she had never tasted it, it was the thought of vodka which left such a bitter taste.

Opening the freezer, Connie filled a glass with ice and then switched to the refrigerator. After filling the glass nearly full with tonic she poured in a few swigs of vodka. She searched for, but could not find, a lime, settling for a wedge of lemon instead.

Connie sat down in the living room with the remote control, and flicked on the tube. She cycled through the channels quickly before honing in on a rerun of *Jeopardy*. Just as quickly as she had turned it on, Connie flicked the remote, and turned it off.

She dragged herself off the couch, and headed back toward the bedroom. She pulled out a package of pictures which she kept in the drawer of her night table, and brought them with her back to the living room.

After opening the envelope of pictures, Connie began thumbing through them. She had grabbed an eclectic bunch. Some were of Connie and Stuart, others of Connie and guys she had picked up and held onto for a day or sometimes a week.

One stack showed she and Stuart, with a few other friends strewn in during a period oh, maybe three months ago. One night, Stuart had brought the camera along with them to the Silver Diner, and snapped shots all around the place. It was well after midnight, and the denizens of the diner were in rare form. Connie remembered that there was a guy with a shock of slicked back bright orange hair who kept popping quarters into the jukebox and playing Elvis songs. Each time a new song came on, he and his friends would take turns pretending to croon out the lyrics to the table of young women sitting next to them.

Connie smiled at the remembrance. They had talked, she and Stuart, on the way home, about the unabashed way the young men had sung. Stuart had attributed it to their state of inebriation, but Connie had disagreed. She had been drunk, she said, on rare occasions, but would never have had the nerve to get up and sing like they did. No, she remembered arguing, it's more than just the drink, it's a personality, an easiness or something else, that she knew she most definitely did not share.

When she was finished looking through the pictures, Connie curled her lip a bit, gave out a wry little snort, and placed them back into the envelope. She stood up from the couch and headed back into the bedroom. She padded into the large walk-in closet, and took a shoe box down from the top shelf. Heading out of the closet, Connie plopped down on the corner of the bed, and took the cover off the shoe box. It contained dozens of old Parker family pictures. Connie thumbed through them until she found her favorite. She smiled as she looked at the picture of herself as an eight-year-old sitting with her father. They were all dressed up, Carlisle—daddy—in a black, pinstriped suit and white shirt. Connie in a flowery, long, blue dress with white tights and patent leather shoes. The old man actually looked kind of stiff come to think of it. The smile vanished from Connie Parker's face. She popped the photos back in the box which she quickly put back up on the shelf. The phone was ringing again. Connie let it ring twice, willing it to stop, but it wouldn't. On the fourth ring, afraid it might be her father calling about her mother, or someone else she might not want to miss, she lunged across the bed, and grabbed the receiver.

"Yes, hello," she said in a jittery staccato.

There it was again, only this time it sounded like the part of the theme song that they played during Final Jeopardy. Connie started to hang up, then changed her mind. She put the phone down and grabbed her briefcase. She pulled out her tiny dictaphone and pushed the record button.

"Listen," she began, "this is getting silly."

The music continued.

"George, are you there? Is that you? Or is it Mo? Or Jim? Or Bill?"

Nothing but the *Jeopardy* theme song just about ending. Connie slammed down the receiver, and immediately regretted having spoken, and having displayed concern. Her little outburst certainly wasn't going to put an end to the calls.

Connie picked up the phone.

"Hello, operator, yes, I'd like to get a new telephone number. Unlisted please."

"Yes ma'am, you'll need to call back in about a half hour, all of our computers are down right about now."

"Well I'm being harassed, how do you suggest I handle that?" Connie screeched, her voice taking on a life of its own.

"It's only a half hour, ma'am, I'm sorry. Why don't you try unplugging the phone?"

Connie slammed down the receiver. She stormed

back into the living room, and picked up the vodka tonic which she hadn't yet started. She took a deep swig, and licked her lips. It was awful. She took one more tiny sip, and walked to the kitchen where she poured the rest down the drain. Must be an acquired taste. With a feeling of gloom beginning to envelope her, Connie headed back to the living room and plopped down on the couch. She stared briefly at the phone which resided on the coffee table directly in front of her. She picked it up and punched in Jayne's number.

"Hi, Jayne, this is Connie, how are you?"

"Fine, Connie, and you?"

"Okay, I guess. I just got a call from Evans. The grand jury indicted the barber today."

"Do you want to get together and talk about it?" Jayne asked.

"That'd be great, that is, if you're not too busy."

"No, I'm okay. Meet me at the Saxophone Club, say at, five?"

"I'll be there. Thanks."

Connie looked at her watch. It was four o'clock. She had a half hour to kill. She went back into her bedroom and reached into the cabinet underneath her night table. She pulled out the folder which she had brought home with her earlier in the day. It contained a bunch of letters. Most of them were from George Moran, and dated back a year or more. But two of them were unsigned, typewritten letters. George had signed all of his letters. It was difficult to tell if these two were from him, and it was just some kind of weird ploy, or if they were from someone else. They weren't nice letters.

She began spreading the letters out on the bed. The early letters from George were innocent enough. Actually, very business-like, with an innuendo or two thrown in, but not threatening in the least. But as Connie turned down his repeated advances, George's letters took on a harder edge.

But the two unsigned letters were altogether different in tone. She shook her head as she began to scan through the first one for the hundredth time.

"Dear Connie:

Can't understand you. You know what I want from you. It's very simple. I know you want the same from me but you're afraid to admit it. We could have a great time together. But if you don't say yes soon, I'm afraid it could get ugly. You'd better think about it long and hard, babe."

It was signed: *"I'll be in touch."* It was dated the prior summer.

Next, she pulled out the second anonymous letter, which was dated almost exactly a month after the first one.

"Connie:

It's really too bad you can't admit your true feelings for me. Why are you such a bitch? I know you're giving it to lots of other guys, but that's about to stop. If I can't have you, neither can they."

She remembered the letter well. It wasn't signed, but it was clearly composed on the same typewriter as the previous letter. She thought about calling the cops when she got it, but then thought better of it. She thought about calling George, too, but what if it wasn't him? What if he was actually leaving her alone? A call from Connie would undoubtedly set him off again. Then she'd have two deranged lunatics on her case instead of, perhaps, just one. Who knew, maybe the last two were from Mo Buell. It was anyone's guess, so why antagonize George, especially since she might need him someday.

Connie had never shown the letters to anyone, not even Stuart. By the time Stuart and she had become an item, the letters were a thing of the past. She hadn't even looked at them during the whole time she knew Stuart, and she hadn't heard from Moran, or for that matter anyone else who could be remotely considered to be a threat, for some time. Once or twice she thought about throwing them away, but that would be admitting defeat, something she was not willing to do. No, as long as she had the letters, she was a player in the game, whatever the game might be.

After thumbing through the strange documents another time or two, Connie slipped them back in the file, which she then placed on the bed while she got dressed. When she finished dressing, Connie walked over to the bed and picked up the file. She headed towards the front hallway closet where she usually kept her briefcase. She opened the closet door, and began searching for it, before realizing it was still in her bedroom. She straightened back up, thrust the folder under her arm and headed for the door.

"I still can't believe you never showed these to the cops," Jayne said over the happy-hour din as she glanced through the letters a second time.

Connie shook her head. "It's like I told you, once I threatened him he completely dropped out of my life. So there was really no reason to turn the problem into something bigger than it was. You know, I agree with you that Moran is offbeat, but he had a weird family life, and I can relate to that. I mean, I just couldn't believe he would harm me. Still can't. So there really was no way I was going to the cops."

"Look, the guy is definitely not playing with a full

deck. So it's probably not real easy to figure what's a bluff and what's real."

"True. But I'm not convinced he's violent or anything. He's a big talker who happens to be horny as hell. You know what he always says, his favorite expression?"

"I think you might have told me, but I forget. What is it?"

"He says 'I make the rules' when he does something, you know, offbeat or weird, like that excuses his behavior."

"That's exactly what scares me about him, Connie!" Jayne was all eyes, big brown ones that matched her long brown hair. "I'll tell you one thing, if I had gotten those letters I would have been scared shitless. I know I would have told someone, particularly about those two unsigned jobbies.

"You know, Connie, when you called me, you said Evans told you that the barber was indicted. But we've been talking about these letters all night."

Connie took a deep breath and exhaled very slowly. She tightened her lips a bit, started to speak, then paused.

"I'm sorry," Jayne cut in. "I, I didn't mean to put you on the spot."

"It's okay. The thing is, I keep getting these calls all the time," Connie stammered, her voice faltering.

"What calls? What do you mean?"

Connie looked down at the floor, and scuffed the heel of her left foot against the side of her chair. She looked back up at Jayne, who leaned forward, waiting.

"Harassing calls."

"From who?"

"Moran. And Buell."

"What?" Jayne's eyes nearly popped right out of their

sockets. "Didn't realize you knew him," she replied, her voice trying to hide what her eyes could not.

Connie sighed, swiveled her head from side to side, and then slumped down in her chair. Before speaking, she scrambled back up to a full, upright position. Blushing deeply, Connie said, "it must seem like I date every guy in Washington."

"Nah, not every one. Just the rich and powerful ones!"

"Oh, hey, like that's much better?"

"What's the deal with Buell?"

"I don't know. I mean, I actually dated him for a while, as opposed to George, who I just kept putting off."

"Oh, I thought, for some reason, that you dated George."

"Actually, I did, but just a couple of times," Connie leaned in, "though I thought about sleeping with him more than once."

Jayne looked shocked. "Connie I've only seen George a handful of times, but, I mean, you can't tell me you think that pig is physically attractive?"

"No. I guess, looking back on it, I don't think it was so much that as a combination of how exotic he seemed and how well he seemed to be doing. You know, somehow, I seem to measure guys' attractiveness, at least a little, by how different they are or how successful they are. Or how big their egos are. Then, I have to admit, I sort of get off on taking them down, you know, controlling the scene."

The conversation lulled momentarily and the waiter, who had disappeared for what now seemed like a fantastically long period of time, returned. But Connie wasn't particularly hungry, and Jayne wasn't all that picky, so they stuck to hors d'oeuvres and drinks.

Connie felt a pleasant buzz as they got up to leave.

She almost forgot to take the file containing the brilliant writings of George Moran, and possibly some other deranged maniac, but Jayne reminded her about it just as they were leaving.

She picked up the file with just a trace of a giggle, never noticing that one of the two unsigned letters had slipped out, and slid under the table where she and Jayne had been sitting. She had had just enough to drink to not miss it.

Chapter Eighteen

Gary Schofield picked at his fingernails while he waited for Mo Buell to finish his show. There wasn't much to look at in the waiting room, a wimpy looking ficus tree, two plastic seatcovered chairs, and a plain, brown, wooden coffee table which housed a half dozen magazines, none less than six months old.

Sweating profusely and mopping his huge forehead with his fleshy palm, which wasn't exactly the most absorbent thing around, Mo burst forth from the studio.

"Hey, pal, you got an appointment," he called out as he brushed past Gary.

"Actually, Mr. Buell, yes. Yes, I do," Gary said, as he fumbled in his pocket for a business card.

Buell stopped, his eyes narrowing as he scanned up and down Gary. "You the reporter from the *Sun*?"

"Yes, Mr. Buell," Gary replied unctuously. "Yes, I am." Gary thrust out his hand, and grabbed Buell's sweaty palm and began pumping it. "Jack Metzer's the name. Writing a story about shock jocks. Just wanted five, maybe ten minutes of your time."

Buell ushered Gary into a small, though tastefully decorated, dressing room. The two chairs looked comfortable, and Gary thought about sitting but waited for Buell to permit him. The narrow, white formica makeup table was cluttered with cosmetics and deodorants which Gary found amusing given that this was radio.

Gary imagined that his father, who was a real reporter, had probably been in this situation a hundred times in his life. It was the boredom brought on by that very fact that had caused the old man to accept the *Baltimore Sun's* offer to do some reporting in Vietnam. Gary was thirteen when his father stepped onto the military transport plane at the Andrews Air Force airport in suburban Maryland. It was the last time Gary ever saw the old man. He was reported as missing for a while, before the government finally told Gary's mother that a soldier had seen her husband killed while covering a battle.

The radio personality motioned toward the plush red-cushioned seat backed up against the left wall, and Gary plopped down into it. Buell, who was 5'5" on a good day, pulled up the chair from his dressing table, twirled it around so that it was facing him, and sat on it, propping his elbows on the chair back.

"First," Buell sneered, pointing his finger at Gary, "I don't like the phrase 'shock jock.' Anybody who's shocked by my stuff must be like a two-year-old. Other guys, maybe they're shock jocks. Not me, pal. Next question."

"Mr. Buell, how can you say you're not a shock jock when you keep talking about things that offend people's sensibilities?"

"Okay, look, Jack, stop with the 'Mr. Buell' bullshit, okay? And you know what else? I don't care if I offend their itty-bitty little sensibilities, okay? I get paid good money so somebody must be listening and liking it, right?"

Gary smiled. "Mr. Buell—"

"Ah, ah, ah," Mo interrupted, wagging his finger at Gary.

"Sorry, Mo, one of the stranger things you've done

lately is all this talk about Connie Parker, the poor woman who—"

"Hey," Buell snapped, "I know exactly who she is, and one thing's for sure. She ain't poor. Besides, what's so strange about what I said about her? That I'm not broken up over Katcavage's death? Big deal. Print that, Jack. Big deal," Mo continued, waving his arms in a wildly exaggerated manner. "What am I, the first guy who ever admitted that he was happy that someone standing between him and pure happiness got knocked off by some loser?"

Gary smiled again. "Can I print that?"

"You bet. All of it."

Gary shook his head, and scratched the hair behind his left ear as he climbed back into his car. He called Mark from his cellular phone, and reported on the conversation.

"I guess we should keep an eye on him," Mark said when Gary finished his briefing.

"Damn right," Gary replied. "Damn right." Then he smiled. Next stop, Bermuda!

Gary snapped his fingers and did a clumsy two-step as he made his way through the airport. He was heading to Bermuda. On business. In February. That's right maggotry, he thought, Bermuda. Not Manitoba. Not Florida in August. Bermuda. In February. Okay, it might be warmer in, say, St. Thomas, but this wasn't bad.

The eternity in the friendly skies ended, and Gary hailed a cab outside the Bermuda airport. The cab was adorned with the omnipresent blue bonnet which assured that its driver was a qualified tour guide.

The airport, on the northern edge of the island was a

short distance from the luxurious Marriott Castle Harbour Resort. Normally, Gary preferred to drive himself, but private vehicles, other than motor bikes or mopeds were unavailable on Bermuda. Made it eminently livable, but tough to be a private investigator.

Gary wasn't used to such posh accommodations as the huge white-and-pink tinged sprawling resort, but he needed to be in a place where he wouldn't arouse suspicion, and where he might luck into Moran or Caulfield. Gary booked a room under the name Evan Jameson. He paid in cash.

The next morning, Gary set out early. Following the only lead Joseppe had given him, Gary began asking around about the possibility of buying real estate on the island. He quickly learned that he would need to head south and east toward Hamilton, so he rented a motor bike and set out on North Shore Road.

The views of the crystal-clear Atlantic from Crawl Hill were a spectacular azure, the sand of the beaches pristine. But the ride was broken up by Shelly Bay, a major shipbuilding area. Riding a motor bike was pretty cool, but the road was narrow and windy, not meant to carry the automobile traffic which had lately found its way onto North Shore Road. That made for a number of harrowing twists and turns, and a less than relaxing trip.

Once in Hamilton, Gary parked his motor bike and landed in the brilliantly named "Island Real Estate" office. He spoke to Mr. Inola, who kept trying to get Gary to buy a time share. Mr. Inola wore a shiny, black, polyester suit, with a wrinkled white shirt and an open collar. He was quite insistent that he had no real competition on the island and he hadn't heard of either Moran or Caulfield. He explained in limited fashion that Island Real Estate was a Bermuda institution. No upstart agency was going to cause it any real harm. Yeah, thought Gary, especially one which has no intention of doing any business.

Next, Gary headed over to the Recorder of Deeds' office. He looked through recent land transactions and real estate sales. Bupkus.

After two futile hours spent on this little exercise, Gary decided to change tactics. He went to the island government's Corporate Affairs office. There, he reviewed information concerning all recently formed corporations. As he suspected, the boys were nowhere to be found.

Gary knew these guys weren't simply going to show up on some form somewhere. But if he hadn't looked, and later found out he could have tracked them down through, say, the Recorder of Deeds office, he would have slit his wrists.

Two more real estate offices visited that afternoon proved fruitless as well. As evening approached, Gary headed back to the hotel. He spent a few minutes washing up, made some telephone calls back to Washington, and headed downstairs. He walked into the courtyard behind the main building which gave way first to the main pool which was partially surrounded by an old stone wall, and then to a wide expanse of grass and trees. He could just barely make out the turquoise water of the Atlantic a couple hundred yards in the distance.

Gary walked past the pool where a few stragglers were still lingering, and onto the immaculately manicured, soft green grass. He covered the short distance to the ocean and walked along the moss-covered rocks which separated the land from the water. There was no sand here, that being reserved for an area beyond the second pool, maybe five hundred yards down the coast.

After wandering around a bit, Gary made his way back to the Terrace Cafe, took a table overlooking the ocean and ordered a drink. Gary struck up a conversation with his waitress, but he struck out again. Either Caulfield and Moran hadn't been around, they had paid off people to keep their mouths shut, or these people had the worst memories of anyone in history!

Gary ordered dinner and had another drink. Shortly after nine, he decided to head out. He pulled the waitress aside and handed her two hundred dollars U.S.

"I need to borrow your car for a few hours," Gary said, "that is, assuming you have one. There is a little woman I am interested in, and I simply cannot have her think I am unable to provide for her."

This no car rental crap was for the birds, but the pert little blonde who had served Gary had a Miata which she was only too happy to loan to Gary for his room key and the up-front cash.

Gary headed out to try to find some local hangouts. He eventually found a little gray-looking, pub-like joint which didn't look too touristy.

The place was noisy, smoky, and, frankly, rancid. There wasn't a tourist in sight. He stifled his urge to leave, and somehow found a seat at the bar. He could feel eyes, lots of them, boring holes through him. He ordered an island drink and looked up, deflecting the glares of all but the boldest.

Shortly after he arrived, Gary noticed a man and woman engaged in a rather heated discussion at a booth two-thirds of the way towards the back of the bar. Although it was dark, and Gary had nothing more than a description to go by, his gut told him that the man bore watching. He looked different from all the others in the bar. His coloring, his manner of dress. He was trying to fit in, and not totally succeeding.

After a brief lull, the woman screamed, "leave me alone, Jack," and bolted for the door. The man followed in hot pursuit. Gary decided to make it a ménage à trois. He hopped into the borrowed Miata, and sped off right in the tracks of the second car which was just then screeching out of the parking lot.

The others knew the way, but Gary did not. It made for a less-than-fun chase. Somehow, he managed to stay with them as they blasted down North Shore Road and over to Middle Road. They eventually came to a small group of pastel houses. The woman leapt from the first car, the man from the second, both blissfully unaware of Gary's presence.

The man Gary thought might be Jackson Caulfield tore after his prey. The whole bizarre scene was playing itself out in surreal silence. The woman scurried up to the door to her little pink house, opened it without a key, and slammed it shut. Gary could hear the deadbolt click behind the door.

The man turned on his heels, defeated. No screaming, no histrionics. Just a hang dog look of defeat. He walked back to his car, hopped in, and sped away.

Gary quietly followed as he turned onto South Road on the other side of the island. After about fifteen minutes, the man pulled up to a nondescript, small, house-like building in a residential area on the outskirts of Hamilton. He let himself in through the front door and walked rapidly down the hall. Gary waited until the man entered a door on the right side of the hall. Then the private investigator hopped out of the little red convertible, and peered in through the glass door.

On the left-hand side, just inside, was a directory. The glare from the lone streetlight made it difficult to decipher. Gary squinted. He cocked his head to the left and knelt down a foot or so. Finally, he could make out some, but not all, of the words. He peered at the rather scanty listing of tenants. Jonathan Bonor, CPA. Smith & Lewis, Attorneys-at-Law. M & C Real Estate. Bingo!

Chapter Nineteen

The outburst of a couple of days ago seemed in many ways to be ancient history. Donald Lubins had resigned himself to staying with Mark and Carol for at least a couple more days. The high temperature was 17 degrees earlier today, and Lubins knew that Mark was right, whatever his motivations for wanting Lubins to stay. In two, maybe, three days it was supposed to warm up considerably. Lubins had figured he could leave then, until the phone rang and changed everything.

Lubins had just hung up the phone in Mark's living room, what was it two, three, ten minutes ago? He kept hearing the words reverberate in his ear. "We found your wife, Dr. Lubins. Julie, isn't that her name? Two kids? Yep. They're in Dayton. Nope. S'far as we can tell she's still single. Yep. Sure, we'll send you the address, phone number, the whole nine yards just as soon as we get it written up from the field investigator. You bet. You're welcome."

So there it was. A mystery no longer. In a day or so he'd have the actual address and telephone number. He grabbed his left hand with his right to stop the shaking. But it was no use. He headed for the refrigerator, and popped open a beer. He tilted back his head and took a huge swig. He nearly choked on it, and ended up spitting the half that didn't flow out of the sides of his mouth into the sink.

He grabbed the sponge and cleaned up the spillage from the tile floor. He tried to take another swig from the bottle, with much the same result. Wincing, he poured the rest of the bottle down the sink, and ran the faucet to wash away the evidence. He noticed he was still shaking as he let himself out of the apartment to walk down the hall to the trash disposal. He dropped the bottle into the chute, waiting while it clanged its way down to the basement before shattering upon impact. He turned, and padded back towards the apartment. His heart raced when he noticed the door, which he had failed to prop open, appeared to have swung shut. He began trotting towards it before breaking out into a full-blown run. Sweating, he pushed against the door with his shoulder. Luckily, it hadn't engaged. It swung open freely.

Lubins flopped onto the couch. He twirled the piece of paper containing the P.I.'s phone number in a circle, then began rolling it up and unrolling it.

Mark and Carol would be home soon. Lubins jumped up. It was nearly six o'clock, and Crisfield hadn't been out for a few hours. Lubins grabbed his coat and the leash, and called for the golden retriever.

Crisfield bounded through the living room and ran directly to the front door, pawing at it with excitement. Mark generally worked long hours, and Lubins could tell that Crisfield wasn't used to all of the attention during the day.

Lubins put Crisfield on a leash only long enough to get him out of the immediate neighborhood. Once they hit the park, Lubins let the dog run free. Crisfield leapt and bounded along sniffing this and pawing that. The cold didn't seem to bother him, though Lubins felt the chill right through the coat Mr. Liberal Help-the-

Homeless, Mark Clifton, had given him. Ah, yes, the coat. It was a Brooks Brothers special, camel's hair, full length, and at least two sizes too big, but in much better shape than the piece of trash that Lubins had been wearing.

Lubins frolicked with Crisfield for nearly a half hour. As the cold began to become unbearable, Lubins called for Crisfield, and the two headed home. Lubins grabbed the dog and held him against his chest. A tear came to Lubins' eye and he wiped it away with the back of his gloved hand. He breathed deeply twice as he approached the door and tried the handle. To his surprise, Mark and Carol were already home.

"Hi, Donald, thanks for taking Crisfield for a walk. I think he really loves you!" Mark said with a smile.

"I never had a dog before. It's kinda nice. I love him too," Lubins said, as he blushed.

"How was your day?" Mark asked.

Lubins took another deep breath, then exhaled slowly. "Well," he began, "actually, I spoke with a guy from Schofield's office. I think his name was Tim something or other. Anyway, he tracked down Julie and the kids."

Lubins saw Mark and Carol exchanging glances, so he averted his eyes.

"Where are they?" Carol asked.

"Dayton, Ohio, of all places."

"Is she remarried?"

"I don't know for sure, but it doesn't sound like it," Lubins said, shifting from one foot to the other.

"What are you gonna do?" Mark interjected.

"I'd love to see the kids, that's for sure, but I don't know if she'd let me. I mean, I'm really not in too impressive a condition," Lubins began with a snicker. "I'd love to work something out. But I'm not sure I'm ready for it either. Besides, I, I really don't know how to go about it. If I can get my feet on the ground, you know, a bit steadier, maybe, I think it would be easier."

"What comes first, Donald?" Mark asked, his fists clenched by his sides. "Getting your feet planted more firmly on the ground or seeing your kids?"

"Yeah, I know what you're saying, but it's only going to help to see the kids if I'm ready for it, and I'm not sure if I am or not." Lubins shrugged his shoulders, and turned to leave the room. "I'm gonna go get ready for dinner, you guys. I'll be right back."

Over dinner the conversation shifted to Mark's defense of Joseppe. Lubins found the case fascinating. As he was pummeling Mark with questions, the lawyer suddenly smiled and interrupted. "You know, Donald," Mark began. "I know what your skills are and everything, and I hope you won't think that I'm being demeaning, but maybe you ought to try to get back to work at a nonthreatening level."

"Such as?" Lubins asked, a twinge of suspicion evident in his voice.

"Please don't take this the wrong way, I know you have a Ph.D. and all that. But Joseppe needs help around his shop."

"And?"

"Well, he used to have a guy there who did all sorts of stuff. I mean, don't get me wrong, it's totally menial stuff. Like shining shoes for customers, sweeping up hair, running errands, that sort of stuff. But it's a paying job and it'll get you out of the house during the day." Lubins could see Mark was getting excited. "You know, he's still got some high-powered customers, and maybe you could meet someone who could help you out in getting a higher-level job."

"Look, I just came from being a circus roustabout. Shining shoes is no worse, that's for sure. I'm not insulted. We had our little go 'round the other day, but I appreciate everything you've done for me, and I don't want to sit around the house like some dude on welfare. So, if you think Joseppe would be willing to talk to me about the job, I'll do it."

The following day Mark called Lubins around noon. The lawyer explained that he had spoken to Joseppe. It was all set. Lubins could start tomorrow. Lubins smiled. It felt good to have a job. Okay, so it wasn't quite the same as teaching Comparative Lit., but he didn't even have to interview for it. It was a start. Yep, yet another start.

Chapter Twenty

George Moran's spies told him. The two guys he paid fifty bucks a day to make sure nobody found George without George finding them first. The boys described Gary Schofield, ridiculing his tight little ponytail, and said he was posing as one of George's old college buddies. He was using the name Jay Pruitt.

Moran's spies were paid handsomely when they provided tips. George knew the meaning of incentives. Cash incentives worked with island beach trash, they worked with Wall Street investment bankers, and they worked with Joseppe Giavonni. Yes, incentives cut across all socio-economic lines.

Unlike Caulfield, Moran had a lot more to lose than the ill-gotten gains of one simple transaction. In fact, the fraud which Moran had perpetrated with Caulfield was merely a clone of the other twelve which Moran had pulled off in various cities on an almost simultaneous basis. Moran was sitting on nearly $100 million.

The other thing was the time and ingenuity that had gone into earning all that money. It would be an absolute crime to have it all slip away because some pesky investigator or government bureaucrat wanted his or her own set of rules to be followed. George smiled. I make the rules, he thought. I make the rules.

George didn't particularly want to deal with Schofield

right now. Life was too good, and George didn't want to get involved in a scuffle. Besides, he was getting antsy.

Growing up, the Morans had always moved around. When Mom was performing with the circus, walking the highwire first, then later as she got older, working with her performing dogs, they were never in one place for more than a week. Usually they moved every two or three days.

George got used to the movement, the travel. It gave him a way to leave behind whatever problems he might have caused the locals. There was the time George beat up a little kid, only to learn that the kid was actually mentally disabled. Worse still, the kid's father was the mayor of the little town where the circus was performing.

Of course, there was always next year, when the show would come back, but none of the petty crimes which George perpetrated, even beating up the mayor's son, was likely to be remembered by then.

Movement was redemption. And it was escape. Sure, there were times you had to stay and make a stand, but it was usually easier, much easier to simply move on.

It was actually kind of funny, but having all the money didn't really cause all that much of a change in George. For a while he had bought fancy cars, and sleek European suits that cost the equivalent of some people's monthly income. But his desire for those status symbols faded as the items themselves wore down, and he never replaced them.

Once George thought about starting his own business. Maybe bringing mom and dad over to help out. It was a fantasy of course. To start a business he might have to fill out some forms, maybe comply with some business registration nonsense. Still he thought about it every so often, not because he desired legitimacy, quite the contrary. He wanted to run something entirely on his own terms. No interference from people for whom he had no use. A place where he made the rules, and everyone else blindly, obediently followed.

There was no need to hurry away, at least not yet. Moran figured he had at least another few days before the investigator began to get close. So there was no reason to hightail it off the island, or to even contemplate ways of deterring Schofield. No, if he decided to leave, he could pack and go at his leisure.

The more thought Moran gave the matter, the more he decided he didn't want to confront Schofield. Because if he did, he might have to kill Schofield and that was something George Moran did not want to do. At least not while he was in Bermuda. It was way too nice a place to have to leave on a permanent basis. Of course, if Schofield followed him elsewhere . . .

—

The man who had forgotten to take lessons at charm school didn't bother telling his supposed partner where he was going. In fact, Moran didn't even bother to tell Caulfield he was leaving at all. It wasn't his business anyway.

George figured he'd be gone for a few weeks at the very least, and he didn't want Caulfield snooping around in anything that wasn't Caulfield's business. So George went to the post office and put in a change of address form. Good old P.O. Box 2812 in Lakeland, FL. Whenever he wanted to hide, it had come in handy. Might as well go with something you knew. Something comfortable.

Next, he went to the liquor store. Duggie had put aside a case of his favorite Cabernet Sauvignon, the one that didn't cause a massive headache, and a case of

Mouton-Cadet. The two cases would have to be shipped now, but that was okay. Duggie was used to special orders. And he never, ever asked questions.

After the post office, George headed back home. He threw together a suitcase worth of clothes, all casual, walked out the back door, looked at the Atlantic, then quickly turned and headed through the house and out the front door. George made sure everything was locked securely and then he placed a note on the door. It read:

"Dear Inspector Schofield:
 Good try. Better watch your butt.
 Remember, I make the rules.
  Love, George."

George hopped in his car, a dusty brown Porsche, and sped off along South Road towards the airport. He didn't have a reservation, they really weren't necessary if you knew what you were doing. And reservations and airline clerks were such a pain to think about when you were preparing to go into hiding.

The large, deeply tanned man at the ticket counter who was helping George was clearly an American on a lark. An airline ticket clerk, no worries, lots of free time in the sun. The problem was that though the clerk was friendly, he was unyielding too. There were no seats on the next flight out to Tampa, period. After attempting, but failing, to bribe the young man, George settled for a ticket on the following flight which didn't leave for another three hours.

Moran found an empty locker and flung his suitcase into it. He walked back past the ticket counter and flashed a disgusted face at the clerk who smiled in return. Moran wandered outside and meandered back in the general direction of his car. Locating it, he hopped in. Three hours is a long time to sit in one place, better to keep moving.

He drove away from the airport at breakneck speed towards St. George's Harbor, the cradle of Bermuda's civilization. But he had no desire to see the beautifully restored town hall or any of the other attractions.

Once away from the airport, George drove aimlessly along. After fifteen minutes, and just shy of St. George's, he pulled over and got out of the car. He pulled his pistol out from the glove compartment, and cleaned the short barrel with his shirt tail.

It was a crystal clear day, and the wind was unusually light, blowing gently from the east. George leaned against the hood, not sure if he was enjoying or loathing the momentary solitude resulting from his inability to bribe the ticket clerk at the airport.

George finished cleaning his gun and held it up toward the sky. As he squinted toward the sun he saw three small birds gracefully floating into his view. He smiled tightly, narrowed his field of vision, aimed, and fired at the birds. A split second after the report sounded from the gun, he heard raucous, angry squawking from the birds. He followed the sounds with his eyes and saw one of the birds tumbling out of the sky, like a fighter pilot who has taken enemy fire.

George cracked each of the knuckles on his left hand twice, and those on his right hand once. Then he picked up his right foot and cracked that ankle. He tried next to do the same with his left ankle, but was unsuccessful. Irritated, he kicked at the dirt beneath him. Then he looked at his watch. It was getting late. Time to head back to the airport.

Chapter Twenty-One

Connie Parker woke up feeling slightly more than just a little groggy. She tried to sit up in bed, but her head, not to mention the rest of her body, rebelled. She plopped back down on the pillow, exhaling mightily as she landed.

The effort to get herself up and out of bed hardly seemed worth the struggle. She had a meeting with her favorite prosecutor in one hour. He'd wait.

As Connie showered, she tried to massage some of the feathery feelings out of her brain. She stepped out of the shower feeling a bit less dizzy, only to realize that she had forgotten to replace the bath towel which she had thrown in the laundry basket the previous day. Shivering, she stumbled out into the hall to the linen closet.

As she wrapped the towel around herself and fought off the cold, she nodded her head back and forth. She let out a short sigh of resignation.

Still dripping, she made her way back into the bedroom and pulled out the file she had taken with her to the Saxophone Club the night before. She pursed her lips and smiled at the thought of the look on Evans' face when he saw the letters. Not just the ones from Moran, but the other unsigned ones as well. Who the hell knew what they meant for the case, but they'd undoubtedly send Evans into a tizzy!

She began looking through the file, slowly at first,

then more rapidly. Unable to put her hands on the two unsigned letters, she began to rifle through the file, throwing papers across the bed as she searched. Finally, she found one of the two unsigned letters, but it was crumpled, the ink was smeared, and it stunk from alcohol. She couldn't show that letter to Evans. She continued searching for the other letter.

After ten minutes she dumped the file and stood back up. Okay, so maybe she wouldn't show Evans the letters after all. Then she snapped her fingers. Maybe Jayne had kept the other letter. But she shook her head. That made no sense. And right then and there, she knew she couldn't tell Jayne, couldn't admit that one letter was virtually destroyed, and the other one was missing.

No, Connie couldn't talk to Jayne or anyone else about the letters. It was as simple as that. Time to move on to something else.

The cold morning air actually did Connie some good. She dressed quickly, shivering a bit with the cold, but not really minding. Her momentum was increasing. She dried her hair, applied just a touch of makeup, and headed out the door.

As soon as Connie arrived in U.S. Attorney Jim Evans' office, she was overcome by another wave of nausea. She hadn't eaten breakfast. She wasn't in the mood. Now she was paying for it. As soon as he saw Connie, Evans started in.

"I'm concerned, Connie. You don't look very good."

"A hangover, Jim, nothing fancy. You gonna prosecute me for that?"

Connie ignored, or at least tried to ignore, the fact that Evans left his eyes directly focused alternately on her legs and breasts. She followed him into his office. She sat down and purposely put her winter coat on her lap. She deflected a few personal questions, and then Evans became more business-like.

Evans questioned her in detail about the final night of Stuart Katcavage's life. Connie felt distant, almost like she was watching herself as she spoke. She told Evans for the third time about the party. Only this time, the prosecutor was very direct and very thorough. He took what appeared to be excruciatingly detailed notes as they spoke, Connie responding to most questions in a dull monotone. If the prosecutor felt any doubts as a result of Connie's apparent lack of emotional involvement, he didn't let on. He continued to question her, so she told him about every conversation she could remember from that night.

At times, the lawyer referred to notes from previous conversations, and on more than one occasion, he reminded her of people with whom she had spoken or things which had been said. In each instance, she was able to reconstruct a conversation more fully after Evans' prodding, but that didn't mean she was enjoying herself. Far from it.

Evans spent nearly an hour and a half going through Connie's entire relationship with Stuart, paying particular attention to anyone who might want Stuart dead. Connie answered questions about lobbyists on opposing sides of issues, and she told Evans about some of Stuart's failed business relationships, though there were few of which she was aware.

It was obvious to Connie that of the people who might somehow be considered suspects, not many had been at the party that night. But that was the focus of Evans' incessant questioning, and Connie had no inclination to change the topic.

After Evans was done grilling Connie, he explained

that he would have all of his notes and the various things they had discussed drafted into the form of direct testimony. That is, questions from him, and answers from Connie, to be used at the trial. He would send it over to Connie's office so that she could begin studying it. Her debut was less than a month away.

"You know," Evans said, with a hint of something Connie couldn't discern, "even Katharine Hepburn studies her lines before her show debuts."

And then Connie understood, like the proverbial light bulb going off. Glee, that's what it was. Evans loved the courtroom, that was clear all along. But this impish grin, this irritating almost contorted look on his lips, was more than just a love for the courtroom. It was, at some level, a blatant disregard for the pain of virtually everyone else involved in the process.

The analysis had taken a while. But now that Connie had figured it out, had at least expressed to herself what made Jim Evans act the way he did, the situation became a bit more tolerable.

Connie slipped into her coat before the obsequious prosecutor could help her. After promising she would look over the direct testimony as requested, she strode out the door.

Connie sauntered out into the bright sunlight. She hadn't been expecting it, and she squinted against the relentless rays which seemed aimed directly at her, and her alone.

She started to hail a cab, then pulled her arm back down. She headed slowly down the street for a half block, then abruptly turned around and headed back in the other direction so the sun would be at her back.

When she got back to her office, Connie immediately glanced over at her calendar. At first it seemed entirely foreign to her. Then she realized it was on the wrong week. She flipped the pages quickly at first, slowing down as she approached the right page.

She had two afternoon meetings and was free after five. She picked up the phone and dialed Jayne's number. Jayne answered on the second ring. She had tentative plans. Damn it. Wait, she would see if she could break them. She would try and call back later.

Connie took off her coat. Disdaining her closet, she draped it over one of the guest chairs. She picked up a stack of mail from her in-box, and began glancing through it. Numerous letters from clients. Some asking about the status of projects long overdue. A few expressing belated condolences. Hard to write letters. Both kinds. Connie knew.

She put down the stack of letters without dictating or directing a response to even one. She stood, put on her coat for the billionth time in the last few days, and headed back out the door. As soon as she hit the street, Connie realized the coat was superfluous. It was a gorgeous, bright afternoon, winter's cold having finally lifted a bit. She stopped walking, tugged at her lapels for a second, and then, smiling wryly, left her coat on.

Chapter Twenty-Two

Time to get to work. Mark Clifton had handled enough cases to know when the time to shift to high gear was upon him. And he knew it was now. He hummed a song whose title he couldn't remember, as he ushered his client into the office.

Joseppe didn't understand. Why did there have to be two trials? Oh, Mark had explained that in the first place the wonderful think-ahead prosecutors had brought two separate indictments. Besides which, the two allegations were based on very different facts, and would require very different witnesses and defenses. To have the same jury decide both cases would be ludicrous, not to mention that it might not even be legal.

And there were tactical reasons for having separate, back-to-back trials. Joseppe, not to mention anyone else who might testify at both trials, would have a broader range of things about which testimony would be permissible if the counts were tried separately, and the second trial started before a verdict was reached in the first trial.

But the immigrant wanted his horror story to end. To Mark's utter dismay, Joseppe kept mentioning that he had an abiding faith in the American justice system. Brilliant, Mark thought, just brilliant.

What Mark and Jim Evans had finally agreed to, with a little help being given to Mark by the judge, was that the two trials would be held back-to-back. First they would try the fraud case. It would be tried in front of Judge Robinson, an elderly, no-nonsense jurist who generally seemed to believe that the only good defendant was one who was behind bars. While at Justice, Mark had loved the judge. Now he knew his former ally would skewer him.

Mark and his less-than-favorite associate, Peter Long, were working late into the night. February was almost at an end. The trials were three-and-a-half weeks away. There was a ton of research to be done, not to mention witness and document preparation. But Mark was used to it. He had tried cases for the Justice Department for nine long, arduous years, the last four as first chair counsel. He knew the program.

Despite their differences, Mark and Peter actually worked reasonably well together. Oh, there was always a bit of tension in the air, which Mark did nothing to relieve. But, somehow, some way, the work always seemed to get done, and the final product wasn't half bad.

At first, Mark worked mostly on witness statements, and he spent much of his time talking to potential witnesses. The character witnesses would be easy. There were a zillion old friends who would vouch for their buddy, Joseppe. Of course, customers were the best. For it was customers who had lost a combined fortune in the real estate scam. The ones who were willing to testify on behalf of their barber would be very helpful.

So far, Mark had found plenty of customers who hadn't been bilked out of their hard-earned money who were more than happy to talk about the raw deal Joseppe was getting. But Mark had yet to find one customer who had invested in the program at Joseppe's request who would testify for him. It would be a miracle if such a soul appeared. Mark tried to put himself in their position. He was quite certain what he would do. He would tell Joseppe's lawyer to go to hell!

Despite the supposed prohibition imposed by senior partner Jack Christian, Mark had kept Carol abreast of the case. And despite the prohibition, she had conducted a bit of research on her own. Of course, they couldn't bill for her time since she wasn't allowed to be working on the case in the first place, but what the hell, Mark knew he could use the help.

Early one morning, way before Jack Christian graced the halls of the firm which bore his name, Carol came upon a potentially important discovery. There was a late 1992 case out of Alabama in which the defendant was found guilty of murder under circumstances remarkably similar to Joseppe's case. In the Alabama case, the defendant was a woman. She was a hairdresser by trade and she had gotten a whole bunch of her customers involved in an illegal numbers game. Most of them had lost miserably, and one began to suspect that the hairdresser was reaping a piece of the action. Suddenly the one with the suspicions wound up dead.

The hairdresser was convicted of first degree murder, which was bad enough. But what was worse, was the fact that the judge had allowed instructions to the jury permitting them to speculate liberally.

As Mark listened to Carol describe the case, its impact became immediately clear. The instructions were such that the burden of proof had become much less than the usual "beyond a reasonable doubt." Carol was certain the judge had screwed up. Royally. She promised Mark that she would call the defense lawyer and find out whether the case had been appealed. They could only hope so.

Although a judge in Washington, D.C. would not be

compelled to follow a case decided under the laws of the State of Alabama, a good prosecutor would be certain to point it out again and again and again. Of course, your honor, such a case is only instructive, and your honor is not bound by it, such a prosecutor would say. The message would get across, loud and clear. Not to worry. Evans was not going to miss the opportunity.

The case set such a terrifyingly bad precedent that Mark decided not to discuss it with Joseppe. Not yet anyway. Oh, Mark knew he needed to speak to Joseppe. There comes a time in any trial when the client needs to be educated. For the most part, that time was now. But the Alabama case, well, it might be better left alone with respect to Joseppe. There wasn't a darn thing he could do about it anyway.

When the barber sat down in his lawyer's office, small talk evaporated. Mark got right down to business.

"Let's talk about the murder case first. As you know, the prosecution is trying to prove that you killed Stuart Katcavage by poisoning him on the night of December 12, 1992, by supposedly giving him a drink laced with cyanide. I have spoken directly with about twenty people who were at the party that night. Everyone is in agreement that there was no knock down, drag out battle between you and Stuart. A few people remember that you guys exchanged some words, but nobody remembers anything extraordinary. I'll plan to call, oh, maybe two of them as witnesses. But we'll have to wait and see what the other side does.

"My associate Peter has been doing a ton of research on the cases that have come down in the past that are like yours. You know, as we've discussed before," Mark continued, his voice becoming professorial in nature, "that the American legal system is based on the idea of precedent cases, you know, what happened before.

"Basically, we need to show the judge that there's a precedent for what we're asking him to do. So, if we want to have the judge tell the jury to disregard certain testimony, or if we want him to disallow a witness, we need to either show that there is a statute or law which requires him to do what we say or that it's been done before. Now cases from the court where your case is being heard have the most precedential value, but a judge will at least listen to cases from other jurisdictions. So, we've been looking at all the cases out there. The cases in D.C. are fine. In every one we've seen so far, the prosecution has been required to prove beyond a reasonable doubt that the defendant did whatever it was that killed the victim. That's the usual standard. In your case, the jury would almost have to speculate, unless the prosecution could, say, find someone to testify that he had sold you cyanide the day before."

Joseppe put up his hand. "Markie, you don't need to explain to me about cases. People I understand. Or at least I used to. When you're ready to pick witnesses I want to be involved. But you do the case stuff. That's why I hired you. Now, what do I need to know about the fraud charge?"

"Well, for starters that it will be the first case tried. There will be a totally separate jury, and we may or may not know the outcome of that trial when we start trying the murder charge. The judge is likely to want the jury sequestered in the fraud case. Actually, the juries in both cases may be sequestered. Anyway, the fraud case is actually more complex, even though it's totally under control and a lot less serious in any event. You've got the securities fraud issue which we've been researching, and trying to convince Evans that he has no chance on, and then there's the common law fraud claim.

"The securities fraud issue is the one that is controlled by a federal statute. That's why that case is in federal court.

"The common law fraud charge requires the government to prove that you intended to bilk these people out of their money. I think the government's burden of proof is tough on that claim. The securities issue is a little different. For instance, what you were selling is being characterized by the government as a private placement. Normally, those kinds of securities can only be offered to 35 people, otherwise you have to do all sorts of things in the way of compliance.

"Anyway, you don't want to hear about all of that. As far as people are concerned, I'm gonna want to talk to your wife and some of your customers. Obviously, I'd love to talk to Caulfield or Moran, and that's why Schofield went to look for them. But, I gotta tell you, as good as Gary usually is, I can't rely on him to find them.

"Regardless of whether we find those guys, we need to prove that you didn't know what you were doing. You're gonna be the lead witness, that's for sure!"

"Markie, this is really too much for me to understand. I don't know why anyone would want to do this to me. I'm a poor immigrant who saw a chance to make a few bucks. Believe me, if I had known that people would lose money, I never would have done it. Never. And that murder charge! Once I got over the shock, all I could do was laugh. I mean it's totally absurd. Totally!"

Mark wanted to tell Joseppe to save it for the stand. If his client could repeat this performance, Mark felt sure he would win two acquittals.

"Listen, Josep, I hear ya. We're gonna keep on studying, preparing, and researching. We'll talk to everyone we need to. Twice. Then we'll kick some ass in the courtroom." Mark stood as he spoke, and put his arm around the barber's shoulder. Joseppe managed a weak smile, and Mark squeezed his client's shoulder. The two men shook hands, and Joseppe gave Mark a troubled, knowing look. Mark smiled, gave Joseppe the thumbs up sign, and headed back to his office. Although he was whistling and trying to keep up the bravado for his client's sake, Mark knew that time was growing short.

Mark plopped down in one of the guest chairs facing his desk only to realize that a small file had beaten him to the spot. He jumped up, snatched the file off the chair, and sat back down. He tossed the file onto the other guest chair, already home to two larger files.

Mark propped his feet against his desk and pressed hard, forcing the two front legs of the chair into the air as he leaned back. He sat in this position, balanced against the desk, pondering his case.

While at Justice, Mark had often argued with colleagues about the wisdom of looking at the big picture in a case. In this case, the big picture had to do with who killed Stuart Katcavage. Those in favor of looking at the big picture would argue that if you could prove that someone other than Joseppe killed Stuart, then you were serving your client well. Those taking the opposite side of the argument, believe that by focusing on who else might have committed the murder, defense counsel is actually wasting time. The only real issue is proving that it wasn't Joseppe.

Mark didn't really subscribe fully to either school of thought. He saw both sides equally, and tried to balance the need for looking at the big picture with the exigencies of defending a client against a murder charge.

To this point in the case, Mark hadn't let his focus wander even for a second from Joseppe. Mark truly believed his client was innocent. But if that was the case, then who was guilty? George Moran was certainly a likely suspect. So too was the ranting Mo Buell. And what about Connie Parker? Was she above reproach? Early on, Mark had spoken briefly with David Moore, the police sergeant assigned to the case about Connie. Moore had indicated that he doubted Connie's sincerity, but hadn't said why. A gut instinct based on his years on the force no doubt.

What about motive? Joseppe's was clear. Fearful of the potential ramifications of the investment scam, Joseppe had panicked. Motive would be Evans' strongest argument.

Moran's motive might be the same as Joseppe's, although having already fled the country, Moran would be less likely to be concerned about legal proceedings which Stuart might bring.

Buell would have unrequited love as a motive. And like Moran, Buell wasn't altogether sane, so other less obvious slights might play into the mix as well.

Perhaps the single most interesting thought, was the idea that Connie Parker could somehow be behind the whole fiasco. Motive was awfully tough to figure, but who knows what goes on behind closed doors. Maybe Stuart was cheating on her. Maybe he had told her he'd never marry her.

Joseppe and Connie were the only two among the main suspects who had access to Stuart the night of his death, and that made each of them that much more likely to be involved. Either Buell or Moran would have needed to hire someone to carry out the actual murder. Mark didn't know enough about either one to determine if they were capable of such planning, though both certainly had the financial wherewithal to pull off such an outrageous act.

Mark shook his head and gently released the pressure his feet were exerting on the desk. The chair slowly found its way back down to the floor and Mark clambered off of it and around his desk. He ran his hands through his hair, took a deep breath, loosened the knot on his tie, and grabbed a file marked "witnesses." The lawyer had a lot of work to do, and time was evaporating.

Chapter Twenty-Three

Gary Schofield burst into the phony real estate office being run by George Moran and Jackson Caulfield. He glared at the receptionist. "Where's Caulfield?"

She looked up impassively from her perch. "Who wants to know?" she replied between the crackling and smacking of gum.

"John Jennings," Gary snapped.

"Look, pal," came the sassy reply from the receptionist, "I know a John Jennings and you aren't him."

"Listen, sweetie," Gary hissed, "pick up that telephone and buzz Caulfield." Gary's voice was now down to a whisper.

The receptionist nodded coolly, and picked up the receiver. "Jackson," she began, "there's a John Jennings out here to see you."

Caulfield opened the door to his office. No sooner did he have one foot through the opening then Gary pushed him back in and pulled the door shut behind them. Gary grabbed Caulfield's shirt, twisted it and rammed the real estate shyster up against the wall. "Where's your partner?"

Caulfield tried to struggle, but to no avail. As he attempted to wriggle free, Gary rammed him against the wall a second time. The bug-eyed Caulfield went limp in Gary's grasp. "I asked you a question, Jackson," Gary said derisively. "Now where the fuck is he?"

"I, I, I don't know," came the reply.

"Now you don't expect me to believe that, you little fuckin' putz, do you?"

"You can believe what you want," Caulfield began, but before he could get out another word, Gary slammed him up against the wall a third time.

"Listen you squirmy little shit," Gary hissed. "I've had enough of your two-bit horseshit. If you don't tell me where Moran is I'm gonna assume you don't want to cooperate. And I have ways of treating people who don't want to cooperate with me. Now do I make myself clear?" Just for effect, Gary tightened his grasp on Caulfield and shoved him, though this time more gently, into the wall.

"Look, pal, I have no idea who you are for starters. Besides which, I swear to you, on a stack of bibles, that I don't know where Moran is. He left here a while ago, and I haven't heard jack shit from him. If you don't believe me, go ask Lindy, the receptionist."

"Now that's your first good idea since we met," Gary said. "Why don't you get my good friend, Lindy, to come in here and join our little party. Then I can ask her myself. And don't try and give her any warnings about what I might ask. `Cause if you do, you'll regret it. I promise."

Caulfield buzzed his receptionist, who then entered the office still chomping on her gum. She stared at her shoe tops while Gary asked her questions about Moran's whereabouts. She was about as talkative as a corpse.

Gary finally began to believe the two impostors. They might not be running a real estate operation, but it actually did appear as though they had no idea where Moran had gone. Furthermore, they didn't seem to have any idea as to why he had left. Gary had his own ideas on that score.

When he had satisfied himself that his new friends had no further information concerning Moran's whereabouts, Gary took a slightly different line of questioning. "Has Moran gotten any mail delivered here in the last few weeks?"

The two coworkers looked at each other. Finally, it was Caulfield who answered. "None that I can recall, do you remember any Lindy?"

The phony receptionist just shook her head.

"Well, I've got an idea, Jackson, old buddy," Gary began. "How 'bout you and me taking a little trip down to the post office and you tellin' the busybodies who work there that I'm a long-lost relative of George's, and that I need to find him. Tell 'em it's a family emergency. And tell 'em we need his forwarding address, right now. What do ya think of my little idea, Jackson?" Gary asked, as he kicked Caulfield in the shins.

Caulfield glared straight at Gary, then looked for help from Lindy. "Fine," he said, "you're the boss. By the way, do you have a name?"

"Yeah, but you can just call me 'sir'."

"Well, sir," Caulfield began, "it might be helpful if I can call you by your name when we go to the post office."

"Just make one up, Jackson, I'm sure you'll do just fine. After all, you've made a pretty damn good living out of conning people so far. It shouldn't take much to do it one more time."

The main post office was in Hamilton, too far to walk. Gary forced Caulfield to give him the keys to the Ford Taurus sitting in front of the office. Gary drove toward Hamilton with Caulfield giving directions from his perch in the back seat with each hand cuffed separately to a different part of the car. Since his right hand was handcuffed to the bottom of the seat, Caulfield was hunched over in a most uncomfortable pose.

Every five minutes or so Gary slammed on the brakes and sent Caulfield sprawling into the back of the front seats. The first time or two, Caulfield screamed out in pain, but eventually Gary was unable to elicit any response from his weak-kneed adversary. Too bad. It was fun while it lasted.

When they got to the island's main post office, Gary released his POW. The private investigator pulled a baseball cap out of his back pocket and pulled it on making certain to tuck in his stubby little ponytail.

"Hey, Jackson, by the way do you prefer, 'Jack' or 'Jackson'?" The prisoner didn't respond, so Gary continued. "Make sure you're cool when we get to the post office, good buddy. Remember, my little gun is loaded, and I'm just sick enough to use it."

Caulfield led Gary into the post office, and Gary asked his prisoner if he knew any of the clerks. Before Caulfield could answer, however, one of the clerks waved a greeting and called him by name. Gary nudged Caulfield in the direction of the friendly woman with the lilting island accent and the red bandanna.

Caulfield bit his lip, then began to speak. "Hi, Germaine, this here is George's cousin Harvey."

The clerk nodded a greeting.

"You know, George left a few weeks ago, and he never told me where he was going. One morning he just didn't show up for work, and when I checked his house he was gone. Harvey here," Caulfield nodded at Gary, "came down here looking for George because they have a bit of a family emergency on their hands. He asked me if I might be able to help him track down just where George took off to. I thought maybe you'd be able to help us."

"Well, Jackson, I'm really not supposed to give out any information that I get in my official capacity as a government employee here," Germaine began, with the bureaucratic doublespeak sounding stuffy and silly at the same time.

"Here," Gary said as he pulled an American $50 bill out of his pocket and handed it to Caulfield. "Perhaps this will change your friend's mind."

Caulfield rolled the $50 bill into the palm of his hand and reached across the countertop and shook hands with the clerk. Suddenly her tune changed. She winked at Caulfield and said, "I'll be with you in a minute, Mr. Caulfield, please wait here."

The clerk returned and slid a piece of paper across the counter. Just as Caulfield reached for the paper, Gary dug a fist into Caulfield's back.

"I'll take that," Gary intoned.

George Moran's former partner and his current pursuer walked together out of the island post office. When they got back to the car, Gary grabbed Caulfield by the side of the arm and shoved him into the back seat. Gary took out the handcuffs which he had used on the trip down to the post office, and secured the by-now-compliant Caulfield in a position that even a contortionist might find uncomfortable.

Caulfield did not make a sound as they headed out North Shore Road in the opposite direction from M & C Realty. After having driven a couple of miles, Gary suddenly made a right-hand turn, driving away from the ocean on a deserted dirt road. He turned back towards his prisoner. "Listen, Jackson, I don't know whether I'm gonna come back for you or not. If you know what's good for you, you'll keep your nose clean from now on. Don't try to report me to anyone 'cause there's no one you can report me to. Now that I've found you, one of my people—a different one every day—is gonna follow you," Gary lied. "If you try any monkey business, I'll make sure you're taken care of. And you'll be taken care of, but good, if I have to do anything. So don't fuck with me, Jackson."

Gary pulled the car over to the side of the road, put it into "park" and, leaving the engine running, got out and opened the back door. He unhooked the handcuffs from Caulfield's hands. He looked at Caulfield and momentarily thought about handcuffing the man's hands behind his back. Then he thought better of it.

"Get outta the car, you scum!" Gary screamed at the semi-cowering man.

"But, but, that's my car, and besides, I'm nowhere near my office. We must be two miles away!" Caulfield seemed to be feeling a bit stronger.

"Look, pal, you're lucky you're not handcuffed. You got feet, now start walkin'!"

Chapter Twenty-Four

Donald Lubins heard the phone ring. His first instinct, which he quickly quelled, was to answer it. He had only had two beers, but no one was around, and he felt perhaps more drunk than he really was. After the third ring, Mark's altogether-too-serious answering machine kicked in. Lubins listened. It was the private investigator who was helping Mark with his case. Lubins knew the call was none of his business, but he listened anyway. He was mesmerized.

"Anyway," Lubins finally heard the voice say, "the woman in the post office finally gave us the address which Moran left. It's a P.O. box, of course. Moran's pretty shrewd. It's box 2812 located in Lakeland, Florida. I'm heading for Lakeland as soon as I can get outta here. I know time is running short, but I think Moran would be much better for you, so I let Caulfield go. I can still go back and get him if I don't track down Moran in time. I mean Caulfield was pissin' in his pants he was so scared. He's not goin' anywhere. He'll be there if we need him. I'll try you later or tomorrow."

Lubins stared at the answering machine. He picked up the beer bottle he had been working on, and sucked in some foam. Then he put it back down again, nearly missing the countertop. His heart rate had jumped perceptibly, and his hands had begun to shake from side to side despite his clenched fists.

Lubins felt sick. He ran to the bathroom in preparation for a ride on the porcelain bus, but like a quickly approaching thunderhead that peters out before amounting to anything, the nausea passed. Lubins was so drenched in sweat, it was as if someone had turned a hose on him. Trying to gather himself, Lubins stood in the bathroom doorway, gripping either side of the door frame, and rocking back and forth. Finally, he decided to take Crisfield for a walk.

During the walk, Lubins began theorizing, thinking, analyzing. In a way, nothing had really changed. He didn't have to tell Mark that he'd heard the call. Sure, there were implications to that, but, so what? Did he really owe anything to Mark?

Mark and Carol were home when Lubins and Crisfield returned. After Mark hugged, then fought off the dog, Lubins turned toward the lawyer and asked, "Anything new with the case, Mark?"

"Nah, not really," the defense lawyer answered. "How was your day?"

"Not bad. Nothin' special, you know, just a day," he said, as he swayed back and forth, hovering in the doorway to the living room.

A bit of small talk ensued, after which Lubins made an excuse about feeling tired and headed off for bed. Once in bed he tossed and turned, gently at first, then more violently as the sleepless night wore on.

Lubins made up his mind. He was going to go to Dayton. He had over a thousand bucks saved up from working for Joseppe. With that much to his name, he could well afford to give Julie five hundred, maybe more. That way, maybe she wouldn't boot him out as soon as he got there. That would really hurt. He knew Julie wasn't going to welcome him with open arms, but he hoped, for the kids' sake if nothing else, that she would be cordial. He could use a nice visit with the kids. After all they were his children.

The following morning Lubins shared his plans with Mark and Carol.

"We'll miss you, Donald," Mark said through pursed lips. "I mean, we always knew you'd go. I guess I just didn't think it would happen this quickly, despite it all!" Mark snapped his fingers. "Is Joseppe okay with it? You're not leaving him in the lurch are you?"

"No, of course not. I've already spoken to him, at least in general, about it. He said he can always find someone on pretty quick notice, not to worry. He said family's first."

"Listen," Carol chimed in. "Keep in touch. Please let us know how it goes with your wife and kids. Okay?"

"Ex-wife," Lubins said. "Ex-wife," he repeated, studying his shoe tops.

Lubins headed for Union Station and the Amtrak terminal. No more buses for this boy. He was feeling flush. A thousand dollars to a recently homeless man is like a million to your average Joe. Hey, Lubins even had dumped his signature duffle bag, though not without a twinge of regret. Carol had helped him pick out the new denim suitcase he was carrying, and it would forever remind him of her. That alone was enough to make him put the duffle bag out of his mind.

The train ride to Dayton was going to be a long one. Amtrak stopped in every two-bit town along the way. It was almost as bad as riding the bus, but the clientele was a bit more upscale.

Lubins was lucky enough to find a window seat. He curled up into a little ball against the gently rocking car and tried to fall asleep. When he couldn't, he began looking around. Yeah, the calibre of the people on Amtrak was a lot better than it was on the bus. Business people in suits. Students, obviously from families with money. And young families. No down-and-outers. Lubins smiled as he looked around. He thought about how easily he had gotten used to the other world, where people somehow were treated, and therefore they acted, like less. Less important, less human. Just less.

His smile evaporated. He began thinking about Mary. And Tiny. He dabbed a tear from his eye. Then he rubbed his eye more vigorously, and shook his head as though that could somehow remove the demons and make him forget.

The trip took fourteen hours. Lubins arrived in Dayton at seven in the morning, clutching the piece of paper with Julie's address. It was Saturday. The kids would be off from school, and Julie was likely to be off from work as well. It was as good a time as any to try to see them.

Lubins got directions, and found the local bus stop. He would have to take two buses from the station. He thought about hailing a cab, but there were none in sight. This was Dayton, after all, not Washington.

It being Saturday, the buses were running only once an hour. So he waited. Needless to say, he had just missed the first bus he needed to take. It would be fifty-five minutes before another one would arrive. He bought a newspaper and a cup of black coffee, and settled in for the wait.

It was strange sitting in the waiting area. He saw the cops shoo a couple of homeless guys out of the city's main bus stop. He thought briefly about getting involved, or even offering them some money. But he thought better of it. He had to conserve cash. It might be a while before he was working again, and he knew he would have to give Julie a big chunk to bribe her into letting him see the kids. Not that she was a jerk. After all, he owed her a hell of a lot more than he was planning to pay, if you believed the courts, which he was sure she did just the same as he didn't.

He glanced through the local rag, and the time passed. Slowly. Excruciatingly slowly. Finally he boarded the bus which would take him one step closer to his destination.

As the bus rolled on, Lubins tried to predict what would happen. It reminded him of the times in high school when he had wanted to ask a girl out on a date. He would run through every possible permutation, though it never turned out like any of his expected scenarios.

Lubins' son, Robbie, who was now eleven, would greet him with open arms and unabashed excitement. They had always been close, and somehow Donald knew that Robbie would forgive him his transgressions, and welcome him home. Laurie was another story. She would be nine by now. She had always seemed standoffish and distant, even when Donald was the nominal head of a supposedly perfectly functioning family unit. Somehow, he figured, that would mean she would be distant, even unfriendly towards him.

Julie was the wild card. She loved the kids. She wouldn't want them to be hurt. She would see Robbie's reaction and she would want to protect his feelings. Lubins hoped that would be her overriding sentiment. He predicted a cool reception with more curiosity than hostility from his ex.

His instincts were generally good. If they proved to be correct this time, he would be happy. Two out of three would be decent. About the same batting average he had before he disappeared.

The first bus ride finally ended. Lubins then had to wait in the bitter cold for twenty minutes for the next bus to arrive. He fleetingly thought again about taking a cab, but again he couldn't find one. He was headed for the suburban parts of Dayton, and it was early on a Saturday, not great cruising opportunities for a cabbie.

The second bus finally arrived five minutes late. The nondescript city carrier had one passenger. An old black woman carrying a huge pocketbook and reading the Bible. Lubins nodded to her as he boarded. She smiled and praised Jesus, her savior. Lubins returned the smile, but not the praise.

The bus dropped him off a block and a half from Julie's apartment. The neighborhood appeared to be working-class. The homes were modest, but well-kept. There was a mixture of single family homes and low-rise apartment buildings, each seeming to hold about ten to twelve units.

Lubins couldn't tell what the racial or ethnic mix of the neighborhood was since it was so early that almost no one was out and about. He wasn't about to dally. He walked immediately up to the apartment building. Just as he was about to press the code to reach his ex-wife and children's apartment via the intercom, someone headed out of the front door to the building, and he was able to slip inside. The heat in the little alcove soaked through his coat and immediately improved his state of mind. He stood, rubbing his hands together, in the small lobby for just a second.

Lubins soon despaired of being seen, so he headed upstairs to Apartment 3C. He was amazed when he realized that he was sweating. Profusely. It was about 27 degrees, he had just been outside for an extended period of time, and he was sweating. Go figure.

He knocked gently on the door as his pulse quickened. He began tugging at his hair, then twirling it in his fingers. He felt a sudden overwhelming desire to fart, but miraculously he was able to quell it. After an eternity, Robbie, who seemed a foot taller than Lubins remembered, opened the door.

"Dad!" the wiry boy screamed with delight, as he jumped into his father's arms. "Maaah, Laurie," he screamed, "Dad's here!" The young boy, whose arms had grown dark brown hair, and were actually showing a touch of definition since his father had last seen him, held onto Lubins as if the man was an apparition, and would disappear unless held tightly. Lubins returned the hug, and began to cry, though he tried desperately not to.

Laurie was the first to join Robbie at the door. "What are you doin' here?" She had grown too, and she looked more like a teenager than a little girl, despite being only nine. Her voice, which was still a tad high-pitched, was surprisingly devoid of the venom which Lubins expected.

"I know it's been a long time," the father said to his children, "and there is really no excuse for any father to not see his kids for that period of time. But I was out of work, and I was ashamed to let you kids see me, or to see your mom." Lubins had rehearsed for quite a while. He had opted for honesty. Kids can tell.

"It was a real rough time for me, but with a little luck and some help from some great people I got through it. And once I got back on my feet again, the first thing I wanted to do was see you kids.

"There are a lot of things you'll never understand," Lubins continued, his voice cracking. "And I know I let you both down. God, do I know how I let you down. But the one thing you need to know is that I love you both very much. My being away for so long never changed that. If anything it made me love you even more. I mean that, really I do. I hope you can believe that."

Lubins looked down at his feet momentarily. Then he looked up at his children. Laurie still had the biggest chestnut-colored eyes of anyone he knew. And Robbie still had that puckish, "I'll snag you yet" grin.

"I, I was gonna bring something for each of you, but I've been gone so long I didn't know what you liked. So if your mom says it's okay I thought maybe we could all go out and find a little something for each of you."

Robbie was smiling broadly by now, but he still refused to let go of the parent he hadn't seen in over two years. He stayed glued to his father's leg, and Lubins didn't mind one bit. Lubins could tell that his daughter wasn't sure how to react. Finally, she gave her old man a grudging hug.

Lubins was aware that Julie was watching the reunion between her ex-husband and her children from the hallway. After hugging his somewhat reluctant daughter, Lubins looked up and caught his ex-wife's eye.

"Hi, Donald," she said. "This is certainly unexpected."

She looked great. She had always had pretty features, but she had gained a tremendous amount of weight in the latter years of their marriage. It was all gone now, and her hair, always a pretty shade of sandy blonde, was pulled back in a long ponytail, and shone radiantly.

"Hi, Julie," he said, averting his eyes.

"Donald," she replied with a cautious nod. "It's been a long time since you've graced us with your presence." Her narrow blue eyes were inquisitive, though not angry. "Where have you been hiding?"

"Actually, I've lived in a lot of places. Like I was saying

to the kids, I've been kinda down on my luck till recently. That's why I haven't been by sooner."

"What happened? You win the lottery?"

"No," Lubins maintained his cool and deflected the sarcasm. "I ran into someone I hadn't seen for years, and he helped me get my feet back on the ground again."

"So you decided to just drop in and see how the ol' family was doin' without you?" She was caustic, though not really biting.

"This wasn't a decision I made lightly. Believe me there were plenty of nights when I was certain I was never going to see you again. Any of you. But once I got a roof over my head I was able to think a lot better. Anyway, Julie, isn't this a conversation we could have alone, some other time?"

Lubins saw the hopeful look in the kids' eyes. They were watching, searching for a sign from their mother. But aside from a touch of sarcasm, she hadn't let her feelings be known. She hadn't thrown him out, so that was some indication of progress. But she hadn't exactly greeted the man to whom she was married for thirteen years with open arms either.

"Wait a minute. Did you say 'once I got a roof over my head?' Were you homeless?"

Lubins looked down at his new Nikes. An eternity later he looked up. Julie apparently didn't care if the kids heard this. "Yes," he admitted. "But, thankfully, only for a very short time."

"We were just on our way to the mall," Julie replied abruptly. "Would you care to join us?"

The reunited family piled into Julie's Chevette, and headed out. They made small talk as they drove. Lubins asked his children about school, and tried to remember their friends' names. But they had each made new friends since coming to Dayton for a "new start" two years ago.

Lubins bought Robbie a football and Laurie got a special new doll. They looked for all the world like the perfect American family.

Julie was good. She let her former husband feel like a dad for the first time in years. She didn't harangue him about the child support. As Lubins was all too well aware, there would be plenty of time for that later.

They had pizza and cokes before heading home from the mall. Lubins was thrilled with the outcome so far, but he hadn't spoken to Julie alone yet. That was to come soon, and Lubins knew it wasn't going to be easy. In the first place, he needed to know if he had a place to stay for the night. He wasn't looking forward to sleeping in yet another YMCA. He had come too far for that. On the other hand, he didn't want to blow too much cash on a motel, especially if he was going to be around for a few nights. He had felt rich when he set out for Dayton, but no more. Reality had set in pretty quickly.

When they got home, Julie asked the kids to play on their own for a little while. Lubins tugged at his hair, and also at the spot on his upper lip that used to house his moustache. He flicked some dead skin off his lower lip as he waited for the kids to make themselves scarce.

"Start at the beginning and give me the big picture," Julie said. "You can spare me the gory details, but at least let me know why I haven't seen a check in two years. At least tell me where you disappeared to so I can tell the kids why you abandoned them. You know, I stopped making excuses for you about six months ago."

"I'm surprised you continued for so long," Lubins tried to remain calm. "It was good of you. I stopped making excuses for myself somewhere about that time too.

"Listen," he continued, palms facing upward, eyes wide open and honest. "There is no excuse for what I've done. But there is an explanation. The last time we saw each other, you were living in Jamaica Plain, near our old house in Boston. I had just been fired from my teaching job at Madison High School in Stillburg. I don't think I told you at the time that I got fired. I guess I was too proud to tell all of you.

"After that I had a series of restaurant jobs, each worse by half than the one before it. I started as a waiter in a decent place and made decent tips. I just couldn't face you guys while I was working as a waiter. But that restaurant fell onto hard times, what with the recession and all. I was the last one hired, so I was the first one let go. The next place got shut down by the health department.

"After that, things got a bit more desperate. I ended up running the back of the kitchen in the next place. You know, the supervisor of the dishwashers, the busboys, that sort of thing. That place declared bankruptcy. It was one after another! I guess I wasn't paying attention to the fundamentals of the business, only to the job description and the pay.

"Anyway, you ready for this?" Lubins continued.

"I can hardly wait," Julie replied.

"I ended up at the circus!"

Julie laughed, and so did Lubins. Finally she asked, "What did you do there?"

"I was a roustabout. A workingman for the Flying Ortiz Brothers. They were a trapeze act. I had to be sure their rigging was okay."

"And what kind of training did you have to do that?"

"I have my doctorate in Comparative Literature, and fifteen years teaching experience. Highly relevant, don't you think?"

"Highly," Julie snickered. "What happened after that? Or, I guess I should ask what happened to that. Why did you leave?"

"This you won't believe. Your pacifist husband was fired for fighting."

"Ex-husband, and you're right, I don't believe it. Surely, you didn't start it, did you?"

"Hardly. It was a battle between my group, you know, the Ortiz brothers, and Mora the Great, the female animal trainer. I was sucked into it. I had no choice. Believe me, if I thought I did, I wouldn't have fought. Believe me."

"Homelessness after the circus?"

"Not immediately. I was able to stave it off for, oh, maybe ten days. But my face was all beaten up, so I couldn't very well look for a job. It was really depressing. I mean, really dreadful. Finally, I just flat ran out of money."

"When was that?"

"Six or eight weeks ago."

"Then what happened? You don't exactly look like someone who was recently in such bad shape, you know, homeless."

Lubins refrained from giving his ex the speech he thought she so richly deserved. He didn't ask her, snidely, how she was such an expert on what homeless people look like. No, instead, he gently walked her through the day he met Mark, and the days immediately following that chance encounter.

When Lubins finished, he asked Julie about herself and the kids. Laurie was doing marvelously. Straight As and popular to boot. Robbie, while not quite living up to the standards being set by his younger sister, was doing well too. He had a tremendous sense of humor according to his mother, and was well-liked by most of his peers and teachers, although there were some who thought he was a smart-ass.

Julie seemed to be doing pretty well herself. She was still working as an office manager. This time for a medical office specializing in oncology. She said it was depressing to see all the patients with cancer, but cure rates were up and about fifty percent of the patients who came into the office would make it at least five years.

Julie told Lubins he could stay. For two nights. On the couch.

It was better than the Y. Way better.

They didn't talk money. Julie hadn't asked, and he hadn't offered. It would come up soon enough, of that, Lubins was sure.

The first day and a half passed quickly and easily. Lubins tagged along on their weekend routine. The kids had swim class and Robbie had a birthday party to attend. Julie had dinner plans for Saturday night, which she kept. But she canceled the sitter. She apparently had worked up enough trust in her ex-husband to leave him with the kids. They were always arguing that they were old enough to stay alone anyway. Certainly the three of them would be fine.

Lubins was surprised that Julie wasn't concerned that he might try to run off with the kids. Did he seem that impotent? Or that uncaring? Or was he just that trustworthy?

The evening actually went well. Lubins could tell his kids were having fun, just watching T.V. and eating popcorn. Nothing special for them perhaps, but it was a very special, and long overdue, evening for him.

On Sunday afternoon, Lubins and Julie left the kids with some of Julie's friends and took a long walk.

"I'd like to kick in five hundred toward what I owe,"

Lubins said. "I mean I know it won't really make a dent in the whole thing, but it's the best I can do right now. Once I get working again I'll come up with more, I promise."

"How much do you have, Donald? I mean, I don't want to be the cause of you being homeless again."

"Oh, I don't know exactly," Lubins blushed. "Maybe nine hundred."

"Why not give me three-fifty for now, okay?"

"Thanks," Lubins said with a nod. "Thanks."

As they continued walking the suburban sidewalks, Lubins told Julie about Mark's case, and the overheard telephone message from the investigator. He also told Julie that he hadn't shared with Mark the bit of information about the P.O. box belonging to Stone's Big Top Circus.

"I really want to go back to the show and track down this goon, Moran. I, I know I can do it. But, I've got to tell you, there's something about going back there that spooks me. I guess it's what it reminds me about or something."

"You should go, you know. Otherwise, you'll never be at peace with yourself. The kids will be hurt if you leave town again. And they'll never believe you if you tell them you're only going for a bit. But you need to pay back Mark, and it's not like you can do it in any other way that would be nearly as helpful, or meaningful, to him. I mean, he did something special for you. You need to do something special in return."

Lubins stared straight ahead. "People do things that are special for themselves. Most people don't act selflessly and just help out others."

"That's right, but it seems as if you finally ran into one that did, didn't you? The one person who didn't let you down."

"I'm not convinced, Julie, I'm really not. Helping me made him feel good about himself and all his liberal nonsense. That's why he did it."

"Then don't go. Don't help him. Just take everything he did for granted, and don't ever bother to call him or even ask about him again, since he's happy he helped you and he needs nothing more."

Lubins smiled and exhaled. "Haven't lost your touch, Julie, you know that?"

"Don't sweet-talk me," she laughed, her eyes opened wide, and even giving off a hint of friendliness.

The two glanced at each other momentarily without speaking, and Lubins began walking faster and looked away.

"Maybe you should call Mark," Julie piped up, as though it was a done deal, "and tell him what you're planning to do. It might help for him to know."

"I, I just can't," Lubins stammered. "I just can't let him know that I heard that conversation. Especially now after I never told him when I was there. Plus, what if I don't find Moran?"

"Hey, you didn't exactly commit a capital crime, you know, in not telling him!"

"I know. But I can't tell him now, okay? I just can't."

"In case you decide not to go."

Lubins blushed. "No," he smiled broadly. "My mind's made up, Ms. Day. I'm leaving in the morning. I'll tell the kids tonight. Only this time I mean it. I'll be back as soon as possible. I'm going to be a part of those kids' lives. I mean it."

"I hope so," Julie answered, "I really hope so."

Chapter Twenty-Five

Mark Clifton didn't particularly care for the memo Peter had prepared on the fraud case. The law was a lot more complex than Peter was making it out to be. Maybe the young snotball just didn't get it. Or worse still, maybe he did get it, but just didn't care.

Mark called his associate into the war room, and asked him to shut the door.

"Peter," he began, "let's talk about your memo on the fraud charge."

"Sure, Mark, what exactly is it you want to know about it?" Peter answered, staring straight at Mark.

"For starters, there are two charges in the indictment. One is for securities fraud for violating the private placement law and the other is for common law fraud. Now, your memo makes some distinctions between the two, but it doesn't really set out how differently the law will be applied to each charge in the fraud case.

"For instance, you've got cases intermixed in here. Some cases on the securities issue and some on the common law fraud issue. I mean, Peter," Mark said, as he picked up momentum, "this is basic stuff. You're a fifth year associate. You should be able to distinguish between a common law claim and a statutory claim, and give me two separate memos, one on each. I shouldn't have to ask you to do that."

"I apologize if the format isn't exactly to your liking,"

Peter said through tight lips. "But the fact is, all of the cases are there."

"That may be, but I was hoping to go back to Evans and see if I could get him to drop the securities fraud claim. Joseppe had no idea that what he was selling might fall into the category of a security. He wouldn't know what a private placement was if it smacked him in the face. Now, I know, that technically that's not a defense. But I don't think too many juries are going to attribute the kind of sophistication to Joseppe that most people think is necessary to commit a securities fraud.

"So I think Evans is barking up the wrong tree on that one. Now, I'd like you to take your memo back and separate it out into two documents, one on the statutory claim and the other on the common law claim. Then I'm gonna call Evans and talk to him about it."

Mark could tell that Peter was none too happy with the request. The young man turned on his heels to go. But before he reached the door, which was only three feet away, Mark called out to him again. "How're you doin' with the memo on the murder charge?"

"You'll have it tomorrow. Anything else?"

Mark smiled. "No, Peter, nothing else. I think that's plenty, don't you?"

Peter didn't answer. Instead he turned, clicked his heels, and bolted out the door.

Mark jumped to his feet and followed the young associate out the door. Mark stayed a respectable distance back, not wanting Long to know he was being followed, but wondering just the same where the young man was off to in such a hurry.

Jack Christian looked up from his desk, but continued his telephone conversation as Peter barged in unannounced. The senior partner swiveled slightly forward in his high-backed leather chair, and motioned for Peter to take a seat. Long continued to stand.

Christian terminated his call, and looked up with a terse smile. "What can I do for you Peter?"

"Hi, Dad," the young man retorted.

Christian clenched his jaw. "Shut the door," he demanded.

Peter ignored the senior partner.

"What's this new thing, Peter? I thought we'd reached an understanding long ago. Am I incorrect on that little matter?"

"Not important. I just came to tell you that I want Clifton out of here."

"Now, Peter—"

"Uh, uh, uh," the young man wagged his finger at his father. "You know, I saw that wonderful article about you in *The National Law Journal* just this morning."

Christian could feel his stomach tighten.

"You know, the one about you being this year's choice to receive the bar's highest award for distinguished service? What was it, the career achievement award?"

The senior partner didn't answer.

"When is the banquet? Next month, I believe the article said. You know," Long continued as he walked over to the large picture window and glanced out. "I think my mother would be proud of you, in some absurd way. That is, if she was still alive. But then you'd know more about that than I would. You know, she never did tell me if it was just a one-night stand, or if you fucked her regularly. Which was it, Dad?"

Jack Christian, patrician, paragon of the Bar, sighed deeply and stood up. "You really are a troubled young man, Peter. I've told you all along that I'd be glad to help you out, you know, perhaps with some counseling to help you come to grips with your emotions. It's really not a healthy situation."

"Especially for you, Jack. If crazy Peter cracks, and tells the world he's the bastard son of Jack Christian, it'll just ruin your whole fucking day won't it?"

"You know, Peter, in the first place, unless I choose to confirm what you say, I doubt anyone will give your story much credence. And secondly, all this supposed leverage you have over me will be gone. So don't be so quick to blab," Christian countered as he leaned across his desk and glared at the young man. "It'll end all your fun."

"Hey, Jack, don't be thick. What do you think, I haven't been taping our conversations? I mean come on, don't insult me. As for leverage, you've got a point there, but don't confuse me for someone who gives a shit, 'cause I don't. Now, get this straight. I want Clifton outta here, not just his bitch-witch Keegan. Got it?"

Jack Christian continued to glare at his illegitimate child as the young man turned and stormed out of the office. Christian mopped his brow with the handkerchief which he held in his right hand as he opened the top drawer of his desk with his left hand. He pulled out the diamond studded pistol he kept in the desk for good luck, and for kicks. He'd never used it. Never even fired a single shot.

CHAPTER TWENTY-SIX

Although it was only 9:30, Connie Parker was in bed. Her social calendar had fallen off dramatically in the past few weeks. Mostly her doing. She just wasn't in the mood. She still got invited to all the regular lobbyist affairs, but she didn't have the heart for them anymore. She had gone out for drinks with Jayne a couple of times recently, and made a few "hunting" forays on her own, but that was really the sole extent of her social life for the last month.

The first trial was now only a week and a half away. Connie had spent more time than she cared to remember with Jim Evans hearing about the fraud trial, and preparing for her testimony in the murder trial. Thorough though she was sure he was, Connie somehow doubted that Evans was ever *this* prepared.

Connie was thumbing through the latest edition of *Rolling Stone* and listening to Simon and Garfunkel when the phone rang. She had an unlisted number now, and the *Jeopardy* phone calls had stopped for the time being. Still . . . She thought momentarily about not answering it, but curiosity got the best of her.

"Hello," she said, her voice devoid of emotion.

"Hey, babe, what's a social butterfly like you doing home at this hour? I figured you'd be out at some party or another." It was Mo Buell, and he sounded slightly manic.

"Gee, Mo, this is a surprise. Haven't spoken to you in a long, long time. What can I do for you?" Connie's heart pumped as she wondered how the deejay had gotten her number.

"You can start by not being such a cold bitch all the time," Buell lashed back, venom dripping from his sloppy voice.

"Mo, I think you're drunk, and this behavior is entirely inappropriate. I'm going to make like you never called. Good night."

Connie gently placed the telephone back onto the receiver. She got up from her bed and went into the kitchen. She put some water on to boil, and took out the coffee. She stared into space for a few minutes until the kettle whistled. Then, with a slightly trembling hand, she poured the water into her mug and brought the mug to her lips. But it was still too hot, and she nearly burnt her lips and the inside of her mouth before she was able to stop the coffee from going in.

She sat at the kitchen table shaking her head, and absently picking at a chip in the linoleum table with her pinky nail when she realized the phone was ringing again. Obnoxious little bastard she thought as she glanced up toward the kitchen phone hanging on the far wall. But she couldn't ignore it. Maybe it was her father. It seemed like every time she let the damn thing ring, it was him. Then she would hear the exasperation in his voice on the machine. Sometimes he got so irritated he called her Constance. "Constance, this is your father." Or, "Constance, out again?"

She lunged for the phone. "Yes, hello," she said, the uncertainty evident in her voice.

"Well, now, that's a sweet voice that I haven't heard in a long, long time."

"Who is this?" The voice sounded familiar, but Connie had been expecting either her father or Mo Buell, and she couldn't quite place it.

"Damn, you'll do anything to burst my little bubble, won't you? It would be nice if you had recognized my voice, babe. I'm hurt that you didn't."

Connie warmed to the occasion. "Oh, George, I'm sorry I didn't recognize your voice at first, but actually, I was expecting someone else to call, so your voice was just, I don't know, out of context somehow. It, it's nice to hear from you."

"Well, now, that's better. I'm glad that at least you did recognize me once I talked a bit. How've you been, babe?"

"I'm fine. What's on your mind, George?"

"You, babe, like always."

Connie wasn't biting, at least not tonight. "George, did you want to talk about something specific or are you merely calling to say hello?"

"I wanna talk about you and me, babe. It's a topic I like a lot."

"Look, George, I thought I made it clear the last time we went through this. I do not want to get involved right now with you or for that matter anyone else. I'm sure you heard what happened with my boyfriend, Stuart Katcavage."

"Yeah, I was sorry to hear about that. I knew Katcavage, and he wasn't a bad guy. Although," now Moran's tone hardened, "I still don't understand what you saw in him compared to me."

Before Connie could muster the energy to answer, Moran continued. "I may be coming back to town pretty soon, just as soon as I tie up some loose ends. I want to see you. Just give me a chance and I'll show you that I'm twice the man Katcavage ever was."

"Okay, George," Connie rolled her eyes. "Okay."

Connie stared off into space for a moment after hanging up the phone. Then, smiling vaguely, she disconnected it. Just as quickly, she reconnected it and dialed her old number. Idiots! The phone company had given her a new unlisted number, but they had put a recording on her old number giving out the new one!

Connie quickly dressed and headed out the door. She hailed a cab, and headed up Connecticut Avenue towards an all-night diner. Actually, it wasn't all that late, not even eleven o'clock. But Connie had been in bed for nearly an hour before the two bizarre phone calls, so it felt later. A lot later.

She sat down at the counter and ordered a cup of decaf. She looked around but hardly noticed the rest of the diner's patrons. She had brought her copy of *Rolling Stone* with her, so she thumbed through it. She read an article about Neil Young and didn't realize until she had finished it that she had no idea what the hell she was reading. She didn't even like Neil Young. He was whiny, self-righteous, and old.

The chubby waitress, transplanted directly from midtown Manhattan, called her "hon" and asked her what was on her mind. Connie tried to resist, but this waitress had experience, lots of experience, with people just like Connie.

Connie ordered a second cup of coffee and a piece of Boston Creme Pie. "You know, I just got these crazy phone calls is all," Connie began. "I mean, the one from Moran, well, I could deal with that. He's just different, you know, and I kind of like playing around with him.

But, Buell! He's like this big personality, you know. And he calls drunk as a skunk and starts hammering me. I mean, who the hell needs that. You know," Connie continued between mouthfuls of pie, "I used to have fun toying around with him, but he's a lunatic, he really is."

Connie paused, a forkful of pie poised on her fork. "Oh, what the hell, sorry to be unloading my troubles on you," she said, while raising an eyebrow.

While the waitress helped others at the counter, Connie savored the last few morsels of pie. She left a dollar and some change on the counter, grabbed the bill, and walked towards the cashier. She could feel the eyes, the usual ones, following her as she made her way towards the exit. Only this time she didn't know if it was the regulars leering at her, or if she had spilled her guts too loudly.

She paid the bill, and caught a cab home. The cab driver had a completely indecipherable Middle Eastern name. Connie tried to mouth it a few times, but gave up. She leaned hard against the back of the seat, and bit the inside of her mouth. The street lights clicked past as she stared vacantly out the window.

Connie looked back at the driver's nameplate. How the hell would you ever report this guy, you could never come close to getting that name right, with all the consonants laced together. She smiled softly, and began thinking about the driver. Probably had a wife and some little kids at home, in a tiny apartment in a blue-collar area. Probably was thrilled to be in the U.S. and didn't care about being exploited.

She shook her head. All wrong. Probably a revolutionary. Making bombs for some subversive terrorist plot.

The driver turned and smiled. "We are here, ma'am," he said, his white teeth shining. "That will be $5.50."

Connie handed him seven bucks, and thanked him. He stayed in front of the building waiting for her to be safely inside. Looking back over her shoulder, Connie smiled and waved. Never can tell about people she thought. Never can tell.

Chapter Twenty-Seven

Gary Schofield walked briskly through the lobby of the posh Marriott Castle Harbour Resort on his way back to his room.

"Pssst."

At first he didn't realize the sound was directed at him.

"Pssst. Mister. Hey, Mr. Jennings."

Gary suddenly recognized the voice of his favorite receptionist. He stopped momentarily, expecting a scene.

"Here," she said, as she handed Gary a piece of paper. Then she was gone.

Gary waited until he got to his room to unfold the note. It was short. "Please meet me at my home tonight at eight o'clock. I have some information to share with you about George. I was afraid to talk this morning." It was signed, "Belinda."

Interesting. Maybe a 50:50 chance it was real, at best. But interesting nonetheless. The address was on the back. Hey, looks like I've got a date tonight, Gary smiled.

When he pulled up to the little bevy of pastel pink, purple, and green homes, Gary couldn't see if the lights were on in Belinda's house. It was dark, but Belinda's place apparently was not facing the street.

Gary headed around the back. The numbers were not well marked, most people on Bermuda preferring names for their residences. But Belinda was very clear in her note. Unit 7. Gary found the house and rapped on the door. No answer. He knocked again, this time a bit more insistently. Still no answer.

Gary fished out a few tools of the trade from his pocket, and quickly picked the lock. He let the door swing open, and drew his gun. He headed toward the kitchen. Suddenly, his calf seized up in a monstrous cramp. He pushed his foot down hard and gritted his teeth until the pain subsided. Damn. Gotta eat some bananas, need the potassium.

He refocused his attention on the house. Still no sign of life. He swiveled toward the hallway, which was narrow and unreasonably long for such a small place. Slowly, he was becoming aware of the presence of something in the apartment. He couldn't put his finger on it.

He lurched down the hall toward the bedroom. He stopped to glance in a bathroom. It was empty. Lifeless. He cocked his pistol, and burst into the doorway of the bedroom, arm raised, gun pointing forward.

Immediately, he spotted Belinda, face down on the bed. As he moved towards her, he could hear the gentle swaying sound of reggae music emanating from a neighboring home. He was also aware of the smell of some type of island food being cooked nearby. He approached the bed on tiptoes. He leaned over just enough to see that the sheets were soaked through with blood. Deep red. And fresh. Oh, so fresh.

Gary pulled out a pair of gloves. He began to rifle through her nightstand. He found an address book, and quickly turned to the letter "c." Caulfield was listed. Gary took the book and headed out the door.

Once back in Caulfield's car, Gary pulled out a map of the island. He easily located Caulfield's street, and after a minute to catch his bearings, Gary headed off.

Caulfield lived in a nice place. Stucco looking, sort of. Not purely pastel like most of the rest of the homes on the island. Fairly secluded too, at the end of a dirt road.

Gary got out of the car, and tiptoed toward the front door. There appeared to be only one light on in the house. Gary stopped and looked around. There was a long driveway, but no car. Gary smiled.

Gary turned back toward the house. He rang the bell. No answer. He tiptoed around the side of the house, following the light to the back. Still on tiptoes, he walked up the short set of stairs, and leaned against the door, struggling to see through the tiny window.

At first he saw nothing, but then he hiked himself up high enough to look down on the floor. He gasped for only a second when he saw Caulfield lying in a pool of blood. Honestly, it wasn't that much of a shock.

Gary drove like a wild banshee from Tampa on Route 4 East toward Lakeland. His flight had landed in Tampa shortly after two in the afternoon, and by the time he got his luggage and a rental car it was well after two-thirty. He wanted to get to Lakeland in enough time to find the post office and begin what he hoped would be the not-too-difficult task of obtaining the true forwarding address of George Moran.

The last twenty-four hours had been played out at 78 rpm. But the flight to Tampa had given Gary some much-needed downtime. He was ready to renew the search.

If the post office closed before he got there, Gary would lose a whole day. Time was too precious for that.

Gary got to the post office at twenty to five. He was dressed in long, purple, pink, and yellow madras shorts which were cuffed just above the knee. This was complemented by his yellow-and-brown striped polo shirt and a Chicago Cubs baseball cap to cover his ponytail.

Gary carried with him a large manila envelope with papers hanging out of it. As he got out of the car he made a big fuss about trying to get the papers back into the folder. Just in case anyone from inside was watching, he dropped the manila envelope, and purposely allowed all the pages to come out. He fumbled to pick them up, making certain that they were sticking out at all sorts of odd angles as he picked up the envelope and rammed it underneath his arm. Then he pranced into the post office with a huge, idiotic grin on his face.

"Hi," Gary began, in a voice that mixed a fake Midwestern accent with some other type of speech pattern of an indecipherable, unknown etiology. "My name is Gary Moran, and I've been looking for my cousin George for weeks now." At this point, Gary tried to place the manila envelope on the counter in front of the somewhat bewildered clerk, but he managed to purposely drop it and allow all of the papers to come tumbling out yet again.

"Dang," Gary said emphatically. "I, I, I will be with you in a second. Please bear with me just a minute now, I'm so clumsy." Gary picked up the papers and stuffed them back into the envelope and placed it on the countertop. "This here envelope has all the letters I've tried to send to cousin George to get him to come home." At this point, Gary looked down at his feet and his smile changed to a look of sadness. "Ya' see, George's sister, that is, cousin Helene, is very, very sick. She wants to see George before she passes on. Ya' know, she's really not an old woman at all. Forty-eight years old. It's tragic, really it is. Anyway, I've been lookin' for cousin George for weeks. I finally went to Bermuda—nice place—to try to track him down, and I was able to learn that he's moved to Lakeland. But here's the problem. He's got a P.O. box, and I need to know where I can find him."

The fresh-scrubbed young man behind the counter didn't know how to respond. He looked around helplessly to his colleagues who were all suddenly making themselves very busy, although there wasn't another soul in the place. Gary began pushing letters towards the man who looked young enough to still be in high school. Each one had on it a different type of mark which appeared to be from the post office, but which was placed there courtesy of Gary Schofield, private investigator. The marks read "returned, undeliverable" or "no such addressee."

"The doc said Helene had a month to live. Course she's already made a fool outta that old coot. He said it five weeks ago! Anyway, could you kindly tell me how to find Helene's brother?"

"Have you got the box number?"

"Yes sir. I have it right here on this scrap somewhere," Gary said, as he fumbled through the envelope yet again. "Ah, here it is. It's Box 2812, Lakeland, Florida."

The clerk smiled. "That's easy," he replied. "Your cousin, George, has run off and joined the circus."

"Well I'll be," Gary replied with a laugh. "How can I find the old coot?"

"For starters look in that there phone book, and find the number for Stone's Big Top Circus. They're located right here in town."

"Thank you, my good man. Thank you, kindly," Gary said. "Cousin Helene will be pleased."

He turned to leave, and mumbled under his breath. "This must be a dream! This absolutely must be a dream."

Chapter Twenty-Eight

Although he couldn't quite get over the nagging possibility that what Julie really wanted was simply to get rid of him, Donald Lubins agreed with his ex-wife that he should go back to Stone's Big Top Circus and look for George Moran. For whatever reason, Lubins wanted to repay Mark, despite feeling that Mark's actions hadn't been entirely altruistic. Lubins didn't want a debt, of any kind, hanging over his head.

Lubins still couldn't tell Mark that he had overheard the message which Gary had left the previous week. But he wanted to help, and this was the best option.

A quick phone call to Stone's headquarters had revealed that the unit of the show to which Lubins conjectured Moran had run, was currently entertaining the good folks of Charlotte, North Carolina. Unfortunately, train service to Charlotte was spotty. And Lubins wasn't quite flush enough to afford a rent-a-car, so it was back to the buses. While he certainly didn't revel in the thought of going back to the Greyhound station, at least he had made peace with Julie and the kids, and had a few bucks in his pocket. It was a far cry from the last time he spent 36 hours on a bus.

This time, Lubins was able to concentrate a bit on a magazine, and to sleep on and off. And the ride was only 20 hours.

Less than 24 hours after he had set out from Dayton,

Lubins found himself face-to-face with the marquee sign for Stone's Big Top Circus. His jaw tightened. He turned and looked back at the bus as it pulled away, spewing smoke and sputtering frightfully. He took a step back towards it, then turned again, and trudged towards the arena.

Once inside, he found his way backstage to the general manager's trailer. He knocked on the door. When an unfamiliar face answered, Lubins asked to see Mike McGee, General Manager of Stone's Big Top Circus.

"Hi, Donald, face looks a bit better than last time. What can I do for you?" asked Lubins' former boss as he rounded the corner and came into the trailer.

"I'm flattered that you remember me," Lubins began. "I, I remember you said that I could try back in a couple of months and—"

"Hold on," McGee interrupted putting his hand in the air. "Save the speech. I meant what I said. I imagine that Mora won't get too bent outta shape, she and Manuel haven't been fighting too much lately, so you're welcome."

Lubins retrieved some linens and headed for his newly assigned bed. The many weeks he had spent in Mark's apartment, followed by the nights on Julie's living room couch, had spoiled him. The thought of sharing a tiny room with two other guys, who likely hadn't showered in a week, was not overly enticing.

He knocked on the door which was answered by a guy with long, stringy, greasy black hair. This guy hadn't showered in way more than a week. In fact, Lubins was quite certain the man hadn't changed his clothes in that length of time either.

When Lubins introduced himself, his new roommate merely grunted. Lubins could tell this wasn't exactly going to be an opportunity for late-night literary discourse. He flung his suitcase to the far end of the bed, and began pulling the sheets over the stained mattress. Once Lubins had completely made his bed, he put the suitcase in his foot locker and locked it.

Lubins' new roomie watched the entire proceeding without saying a word or changing the dull expression on his face. Their third roommate, whomever he might be, wasn't present. Lubins tried not to think about where or who roommate number three might be.

"So, what did you say your name was again?" Lubins asked.

"Jarvis, Tom Jarvis. Yours?" he grunted.

"Donald Lubins. Say, Tom, are there a lot of new guys these days?"

"I dunno. I only been here a week. Ain't nobody looked familiar to me."

Lubins was glad he asked. This guy was certain to provide some great leads. Lubins realized for the first time that being a detective might not be all that easy, especially in a place like Stone's Big Top Circus where the majority of people come and go quite frequently, and those who stay don't exactly make a habit of opening up to strangers.

It was going to take more than a few questions, and probably more than a few days, to find George Moran. Lubins certainly hadn't made too many lifelong friendships the last time he was with the show. It was unlikely he could simply start asking people prying questions the moment he returned. But he was determined to try. He knew the first of Joseppe's two trials was scheduled to begin in six days.

The former and current roustabout left his little room with Tom Jarvis sitting right where Lubins had found him a half-hour earlier. He wandered out of the train, and decided to walk the half mile back towards the arena. In ten minutes he was there. There was only one show that day, at 7:30 in the evening. Lubins had plenty of time before he had to report for work. But he figured he'd do some snooping.

As luck would have it, the Flying Ortiz Brothers were set to rehearse in twenty minutes according to the schedule posted near the dressing rooms. Lubins waited for the boys to arrive. Manuel Ortiz was the first to see him. He greeted Lubins with a smile.

"Lubins, that's your name, right?"

"Right, Manuel, that's me. It's nice to see you again."

"You workin' here again?"

"Yep. I'm riggin' for you guys again."

"Hey, that's great, man. We were sorry to see you go last time. You know, man, that Mora, she's been acting mondo strange lately. For a while she try to make peace. You know, she'd invite people back to her trailer after the show for a beer. Then all of a sudden one day she just stop talking to everybody. No more askin' people back to the trailer, no more beer. It's like somethin' happened. But nobody's talkin' about it. Ya' know, man, she's a weird chick, man."

"Any more fights with her and her gang?" Lubins asked.

"Nah. We been layin' off that stuff lately. McGee was pretty pissed the last time," Manuel said with a snort. "Man, you the only one got shitcanned. He have to make a sacrifice at the altar of Mora, eh? The way they deal with her shit jus' blow me away, man."

Lubins walked with Manuel slowly out onto the arena floor. Manuel introduced him to some of the new riggers, and told them to treat him right, that he had come through for the Ortiz family when the chips were down. Lubins merely nodded his appreciation.

Lubins helped during the setup for rehearsals and then simply hung around, listening to the other workingmen talk. The more gossip he could pick up, the better. He needed to be a sponge, but an innocuous one.

Just before the evening performance, one of Mora's henchmen approached Lubins.

"Hey, perfesser," the oversized gorilla began, "didn't realize they let you back."

"Nice to see you too, my friend," Lubins retorted.

"Listen, smartass, things is different now, instead of before. Keep ya' nose clean, ya hear?"

"Got it, my man," Lubins replied. "And, hey, thanks for the warning."

Lubins did just fine on his first night back. Aside from the little warning from Mora's "bodyguard," all went smoothly. The Flying Ortiz Brothers' act went off without a hitch and was well-received by the sparse crowd. There was little that Lubins could do about the fact that Mora was still the star of the show, receiving applause that was somehow a notch, or even a notch and a half above that received by the Ortiz. All Lubins could do was make sure that the Ortiz didn't tumble through the air when they weren't supposed to. On his first night back, Lubins accomplished his task.

Long after the show was over, Lubins sauntered around backstage.

"Say," he said to one of the clowns removing makeup, "small crowd tonight, eh?"

"Who gives a damn?" came the response.

So he tried another avenue with a different performer.

"Hey, felt a bit warm out there tonight, eh?" he said to one of the showgirls.

"Not in what I was wearing," she smiled.

But Lubins couldn't think of a follow up. He smiled

back at the showgirl who sat, waiting and smiling. He shook his head a bit, and, still smiling, said goodnight.

Lubins walked past the rest of the dressing rooms and headed back for his palace on the train. Tom Jarvis was sitting on the edge of his bed picking at his teeth with a match. Roommate number three was present as well. Lubins recognized him from a few months ago. He was Charlie McFerrin, a kindly, old, black man with a winning smile and a gray stubble of a beard. McFerrin was mostly bald with a slight fringe of salt-and-pepper hair. He stood five feet ten inches tall and weighed well over two hundred pounds, having been raised on good ol' southern cooking, and from what Lubins could gather, never changing his eating habits. He looked and spoke as if he had come to the show directly from the cotton fields of Mississippi or maybe from some sharecropper's farm in rural Alabama.

McFerrin nodded at Lubins with recognition. "Welcome back," the rigger said. "I see lotsa guys come an' go through here, but I never thought you wuz one who would come back."

"You never can tell, can you?"

Lubins looked at McFerrin, and then looked back at the greasy Jarvis sitting on the third bed. Lubins stood, stretched his arms a bit, and said, "You know, I think I'm gonna get a bit of fresh air before turning in." He looked at McFerrin. "Wanna take a walk?"

McFerrin jumped up from the edge of his bed. He nodded his head, and without looking at Jarvis, followed Lubins out the door.

Once they were outside, McFerrin spoke. "That dude gives me the willies!"

"How long have you been living with him?"

"I don't know, exactly. Not long. Maybe a week. But I

stop keepin' track o' time a long time back. But I can tell you this, it's longer than I wish it was."

"Have you told McGee you'd like a new roommate?"

"Nah, I don't like to rock da boat, if you know what I mean."

Lubins nodded his head. The two walked on in silence, with the old man gently pawing at the dirt underfoot, occasionally sending stones screaming out in front of them.

It was Lubins who finally broke the silence. "You know, I'm not really all that thrilled about seeing Mora again. One of her henchmen has already made some threats in my direction. That fight wasn't my idea, you know. I had no choice but to get involved once Manuel came to get me. You know, I hear things have changed over Mora's way. You have any idea what's going on?"

McFerrin shook his head. "Not really sure. But da other day I seen this dude walkin' with Mora. It wuz really late at night, and I guess they didn't think anyone else'd be out. But I like ta walk, and get fresh air. Soon as they saw me, they turn around real quick like, and start walkin' in the other direction."

"Hmm," Lubins replied.

"Ya know, I seen a lot a crazy shit 'round here. I don't get to thinkin' 'bout it too much. I just go 'bout my business. It's like, there was this time, 'bout twelve or thirteen years ago, guy murdered his roommie just 'cause the guy looked at him wrong. Now, I didn't see him do it or nothin', but I knew 'bout it just the same.

"Cops come. They start askin' questions and stuff. I just didn't say nothin'. People here, they thank me for it later. Ya' know, it's just like that here. Lots of people, they here 'cause they hiding from something. That's just the way it is on the road."

Lubins nodded silently and began circling back towards the train. Good ol' Jarvis was probably still sitting on the edge of his bed, picking at his teeth. Or, maybe he was cleaning the bottom of his boots with the same wooden matchstick.

Chapter Twenty-Nine

George Moran leaned back against the fake wood paneling on the inside of his sister's RV and pushed the window opened slightly. He flicked an ash off his cigarette through the window and glared at his sister. Mora the Great glared right back at him.

"You know," Mora began, but she stopped in disgust to let Moran finish cracking his knuckles. "I told you you could stay as long as you need too, but it will be a relief when you leave."

"Nothin' like a little sisterly love, eh, Mora?" Moran said, patting down the already greased back remainder of what passed for his hair.

"You remember what Mom used to always say? She said 'I always love you, but I may not always like you.' Well, that goes for me too, George. I don't think mama would approve of you one bit."

"Would that be before or after she breaks the chair over some guy's head in a bar? I mean come on, Mora, my heart's breakin'. Really it is."

"Look Mom did okay with what she had. She was one of the best tightrope walkers in Italy, and you know it."

"Yeah, until she started boozin' and raising hell, then all she did was beat up any guy who made eyes at her, after she basically begged them all to do just that."

"Not true," Mora replied with a wave of her hand.

Moran smiled. "You remember the time we were in

Florence, I think it was. Yeah, Florence. Remember, I was like nine, maybe ten years old.

"It was the night I followed mom into the bar, and she's talking to some guy, you know, some guy from the show, or maybe he was the local promoter. Anyway, I got into it with some drunk at the bar. Remember?"

"Yeah," Mora answered. "I remember. I was about twelve. The guy didn't like circus folks. Called us gypsies, so you pulled his chair out from under him. Boy, that was brilliant!"

"Hey, Mora, how can you say that? I mean you just don't seem to give a shit if people put you down solely on account of who you are."

"Exactly right!"

Moran glared at his sister but his piercing stare was interrupted by a rapping on the door. Feeling disgusted, Moran stood up, stopped momentarily to crack his ankles, and began walking toward the bedroom. Halfway there he stopped to yank up his pants which had fallen slightly from his protruding, plumber-like belly, and needed some convincing to stay up. In no big hurry, he sauntered into the bedroom, pulling the door shut behind him.

As far as Moran could tell, the only person who had spotted him in the weeks he had been living with his sister was the old black man who was out walking at two o'clock in the morning. And Moran wasn't too worried about him.

Moran peeked through a crack in the bedroom door, trying not to bust it open with his all too prosperous girth. He was surprised to see the old man standing there. Mora didn't invite him in. Instead she brusquely asked the longtime employee what was on his mind.

"I'm sorry to bother you Miz Mora. But I'm bunkin'

with this white dude, Lubins. You'd know him if you'd seen him. He was here when you guys fought the Ortiz. Anyway, he's back, and I'm bunkin' with him. He ask me to tell you that he didn't want to be in that fight and he don't want no trouble. He say one of your guys been threatenin' him already and he only been back one day.

"Like I said, I'm sorry to bother you with this, Miz Mora, but I don't want no trouble and he seem like a nice guy."

"Thanks for letting me know Charlie, you're a good man. I'll try to make sure there are no more fights. You can go now."

"Thank ya' Miz Mora. Lubins, well, he'll be real happy."

Moran sauntered out of the bedroom, a half-empty wine glass in his hand. "Who the hell was that?"

"None of your damn business, George," Mora exploded. "You're lucky I haven't kicked your ass out of here yet, especially with all that damn wine you're drinking. And it's none of your business who comes to talk to me."

Moran looked down at the glass in his hand, swished the wine around a bit and smiled. "Touchy, touchy, touchy," he replied. "It's only my business if that black dude was up to no good," he continued. "When was the last time a workingman who wasn't assigned to you knocked on your door?"

"Charlie's been with the show for over twenty years. He goes where he wants. Everyone likes him, and I don't think there's anything wrong with him knocking on my door."

"You sound like someone who's tryin' to convince herself of something she doesn't believe. You think it's weird that that old man knocked on your door, but you just don't feel like talking to me about it. That's okay, I'll just kill the fucker."

"How did you become so screwed up, George?"

Moran didn't respond. Not immediately. Not at all. Instead, he sat back down on his chair, picked up the pencil he had been using for the crossword puzzle, and began drawing pictures on the corner of the newspaper. First, he sketched two stick figures copulating. Then he drew a heart with the initials "G.M." and "C.P." inside it. Then he put an arrow through the heart.

Chapter Thirty

The trial date was looming. Peter's lack of help was making Mark Clifton nervous. He could tell Joseppe was getting nervous too, though the barber's emotions had nothing to do with a lack of trial preparation. Mark gazed at the files and books spread out around him. He began chewing absentmindedly on the inside of his mouth and humming an old Beatles favorite, "Yellow Submarine." He made a fist and pounded the table, gently, at first, and then harder. After chewing the first layer of skin from the inside of his mouth, he picked up the telephone on the conference table and buzzed Carol's office. He smiled when he heard her voice.

"Are you real busy right now?" Mark asked, trying not to allow his tone to betray his concern.

"I'm okay, what's up?"

"Can you meet me at Nick's? I know this is ridiculous, but you know Christian."

They met at Nick's. Mark smiled as Carol, wearing her trademark teal scarf strode in. Then he was all business. "I just met with that sniveling dog, Long," he began. "I've had it with him. His memo sucked and his attitude was even worse."

"I'm sorry, honey," Carol replied. "You know what I think of him. But I've never really worked with him. I thought you used to be satisfied with his work?"

"I did. That's what pisses me off the most. You know,

the fraud indictment has two totally separate parts, one pertaining to potential statutory violations and the other pertaining to common law fraud. Instead of giving me either two separate memos or, at least one memo with two separate parts, he just blurred the whole damn thing together. It was like he didn't even know there was a difference. And when I called him on it, he acted like a total prick."

"Why don't you just throw him off the case?"

Mark thought about telling Carol of the conversation he had overheard between Long and Christian. Then he thought better of it. Instead, he said, "and do what? There's no other associates, other than you, who could pick this stuff up quickly enough to help me. The trial is six days away, and I need a shitload of research done. It's got to be insightful and it's got to be done by someone who knows the fact pattern inside out. I can't take myself away from what I'm doing to bring someone up to speed at this point. It's really pissing me off!"

"That's obvious," Carol laughed. "Listen, I've got an idea. I'm not working on anything earth-shattering right now. It's plenty to keep me busy but my deadlines are pretty loose. We don't even have a trial date in the Simmons case yet. So, why don't you let me help you? I know I can't bill for it 'cause Christian would find out, besides which, it wouldn't be fair to Joseppe. But, I hate to see you like this. Besides, it'll be fun!"

"Talk about a fucked-up situation! I've got the best damn associate in the world wanting to work on my case, but my partners won't let me so we have to do it without billing, or even telling anyone."

"Who is your highest obligation to?"

"My client."

"So?"

Mark looked up and stopped studying his shoe tops. "You're on," he said.

Mark knew that Carol, having finally been unleashed, would attack Joseppe's case with a vengeance. Oh, he knew she had to be careful, very careful. She would need many of the same casebooks and other research materials that Peter would be using, so she would have to be circumspect. She also couldn't neglect her current workload, light though it might be. Within these boundaries, however, Mark was certain she would be a research terror.

Carol quickly uncovered numerous helpful cases and statutory citations on the fraud charges which she dutifully reported to Mark. And she followed up on the Alabama murder case. She spoke with defense counsel, a public defender in Montgomery, who advised her that the case was on appeal with the eleventh circuit, and that oral arguments had been held a few weeks earlier. A decision was expected any day, and counsel agreed to contact her as soon as he heard.

Before nightfall the following day, Carol provided Mark with three separate memos. The first dealt with the murder charge and the law surrounding it. The second dealt with the statutory fraud charge, and contained significant case law to the effect that Evans would never be able to gain a conviction of Joseppe. Carol suggested in this memo that that should be reason enough for Evans to drop the claim. Why would he want to dilute a potentially stronger claim by bringing the weaker one as well? Mark hoped she was right.

The third memo pertained to the common law fraud charges. The basic issue there went to Joseppe's state of mind, and whether or not he had the requisite intent to defraud his customers. He had certainly provided them with information, and they had relied on it to their detriment, so all that mattered was whether Joseppe had intended for his customers to lose money, or at least could be said to reasonably have known that they would lose their money. It was a question Mark had asked himself before.

With the trial exactly five days away, Mark and Carol began to discuss strategy for choosing the two juries for the separate cases. Mark had convinced Evans that Joseppe's cases would be seriously prejudiced by trying the charges at the same time. Information about the fraud could certainly have a prejudicial effect on the murder trial and vice versa. Besides, if the murder trial began before a verdict was reached in the fraud trial, Joseppe could testify more freely, without the concern that his testimony from the first trial could be used to impeach him. Mark would, at least to some degree, have the opportunity to see the jury react to certain information, and to certain trial tactics before deciding whether to use them again in the more serious murder trial.

Mark knew that the issue of prejudice was clear. So it didn't surprise him when Evans consented to separate trials. Besides, it would give the pompous ass two separate soapboxes. Who could ask for more?

Mark's true concern in seeking separate trials was the very real possibility that his client might do poorly in the fraud case, where the evidence was much more clearly against him. That, in turn, could hang him in the murder case if the same jury heard both.

Of course, Mark knew that the converse was true as well. If Evans screwed up the fraud trial, where he was expected to prevail, it could do wonders for Joseppe in the murder trial. When it came down to it, Mark did what he always did. He went with his gut. Two trials. Fraud case first. It was a decision the judge may have made anyway, without concern for Mark or Jim Evans, but it was better to think these things were within your control, not outside of it.

Enough with the pretrial administrative crap. Sometimes all the jockeying made Mark sick. It was time to start thinking about strategy. Strategy that would matter. Like picking a jury.

Middle-aged immigrants would make wonderful jurors. Well, that was pretty obvious. But it wasn't like Evans wouldn't just use all of his peremptory challenges to strike anyone with that profile from the jury panel. So what or better yet, who, would come after middle-aged immigrants? How would poor people feel if they were sitting on this jury? Mark argued that they might understand any potential motivation Joseppe had to make a few dollars. But Carol countered that if they were poor, but basically honest, they might be appalled at what Joseppe had done, and have a visceral reaction to it.

The juries, both of them, would be chosen from citizens of the District of Columbia. They likely would be predominantly black. In cases where the defendant was black, the advantage of a predominantly black jury was readily evident. In this case, it was unclear what effect the racial make up of the panel would have on the outcome of the case.

When all was said and done, Mark decided that the lower the socioeconomic class of the potential juror, the more desirable that person would be. It was a gut instinct, just like all the others Mark had lived by.

They wouldn't have a hell of a lot of information about the jury panel until the day the jury was going to be chosen. But that didn't mean that a profile couldn't be drawn of the so-called perfect juror. So Mark and Carol began setting out various pieces of demographic information and character traits which they believed would be telling. Then they began drafting questions for the judge to use on *voir dire*, the choosing of the jury.

After drafting a profile of the so-called perfect juror, it was time to finalize the process of sorting through the potential witnesses. Mark had spoken to all of them, either in person or on the phone. In the case of potentially key witnesses, Mark had made extensive notes while interviewing them. He began reviewing his notes, and discussing the possibilities with Carol. All had been told they would be called. It was easier that way.

Witnesses for the defense, in both cases, were actually few. Joseppe himself would be the main witness in both cases. In the fraud case there would be character witnesses, but only a few so-called fact witnesses, people who would testify to actual occurrences or dealings with Joseppe which might provide evidence about the case itself, as opposed to the defendant.

In the murder case, Joseppe's wife, Carlita, was a key witness. She had spent virtually the entire day and evening of Stuart Katcavage's demise with her husband. She would, in effect, be Joseppe's alibi witness. And although she hadn't actually accompanied him when he got the drink for Stuart Katcavage, she had been by his side for just about the entire night in question. State of mind would be an important factor, and Carlita could bolster Joseppe's own testimony.

Were it not for the bizarre case decided in Alabama, which included the instruction from the judge permitting the jurors to essentially speculate as to the way in which a particular murder may have been committed, Mark would have been confident in his ability to gain an acquittal on the murder charge. Oh, sure, anytime you have a client on trial for murder, you're a fool if you're confident and relaxed. But this case, at least on its face, seemed better than most. Joseppe was an upstanding citizen, well-known in the community, and had lived an exemplary life. He wasn't a drug dealer or a gang member. No one had seen him commit the alleged crime, and there was really no concrete evidence that, in fact, he had done so.

Joseppe hadn't told anyone he was planning to kill Stuart Katcavage, and the motive, while possible, wasn't the absolute strongest in the world. In short, there was a crime, and there was a body. There wasn't much else. There was no evidence, and there were certainly no witnesses, to tie Joseppe to the murder of Stuart Katcavage "beyond a reasonable doubt."

Unfortunately, the judge in Alabama had changed the rules. He had said that in a case remarkably similar to Joseppe's, if you had a motive and you had the crime and you had at least one other factor, such as physical proximity or something else to raise your suspicions, you could speculate as to the exact circumstances of the case. The Alabama judge was trying to tell his jury members to open their eyes to the facts of the case they were trying. But in so doing, he had gone too far. Way too far. All criminal cases, not just murder cases, are based on the American ideal that a defendant is innocent until proven guilty. And to be proven guilty, a jury of the defendant's peers must believe in his guilt beyond a reasonable doubt.

Judge Alabaster A. Samson, federal district court, Alabama, apparently didn't ascribe to such lofty ideals. In one fell swoop he took away a protection which all defendants being tried for alleged crimes in the United States had always enjoyed. Sure, the D.C. court could choose not to follow the Alabama decision. Particularly if it felt the decision was wrong. But it could also choose to follow it. Follow it exactly.

Mark knew Judge Samson's decision was wrong. Dead wrong. He also knew it would be overturned on appeal. Either that, or it would find its way to the Supreme Court where undoubtedly it would be overturned. But that was of no great solace at the moment.

Evans had to be aware of the case. Either that, or his researchers were as bad as Peter Long. Assuming Evans knew about the case, he would ram it down Mark's throat at every opportunity. Mark would need to demonstrate to the judge that the case was wrong, and that the judge should not rely on it. Otherwise, the burden of proof which Evans would need to achieve would be dramatically lessened.

Carol reported to Mark on a host of other cases which appeared to contradict the Alabama case. But none of them had a fact pattern so incredibly similar to Joseppe's case. And that was what the law was based upon. Finding cases with similar fact patterns.

Mark knew, just knew, that Evans would rant and rave to the judge that Joseppe's murder case was "on all fours" with the Alabama case. That is, the facts were exactly the same. Evans would back the judge into a corner, and tell him that he was required to follow the Alabama case. Mark would argue to the contrary that it was a case decided in another jurisdiction with a different set of laws. But Evans would counter, correctly so, that the standard of proof in each jurisdiction was similar, and each jurisdiction followed the same rules in trying murder cases.

It wasn't going to be fun, Mark knew that much. The thought of Joseppe serving time in a maximum security federal prison was enough to make Mark physically ill. The barber would undoubtedly be defiled and beaten by the inmates who would each desire to be his very close personal friend.

Mark tried to put such thoughts out of his mind. He needed to begin prepping witnesses, probably should have started already. He also needed to see if Gary was going to deliver Moran.

As he was thinking about Moran, Mark suddenly remembered the phone call he had gotten the night before from Julie Day, Lubins' ex-wife. It was almost like it hadn't happened. Mark had completely forgotten about it in the crush of preparation. Julie had called to thank Mark for what he had done for Lubins, and to tell Mark what Lubins couldn't: that Lubins had overheard the phone message from Gary, and had gone to try to track down Moran.

Mark felt a sudden surge of adrenaline course through his body. He quickly dialed Gary's phone number and asked the investigator's assistant, Susan, to get a message to Gary to call Mark in the office. Gary wore a beeper, so it usually only took a few seconds for him to call. Today was no different.

"Hey, Gary," Mark began, trying to sound nonchalant. "Where are you?"

"You wouldn't believe it if I told you," Gary replied.

"Try me."

"On my way to the Big Show, Stone's Big Top Circus!"

"Good. Great, in fact."

"Well, I guess you figured out that that was the P.O. box that Moran left as his address."

"Right. I didn't figure it out, Lubins did."

"Is he back so soon?"

"No. Actually, that's why I called you. He's out at the circus too, looking for Moran."

"Whatsa matter, you don't trust me?" Gary laughed.

"Hardly. He apparently overheard your message to me and recognized the address. So, after he saw his family, he decided he wanted to do something to help me."

"Touching. Absolutely touching."

"Listen, I think he's in over his head."

"Of course he is. And he's just gonna get in my way."

"So send him home. Tell him I thank him, but get him out of there."

"You got it. By the way, Caulfield's history."

"As in dead?"

"Yep."

"How?"

"Killed. I assume Moran had him killed, though it seems like Moran himself was off the island when it happened. But you remember I told you about my conversations with Caulfield?"

"Sure."

"Good ol' Georgie boy must have figured Caulfield was gonna turn him in, so he didn't want to take any chances."

"Great guy."

"The best Mark, simply the best. Hey wait a minute. Did Lubins' wife tell you which unit Donald was going to?"

"What do you mean?"

"There are two units of Stone's Big Top Circus. The silver and the gold. They play in different towns on the same days."

"Really. I didn't know that."

"You learn something new every day. Did she say where he was heading?"

"Come to think of it, no, I don't think she did."

"All right, I'll try to reach her and find out."

"Hey, how did you know that about the circus anyway?"

"I did some time there in a previous life, remember?"

"Yeah, sort of."

"Sort of? Not the kind of thing a guy like you would forget."

"True. I guess I've got a lot on my mind lately."

"I guess so," Gary came back in mock horror. "I guess so!"

"Hey," Mark shot back, "how come you didn't recognize the P.O. box?"

"It's different. The show used to be wintered in Tampa."

"Yeah, yeah, yeah," Mark laughed, "a million excuses!"

Chapter Thirty-One

Another night at home alone. Jayne was busy. Connie couldn't stomach the idea of going out to look for a man tonight, it just didn't feel right. For whatever reason, the few girlfriends she used to have, had stopped calling. It probably wasn't that difficult to figure. She just wasn't much fun lately. Let's face it, none of the friendships was exactly deep.

As Connie mulled over her sad state of affairs, she was interrupted by the telephone. It rang twice as she stared at it. Finally she decided to pick up the receiver. She could always hang up if the call was obscene or harassing. Or if it was another *Jeopardy* call.

"Hello."

"Well, Constance, finally you, and not that god-awful machine."

"Hi, Dad," Connie replied, trying to sound upbeat.

"When is the Italian's trial?"

Connie winced. "The first one starts on Monday. But first they have to pick the jury."

"What do you mean the first one?"

"I guess you don't remember, we spoke about this last time—"

"Constance," Carlisle Parker interrupted, "don't patronize me. I'm still your father even if you are some independently wealthy high-class call girl."

Connie bit her tongue, choking off the urge to

scream. Instead: "I know, Dad, that you disapprove of the line of work I'm in, but lobbying and whoring are hardly the same."

"Yeah, so you say, but the reporter for that *New York Post* equivalent you've got there, what is it *The Washington Gazette* or something? Anyway, he didn't see the distinction between what you do and what a high-priced call girl does. Now, mind you, I understand you are at the height of your profession. I would never refer to you as a 'whore.'"

"If I could change it all I would, Dad, really I would. But I can't change what's been done."

"You always listened when I said, 'Whatever you want to do is okay, so long as you do it well.' And you're at the top of the line. Hell, you could probably buy and sell your old man fifty times if need be, huh?"

"This is going nowhere. I've got some things to do."

"Gotta do some work, Con?"

"What difference does it make?"

"Look, sweetie," Carlisle began, suddenly softer. "I apologize. I just don't like the way you were described. It made it seem somehow less than honest. You know my feelings about that. Honesty is paramount to me. Always has been. But, hell I've told you that already, haven't I?"

"Three, maybe four hundred times a year, Dad."

"I never could count, sweetie, you know that. That's why I went into banking!"

Connie managed a smile. "You know, the last few months haven't been particularly easy. Between Stuart and the trials, I could really use your support. I really could."

"Now, you know, your mother and I have always supported you in whatever way we could. That doesn't change no matter what we might say in an unpleasant moment."

"Speaking of which, how is Mom? I owe her a call."

"Well, Constance, you know, your mother and I don't really speak, though we have during her recent illness. But she's better now. Don't stand on ceremony. Call her up. I know she'd love to hear from you."

Connie hung up the phone and walked over to the refrigerator. She pulled out a bottle of chardonnay from which one glassful was missing. Next she took down a wine glass from the cabinet.

As she sipped her wine, Connie clicked through the channels on her remote control. Gee, cable is great. Now there's nothing to watch on 56 channels instead of 13. Such a deal!

Connie finished the first glass of wine and poured herself another. She took it with her to the bedroom. There, she reached into the drawer of her night table, and pulled out the copy of *The Washington Gazette* that at first seemed so flattering, so fun. She opened to the article and saw a picture of herself, along with two of her colleagues standing on the steps of the Capitol. Instinctively, she tore the picture out, crumpled the page, and threw it across the room. Then, slowly, methodically she began tearing out the article, page-by-page, and ripping it into tiny little pieces. When she finished this little task, Connie threw the remnants across the room where they fluttered to the ground like so much confetti.

Chapter Thirty-Two

Donald Lubins was excited to give Mark the news about the sighting of George Moran. While Lubins couldn't be one hundred percent sure that the mystery man living with Mora the Great was the man that Mark and Gary Schofield were seeking, the old college professor was pretty sure.

Lubins broke into a broad grin as he hung up the telephone. It felt great to be able to return the favor for Mark.

As he walked away from the bank of telephones in the Greyhound station clutching the bag of groceries he had just purchased, he sensed that the man who had been speaking on the telephone next to him might be following him.

Lubins tried to act casual at first. He walked slowly away from the bus station, until it became obvious that he was being followed. He began to pick up the pace, but he couldn't shake his pursuer. It was nighttime, and the streets of the mountain town of Asheville, North Carolina were deserted.

Lubins glanced over his shoulder. The man following him seemed not to give a damn if his prey knew. Lubins ran his hands through his hair. Turn and confront, or run? What did the fucker want?

Lubins whirled around on the deserted street holding the package in his right hand, and put his left hand on his hip. He waited for the man who was no more than twenty yards away to approach him. But instead of confrontation, Lubins was met with a quizzical look from the man he believed to be his pursuer. Lubins suddenly felt ridiculous. Obviously, the guy's not following me, thought Lubins, I'm just too caught up in the whole intrigue of what I'm doing.

Lubins whirled around again, and without a word, walked on. Before long, he was approaching a set of train tracks. He was on the right course. All he needed to do was follow the tracks back to the railroad siding which held the circus train.

Although it was dark, following the tracks was easy. And from what Lubins remembered of the walk into town, it was no more than a mile back to the train.

As he began picking his way along the side of the track, Lubins looked alternately behind and to the side. He no longer felt the presence of anyone else. He shrugged his shoulders as he thought about the occurrence of just a few minutes earlier.

He was probably halfway back to the circus train when he heard a whistle signaling the approach of another kind of train, most probably a freight. He paused momentarily to listen before determining that the train was approaching from the rear. Satisfied that it was still some distance away, Lubins continued his slow return to the circus train.

The whistle grew ever more insistent. Lubins realized that the train was close. Man, he thought, it must not be going very fast, it seems to have taken forever to get here.

As it came into view, the train seemed to be picking up speed. Lubins saw it over his shoulder, and began moving away from the tracks, further down the gentle incline on the side on which he had been walking.

The train was no more than twenty yards away when Lubins felt himself stumble towards it, the grocery bag slipping from his grasp. He glanced up just in time to see the man who had been following him, arms outstretched from having pushed Donald, grinning and laughing.

Lubins tried to right himself, but the man shoved him again. Arms flailing, and left foot splaying out wildly, Lubins looked up in terror as he stumbled directly into the path of the oncoming freight train.

"Ian, Scott," Lubins cried out, "help me!"

George Moran burst through the door of his sister's comfortable home on wheels.

"Hey, where've you been? I thought you weren't going out?" Mora the Great asked him.

Moran cracked his knuckles two at a time. "I got antsy," he snapped. "Hey, for some reason, I think my cover may have been blown. That black dude who's been nosing around, I don't trust him. Can you get him shitcanned?"

"Hey, he's been with the show for something like twenty years," Mora the Great protested, as she pulled back her thick blonde hair, and methodically brushed it. "I'd have to be able to show that he did something pretty awful to get McGee to can him."

"Well can't we make something up?"

"Nah, I just don't think Charlie is involved in anything, and I really don't want him to lose his job."

George squinted at his famous sister. "Listen, Mora the Great," he sneered, "don't forget about your obligations to your family. I'm telling you, this guy is trouble! If you don't take care of him, I will!"

George stormed out of the RV's living room and into the bedroom where he was living. He flung himself down on his bed, and raised his feet up to remove his shoes. He cracked each of his ten toes with the palm of his left hand, and then proceeded to crack each of his ankles a dozen or so times.

After he finished this little bit of self-flagellation, George bounced off his bed and made his way back out to the living room. It pissed him off that Mora only had one telephone. It made it hard to make telephone calls in privacy. But Mora spent much of her time out of the RV, so there were opportunities. In fact, George was noticing that Mora was spending more and more of her time out of her luxury home on wheels. Too bad.

Chapter Thirty-Three

Irritated didn't even begin to describe Gary Schofield's state of mind. Aggravated gets a bit closer. Totally pissed off, well, that's certainly getting at the way Gary felt when Mark called him with the news.

Gary couldn't believe it. He had tried to reach Julie Day to find out where Lubins had headed, but he simply couldn't raise her. That had left him with two choices. He could try the gold unit of the circus or the silver unit. He knew both traveled most of the year, and they were considered equal in talent and stature. So the choice wasn't easy.

Gary determined that the silver unit had twice the amount of turnover as the gold unit over the last two months. So he had gone with the odds, and headed for Arkansas.

There really wasn't any reason to second-guess himself, even with the news from Mark that the homeless guy-cum-amateur sleuth had tracked down Moran. But it was irritating to think about. First, the guy's ex-wife called Mark, but she didn't tell him which unit was having all the fun. Now Gary learned, the guy himself had called Mark, and Mark was telling Gary that the elusive fat bastard, Moran, was with the gold unit. And Gary was not. Another precious day lost.

Gary flew to Greenville, South Carolina, rented a car, and made his way to the Civic Center where the gold unit of Stone's Big Top Circus was to begin performing that night, having just completed its run in Asheville, NC.

He found a few workingmen knocking around the arena even though it was only 2:30, some five hours before show time. It had been nearly eleven years since Gary's stint with the show, and Gary had been with the silver unit. Nothing looked familiar. Gary asked the men how to get to the train, and they directed him along a worn dirt path which they said would lead to it in about fifteen minutes. They told him that Mike McGee, the general manager of the gold unit, was likely to be there. He was the man to see about work.

Gary made it to the train just in time to learn that McGee had headed over to the arena. Gary turned around, and trudged back to the Civic Center where he found the general manager in his trailer. Gary introduced himself and produced a letter of reference from the general manager of the silver unit. Okay, so it might have been a slight forgery. McGee made a phone call while Gary cooled his heels, and moments later, to his surprise, Gary was hired. Either the call had nothing to do with checking references, or these guys needed all the warm bodies they could find. McGee left Gary with the assistant general manager to fill out the paperwork.

Gary was told he shouldn't work that night. Rather, he should sit in the stands and observe. There would be plenty of time for manual labor, a little brain work was in order for now. Gary didn't mind a bit. It would give him a chance to scope out the situation, to get a feel for the way the unit worked.

Gary thanked McGee and his assistant, and headed back towards the train. His shoes were already caked with a bizarre combination of mud, dust, and gunk. The runoff from the RVs was forming a mini-stream alongside the dusty path between the arena and the train causing the bottoms of Gary's shoes to collect gunk, while the sides were caked with mud and the tops were showing off dust. Gary shook his head and tried not to think about what exactly it was that made up the runoff.

The routine at the train was the same as Gary remembered from his prior stint. He got his linens and made his way to car 36. He knocked gently and went in. On the far bed, laying down and staring at the ceiling was a graying, kindly looking old black man. The middle bed contained a screamingly dirty, grimy white-trash type who was using a Swiss army knife to scrape mud off his boots. The black man looked over and nodded.

Gary nodded in return, and said, "Howdy," hoping it didn't sound as phony as it felt.

"Name's McFerrin. Charlie."

"Nice to meet you. I'm Lyle. It's actually my last name, but that's what folks call me," Gary said, as he shrugged his shoulders and smiled good-naturedly. The other guy kept cleaning his boots without acknowledging Gary's presence, so Gary decided not to push it. Gary began to lift the shoulder strap on his duffle bag to place the luggage on the vacant bed when his thus-far silent roommate mumbled, "Bed's spooked."

"Excuse me?" Gary replied.

But that was as much information as Tom Jarvis appeared to have any intention of sharing. He was back to scraping the dirt off his boots, although, for the life of him, Gary couldn't understand why.

"What he's telling you 'bout the bed is the truth," Charlie interjected. "The last guy who had that bed just croaked."

"In the bed?"

"Nah, somewhere in the field, I guess."

"What happened to him?" Gary asked, his curiosity piqued.

"They told us he got hit by a train. Me, I don't believe that."

"What do you think happened? I mean," Gary laughed, "wouldn't it be pretty easy to tell if someone was hit by a train?"

"Let me explain. He maybe was killed by the train, okay? Paper wasn't even sure 'bout that. Guy who read me the article said they wasn't able to find the body but there was some skin and bone, blood and hair and stuff on the train's cowcatcher, and the conductor say he saw somebody and felt something hit the train. Anyway, guy never came back so I guess he is dead and gone."

The old man paused a moment before continuing. "Oh, yeah," he said as he snapped his fingers. "What you asked me, I think somebody helped him get in front of it, if ya' know what I mean."

"Yeah, I get the picture. What happens when someone dies out here anyway? I mean, most people out here aren't traveling with their families or anything. Who takes care of everything?"

"A coupla us guys pulled together Don's stuff and we got his last pay from the general manager and—"

"Wait a minute," Gary interrupted. "What did you say his name was?"

"His name was Don. Last name of, let me remember, Rubin, or Lubins."

Gary blanched, but maintained his composure.

"You turning even whiter than you normally is. You didn't know the man, did ya'?" Charlie asked.

"No," Gary said truthfully, for he had never actually met Lubins. "No, I did not."

A Place to Hide

Gary suddenly felt the need to leave the friendly environs of his new home. Immediately. He kicked the duffle bag under his bed, dropped the sheets onto the top of the bed, and nodded at McFerrin. Gary quickly made his way through the impossibly narrow hallway to the nearest exit. He began heading back towards the arena. It was still a while before show time. Time to have a look around.

Gary kicked at the dirt as he made his way back to the arena. When he reached the parking area he began sauntering around among the RVs parked in the back. He knew one of them belonged to Mora the Great. He also knew, thanks to what Lubins had shared with Mark, that George Moran was likely to be in that RV at this very moment.

And it didn't take a rocket scientist to speculate that Moran had killed Lubins. What was the deal? Was this guy keeping notches on his belt?

Before Gary knew it, the show was under way. Since he wasn't working that night, Gary got to watch from the cheap seats, although no seat in the Greenville Civic Center could honestly be characterized as bad.

The show opened with three clowns horsing around on the tightrope. As Gary watched them frolic, one of the clowns lost his balance. The other two looked on in horror as he fell, missing the net by a full two feet. The crowd was stunned into silence, but before the mood became irretrievably somber, a clown ambulance, populated by clown nurses and doctors, roared into the fray. The crowd, momentarily fooled, loved it.

Next a wild animal act, which Gary thought was only so-so, performed. Then it was time for the Romanian acrobats working on the teeterboard. The ringmaster bellowed out one superlative after another about the legendary performers who had spent the early years of their lives toiling away for some long-forgotten Communist regime for the collective good.

Immediately upon the heels of the two groups of Romanians came three acts from Mongolia. Horses were featured prominently in the display. Gary stifled a yawn.

Gary woke up a bit just before intermission when the Flying Ortiz Brothers and the Flying Marvellas took rings one and three by storm. Despite his utter disinterest, Gary had learned that the Ortiz brothers were the undisputed champs of the trapeze.

The Marvellas were a bunch of nice kids. But they couldn't begin to compete with the Ortiz brothers. In fact, the Ortiz brothers seemed to blow them off like so many pesky little gnats.

Gary watched with amusement as Manuel and his brothers pranced about 25 feet over the hippodrome track. McGee had told Gary about the on-again-off-again war between the Ortiz brothers and Mora the Great. He had also assigned Gary to a position where he would have little to do with either.

After the Flying Ortiz Brothers finished their highly athletic routine, the show took a twenty-minute intermission. Gary watched as the concessionaires gently plied their wares, much to the delight, no doubt, of the already thrilled parents populating the crowd.

Immediately after the intermission, the ringmaster raised his voice, and with it, the expectations of the masses. Suddenly, seemingly from nowhere, sprang Mora the Great, followed by twelve snarling Bengal tigers. The excitement grew as the beasts were released from their individual cages and allowed to run free inside the gigantic metal globe cage in the middle of the center ring.

Gary had to admit it, the animals were majestic. And

so was Mora. She controlled their every move with a wave of her hand, or a simple voice command. The crowd "oohed" and "aahed" as Mora put the cats through their paces. They rolled over as one, and then jumped through hoops of fire. She was impressive. Charismatic and totally under control.

Gary slept through most of the rest of the show. There were a number of mediocre clown routines which the kids loved, and a few more decent high-wire routines. But Mora was the obvious highlight of this show.

As he slowly made his way back to the train, Gary pondered his problem. He somehow had to get into Mora's trailer and sniff out Moran. And he had to do it quickly. But how could he do it? How could he do it?

Chapter Thirty-Four

Mark Clifton was deeply engrossed in his research for the trial. It was mid-morning on Thursday, and jury selection for the fraud trial would begin on Monday morning, less than 96 hours away. Earlier in the week, Mark had written out the questions he would ask Judge Robinson to pose to the prospective jurors, and he was honing them down now. Carol had provided him with three memos on the sly concerning various possible defense tactics.

Peter Long had provided Mark with an updated memo in the format Mark requested. The new document contained some case citations and other references which were directly contradictory to those provided by Carol. Mark wasted close to an hour checking some of them out on his own, confirming his suspicions that the fabulous Mr. Long was purposefully sandbagging him. Mark shuddered to think what shape he would be in now were it not for Carol. Long would have to be dealt with, that was for sure. But a decision on just how to do such a thing would have to wait until after the trial.

The phone, the wonderful little device invented to interfere with productivity and in general harass people, interrupted Mark's preparation. It was Jack Christian's secretary. Mr. Sanctimonious was requesting the honor of Mark's presence. Now.

"Come in, Mark, and close the door behind you, please," the courtly senior partner began. Jack Christian

A PLACE TO HIDE

was in his late fifties, and Mark had to admit, the man had aged gracefully. His hair was mostly gray, but a silver gray and very full. He wore conservative suits, befitting his conservative style. He rarely removed his suit jacket, but somehow it never appeared wrinkled.

Mark looked at Christian in a different light now. The senior partner's hands which rested gracefully on the top of his desk, were long and fine, with manicured nails. They had obviously never touched a gardening tool or a spark plug. Ever. In the two and a half years Mark had practiced with him, he had never seen Christian raise his voice or lose his temper.

There was a story that Christian had lost his temper once, when a young associate made a rude remark to a trial judge in chambers. Christian apparently rebuked the young man, apologized to the judge, and quickly regained his composure. The story was legendary at the firm, not because it was so outrageous, but because it was apparently the only evidence of human emotion anyone had ever seen Christian display.

"Mark, I'm going to be very blunt about this. You've created an untenable situation in the firm which needs to be addressed immediately. I recognize that you have a major trial in a few days but this cannot wait. I have learned that Carol Keegan has been working, feverishly I might add, on the Giavonni cases.

"I don't think I need to tell you that this has created numerous problems, both internally and from a client relations point of view. I will try to enumerate the major ones, although I am certain that if you gave it a moment's thought, which you apparently haven't, you would see all of them yourself."

Mark took a deep breath, and let it out slowly. This was obviously a prepared speech. And a long one. Mark thought about interrupting, and confronting the pompous ass. Instead, Mark sat back and tried to control himself. As he averted his eyes from Christian's imploring glare, Mark caught a glimpse of something that looked familiar on the corner of Christian's desk. He tried to conjure up an idea of what it was as Christian launched into his remarks.

Just as Mark was about to forget about the item on Christian's desk, he remembered where he had seen it before. It was the invitation to the bar dinner honoring Christian. What a hoot! The man was being honored for caring about clients, work-product and all the rest of it. Man, that rankled!

"In the first place," Christian was saying, "you've created a very sticky situation between two of our better associates, Carol and Peter. Additionally, we have an associate putting in substantial time for which we will never be remunerated. That is, of course, unless you plan to bill Giavonni twice. Thirdly, Carol is being taken away from her other cases to work on the Giavonni cases.

"There are more problems that arise from this situation including the fact that you and Carol have your ongoing personal relationship muddying up the professional waters. I have spoken, at least informally, with all the other partners. We considered not discussing the matter with you until the Giavonni cases were over because we didn't want to do anything that might affect your performance. But the fact is these problems need to be addressed now.

"You need to stop using Carol on this case immediately. That's number one. If you have problems with Peter, then you should let someone know. But trying to go in through the back door and use Carol is unfair to him as well as to everyone else involved. We can discuss the rest of the ramifications of your behavior after the Giavonni cases end. Do I make myself clear?"

Mark cleared his throat and began to speak. But nothing came out. He stood and tried again. "I'm not sure you're getting the whole story. In fact, I don't know where you got any of your story. But for now, you have made yourself perfectly clear. I will follow your instructions, and we can revisit the issue when the Giavonni cases end. Now, if we're through, I've got a ton of work to do before the trials start next week." Mark shifted from one foot to the other as he waited to be dismissed. The senior partner nodded his head towards the door, and Mark was on his way.

Mark headed back for the war room where he was preparing for the cases. He sat down and began leafing through the questions he was readying for voir dire. He read three questions then stood up and began pacing the floor. He walked towards the door, but did a quick about-face just as he got there, and slumped back down in the chair next to the one where he had been working.

He flicked on the radio. Peter had been listening to some punk rock station. Mark began turning the dial as he looked at his watch. It was 10:45. Still time for the Mo Buell show.

"Yeah, so what's the point of your question," Buell was harassing a caller.

"The point is that, yeah, maybe the barber could be found guilty of fraud, but not of murder, so it makes sense for there to be two trials."

Mark grimaced as he dropped the papers he was holding.

"You know, if it gives me the opportunity to see my beloved, Connie Parker, twice, under circumstances where she can't leave, then I agree with you it makes sense for there to be two trials. Honestly, though, I don't really give a damn about the barber. He's probably guilty as sin anyway. Next caller."

"Yeah, hey is this Mo?"

"What's on your feeble mind, ma'am?"

"Mo, I can't believe I finally got through."

"You're gonna get hung up on if you don't start believin' it, my fair lady. Now talk about somethin', anything but the fact that you can't believe how you finally got through, okay?"

"Okay. Listen, I'm a big fan of yours, and I'd love to meet you. But, well, you know, you keep talking about that Connie Parker. Don't you have any interest in other girls?"

"What do you look like, honey?"

"Friends tell me I'm cute."

"Cute? Have you ever seen Connie Parker? She's not cute. Cute is for little girls. Cute is for, like, junior high. Connie is gorgeous. Beautiful. Sorry sweetheart. Call back when you grow up.

"Well, folks, that about does it for today. Keep those cards and letters coming. Especially the idiotic ones which seem to make up a disproportionately large number, I must say."

Mark shook his head as he snapped off the radio. He picked up the phone and began to push the buttons for Carol's intercom. Just as quickly he hung up the receiver. He absent-mindedly picked at some dried skin on his cuticles as he fished for the papers which he had dropped on the floor.

He picked up the phone again and buzzed Carol. "Free for lunch?"

"Yeah, but not now, it's not even eleven."

"True, but we need to talk."

"Forty-five minutes, and that's my best offer."

"Deal."

Mark breathed a sigh of relief as he hung up the phone.

Moments after they were seated, Mark recounted in gory detail the conversation he had just had with Jack Christian. Carol sat quietly. Finally, she asked, "How do you think he found out?"

"There are only two possible ways. One is if someone was able to figure out that the computer research you were doing was for the Giavonni cases. Now, I guess that's possible because Lexis gives all sorts of information on their bills. But the way I see it," and here, Mark paused for effect. "The way I see it, there are a couple of problems with that. First, the bills probably only come in once a month, so it's doubtful any have come in with enough info to hang us. Second, I don't know who sees those bills, but I guess Jan does," Mark said, making reference to the office manager.

"The only other way is if our close personal friend, Peter Long, somehow figured it out and told him," Mark offered with a sneer. "I didn't ask the old patrician bastard and he didn't offer any explanation."

Carol twirled her teal-colored, striped scarf and tapped her finger on the table as she gazed at her lover. "We knew there were going to be problems when we first started seeing each other, but I guess I was naive on this one. I never figured anyone would give a shit if I researched the Giavonni case to death. I mean, you've got more experience in this political bullshit. Is Christian right, or do you think he's taking a self-righteous, holier-than-thou attitude?"

"I don't have the slightest idea what's eating him, really I don't," Mark lied. He just couldn't bring himself to tell Carol about the conversation upon which he had eavesdropped. "Maybe I'm just too close to the situation, but I don't know what the problem is, really I don't."

"So, what do we do?"

"Well, that's the question isn't it? The trial's only a few days away. You know, I basically have all the information I need at this point, and what little else might come up I can always ask Long to get for me.

"I definitely don't want you doing any more work on the case. If we got caught at this point doing it, I'm sure there would be big-time bullshit. What I need to do, is to forget all about Jack's little shit-ass speech and concentrate on preparing for the trials.

"But I gotta tell ya', regardless of what he feels, or the other partners for that matter, I really think he could have waited until after the trials. You know?"

"I agree, but you're right that you need to put it out of your mind. We'll deal with what it all means later. In the meantime, you owe it to Joseppe to be totally functioning and not worrying about some stupid internal matter."

Mark paid for lunch and they headed back. It was nearly three o'clock. He sat down and pulled out a new pencil. He sharpened it with his little school-kid sharpener. He began to craft a line of questioning and immediately broke the point. He held the pencil over his head and began to bring it down toward the desk in anger but caught himself.

Mark took a deep breath at the same time he took a new, but previously sharpened pencil from the box. He leaned over and began to write. After completing two further questions, he stood. He stretched for a moment and headed out for some coffee.

Later that night, Mark and Carol scarfed down a pizza on the way home from work.

"So, how's life?" Carol asked when they were finally seated.

"What do you think?" Mark answered, rubbing his chin.

"Have you gotten any work done?"

"Oh, yeah, don't get me wrong, I've done plenty of work, though it never feels like there's enough time. It's just that every ten or fifteen minutes my train of thought gets interrupted, and I try to figure out just what the fuck Jack's up to. I mean it won't exactly reflect all that great on the firm if we get blown out of the water on this, I mean these, cases. So why didn't he just wait to give me his little ethics speech? Why play out the little passion play now? It makes no sense."

"I agree. I haven't done a damn thing all afternoon and evening except try to figure it out. By the way," Carol spluttered, "I don't think anyone else knows about your little talk with Jack. I did a bunch of pokin' around to try to get some scoop, but nobody said anything."

Mark felt his stomach tighten. "You didn't tell anyone what's going on did you?"

"Geez, give me some credit will ya'? Of course I didn't. What do you think I did, say 'Hey, Christian chewed Mark's head off before 'cause I'm workin' on the Giavonni case. Got any idea what's gotten up his ass?'"

"Okay, okay. Sorry."

Mark awoke Friday morning, shaved and quickly showered. He threw on a pair of casual pants with a sport coat and tie and trotted out the door. It wasn't a bad day to walk to the office, but he didn't have time. He hopped in his car and headed off for the short trip.

He began plotting strategy. Having not heard from Gary Schofield in a few days, Mark could only assume that George Moran was not going to be available for trial. That was too bad. After all, Moran was the brains behind the real estate scam, about that there was no controversy. And there was most certainly a chance that he was involved in the murder too.

Shortly before lunch, as Mark was completely immersed in preparing his opening statement for the first trial, his secretary buzzed him. He had told her he did not want to be interrupted. He took an exasperated swipe at the intercom button and called out to the speaker phone to find out why she was interrupting him. He had a phone call she informed him. It was Gary. Mark took the call.

Chapter Thirty-Five

When Connie Parker opened her eyes to greet the day on Thursday morning, the room was spinning and her sheets smelled like wine. Chardonnay if she remembered correctly. Or was it Chianti? She tried to get up, but immediately fell back into her bed. She felt a violent pain in the pit of her stomach. She was able to make it only as far as the wastepaper basket on the far side of her room, just short of the bathroom, before she began retching and heaving the prior night's entire intake of food and wine.

Long after the contents of dinner and her little binge had settled safely into the bottom of the trash can her insides continued to pulsate. She winced with each passing spasm, noticing they were becoming fewer and farther between. She laughed, to the extent she could, at the thought that it was almost like reverse labor. Eventually she was able to crawl back towards the bed and climb up on it. The stench of vomit permeated the air, sending Connie into a Catch-22 tizzy. If she didn't get up and get the trash can out of her room she was going to get sick again. But she was too sick to get up and remove it!

Connie gathered herself for an assault on the trash can. She gently swung into a sitting position with her legs dangling towards the floor. Using her hands, she pushed herself into a standing posture. She steadied herself and shuffled off towards the offending basket. It was light, bearing nothing but last night's dinner and wine. She picked it up, but couldn't quite decide what to do with it.

Her energy quickly waning, she flung it in the shower and turned on the water. She put her hand against the tile wall to brace herself as she waited for the steamy water to cleanse the poor pail of the remains from the eruption of her innards. The spasms were stopping. She still felt nauseated, but the intensity was lessening.

Somehow she was able to make her way to the second bathroom in her apartment. She certainly wasn't going to go in the shower where she had just dumped the trash can! She turned the shower on as hot as she could stand it, and stood underneath it as torrents of water spurted forth from the slender silver nozzle. She began to regain a bit of a sense of equilibrium. Occasionally her stomach would spasm and she would retch again, but it was dry now, there being nothing left to vomit.

Connie toweled off, but again began feeling faint. She sat down on the rock-hard top of the closed toilet and waited for her senses to normalize yet again. She fished a toothbrush out of the medicine cabinet and found some toothpaste in a small travel pack. She vigorously brushed her teeth, using gobs from the small tube of toothpaste to rid herself of the horrible stench which still wallowed in her mouth.

She stood up and began inching her way out of the bathroom. She shuffled along the hallway like an octogenarian. Once back in her bedroom, she began dressing. She knew immediately she would not be able to stomach pantyhose, so she put on a pair of simple black, wool pants with an equally plain off-white lamb's wool sweater. She made her way back to the bathroom off her bedroom, where the odor was still readily evident. She gagged slightly, and picked up her makeup and brought it to the other bathroom.

Concentrating heavily, she was able to do at least a modicum of justice to her makeup. Just as she was finishing with her eyeliner, she stopped and looked in the mirror. Had Buell called again last night? Or was it just a dream? She shook her head gently, but instead of clearing the gathering cobwebs, it sent a searing pain through her forehead. As the pain let up ever so slightly, she experienced a wave of nausea so severe that she thought she would faint. She plopped down on the closed toilet seat to gather herself.

There was no way she was walking to her office today. Nor did she relish the idea of driving. She made her way down to the street and hailed a cab. Her appointment with Evans was scheduled for eleven o'clock. The prosecutor had taken to conveniently scheduling appointments around lunch. She smiled at the thought. It would certainly be at Evans' risk!

Once in her office, Connie closed the door. She picked up the telephone and called Jayne. She told her friend in a hushed tone about the way she felt. Jayne counseled her to cancel the eleven o'clock appointment with Evans.

"What could possibly be so important at this point? You already know your lines as well as you're ever going to know them. Evans just wants to spend more time with you. It's not right already. It's just not right."

"Somehow, I feel like if I don't go, and then something goes wrong at trial, I'll blame myself for as long as I live. I keep telling myself that I'm doing it for Stuart. But I guess it's pretty obvious that I really don't know what I'm doing anymore."

Connie tried to choke back the tears, but it was no use. She began crying gently at first, but then her sobbing became more fully realized. By the time she hung up from her conversation with Jayne her stomach was spasming again. Her body was heaving as she wailed uncontrollably.

As she tried to regain her composure, she heard a knocking on the door. Gentle at first, it became incessant. Finally, she was able to hold back the tears long enough to open the door. To her surprise it was Jayne. Connie embraced her friend, and cried. Long and hard.

When she gained control, Connie spoke. "Headline news: control freak loses control!"

"Happens. To everyone. I think it's amazing that you held up this long."

The phone rang, followed by the obnoxious ringing of the intercom buzzer. Connie ignored it.

"You know, I don't think I could have survived the last couple of months without you. I want you to know how much I appreciate it. I mean it."

Jayne put up her hand. "Enough said."

"Thanks. You know, I was thinking about what you said on the phone and I don't see any choice other than to go to Evans' office and subject myself to a few more hours of his leering. If I don't do it and he loses the case, either of the cases, he'll blame it on me forever, even if I'm perfect on the witness stand. And I know myself well enough to know that I couldn't take that."

"Well nothing says that you have to have lunch with the asshole, and nothing says you have to give him even one second more than you feel is absolutely necessary. I'd stand my ground with him, if I were you. I really would. Enough is enough with this guy already."

Connie looked at her watch. Incredibly, it was 10:45.

She stood and looked over at her friend. "I'd better go. Do you want to share a cab?"

"Sure. I think between the two of us, we're keeping all of the D.C. cabs in business!"

As she settled into the cab by herself after Jayne got out, Connie pulled her mail out of her pocketbook. She wasn't all that interested in it, but her secretary had handed it to her on her way out the door with Jayne.

A couple of promotional solicitations led the way. A bill from a P.R. firm she had subcontracted with on a big case just before Stuart's death made it to the "action" file. A few more pieces of junk mail followed. The final piece of mail appeared to be a personal letter, though it bore no return address.

Connie tore open the envelope. The letter was short and to the point. It read:

"Dear Connie:
I guess we're all in Jeopardy, hey babe?"

It was unsigned.

Chapter Thirty-Six

Mark Clifton told his secretary to hold the call for a minute. He wanted to get back to his office to talk to Gary. He bounded out of the war room, and headed down the hall. He depressed the blinking button and picked up the receiver all at the same time.

"Hey, Gary what's the good word?"

"I'm afraid there aren't any, Mark." Gary sounded somber.

"Listen, forget it. You tried. If you can't find Moran, or get him back here, it's not the end of the world. We'll do the best we can."

"It's not that. Mark, I'm sorry to have to be the one to tell you this, but I think your friend Lubins was killed the other night."

Mark gasped. "Wha', what happened?"

"Yeah. They said he was hit by a train. But the scuttlebutt is that he was pushed. Probably by your buddy, Moran, but no proof, and no body."

"I, I don't know what to say. I mean, this is all my fault. He never would've gone back if not for me. Damn. Damn! Wait a minute. How do you know he's dead if there's no body?"

"I spoke with the cops who filed the report, and I spoke with the conductor of the train. Seems he was walking or running along the side of the track when he was pushed or maybe fell in front of the train. Cops found skin and hair fragments on the cowcatcher. And they also found bone fragments and blood, both on the cowcatcher and nearby. I spoke with the conductor. He said he saw something and definitely felt something hit the train. There was a bag of groceries which got whacked, and the checkout girl at the market described Lubins as having just been in."

"Yeah, but no body?"

"Right. I checked that out with the cops, too, believe me. The train traveled seventy-three miles after this point before coming to a stop. Conductor says it's possible Lubins got thrown at almost any point between here and there."

"What? That's outrageous. Why didn't he stop if he felt something?"

"I asked him that too. Said they almost always feel things hitting the train. Kids put bags of shit on the tracks all the time for yucks. Said he didn't think he'd hit a person, so he kept on going."

"Well," Mark said softly, "you're probably right. But I'm not giving up until we find the body, okay?"

"Listen, you're the boss, Mark. Always have been. But you got a trial coming up. Make that two trials. So tell me what you want me to do, look for Moran, or look for Lubins."

Mark considered for a moment. "I've got an ethical obligation to Joseppe, he's my client. You better look for Moran."

"Okay," Gary replied, and Mark was taken by how subdued the investigator sounded.

After the initial shock began to wear off, Mark had some practical issues to deal with. In the first place, he had to call Lubins' ex-wife. She and the kids had been deserted before. Mark didn't want them to think it was happening again. On the other hand, he wasn't sure he wanted to tell her he thought Lubins was dead when he wasn't certain himself. Maybe he could get hold of the newspaper article, or have the cops get in touch with her. Something had to be done.

Next, he had to determine whether to tell Joseppe about Lubins' demise. And he had to try to continue preparing for the trials. Finally, he had to assume that Moran wasn't going to be testifying.

Mark took a deep breath and let it out ever so slowly. He swiveled his chair around and flipped on the radio.

"Yeah, coming to you live from the Nation's Capital, it's the Mo Buell show. When you wanna go home, you're goin' Mo Buell! So, here we are just days away from the big barber trials, and I can hardly wait. I haven't seen Connie Parker in longer than I can remember, and she'll have to be dressed to kill I figure, for the jury's sake. Hey, I guess that was a bad word choice for a murder trial, eh?"

Mark turned off the radio, and called his paralegal, Linda Deloitte.

"Linda, can you please prepare a subpoena for Mo Buell for the murder case, and hold onto it, in case we need him to testify?"

"Sure, no problem."

"Any luck tracking down that bartender from the party that night?"

"None. I checked with all the witnesses, the company that catered it, and the host. And Gary's guy checked too. But we're not giving up. At least not yet."

"Thanks, Linda. Don't kill yourself looking for that guy. He's probably long gone, and has been since the night of the party."

Mark hung up the phone, and decided against telling

Joseppe about Lubins. There was nothing Joseppe could do about it, and nothing to be gained by telling him.

Mark spent the weekend alternately strategizing and trying not to mourn. Before he knew what hit him, it was Monday morning, day one of the fraud trial. Jury picking day.

It was going to be an intense couple of weeks, of that Mark was certain. He had tried numerous fraud charges, and he felt reasonably well-prepared for the first trial. But the murder case was only his second one.

Over ten years ago, just before joining the Justice Department, Mark had defended an accused murderer on a pro bono basis. It was far different from the case of Joseppe Giavonni. In Mark's first murder defense, the man he was defending was scum. He had been convicted on three prior occasions of assault and battery, once with a deadly weapon. This time he was brought up on charges of having murdered his ex-girlfriend. Although the evidence was circumstantial, it was fairly damning. On the third day of that trial, with the outcome still very much in doubt, Mark and the District Attorney reached a plea bargain agreement under which Mark's client was to spend thirty years to life in prison. Mark's client accepted the plea, and told Mark he was relieved to be going to prison. At least there he would stay out of trouble. Mark never did learn if the guy was guilty. It was just as well.

Now, ten years later, in many ways, Mark felt like a novice. Oh, sure, he had prosecuted hundreds of criminal cases while at the Justice Department, and had defended more than his fair share of other types of criminal cases both before and after his stint at Justice. He told himself that murder was just a more serious offense, otherwise there was no real difference. Right. And the Grand Canyon is just a big hole.

The painful process of selecting a jury for the fraud case was under way. Each side was entitled to innumerable challenges of potential jurors for cause. So any time a juror said that, for instance, he didn't like Italian Americans, Mark would have the right to strike that juror from the potential pool. And each side had the right to ten peremptory challenges as well. That is, in ten instances each party could blow off a potential juror for no reason at all, or for a reason that didn't constitute cause.

Oh, maybe the defendant doesn't like the way the prospective juror combs his hair. Or maybe he doesn't like the look in the prospective juror's eye. Fine. Slash him. Gone. But only ten times, so be careful who you nix.

Mark had spent many hours putting together the profile of the perfect juror. A middle-aged immigrant with little or no education. And even less understanding of the securities laws. Now, as Monday morning turned into Monday afternoon, Mark strived to come as close as possible to picking just such a jury.

Of course, Jim Evans had completely different thoughts. He used his peremptory challenges wisely to strike immigrants. He also struck a less-educated potential juror.

By the end of the day Monday nine of the eventual twelve jurors had been chosen. Mark had managed to slip one Jamaican immigrant through after Evans used his tenth and final peremptory challenge. Kind of early to be out of peremptories, Mark thought. Sort of like running out of timeouts in the third quarter.

Overall, Mark felt okay about the nine jurors chosen so far. Not great, but okay. The jury chosen was a mishmash of Joseppe Giavonni's alleged peers. In fact, of the nine chosen so far, seven were women only one of whom was employed outside the home. And of the two men, one was retired. So seven of the first nine jurors chosen were not employed outside their home. Not unusual. Everyone else always comes up with an excuse for not serving!

Mark spent early Monday evening in the office, and as distasteful as it was, he spent the time with Peter Long. They went through the jurors who had been selected, and agreed that as a whole they had done pretty well. They continued to strategize and talked about things such as the tone Mark should strike in his opening statement, and how aggressive he should be during cross-examination of the prosecution's witnesses. Mark wanted more than anything to call Peter on the memo he had prepared, to straight out accuse him of trying to undermine the case. It was distracting to even think about, so Mark tried to put it out of his mind. There was sure to be plenty of time for confrontation later.

As they were discussing the case, Mark with passion, Peter without, Mark noticed the young attorney's eyes wandering across Mark's desk. Peter looked up in time to notice Mark eyeing him, and he blushed just slightly.

"I, I couldn't help but notice the invitation to the bar dinner honoring Jack. You going?"

"Hadn't thought about it," Mark lied. "We have a case to try."

The prosecution's case would be based upon the testimony of a number of witnesses who would claim that Joseppe, through his personal relationship with them and the trust they had in him, had convinced them to invest in a scheme which he knew would not provide them with any return.

The key to the case would be Joseppe's state of mind. That he had convinced many of his customers into investing in the real estate partnership was beyond question. In fact, Mark had tried to stipulate to that fact to avoid the problem of having the jury listen to witness after witness discuss Joseppe's sales pitch. But Evans was too smart for that. He didn't accept the stipulation.

So if it was a given that Mark wouldn't fight the fact that Joseppe had "convinced" the victims into their investments, the whole case would turn upon whether the barber had done so knowing that Moran and Caulfield had no intention of providing the investors with any return. Ever.

The fact that Joseppe had received payments in return for each investor he brought into the picture did not help matters. But it didn't toll the death knell either. Certainly none of the so-called victims of the scheme could testify as to Joseppe's state of mind. As far as Mark was concerned, only Joseppe, and possibly, but only possibly, some of his closest confidants or family members, could testify as to the defendant's state of mind at the time he encouraged his customers to invest.

So Joseppe's credibility was what was really on trial in the fraud case. Evans likely would try to tear Joseppe apart on cross-examination. The prosecutor was good, and ruthless, and he wouldn't hesitate to ask Joseppe all of the difficult questions which came to mind. Oh, sure, Mark would have the opportunity to bolster Joseppe's testimony on redirect, but the barber was really going to have to go it alone during cross.

There were a few witnesses that Mark couldn't quite

figure out, most particularly, the Mercedes Benz salesman who had recently sold Joseppe a car. Mark was quick enough to figure out that Evans wanted to demonstrate that Joseppe hadn't exactly been reluctant to spend the fruits of his ill-gotten gains. But so what? In fact, if that was what the car salesman was going to testify about, Mark figured it might be helpful. He would paint Joseppe as the kind of guy who would have returned the money, if only he had known about Moran and Caulfield's abhorrent scheme. No. Evans was too smart. The salesman had more.

The overwhelming female majority on the jury was cut into slightly on Tuesday morning. Two out of three of the final jurors chosen were men. To Mark's utter delight, he was able to get another immigrant on the panel. This time a 45-year-old nurse from Ireland. She was joined by a 57-year-old dentist and a 23-year-old unemployed day laborer.

The engineer chosen Monday was picked by Judge Robinson as the foreman. Judge Robinson gave some last-minute instructions to counsel and the jurors. Then he told everyone to have a hearty lunch. The fun would begin at one o'clock.

Chapter Thirty-Seven

Gary Schofield strode boldly up to Mora's trailer. He rapped three times on the door. He heard some rustling and the gentle closing of a door, and then: "Who is it?"

"My name's Howard Corcoran," Gary called out. "You'd probably recognize me as a workingman, although I'm really a newspaper reporter. I've been undercover here for a bit of time, and I'd like to talk to you."

The door to Mora's trailer opened to reveal the Great One in extraordinarily tight-fitting, stone-washed jeans and a white T-shirt with a pocket. She seemed dramatically smaller in person than she did when she performed.

Gary pushed his way past Mora and plopped himself down on the brown, formless sofa in the corner. He quickly pulled out a notepad and pen, and glanced up at Mora who was still standing by the door.

"Mind if I ask you a few questions?"

"As a matter of fact, I do. I think you'd be better off if you just left."

"Well, that's just fine. I've already spoken with Manuel Ortiz, and gotten his side of the story," Gary lied. "If you want my article to just reflect his side of your battle, that's okay with me. I'll just say you were unavailable for comment."

Mora slammed the door shut, grabbed a kitchen chair and dragged it into the living room. She flung the chair around so that it was facing backwards, and she sat with her arms slung over the back of the chair as she faced Gary. "What did that little Chicano bastard tell you?"

"Not important. Let's just get your side of the story."

"No. I want to know what Ortiz said about me before I'm gonna say a word."

"Well, for one thing, he said you were the greatest animal trainer he had ever worked with," Gary said, trying to disarm the woman who was not intimidated by twelve ferocious tigers, and was unlikely to be intimidated by one fake reporter.

"What else did he say?"

Gary decided to get down to business. "He said something else that struck me, anyway, as being kinda strange. He said he thought you had somebody living in here with you," Gary said as he motioned throughout the trailer, "although it doesn't look like it. He said it was a guy. I don't know what he was intimating, maybe that you were having an affair with somebody you didn't want the world to know about or something."

"He has quite an imagination," Mora laughed. "I will admit that sometimes I have had people here, but never one person living here with me."

Gary shook his head. "It didn't sound too plausible to me, Mora," Gary confided. "But, you know, as a good reporter, I have to follow every lead, and try to track down as much information as I possibly can."

It was almost imperceptible, but Gary saw the door to the bedroom open slightly. Mora had done a good acting job. After all, she was a paid professional. But Moran was in the trailer. The homeless guy was right.

Gary's momentary shift of attention caused an uncomfortable lull in the conversation. Before Gary could come up with another inane question, Mora seized upon the silence. "What exactly is the purpose of your article anyway, my friend, and who do you write for?"

"I write for the *Charlotte Observer* out of North Carolina. The nature of my story is behind-the-scenes at The Big Show. People love to know what goes on before and after the show."

"Well let 'em come and see, that's how they get their kicks. I don't really see why this stuff would be of much interest to anyone out there."

"How would you characterize the nature of your relationship with Manuel Ortiz?"

"That's between me and Ortiz. I'm not gonna air my, what do you call it, 'dirty laundry,' eh, in public. It's all overblown anyway."

"An employee of the circus was recently killed when he was hit by a train. Rumor has it that his death wasn't an accident. Do you know anything about that?"

"I didn't really know the guy, but I feel sorry for him. I heard he was only with us for a short time. It is a tragedy."

"Do you still enjoy performing, Mora?"

"Yes, yes I do." Mora became animated.

Gary didn't want to stay in the trailer any longer than necessary. He also didn't want to blow his cover. "How much longer do you see yourself doing this?"

"Oh, I don't know, seven, maybe ten more years. As long as I am still reasonably popular, and Mr. Stone will have me."

"Oh, I'm quite certain you'll stay the most popular circus entertainer in history as long as you want to. I'm also quite certain that Mr. Stone will want you to perform as long as you possibly can. Thanks for your time. I'll get out of your hair."

Gary shook Mora's hand and headed out the door. Gary began walking away, but as soon as he got to the next trailer he doubled back and snuck behind Mora's vehicle. He pressed his ear to the wall. He couldn't make out exactly what was being said, but it was quite obvious that more than one voice was talking inside. In short order, Gary, afraid of being caught, tiptoed away from Mora's trailer, and headed back towards the train.

As Gary let himself into the cramped room he shared with McFerrin and Jarvis, he sighed with relief. Neither of his roommates were there. It was nearly dark, and the evening's show would be beginning in a little under two hours. Gary knew he needed to head back to the arena as soon as possible. He removed the tape from the tiny tape recorder he was wearing during his conversation with Mora, and placed it in the inside pouch of his duffle bag. Gary knew it was probably meaningless. But if he hadn't worn the wire, there's no telling what would have been said.

He quickly changed clothes, and began heading back to the arena. Once he got there, Gary participated in the tedious task of rigging the show. He was acting as a general rigger, and tonight he was working with the high-wire crew. They stretched the wire from one side of the arena to the other, pulling it taut, and making certain it was securely fastened from the girders. They tested it two, three, four times. This was one act which had no room for error.

The head high-wire rigger took his work seriously. Most of the others did not. They were a transient group, and their boss was lucky to keep anyone for more than a few weeks at a time. As he helped prepare for the evening performance, Gary could only smirk at the ineffectiveness of the workers, all the while reminding himself that it wasn't his job. At least not really.

The show, including the high-wire act, went off with-

out a hitch. Gary had never realized before how much
the performers depended upon the workingmen. Given
the nature of some of the laborers on The Big Show, it
was a scary thought.

Gary hustled back to the train after helping to dismantle the rigging which couldn't stay up all night. Jarvis, stringy greasy hair and all, was sitting on the edge of his bed, participating in his favorite boot-cleaning routine when Gary got back to the room. McFerrin was nowhere in sight. Gary acknowledged his roommate's presence with a nod which went unreturned. Not a big shock.

Gary sat on the edge of his bed, pulled the duffle bag up from the footlocker, and glanced over at Tom Jarvis to make certain he wasn't watching. But Jarvis was watching. When he saw Gary look up, he averted his glance. Gary took the opportunity to remove the tape from the duffle bag. He placed it quickly, but gently, in his pants pocket.

Gary grabbed a fleece-lined jacket from the bag, placed the bag back inside the footlocker, and headed for the door. He let himself out of the room and trotted down the hall to the exit of the train. He nodded to the few people he saw coming and going, and slipped off the train car. Wishing he was invisible, Gary headed around the side of the train, and went back towards the outside of the car where he lived. He sat down, leaning against the side of the train. He patted the inside pocket of his jacket, and felt the handle of his little Saturday night special. He smiled. Then he leaned back to wait.

Gary was dozing off when he heard the ruckus begin. He pressed his ear up against the train, but still was barely able to make out what was going on.

"Where's your roommate?" Gary heard Moran scream.

"I dunno," came the reply from McFerrin.

"Listen you old coot," Moran continued to scream, "if you don't tell me I'll beat the living shit outta you."

Gary stood and searched for a window to look into, but he knew it was fruitless. There were none. The initial screaming was followed by an eerie silence. Gary thought he could make out the sound of boots scuffling on the floor. Jarvis? Doubtful. Not the type.

But then: "The man told you he doesn't know where the city slicker went. That's the end of the conversation, cuz McFerrin don't lie. I don't know who you are, but get your ass outta here, now."

Gary broke into a broad grin. Damn, people surprise you all the time.

Chapter Thirty-Eight

Connie Parker, star witness for the prosecution in the murder case, skipped the first day of the fraud trial. Evans explained that she could watch the *voir dire* and certain other preliminary matters if she wanted, it was up to her. But when the "real stuff" started, the prosecutor wanted her there. He wanted Connie to see what it was like to testify. Get used to the whole trial idea.

Evans promised to call Connie with updates if he didn't see her at the trial's first day. He was as good as his word. The prosecutor, protector of the people, sounded disappointed that Connie hadn't shown, but she didn't really care. Connie wasn't in this for Evans. In point of fact, she wasn't sure why she was involved, but it sure as hell wasn't for the greater glory of any member of the male gender.

The first day actually sounded pretty dull. Evans explained that a jury was chosen, or at least the first nine members of it, and a bunch of other stuff which Evans called "housekeeping" took place. Sounded like she hadn't missed much. Connie was glad she wasn't there. The fewer days she had to spend hanging around the federal courthouse, the better.

Connie met Jayne for dinner at a little pub on the Hill. The place was dark, and Connie knew that it would be empty on a Monday, particularly at six o'clock. In spite of the hardwood floors and the mahogany tables, the place was reasonably quiet, and the owners respected privacy enough to keep the tables an honest distance apart. Connie brought Jayne up to speed on the first day of the first trial as it had been relayed to her by Evans.

"Sounds like you missed absolutely nothing. Glad you didn't go?"

"You got that right. The less time I have to spend at the courthouse, the better. You know what's unbelievable?" She didn't wait for a reply. "I feel, I don't know, like somehow I'm on trial. The barber gets all the benefits of a doubt. We protect the hell out of the accused, but the victim has no rights whatsoever."

"Lot's been written on that subject. Take it up with some of your buddies on the Hill."

"One step at a time. First I need to get through this damn trial. Or I guess I should say, 'these damn trials.'"

"Do you feel sorry for Joseppe? Even a bit? I mean he does have to go through two trials, back-to-back."

"I don't know. I mean, if he did it then no, of course not. But if he didn't do it then, I guess, yeah, I would feel real sorry for him."

Jayne smiled. "You sound good," she said. "Under control. I'm proud of you."

"Thanks. You know, getting together with you has been great. You really have kept me focused."

Connie attended the fraud trial on Tuesday. Just as Jim Evans had requested. The first witness was Ed Olmstead. Connie knew him to say "hi" to, but that was about it.

Evans started the witness off slowly. Name, address, job, that sort of thing. Then: "Mr. Olmstead, do you ever invest money?"

"Yes."

"Do you have a broker?"

"Yes."

"Do you do all of your investing with your broker?"

"I did until recently."

"Then what happened?"

"I made an investment in a real estate trust I learned about from my barber."

"Your barber? Why would anyone invest through their barber? I mean, your broker never cuts your hair does he?"

Olmstead chuckled, like it was the first time he had heard the line. No way, thought Connie. No way.

"I know it sounds strange, but I've known him for just about forever, and he's always seemed very honest."

"What was the amount you invested, and what, if you know, happened to the money?"

"I invested fifty thousand dollars, and it's gone."

"What do you mean 'gone'?"

"Just what I said. The trust, that is the real estate trust I supposedly invested in, was run by two of Joseppe's other customers, and they took the money and left."

"And Joseppe is your barber?"

"Oh, right, sorry, I thought I said that."

"Is Joseppe in this room?"

"Yes," said Olmstead as he pointed at the barber. "Right there."

"Thank you. Now Mr. Olmstead did you have occasion to speak with any of Joseppe's other customers about this investment?"

"Sure. I spoke to Stuart about it."

Defense lawyer Mark Clifton jumped up. "Your honor, may we approach the—"

"Hey," cut in Olmstead, "just ask Connie if you don't

believe me, I'm sure she and Stuart spoke about it before he was killed," he motioned toward Connie. The ladies and gentlemen of the jury followed the motion of his arm, and twenty-four eyes, not counting spectators, rested on Connie.

Momentarily embarrassed, Connie blushed and turned away. When she looked back the scene appeared frozen in time. Evans smiling, Olmstead pointing, Clifton frowning.

"Yes," came the answer from Judge Robinson when Mark spoke up again, "you may approach the bench."

Connie watched the little ritual of the attorneys talking to the judge in private, like they were members of some club or something. You know, we can't speak in front of the children.

As the bench conference dragged, Connie's interest in it waned. She craned her neck around to see if she recognized anyone in the galley. As she squinted over her left shoulder, she picked up the silhouette of Mo Buell. Unmistakably, Mo Buell was in the back of the courtroom.

Connie fidgeted in her seat, straightening her dress, and twirling the end of her hair. Mo Buell. She bit her cuticles, and began biting the inside of her mouth, all at the same time, then she sat bolt upright, took a deep breath, and tried to relax.

The judge banged his gavel, and a startled Connie looked up. He was calling a recess. Connie stood, stretched, and sat back down. She pulled a newspaper out of her briefcase, snapped it open, and began idly thumbing through it.

"Hi, Connie," Buell said as he approached from the rear of the courtroom. "Hope I'm not disturbing you."

"Hi, Mo," Connie replied, as she glanced up from her newspaper only long enough to make eye contact.

Buell shuffled in place for a minute before mustering up the confidence to continue. "What do you think so far?" he asked.

Connie folded her newspaper shut, and glared at the deejay. "What are you doing here, Mo?"

"Hey, trial's open to the public, right? It's an interesting story, might give me some salubrious material for the show."

"Speaking of the show, I hear you've been saying some not-so-nice things about me. How 'bout canning it?"

"On the contrary, my dear. I've said you were beautiful and wonderful, the best I ever had."

Connie blushed. "Look, Mo, that was then and this is now, so I'd appreciate it if you would figure out something else to talk about."

"You know, I landed in the wacky ward when we broke up," Mo said, eyes downcast. "I mean, I just started drinkin' so much that I had to go and dry out."

"I know, you've told me all about it. Look, I'm sorry if I caused you any harm, but your weaknesses are not my problem."

"Do you know what it was like in there? Forty-three days of pure hell. No booze, no coke, no women, no phone calls for Christ sake. Yeah, it's my weakness," Buell sneered, "but it's also my radio show, and it's pretty powerful. So don't be so damn mean to me, and don't be so damn self-righteous. What did I ever do to you that was so horrible? Is loving you a crime?"

Buell turned and retreated before Connie could respond. She shook her head and pursed her lips. Just as she was about to snap open her paper, the bailiff returned. Court was being called back into session.

Chapter Thirty-Nine

Mark Clifton was taken, and he knew the jury was as well. From the moment Olmstead pointed out Connie Parker, Mark knew it was going to mean trouble. It wasn't just that she was attractive. There was a halo-like aura that surrounded her. That was why Mark had tried to head off Evans at the pass. He tried to get to the bench to warn Robinson that the prosecutor was about to do something inflammatory, but he was a split second too late. Sometimes that's what cases are decided upon, split seconds.

Evans had outsmarted him. Tricked him. Mark bristled. He could only hope that a parade of Joseppe's customers, complaining that they had been bilked, would begin to whither away at the jury's patience. Of course, if Evans didn't overdo it, if he played the jury just right, he could bury Joseppe, despite the law.

Okay. So much for the rocket science. Now Mark had a real tactical decision to make. How much to question the witnesses on cross-examination. The contents of their testimony would potentially be significantly more damning to Joseppe's case than thirty seconds of Connie Parker sitting in the gallery. They would need to be crossed, that was for sure, but Mark was cautious. The prosecution still carried the burden of proof. Mark glanced next to him. He saw Peter Long staring impassively into space. Now that was confidence-inspiring, a wonderful associate with whom to strategize.

Evans called a couple more of Joseppe's customers after Olmstead. Each was articulate, and a long-time customer. Like Olmstead, each claimed to have been bilked out of at least fifty thousand dollars. Neither appeared to be the type who would back down willingly upon cross. So Mark kept it simple. Oh, he picked a bit, and got each of them to backtrack a touch here and there, but in actuality he made no real progress.

Robinson called it a day. The first day of testimony would definitely have to go down as a negative. As Mark left the courtroom with Joseppe, it was unclear to the lawyer whether his client realized things had gone badly. Mark decided not to tell him. No use for both to lose sleep.

Day three of the fraud trial began with the witness who was going to testify about something which Mark could not quite fathom. Mark simply had no idea what Hans Mueller, the Mercedes Benz salesman, was going to say. Evans began with the usual nonsense about name, address, and occupation. Then he got down to business. "And did you, Mr. Mueller, ever come in contact with Joseppe Giavonni?"

"Yes, I did," the impeccably dressed salesman responded.

"And what was the nature of your contact with Mr. Giavonni?"

"I sold him a car." Mueller was short and so were his answers.

"And during the course of selling him a car, did you have the opportunity to speak with him on a regular basis?"

"Yes."

"And what was your sense of Mr. Giavonni? Did he seem like someone who had purchased many luxury vehicles in the past?"

Mark jumped to his feet. "Objection, your Honor. The question calls for speculation on the part of the witness."

Judge Robinson peered down from his bench. He looked first at Mark, and then back at the witness. Then he addressed Hans Mueller. "If you can answer the question then you are free to do so. But do not speculate as to the answer."

"I can answer the question," Mueller said, brimming with confidence. "Mr. Giavonni told me it was the first time he was buying a Mercedes."

"And did Mr. Giavonni have a vehicle to trade in?"

"He inquired about the possibility of trading in a Chevy Nova. But we told him that we did not sell that kind of car in our used car lot," Mueller sniffed.

"Did you meet Mrs. Giavonni at any time?"

"Yes, she came in when we closed the deal. She test drove the car once and then we signed all of the documents."

"And do you remember anything in particular about your conversations with Mrs. Giavonni?"

"Yes, Mrs. Giavonni did make one comment that stuck in my mind."

"And can you tell us what that comment was, if you remember?"

Hans puffed out his narrow little chest. "I remember what she said exactly. She said 'Joseppe, I still can't believe you're getting this car from scamming.' " Hans looked around at the jury beaming with delight.

Surprise testimony. Always a pleasure. Mark had delved into the automobile transaction since he knew

Mueller was being called as a witness. But Joseppe had never mentioned anything like this. Hey, Josep, old buddy, thanks for the help.

"Did Mr. Giavonni answer his wife?" The prosecutor pressed.

"No, he just smiled. He just smiled."

Nice effect, Evans. Good coaching. And nice job of acting Hans. That repeat was very believable. Very believable.

Hans was full of himself. He cocked his small head to one side, pursing his lips tightly. This was a cross possibility. Mark reviewed his notes and waited.

Evans finished up with a couple of inconsequential questions, and Mark rose to his feet. "Mr. Mueller, how long have you been a Mercedes salesman?"

"If you heard my testimony," Hans said, "I began selling cars over twenty years ago. I have been a Mercedes salesman for nearly ten years."

"During that time, Mr. Mueller, has anyone ever paid for a car in cash?"

"Of course, on a number of occasions."

"And did you ever question the source of their funds?"

"No, I did not." Hans shifted in his seat.

"Mr. Mueller, if you remember, were any of the people who paid for cars in cash very young men?"

"I, I'm not sure. I don't remember."

"You don't remember? But you do remember that you sold cars for cash?"

"That's what I said, Mr. Clifton," Mueller parried back.

"So you haven't exactly made it a practice of looking into the morality or ethics of your customers?"

"No, I haven't," Mueller shot back.

"Yet, somehow, to use your words, you remember exactly what Mrs. Giavonni said on the day you sold the Giavonnis their car?"

"That's right."

"But you can't even remember whether any of the people who bought cars from you and paid cash were young men?"

"That's my testimony, Mr. Clifton, now if you don't like it, I guess that's just too bad!"

"You know, Mr. Mueller, you're right. If I don't like your testimony it is too bad, because I can't change your testimony. And I can't coach you or tell you what you remember or what you should say."

Evans jumped to his feet. "Objection, your Honor! He can't do that!"

"That's an interesting objection, Mr. Evans," Judge Robinson said with a twisted smile. "I've never heard of an objection called 'He can't do that.' "

"He's badgering the witness, your Honor. And he's making insinuations about the way we prepared the witness."

Tsk, tsk. Poor word choice, Mr. Evans, Mark thought as he suppressed a smile while humming to himself. "Prepared" probably isn't what you meant to say. I mean c'mon, we all know that Hans is going solely by memory.

Judge Robinson raised his arms over his head. He then cradled them behind his neck and leaned back in his chair. Then he rocked forward. "Mr. Clifton, although it was unartfully stated, I think Mr. Evans has a point. You need to get off this line of questioning, or do it in a manner which doesn't make inferences concerning preparation or scripting of the witness."

"Yes, your Honor," Mark replied. "Let me try and rephrase my question, Mr. Mueller," Mark walked back towards the witness stand. Then, looking directly at the jury, and away from Hans Mueller, Mark continued. "In your estimation, Mr. Mueller, does Mrs. Giavonni have much of an accent?"

Evans jumped to his feet again. "I object your Honor, it calls for speculation on the part of the witness."

"I'm going to allow it, Mr. Evans," Robinson said as he directed his attention towards Mueller. "You're free to answer, if you can."

"Yes, Mrs. Giavonni does have a fairly substantial accent," Mueller said, in his own clipped German tone.

Still looking at the jury, Mark continued. "How is her command of the English language?"

"How should I know?"

Mark whirled around. "You're able to tell if she had an accent, and you were able to remember a specific phrase which she uttered, so I would think you would be able to discern how well she speaks the language." Mark glared at the witness.

"Well I don't know!"

"You don't know? You don't know? You don't know!" Mark cried out, waving his arms. "I have to say, Mr. Mueller, that I find it rather amazing that someone could remember the exact words that someone else spoke to them many months before, but that same person couldn't remember if the person speaking the words had a good command of the English language. You certainly do have a selective memory. Nothing further, your Honor."

Mark sat down, folded his arms and winked at Joseppe.

Judge Robinson called for a fifteen-minute recess before the final witness of the afternoon would be called. Evans indicated that he could finish up in under an hour, and that the prosecution would be resting its case that afternoon.

Joseppe would need to testify the following day. And

now, it was certain that his wife would need to testify as well. As they left the courtroom and headed down the hall for one of the tiny strategy rooms, Mark saw Carlita Giavonni ducking into the ladies' room. Originally, she wasn't on the witness list, so she had been allowed to stay in the courtroom. Usually all witnesses, other than the parties to a criminal case, are not allowed to watch the trial until after they have testified. Mark would need to advise the judge of the change, and Carlita would be restricted from watching the proceedings until she testified.

Carlita would need to be prepped. And Joseppe would need to be re-prepped. They had a long night ahead of them.

Chapter Forty

Mark Clifton called Carlita Giavonni to the stand as his first witness. She was middle-aged, plain, and short, and she looked even shorter since she had followed Mark's advice and worn flat shoes. Mark could tell she was grossly uncomfortable with her upcoming role. She fidgeted as she approached the stand, and almost tripped over her out-of-fashion, mid-calf skirt. Her olive skin was already beaded with sweat as she raised her right hand and took the witnesses' oath.

Mark knew Carlita would need a tremendous amount of handholding. He also knew that he didn't want to open the door for Evans to begin probing in areas about which Carlita would not be prepared. He would need to give Carlita a number of easy lobs to begin with to build her confidence. But then he would need to get directly to the point and stick with it.

"Can you please state your full name for the jury?"

"Carlita Antonia Giavonni."

"And where were you born Mrs. Giavonni?"

"In Naples, Italy."

"How long have you been in the United States?"

"Almost 25 years."

"Are you an American citizen?"

"Yes."

"And you are married?"

"Yes."

"And can you please tell the jury who your husband is?"

"Yes, my husband is the defendant in this case, Mr. Joseppe Giavonni."

"How long have you been married to Mr. Giavonni?"

"Next month, 31 years," Carlita beamed as she said the words.

"How long has your husband been a barber?"

"His whole working life. It must be, maybe, 35 years."

"So he was a barber before you came to the United States?"

"Yes."

"And where did you live before you came to the United States?"

"We lived in Toronto, Canada for three years, and before that the whole time in Naples."

"Why did you come to the United States?"

"For a better life."

"And did you find a better life here in the United States?"

"Well, at first, we struggle. Joseppe, he worked in a little shop, and was paid by the hour. During that time, I stay at home and raised the kids. We put away every penny we make until we had enough for a down payment for our own barber shop. Then we struggle to pay back the bank. It is only in the last six or seven years that Joseppe has earned enough money from the shop to put some in the bank."

"Has Joseppe ever made any money other than through cutting hair?"

"Yes. He has made some money through what he calls investments."

Mark glanced over at the jury. *Yoo hoo, boys and girls, wake up call!*

"What kinds of investments, if you know?"

"Mostly in the stock market. In the building where his shop is, there is a big firm that does that. Many of his customers are brokers, and some of them, they would give him tips. Then he would buy stocks like they tell him to."

"Did Joseppe make a lot of many by investing in this manner?"

"Actually, I think he did pretty good."

"What did you think of the fact that Joseppe was investing his hard-earned dollars?"

Evans jumped to his feet. "I object to the characterization of the money being 'hard-earned.'"

Judge Robinson looked first at Evans and then back at Mark. "I'll let it go. I don't find it to be particularly inflammatory or misleading, and I think the jury understands the reference." Robinson looked over at Mark. "You may continue, Counselor."

"Thank you, your Honor. Mrs. Giavonni?"

"I didn't like it. I was afraid he's going to lose it all. I, I guess I don't trust what I don't understand. It's different than working for the money."

"How is it different?"

"Well, it's not like you earn it or anything. You just outsmart the other person. You know, you buy something then sell it for more. That's not working."

"What is it?"

"I call it 'scamming.'"

What does 'scamming' mean?"

"Well, it's like I said, it means any time you get money that you don't work for."

"Like through buying and selling stocks?"

"Objection, your honor, he's putting words in her mouth. She never said that."

"Overruled. This is direct, the line of questioning is permissible."

"Thank you, your Honor," Mark said. "Mrs. Giavonni?"

"I forget the question."

"Do you consider the buying and selling of stocks to be 'scamming'?"

"Yes," Carlita sniffed, "I most certainly do."

"Thank you, Mrs. Giavonni. No further questions, your Honor."

Mark looked over at Evans. He knew what the prosecutor was thinking. Carlita was going to be spared the agony of cross. With a witness like her, Evans stood as good a chance of digging a deeper hole as he stood of getting out of this one. It wasn't worth it.

CHAPTER FORTY-ONE

Gary had spent many nights in many strange places, but he had never, ever spent the night leaning against the side of a train, no less a circus train. When he returned to his room the following morning, McFerrin and Jarvis were more than a little curious. Surprisingly, it was the straggly guy, the one Gary wanted to call "snaggle tooth," who piped up first. "What the hell you been doin'?" he demanded.

"Hey, I found a woman, okay?"

Jarvis looked momentarily stunned, and a bit more than a little uncomfortable. "That, that's not what I meant," he stammered. "I mean who you been pissin' off?"

Gary feigned surprise and hurt. "No one that I know of," he replied. "Why?"

"Some guy I never seen before," Jarvis began, before nodding towards McFerrin, "who Charlie here says has been hanging with Mora, come in here all fired up last night lookin' for you." Jarvis paused, and laughed abruptly. "He weren't lookin' to shake your hand neither!"

Gary continued to act surprised. "I have no idea who or what you're talking about," he snapped. "I didn't think I was here long enough to make enemies."

McFerrin cut in. "He said you was a reporter or something, that true?"

"Nah, I'm no reporter. I couldn't write my way out of a paper bag."

"He's gonna come back lookin' for ya', that's for sure," McFerrin continued. "Let's take a walk a bit," he said, as he got to his feet and pushed Gary out the door.

Gary led the way down the narrow hallway which only had an exit at the far end. He had made a mental note of the corridor when he first got to the show. It was an easy place to get cornered, and a good place to avoid.

As soon as they got out of the train, McFerrin began talking a blue streak. "My man, you know which dude I'm talkin' about. He's the one you ask about before. He's the one killed ol' Don, you ask me. I mean I ain't got no proof, but that's what I figure. Now he's after you. It could be the bed, you know!"

Gary emitted a short cackle. "It's not the bed, Charlie. And don't worry, I can take care of myself. Really I can. He's not so tough. Just acts it."

"Look, man, I don' know what your game is, but I'm stayin' away after this. This is too freaky for me. I know when I'm in over my head, and that time's now. Be cool, my man, be cool."

Gary smiled, shook McFerrin's hand, and thanked him for his help. Then Gary continued to walk. Alone. But he carried his gun. It's like John Lennon sang, "happiness is a warm, yes it is, gun..."

Gary walked back toward Mora's trailer. He might have to kidnap Moran. That was the only hope. It would have to be during a performance when no one was around.

Nah. Shitty idea. Got to come up with something or poor Mark's gonna be left holding the proverbial bag. But trying to kidnap Moran would be suicidal. And that would take all the fun out of it.

Chapter Forty-Two

As he hung up the phone, Mark looked up to see the defendant, as Judge Robinson liked to refer to Joseppe, walk into the office. Joseppe was wearing his best suit, and his most nervous face. Mark could see Joseppe was petrified at the thought of testifying. Mark didn't blame him. Hey, no big deal. In this case it could only mean five, maybe ten years, if Joseppe screwed up. If he was nervous now, Mark couldn't wait to see what he would be like when he testified in the murder trial. If he testified in the murder trial.

Mark led the way over to the courthouse. He watched as his client entered the room first. Although he had been there all week, Joseppe looked for all the world like it was his first time in the courtroom.

Joseppe looked up at the grand, high ceilings. He again asked Mark why there were three judge's chairs, and again Mark patiently explained that every so often, three judge panels might hear a case in this courtroom.

Mark led his client to the leather chairs behind counsel's table, but this time he asked Joseppe to sit in the first row, behind the table. Joseppe would be testifying on the witness stand, not sitting at counsel's table.

It seemed like before Mark even had the chance to let his morning coffee kick in, they were wandering through Joseppe's direct testimony. They were into it for twenty minutes before Mark felt focused. "And, Mr.

Giavonni, what exactly did you say to Mr. Brown?" Mark asked.

"I asked him first if he was still doing any investing."

"And his answer?"

"He said he was doing a little."

"What happened next?"

"I asked him if he was interested in hearing about an investment opportunity a couple of guys I knew were putting together."

"How did he answer?"

"He said there was nothing to invest in. Interest rates were low and everything else had gone sour. He said he would be happy to listen."

"Did you disclose to him at that time that you had a financial interest in whether or not he invested?" Mark knew the answer was unfavorable, and he wanted it out now, when he could control it better. If Evans brought it out first, it would make Joseppe look defensive, like he had something to hide.

"No, I did not."

Mark watched Evans who looked a bit surprised. Mark quickly returned his gaze to the defendant. "Why not?"

"I didn't think it mattered. I knew Moran and Caulfield, and I figured it was a good deal."

"Did you invest in the opportunity yourself?" Another bad answer was on its way.

"No, I did not."

"Why not, if it was such a good investment?"

"Because they wouldn't let me."

"Who wouldn't?"

"Moran and Caulfield."

"Why not?"

"They claimed that it could violate some kind of securities regulations if I bought a unit."

"Okay, Mr. Giavonni, what did you think of that?"

"I believed it to be true."

"Okay. And what did you think of Mr. Moran?"

"He seemed a little harsh sometimes, but he seemed very knowledgeable. Bad hair. Very difficult to cut."

Mark noticed a few snickers, but he couldn't tell if they were from the jury box or the crowd of onlookers.

"And how about Mr. Caulfield?"

"I liked Jackson very much. He was a regular customer for many years. He was friendly, and he seemed to know real estate."

Mark decided to stray a bit. Always a risk, especially with a client who isn't particularly nimble. But what the hell, you only go around once. "Mr. Giavonni, I wonder if you realize you were talking about Mr. Caulfield in the past tense?"

Joseppe looked stunned. "I'm sorry?" the barber said, shifting his weight to the left.

Okay, maybe this was going to be tougher than expected. Mark momentarily thought about skipping the line of questioning. He glanced at the jury. They looked expectant. That made for an easy decision. Mark plowed ahead. "When I just asked you about Jackson Caulfield, you responded in the past tense. You said 'He was nice. I liked him. He seemed to really know real estate.' Do you remember responding in that manner?"

"Yes."

"Why did you respond in the past tense? Is Mr. Caulfield dead?"

"No," Joseppe said, as he emitted a short nervous laugh. "He just disappeared. I mean," the barber continued, blurting out his words, "I guess he could be dead, but he's not that I know of. He left some time ago for Bermuda, and I haven't heard anything about him since."

"You haven't stayed in touch with him?"

"No."

"Why not?"

"He and Moran were running away from the investors. They had taken all this money, and now they had to find a place to hide."

"But you knew these guys. You were working for them. You mean to tell me that they never once told you where they were once they went into hiding?"

"No. You see, it really wasn't the way you say," Joseppe explained. "One day Jackson asked me if I knew anybody that might like to invest some money. I say that, 'Yeah, I probably do.' Then he asked me if I would give information to these people about an investment he and Moran were working on together. I said I probably would. I didn't think twice about it until Moran showed up a few days later. He gave me a bunch of information about this real estate trust that he and Jackson had started. Then he told me that for each fifty thousand dollar unit I sold, he would give me ten grand."

"So, what did you do next?"

"I object your honor," Evans said, as he jumped to his feet trying to break the defense team's rhythm.

Judge Robinson stared down at Evans, his eyes boring parallel holes through the prosecutor's forehead. "Grounds?" he boomed in his most officious tone of voice.

"I'm sorry, your Honor," Evans sniffed. Still unable to muster up a reason, the prosecutor withdrew his objection.

"The witness may answer the question," Judge Robinson directed.

"Thank you, your Honor," Mark answered, as he turned to face Joseppe. Evans had succeeded, at least to a degree. Mark waited momentarily, then said, "What happened after Moran offered to pay you for leads for the investment?" Mark made the mistake on purpose.

"He agreed to pay me for, actually for, investors I brought in, not for leads."

"Thank you for clarifying that, Mr. Giavonni. Now, what happened next?"

"I began talking up the investment to my customers."

"All of them?"

"No. Just the ones I thought might be interested, but that's plenty."

"How many invested?"

"Seventeen."

"So you raised $850,000 and got $170,000 for yourself?"

"No. Lots of people bought less than a fifty thousand dollar share. I got $115,000."

"Okay, and what did you understand to be the nature of the investment?"

"The way it was explained to me, they were going to buy depressed pieces of real estate at bargain basement prices, then wait for the market to turn around."

"Do you know how much they raised altogether?"

"I'm not sure. Between $3 and 4 million, I think."

"And what happened to the money?"

"I don't know."

"Was it ever invested?"

"Not that I know of."

"You said earlier that Caulfield and Moran are in the Bahamas. How do you know that?"

"Actually they are in Bermuda. If I said the Bahamas, I am sorry. Anyway, they sent one report to the investors which was postmarked from down there, and then I just heard they were still there."

"So what happened after they sent the initial report?"

"Nothing that I know of."

"When did the investors start to get worried?"

"Oh, it must've been, maybe two months after the first letter came, maybe April, when some of my customers started asking questions."

"Like what?"

"Like, 'have you heard from Caulfield and Moran?' "

"And what was your answer?"

"It was always the truth. I said I hadn't heard a thing from them."

"What happened after that?"

"I started to get worried that maybe something was up. I was very concerned that I had gotten some of my customers into a very bad investment."

"What did you do?"

"I tried to track them down."

"How?"

"By telephone mostly. I have another customer who was going to Bermuda on a business trip, and he agreed to look them up for me."

"I have in my hand a phone bill which I would like you to take a look at," Mark said as he gave Joseppe and Evans copies of the bill.

Joseppe looked at the bill. Mark began, "Do you recognize this document?"

"Yes."

"What is it?"

"I object your honor. He hasn't entered it into evidence."

Before Robinson could respond, Mark cut in. "If I may, your Honor?"

"Go ahead," Robinson snapped.

"The document hasn't been identified fully yet. I intend to enter it into evidence, barring further objection, once it is identified."

Robinson glared at the prosecuting attorney. "Objection overruled."

Mark got Joseppe to identify the phone bill, and it was entered into evidence.

"So, Mr. Giavonni, you tried to call information in Bermuda and a number of other real estate offices."

"Yes."

"For what purpose?"

"To try to find Moran and Jackson. I was upset for my customers."

"No luck?"

"No luck."

"No further questions at this time, your Honor."

Robinson took a fifteen-minute break after asking Evans how long the cross would be. The prosecutor guessed an hour, maybe an hour and a half. Robinson wanted to finish before lunch.

The break seemed to end before it began. Evans stood up, looked at the jury, smiled a bit woodenly, and attacked.

"Mr. Giavonni, you have testified that the investments your customers were to make were in a real estate trust. What specific properties did Moran and Caulfield have in mind?"

"I don't know," Joseppe replied.

"You don't know!" Evans thundered. "You asked customers, long-term ones at that, to invest in a real estate scheme, and you didn't even bother to ask what properties the investors were looking at?"

"Yes." Joseppe appeared unnerved. The line of questioning was somewhat unexpected, but Mark didn't mind. If anything, it might go to negligence, but this was a fraud trial.

"Why did you stop looking for your friends Moran and Caulfield?"

"It became useless after a while. I mean I just couldn't locate them."

"Why didn't you go down to Bermuda to look for them yourself?"

Good question, thought Mark.

"I must be in the shop or I go out of business like that," Joseppe said as he snapped his fingers. "I work five-and-a-half days a week. It would have been very difficult for me to leave." Mark felt like a boxing coach as he watched his fighter jab back at the attacking prosecutor.

"Have you ever heard of a vacation? Bermuda would be nice for it!" Evans bristled.

"I had just taken a vacation six weeks before this. My customers wouldn't stand for it."

"They won't stand for you defrauding them either!" Evans snapped.

"I object, your Honor," Mark said, as he jumped to his feet. "He's badgering the witness, drawing a legal conclusion and lecturing to my client for the jury's benefit. It's outrageous."

"Sustained," said Judge Robinson, emphasizing and enunciating both syllables of the short word. "The jury is advised to disregard the last comment by Mr. Evans."

Evans continued. "Did you ever offer to pay back your customers out of your ill-gotten gains?"

Mark and Joseppe had talked about this one *ad nauseam*. It was like the old "when did you stop beating your wife" question. There was no good answer. If Joseppe tried to return the money it might look like an admission of guilt. If he didn't, he looked callous. Oh, he could always argue that he was merely being magnanimous, but that was like the people who enter into securities consent decrees which essentially say "we didn't do it, and we won't do it again."

"I had nothing to do with Moran and Caulfield running away," Joseppe's voice was barely audible. "The money I made was not ill-gotten. You know, Mr. Evans, the harm to my reputation, and the costs of this trial, will eat up all of my earnings and much more."

"Is that so, Mr. Giavonni? Are you gonna give back the Mercedes? You know, trade it in for some cash to pay your high-priced lawyer?"

Mark jumped up. Robinson looked over. "I object, your Honor, he's badgering the witness again."

"Sustained. Mr. Evans, Mr. Clifton, please approach the bench."

When the lawyers reached the judge's home turf, Mark could see that Robinson was in a barely controlled rage. "Cut the shit, Evans, or I'll cite you for contempt. Lawyers don't treat witnesses like that in my court."

"Your Honor, I'm not doing anything that horrible. I apologize to the court, but with all due respect I think you are overreacting a bit here." Evans held his ground.

Mark swore he could see Robinson lift off his chair. The old man was ballistic. "Don't question the way I run my courtroom, young man. When it's your courtroom, you may run it however you see fit. Until then, get in line or I'll hammer you."

As Mark was about to leave the bench he felt Robinson turn on him.

"And you, Mr. Clifton, don't get smug. You haven't exactly been the model of decorum. Now get back out there and finish up like gentlemen."

Mark turned at the same time as the prosecutor who

was no doubt wondering, as was Mark, about where the hell the judge got his rage, and what it was really directed at. The old man was usually so calm. And tolerant.

"Mr. Giavonni, do you plan to compensate any of the victims of this fraud," Evans began, a bit more tentatively this time.

"Objection, your Honor," Mark said, a bit more reserved than he would have liked. "The characterization of the investors as "victims" in a sentence about possible compensation from my client leads the jury to the impermissible conclusion that they are victims because of my client. Not to mention that the use of the word 'fraud' is the drawing of a legal conclusion."

"I understand your concerns, counselor," a more subdued Judge Robinson said, as he smiled wanly in Mark's direction. "But, I'm going to allow it."

Joseppe jumped in without making Evans repeat the question. Mark was pleased. The jury had already been reminded twice that Joseppe's customers who invested at his urging were now out substantial sums, they didn't need to hear it again. "I consider every day whether to sell the car. It has brought bad luck. Right now, it would be a bad decision. I would lose a lot of money. Mr. Evans, if I thought, truly believed, that I had done something wrong, I would give back as much money as I could to my customers. And if the jury thinks I should, then I will. I do not want the money. But I do not want this trial, or the loss of business, either.

"You know, Mr. Evans, I have a family to feed. If you want to talk about victims, then talk about them. What they have been through is unbelievable."

Evans was clearly unhappy with Joseppe's tour de force. "Perhaps you should have thought of that a bit earlier," he replied.

"I don't know what you mean."

"I mean that you should have thought about the ramifications of your actions before you began asking your customers for contributions." The sarcasm dripped from Evans' last word.

"I didn't know the consequences of my actions then, Mr. Evans," a fired-up Joseppe replied, "because I didn't know that Moran and Caulfield were gonna head outta town, and leave me holding the bag."

Joseppe had done well. Very well.

Evans wrapped up. It was time for lunch, and then closing arguments.

Chapter Forty-Three

Jayne was busy. No three words bummed out Connie Parker more these days. The fraud trial had gone to the jury. There was to be a one-day break and then it was on to the big one. The trial of Joseppe Giavonni for the murder of Stuart Katcavage. Star witness, Connie Parker.

Connie was sitting in her living room thumbing through the newspaper. She clicked on the television, and just as quickly, clicked it off. She walked over to her CD collection, and glanced through it looking for just the right music to capture her mood. She pulled out her favorite Wynton Marsalis disc, but before she slid it in, she changed her mind. Damn, the apartment seemed small.

She caught a cab to the Donkey and Elephant. The crowd there was eclectic, and though she didn't usually hang out in bars on the Hill, the thought that she might see a familiar face actually held some allure tonight.

Connie suddenly felt somewhat ridiculous dressed in a short, tight, knit black dress. She hadn't worn this particular dress much, it was too short in all honesty. She wasn't even sure why she had bought it.

Glancing around, Connie removed her coat, and headed for a bar stool. It was early, and the place had maybe thirty people in it. The bar was long and narrow, with high wooden square chairs that fit snugly up against the rail. There was just enough room for Connie to cross her legs. Connie nodded knowingly. The designer of this place knew exactly what he was doing.

Connie ordered a Bloody Mary as she looked around. There were two rather large groups, one of kids, maybe 23 years old. First year out of college, working as gophers on the Hill, and out to change the world. The second group was more diverse. It looked like a group out celebrating a birthday, or someone's departure from the office. What a bizarre tradition, Connie thought. Oh, you're leaving the firm? Let's go celebrate! Who is the celebration for anyway, the one leaving or the ones staying behind?

Connie sipped her drink a bit too rapidly as she looked at her watch. She wondered what the hell she was doing, but fairly soon she began to feel a pleasant buzz. She finished her drink, and ordered a second. On the few rare occasions that Connie had gone to a bar alone in the past, she had not sat by herself for too long.

Tonight was no exception. One of the young pups made his way over, sidling up to her like he was king shit. Connie held back the smirk. She was buzzing pretty strongly. This was going to be a blast.

"Hi," he began, with a toothy smile. "You waitin' for someone, or can I join you?"

"What makes you think those are the only two options?"

"Excuse me?" He obviously wasn't used to quick-witted women.

"Well, one other option is that I am waiting for someone, but you can join me anyway. Perhaps I like threesomes," Connie purred, as she curled her lip. "Of course, the other option is that I'm not waiting for anyone, but you still can't join me. Who knows," she said, toying with him now. "Maybe I'm gay. Or maybe I just don't like the way you talk."

The young pup swayed back and forth and picked at his tooth. Connie smiled, but said nothing further for a moment. When the young stud still didn't speak, she could stand it no longer.

"Whatsa matter," she laughed, "cat got your tongue?"

He recovered a bit. "You've got to admit that your response was not something I could've realistically expected when I first asked the question. I figured you'd tell me to get lost, but I figured you'd do it quickly, and not be bothered. I didn't expect to get involved in witty repartee."

"For it to be witty repartee, both of us have to be participating," Connie snapped. "What is the IQ of your average date, about six?"

"Listen," the young man replied as he shifted his weight, "would you like me to crawl back into the woodwork?"

"If you'd like to, feel free. But I'm sure you boys must have something riding on this. I mean you don't want to have to head back and admit defeat so quickly do you?"

The young hopeful could do nothing more than blush.

"Listen," Connie said, a bit more sympathy apparent in her voice. "Go back to your pimply-faced friends, and tell them you think I like you. Tell them that you think I'm playing hard to get. Then I'll motion to you to come over, okay. You'll have some fun. Now, what's your name?"

"Dan. Dan Malloy. And yours?"

"Alice Dodge," Connie said with a laugh. "Now get going."

Connie awoke woozily the next morning. Dan's little apartment was cozy. And despite his drunken state, the young man had proved to be a passionate, and surprisingly sensitive sex partner. Connie momentarily eyed the sleeping Dan, but quickly changed her mind.

She slid gently out from under the covers, and headed for Dan's closet. She slipped on the first shirt she could find, and made a beeline for the kitchen.

Typical single male's apartment. Some dirty dishes in the sink, a six-pack in the refrigerator, and an empty pizza box in the trash can.

Connie managed to find some instant coffee in a cabinet, and sat down to wait for the water to boil. She found a tiny, ancient transistor radio which she picked up and began to fool with. She slid the dial up and down, eventually landing on a strong, clear signal. The commercial that was playing ended at about the same time the water started to boil. Connie put the radio on the kitchen counter and poured the water into the coffee mug which she had retrieved from the sink and scrubbed to a level of cleanliness that, if pushed, could be considered to resemble respectability.

"We're back. Can't say much about those commercials, 'cause hey folks, they're our sponsors. They pay for you to have the right to listen to *Mo in the Morning*, the highest rated show in D.C. Lemme ask you this, dear listeners. Any of you following the Giavonni case? You know the barber of the Hill? Hah. Yeah, I call it the Connie Parker vindication trial. And, hey, this is only trial number one. The big one, murder one, is next.

"Any of you know Giavonni, give me a call. Let's hear about whether you think he could've done it or not. That is, the murder charge. Forget this fraud thing. You know the number here, it's 202-BOSS-JOC."

Connie took a sip of coffee, poured the rest into the sink, and headed back into the bedroom. She gathered her clothes off the floor, quickly stepped into her dress, got herself together just enough to be presentable, and scooted out the door. She stopped outside the apartment, fished a business card out of her pocketbook, scribbled her home number on the back, and slid it under the door. So much for Alice Dodge.

Connie twisted around with her feet firmly planted on the ground, cracking her vertebrae, and stretching her lumbar muscles. She stretched her arms over her head, stopping on the way back down to scratch her scalp. Then she began walking briskly away. Time to get home. Time to shower.

Chapter Forty-Four

Gary Schofield was getting tired of splitting his nights between the arena and the woods outside the circus train. Tonight he was going to hop in the car, and find a nearby motel. Moran was showing no signs of coming out of Mora's trailer. As far as Gary could tell, the lunatic had been holed up there without leaving for four days straight. Gary had only rigged one of the last four days. It was possible that Moran had left then. But other than that, Gary had kept a lonely vigil, waiting for his quarry to emerge.

Shortly before one o'clock Gary hopped into his late-model Ford rental and drove away from the Charlotte Civic Center. Less than a mile away, he found a Comfort Inn. He registered as Mr. Jackson Hole, paid in cash, and hit the sack. In minutes he was sleeping.

At five o'clock sharp, Mr. Jackson Hole was back on the road towards the train. There was another hour until dawn, so Gary stopped for some coffee and a donut at an all-night Denny's on the way. It was unlikely Moran had split, but who knew. It didn't matter. The three-and-a-half hours of sleep were more restful than the previous four nights combined. At this point, the chance was worth it.

Gary wandered over towards Mora's RV and found his favorite spot against an adjacent trailer where he couldn't be seen. He settled in to wait, a private eye's favorite pastime. Oh, the glory of it all!

Shortly after he got there, and still before dawn, Gary saw Moran emerge for the first time in days. Did Moran know he was being watched? He was keeping an awfully low profile. Ridiculously low in fact.

Moran walked quickly towards a wooded area a quarter of a mile from the train. Gary followed at a safe distance. Moran disappeared into the brush, and Gary hesitated momentarily. Gary tiptoed towards the woods. He slipped in five feet to the left of the spot where Moran entered. He stopped, and listened intently. He heard a sound that was distinctly familiar. Moran was taking a leak!

Gary thought briefly about shooting the asshole's pecker off, but decided it would be tough to do in the dark. Think, Gary exhorted himself, think!

Without a doubt Moran was armed. And he was probably just enough off-kilter to use a weapon at the slightest provocation, or even with no provocation at all. Shooting Moran would serve no purpose. If Gary hit him what would he do then, leave him to die? If he didn't hit him, Moran would return the favor of firing into the void. No, it was dangerous, and there was nothing to be gained.

On the other hand, trying to kidnap Moran, and bring him back to D.C. in time for the murder trial—the original plan—still held some allure. Moran wouldn't take too kindly to being kidnapped. He was big, sort of lumpy, and probably fairly difficult to move. Not the best profile for a potential kidnapping victim. Plus, it was starting to get light. How could Gary bring Moran back to where the car was parked without him raising a ruckus?

As his thoughts raced far ahead of his actions, Gary was momentarily startled to hear rustling in the brush nearby. He froze. It was Moran. It had to be. But did Moran know Gary, or someone, was there, or was he crashing headlong through the thicket oblivious to the fact that he had been followed?

Moran burst past Gary in the pale light of the dawn, maybe five or seven feet away. Gary stood totally paralyzed. What little in the way of a plan he had tried to construct slowly crumbled as Moran thundered back towards the trailer.

Gary spit on the dirt. The murder trial was a day away.

Chapter Forty-Five

Peter Long cracked the small piece of gum he kept tucked in his jaw as he leaned back and listened to opening arguments in the Joseppe Giavonni murder case. Too bad we got Judge Dell, he thought. She's pretty liberal.

The courtroom wasn't as nice as the one in the federal courthouse, though it wasn't exactly shabby either. It felt smaller with all the people and press watching, and the lower ceilings. Counsel's table was rounded, like a half moon, and there was circular, recessed lighting to set off the all-wood room.

Geez, if I didn't hate Clifton and Keegan so much, I'd feel kind of sorry for Joseppe, Peter thought. Back-to-back trials in separate courtrooms, with different juries and different judges. And different charges.

But the same lawyers. The same stupid lawyers. Too bad, Joseppe. Too bad Mr. Clifton is going to be relying on some bad cases supplied by yours truly. Too bad he'll get nowhere when he tries to complain to Christian. Clifton's days are numbered. Sorry Joseppe.

Peter smiled as prosecutor Jim Evans told the jury that he would prove that Joseppe Giavonni had murdered Stuart Katcavage by poisoning his drink at the Christmas party the two had attended the prior December. His smile broadened as Evans launched into a dissertation of what the jury should look for, and what the state of the law was. Evans told the jurors all about the case in

Alabama, and how the judge in that fine state had allowed the jury to reach the conclusion that a hairdresser (and here, he paused for effect), was guilty of poisoning a customer even though no one saw her do it.

Peter glanced at Mark. The litigator looked impassive. I hope you lose, asshole, thought Peter. But, either way, you'll be history for sure.

Peter leaned forward feigning great interest when Mark stood to present his opening argument. Joseppe's senior counsel explained his client's side of the story. Joseppe was as shocked as everyone else about the murder. Joseppe didn't even know what cyanide was, no less where to get it. No, the prosecution had this case all wrong. There is absolutely no way the prosecution can prove that Joseppe killed Stuart Katcavage for one simple reason—he didn't.

Peter was just beginning to relax when he noticed a definite change in Mark's inflection.

"One more thing," Mark intoned. "Mr. Evans told you about a case in Alabama. The prosecution is relying heavily on that case for the proposition that you, as a jury, can surmise or speculate about certain things. In fact, the prosecution will undoubtedly ask Judge Dell to instruct you on that very point. But Judge Dell will not do so. There is one very simple reason for that. The Alabama case to which Mr. Evans repeatedly referred was reversed. Now I can only assume that Mr. Evans was unaware of that fact. I certainly don't think he was purposely misleading you. Thank you."

A furious Peter Long scrambled out of the courthouse and quickly made his way back to the office. He stormed into Jack Christian's office unannounced. "You're obviously impotent, Jack," he screamed.

"What is it now, Peter?"

"Clifton just made Evans look sick by telling the court that the Alabama case was reversed. Now I know I didn't find that out, and you know Clifton ain't doing his own research. It's that bitch-witch Keegan. Oh, sure," Long ranted, "you told Clifton not to use her. I can see your instructions mean a lot."

Christian popped out of his chair and pointed his finger at Long. "Maybe you should have found the case Peter," the senior partner said, jabbing his finger at the young man.

"Look, Dad," Long shot back, "when's the big awards dinner? I know it's pretty soon. If you want to enjoy yourself, you better get rid of Clifton and Keegan before that night. Otherwise, the whole world's gonna know our little secret."

With that, the bastard son of Jack Christian whirled around and stormed out of the senior partner's office.

Chapter Forty-Six

It's not often that you get a chance to start over in life with a completely fresh slate, to erase what was bad, and invent a new persona, a new past. In fact, it's so rare, so unlikely, that people generally don't know how to react when it happens. That's why, barely a week earlier, when Donald Lubins was presented with that very opportunity through pure, unadulterated luck, he paused, uncertain about which way to turn.

As Lubins had stumbled in front of the quickly gaining freight train, his foot landed directly on top of a small puddle of soda which had formed when one of the bottles Lubins was carrying in the grocery bag tumbled to the ground, the glass shattering on a rock. The moisture caused Lubins to slide forward more rapidly than he otherwise might have, and most of his body avoided the impact of the train. Unfortunately, Lubins couldn't move his crippled left foot fast enough and he lost two toes in a painful and bloody mess.

Despite the injury, or maybe as a result of it, Lubins spent the night on the hillside near the tracks, disdaining both the circus train and the hospital. He had managed to wrap the stumps with a piece of cloth from his shirt in spite of the searing pain and the pitch darkness.

The following morning, Lubins was able to hop onto the open siding of a painfully slowly moving freight train which took him all the way to Greenville, South

Carolina. There, he purchased some new clothes, wrapped his stump toes in clean bandages, and bought two pairs of shoes, one in size ten for his right foot, and the other in size eleven to accommodate his heavily bandaged left foot.

The Greenville newspaper had a tiny blurb about Lubins being feared dead, and reading the article was definitely one of the most bizarre episodes of Lubins' increasingly strange life. Until he read that article, Lubins had mostly avoided returning to the circus out of fear, and avoided going back to Toledo out of a sense of obligation to Mark. Now, he realized, through a kind of outrageous providence, he was being given a tremendous new lease on life.

Lubins let the impact of his own presumed death sink in as he breakfasted at Hardee's on sausage, eggs, and a biscuit. No child support payments. No debt of honor to Mark. No denials of tenure, no loss of jobs. Hell, no adoption if that's the way he wanted it to read.

Despite the pain in his toes, Lubins began to smile broadly. He stood from the table and limped outside. He breathed deeply, soaking up the cool morning air, and looked directly up at the sun. The sky was crystal clear, and Donald could smell the pine trees in the distance.

Chapter Forty-Seven

Mark Clifton couldn't believe his eyes. Connie Parker was radiant and in mourning all at the same time, if such a thing were possible. Her auburn hair was neatly piled in a bun on top of her head, and she wore a simple, though stylish, black suit. Her skirt just touched her knees, respectfully long, but short enough to allow for her finely shaped legs to be admired by all who wished to do so.

Evans was going for broke, and Mark didn't blame him. There is one school of thought that says lead with some of your less important or weaker witnesses, saving the best for last. After all, the ardent supporters of this theory claim, the last testimony which the jury hears is that which it will remember most.

The opposite school, to which Evans so clearly belonged, believes that the first witness can color a whole trial. If the first witness is weak it makes the prosecution's whole case seem weak. It can be difficult to overcome an ineffective first witness. The believers in this philosophy are of a mind that a strong leadoff witness can have a carry-over effect that can color an entire case.

Mark watched and listened attentively as Evans took Connie through the early days of her relationship with the victim. He was sure to refer to Katcavage as much as possible, though such references barely evoked so much as a sigh from Connie.

Mark wasn't sure at first, but the more he watched Evans and Connie act out their little play, the more convinced he became that Connie was acting in a dull manner on the advice of counsel. After all, what better way to convince a jury that you're heartbroken, and that the defendant has ruined your life and should pay?

If it was an act, she was masterful, and Evans, like a good jockey, was riding her for all she was worth. She was so good that, even to Mark's trained ear she sounded spontaneous, unrehearsed, and slightly depressed all at the same time.

"And did you ever see the deceased in the company of the defendant, Mr. Giavonni?"

"Yes."

"Where was that Ms. Parker?" Evans continued.

"At a holiday party."

"Where and when, if you remember?"

Here, for the first time, Connie showed some emotion. "Of course I remember, it was the last time I ever saw Stuart alive. It was on 34th Street in Georgetown, at the home of someone from the Tobacco Institute. It was during the third week in December. I think on the 17th."

"Thank you. I'm sorry to have to put you through this," said the prosecutor. Mark nearly choked on his breath. Man, this part is barfable.

"What was the nature of the contact between the two men?"

"It began with Stuart confronting Mr. Giavonni about an investment that Stuart had made at Mr. Giavonni's suggestion. The deal never materialized, and Stuart was out a substantial sum of money."

"Why, if you know, didn't the deal materialize?"

"According to Stuart, the deal was a real estate investment. But the so-called general partners in the deal took the money, and never did anything. It was a scam, and Stuart complained to Mr. Giavonni since he was the one who put Stuart onto the investment to begin with."

Mark thought about objecting on the basis of hearsay but held his tongue.

"Did Mr. Giavonni make any money as a result of the investment by Mr. Katcavage?"

"Objection, your Honor," Mark cut in. "It's irrelevant and prejudicial."

"Sustained," Judge Dell said, nodding her agreement to the objection. "Mr. Evans you will please withdraw the question."

"Yes, your Honor," Evans replied, lips pressed together.

Mark held back a smirk as the questioning continued.

"Did Mr. Katcavage fight with Mr. Giavonni that night?"

"Yes, in a manner of speaking. They didn't come to blows or anything. But angry words were exchanged."

"Did the evening end on that note?"

"No. Mr. Giavonni came over, oh, maybe an hour later, and said it was the holiday season and he wanted to bury the hatchet. He offered Stuart a glass which he had in his hand, and offered a toast."

"And what happened then?"

"He and Stuart toasted to the upcoming New Year and agreed to try to work out their differences."

"What did Mr. Katcavage think about this gesture?"

"Objection. It calls for the witness to speak to the state of mind of another individual. It would be pure conjecture," Mark crowed.

"I agree that it might call for conjecture, Mr. Clifton," Judge Dell shot back, her voice betraying some irritation. "But I believe that is because of unartful phrasing, not objectionable questioning. I'm inclined to allow the line of questioning, Mr. Evans, but please phrase it more carefully."

"Thank you, your Honor. Ms. Parker, did Mr. Katcavage give you any clue as to how he felt about Mr. Giavonni's gesture?"

"Yes. He told me he felt it was a classy thing to do, and if Giavonni wanted to try to put it behind them, he was all for that."

"Did anyone else bring a drink to Mr. Katcavage that evening?"

"Not that I'm aware of. In fact, Stuart commented on how out of the ordinary it seemed that the barber brought over the drink even though it shouldn't seem that way."

"Why is it out of the ordinary, according to Mr. Katcavage?"

"Because the host is paying for the booze, so there's no need to buy anyone a drink. A person might get a drink for his spouse or date, but that's really about it."

"I'm sorry to have to bring you through the whole mess again, but it's important for the jury to relive those horrible hours, so please bear with me."

Mark winced. He thought about objecting on the basis that Evans' little soliloquy was prejudicial. But he decided an objection would only serve to underscore just how incendiary the comments really were. Better left unsaid, even if there was a chance he'd be sustained.

"What happened after the toast?"

"We, that is, Stuart and I, stayed for, I'd say, another hour or so. We each had some champagne to toast the holiday season." Connie paused, then continued in a monotone. "Then we toasted our relationship. We each said we hoped there would be many more celebrations together."

"What happened after that?"

"We left. Stuart seemed awfully drunk as we got closer to home, which, in retrospect, should've been a clue that something was wrong. He didn't seem all that drunk when we left. Anyway, I helped him out of his clothes and into bed. His skin was grey. I should have known something was wrong, but I didn't. I just figured he'd had a lot more to drink than I ever imagined.

"The next morning I woke up and he seemed comatose. He had what seemed like vomit all around his mouth. I tried to wake him, but he didn't budge. I checked for a pulse and found a very weak one. I called 911."

Connie was all business. You might say she was on automatic pilot.

"What happened next?" Evans probed.

Connie took a deep breath. "I went with him in the ambulance to the emergency room. They wheeled him right in. I waited out in the waiting area. An hour or so later he was dead," she said, her eyes downcast. "The doctor came out all hot and sweaty and said, 'I'm sorry ma'am, we did everything we could to save your husband, but we couldn't.' And I said, 'He's not my husband.' That's all I could think of."

Mark watched, trying to hide his displeasure. She was good. Damn good. Not too emotional, but the quiet tone, the utter sadness she exhibited did the trick just as well, if not better.

Mark knew he would have to tread lightly on cross. Very lightly. To the jury, Connie was a sympathetic character. The veritable equivalent of a grieving widow.

Evans obviously knew when he had a good thing

going. He declined any further questions. Judge Dell, who was known to be extremely sensitive to the needs of witnesses, ordered a short recess, which was just as well. Connie's cross would begin in fifteen minutes.

Once back in the courtroom, Mark took a deep breath, then began the process which he was dreading. The jury had fallen for Connie, that much was clear. To undo it would be tough, maybe impossible. He couldn't look villainous, yet he had to punch at least a few holes in her testimony.

"Ms. Parker, I know you've been through hell these past few months. And it isn't my intention to prolong your agony even one second longer than necessary. But it is my job to do my utmost to see that Mr. Giavonni receives a fair trial."

Mark looked back at the jury, as Connie sat impassively. She was going to be tough to shake.

"Now, Ms. Parker," Mark continued, "you testified that Mr. Giavonni fought with Mr. Katcavage during the early part of the cocktail party. Do you remember exactly what was said?"

"No."

"But you do remember that they fought?"

"Yes."

"How is it that you remember that?"

"I'm sorry?"

"If you don't remember what was said between the two, how do you know they fought?"

"Stuart told me."

"I'm sorry. I thought from your testimony that you were there. Were you not present when the fight took place?"

"No," Connie said, with not the slightest sign of embarrassment or, for that matter, concern.

"Were you present for the toast about which you testified?"

"Yes. I was there when Mr. Giavonni brought the drink over to Stuart."

"Did Mr. Giavonni offer to get you a drink?"

"Yes. But I had a fresh drink in my hand so I declined."

"How would you describe Mr. Giavonni's behavior at that time? Was he sincere, timid, how did he act?"

"Oh, I don't know how to describe his behavior. I don't really know him, so I don't have any real frame of reference."

"We judge the behavior of people we meet for the first time regularly. I'm sure you've gone into a meeting or a party, met some people, then left and discussed your feelings about those people. I don't mean to be difficult, but surely you must've been sizing Mr. Giavonni up. Mr. Katcavage had just had a fight or misunderstanding with him, and suddenly he approaches the two of you. You don't mean to tell me you reached absolutely no decision concerning this man, made no judgment about his character that night?"

"Look, Mr. Clifton," Connie snapped, "you are very perceptive. Of course I made a judgment about your client that night. But it was filtered through all of the things Stuart had told me about him. I didn't like him very much. I thought he was insincere. Okay?"

Mark had his answer, but it didn't much help. And he had gotten Connie to lose her cool. But she regained it so quickly that he couldn't help but think that it was merely a charade.

"Were you with Mr. Katcavage the whole evening, during the whole party that is?"

"I testified before that I was not present during the time Stuart and your client had their little misunderstanding. Are you trying to get me to say something different now?" Connie asked, her eyes boring in on Mark.

"No, Ms. Parker, I'm not trying to trip you up in that obvious a manner. Surely you give me credit for a touch more cleverness than that?" Two can play the game.

Mark continued. "What I'm getting at, and I'll ask it a bit more directly this time, so there's no question about my motivation, is whether anyone other than my client might have had an opportunity to slip something into one of Mr. Katcavage's drinks?"

"Well, Mr. Clifton," Connie continued, sounding almost unctuous, "no one other than your client brought him a drink."

"But he had more than the one drink, didn't he?"

"Yes. He got all the others himself."

"Couldn't one of the bartenders or someone Mr. Katcavage was standing with have slipped something into one of his drinks?"

"Unlikely, don't you think?"

"I'll ask the questions if you don't mind. Now please answer the last one."

"I already did."

"I see. It is your testimony then that you believe it to be unlikely that one of the bartenders or someone else could've slipped something into Mr. Katcavage's drinks?"

"Not one of the bartenders. The bartender. There was only one. And I think it would've been very difficult for him or anyone else to do it."

"Why?"

"I'm sure Stuart was watching, maybe even talking to the guy while he made the drink. And someone who was just talking to Stuart would have to make certain that no one in the entire place saw him slip something in. The person would've had an almost impossible situation."

"Oh, I don't know. If someone wanted Stuart out of the way, he could have planned with the bartender to have a drink glass with poison just waiting for Stuart. In fact, that kind of scheme would've been easier to pull off with just one bartender than if there had been two or more, isn't that so?"

"Your words, Mr. Clifton, and your conspiratorial mind. Not mine."

Good recovery, thought Mark. A bit on the wise-ass side, but good nonetheless.

Where could he take her now?

"Ms. Parker, did you have any money invested with Mr. Moran or Mr. Caulfield, the gentlemen for whom my client was trying to raise money?"

"No."

Time to take a minor gamble. "Did you know either of those two gentlemen?"

"Yes. I knew Mr. Moran. I did not know Mr. Caulfield."

"What kind of relationship did you have with Mr. Moran, business or personal?"

Evans had apparently heard enough. "Objection. In the first place it's irrelevant, and no one opened the door to this line of questioning. We didn't bring it up on direct, and the witness hasn't brought it up herself on cross."

"Sustained," nodded Judge Dell.

So, thought Mark, she knows Moran. Time to try another angle. "Did Stuart ever talk to you about any of his investments?"

"Just a bit. I only knew him for a few months when he was killed."

"Did you ever discuss the investment he made with Moran and Caulfield?"

"Yes."

"What did you say to each other about it?"

"He explained the nature of the deal, and said how angry he was at having been duped. He really felt taken by Mr. Giavonni."

"What did you say in response?"

"There wasn't much to say. I told him not to get too bent out of shape over it. In the first place, he wasn't alone. Lots of people got duped. People who were savvy enough to know better. And secondly, he had lots of other good investments. I told him it just wasn't worth it to get so flipped out."

"Did you ever tell him you knew Moran?"

"Objection, your Honor. There's been no foundation, and he was told earlier that information about this topic was not allowed to come in."

Judge Dell rubbed her narrow chin. Then she ran her fingers through her thick graying hair. "I'm gonna let it in," she finally said. "I think he has laid a sufficient foundation, and I think the line of questioning is entirely permissible."

Connie looked through narrow eyes at the judge who directed her, gently, to answer the question.

"No," she said without hesitation once the roadblock was cleared.

"Why not? Didn't you think he might be interested?"

"It simply never came up in conversation. I never really thought about it."

"Your boyfriend was being bilked out of tens of thousands of dollars, you knew one of the alleged co-conspirators in the whole shootin' match, and you didn't tell him?" Mark asked, the incredulity apparent on his face and in his voice.

"It wasn't like that," Connie called out. "The fact is

that Stuart talked very little about the situation, or any other investments for that matter. He didn't really share too much of that with me. We'd only been seeing each other a short time, remember."

She was good. She recovered quickly from the few blows Mark struck. She thought quickly on her feet, and had the poise of a veteran. Mark decided to call it a day. The last thing he wanted to do was to help the prosecution by bolstering her testimony during cross. He'd leave that to Evans on redirect.

Evans passed on redirect, preserving his right to conduct it at a later time if he deemed it necessary. Great cross, Mark thought. The prosecution doesn't even feel the need to rehabilitate its key witness. Wonderful.

Judge Dell cleared up a few procedural matters which Mark barely followed. His client was going down in flames, his career at the firm was hanging in the balance, and he wasn't doing jack-shit about it.

Mark's mind wandered while the judge spoke. Where was Gary? Why had Jack Christian gone ballistic about Carol? What was the story with Mo Buell? And why was Connie Parker such a damn good witness?

"She just about killed me, didn't she?" Joseppe asked Mark as they headed out of the courtroom for the afternoon recess.

"Nah," Mark lied. "There's a long way to go, and it's not like she found a smokin' gun lyin' next to the body. It's still a totally circumstantial case. I'd still rather be us than them."

The barber wasn't convinced. "Markie, I know I'm no expert in the ways of the court, but I make a living talkin' to people, and the people in that room, they believed that lady. And you know what? I woulda believed her too if I was sitting where they were." Mark knew his client was right, but he wasn't convinced there was anything they could've done differently. "Well, Josep, would you have gone about it in a different way?"

"Oh, Markie," Joseppe began in a resigned tone, "don't get me wrong, I'm not blaming you. There's nothing we can do now. The good Lord thinks it's time to punish me, so I just have to take what's coming."

"Look, Josep, we've got a few tricks left up our sleeves. They've got a good witness in Connie Parker, I'll grant you that, but that's all they've got. Tomorrow's gonna be our day, you just wait and see."

Washington's most famous murder suspect smiled wanly at his lawyer. He looked like he was trying, but Joseppe had the distinct carriage of a defeated man. He walked slowly, and he sort of shuffled along like an old man with severe arthritis or maybe Parkinson's. It was a pathetic sight, and Mark, who felt at least partially responsible, averted his glance. It was more than he could bear.

Mark's mind raced as Joseppe walked away. Buell.

Mark turned to Peter Long. "Should we bring Buell in under subpoena? The guy's obsessed with Connie. Maybe he was involved in the murder," Mark offered.

"We have absolutely no proof. I think, personally, it would look desperate. I mean what could he testify about?"

For once, Mark had to agree with Long. The guy, Buell, was obsessed, but that didn't make him a murderer. Besides, the point here was to get Joseppe off, not worry about Buell. Of course, if the presence of Buell created doubt . . .

"We could move for a mistrial based on Buell's rantings. The jury probably had a radio in the jury room!" Mark shouted, stopping dead in his tracks.

Before Peter could even respond, Mark waved him off. "I know, I know. We have no proof that the jury's been listening to Buell. But they might be. We need to find out."

Chapter Forty-Eight

Connie strode from the witness stand right past the waiting minions. She had already done enough talking for one day. She headed for the witness room, grabbed her raincoat, and made a beeline for the front door and freedom.

Reporters and camera crews followed. Connie stopped and put up her hand. "It's been a long and difficult day for all of us. I've been asked lots and lots of questions. If you don't mind, I think I'll pass on answering any more."

As quickly as she had stopped, she was off again. A few of the paparazzi screamed inane questions after her, but Connie simply shook her head and kept striding toward the door.

The pack backed off. She thought about heading home for a bit, or even back to the office, just to get someplace familiar, but she thought better of it. No doubt some enterprising young cub reporter would be in those places waiting to get the scoop that was going to change his career. Not at my expense, thought Connie. Go suck someone else's blood.

She hailed a cab, and headed for Jayne's office. Jayne had offered to come to the trial, but Connie had asked her not to. Moments after Connie arrived in her friend's office, the two women had to head back to Connie's office after all to pick up Connie's house key.

"At least give me an inkling of how it went," Jayne begged as they headed out the door.

"The trial went fine. Direct was almost as planned, and cross didn't seem too bad. Plus Evans didn't do a redirect so he must've been pleased. I think Joseppe is guilty, the little shit, I really do."

Jayne just shrugged. "I don't know," she said. "Sounds like he's gonna pay for the crime either way. I'm really sorry I missed your testimony. I wish you would've let me come."

"Forget it. I really don't think you missed much, although the courtroom was crowded as hell. Tell you what, if I ever have to testify again, you can come, okay?"

"Okay," Jayne smiled. "Hey, who was in the courtroom? You said it was crowded."

"Mostly reporters. The little maggots followed me when I left, so I finally had to turn and talk to them."

Jayne looked horrified. "I hope you didn't talk to them without Evans' permission."

"Actually, I did," said Connie, as she put up her hand. "But I don't think I needed Evans' permission for what I said."

"Which was?"

"I said I would give all the men head if they'd leave me alone, and I told the women I'd give them a fifty dollar gift certificate to Bloomie's. I figured the two were about equivalent, what do you think?"

"I think you're nuts," Jayne laughed. "Now, tell me what you said to those parasites?"

"I told them I had spent my day answering questions, and I was sure they could understand if didn't have the desire to answer any more."

"And?"

"And what? They left me alone if that's what you're asking. I hightailed it out of there, and headed to your office."

"Good. When we get to the restaurant, I want to hear all of the details of the day, and for that matter, I want to hear about the whole trial so far. You know, you still haven't told me much about the fraud trial either. I'm really sorry I couldn't go out with you that night between the two trials, what did you do anyway?"

Connie blushed deeply. "I relieved some tension, let's just leave it at that," she said, the embarrassment evident in her voice and mannerisms.

"First time since Stuart died?"

"Was killed," Connie corrected her friend in an attempt to avoid answering. When Jayne didn't speak again, Connie lied, "Yes, it was."

Connie brought Jayne up-to-date over dinner, slowly at first but then with a bit more conviction. Jayne leaned in, her palms holding up her chin.

Whatever the cause of Jayne's silence, it only served to gnaw at Connie. Did Jayne still not believe that Joseppe was guilty? It sure seemed like Joseppe committed the murder, but there really was no direct proof. What if he didn't?

Jayne lived in the exact opposite direction from the restaurant as Connie, so they took separate cabs. As Connie rode home, she thought about other potential killers. Moran was the one Jayne suspected, Connie knew that. And then there was Mo Buell, he was no angel either. Who knows, Connie thought, maybe someone related to Stuart's lobbying efforts for the purveyors of cancer did him in.

The cab dropped Connie off in front of her apartment

building. She decided to take the steps to walk off a bit of her dinner. As she slowly made her way up the brightly lit stairwell, Connie thought about Moran. Why hadn't she told Stuart about him? None of his business that's why. And it was none of Clifton's business either.

Chapter Forty-Nine

Mark Clifton looked like hell when Jack Christian knocked on his door. "How's the trial going, Mark?" Christian asked without emotion.

"Okay," Mark said, flashing a smile. "I think we've got a good day coming up. I, I'm just preparing some last-minute testimony for a witness."

"Kind of late for that, isn't it?"

"New evidence," Mark smiled before looking down dismissively.

Christian sighed heavily and turned slowly before leaving. He continued down the hall to the elevator which he took to the street.

"Taxi!," the senior partner called out as he bolted out of the door, "taxi!"

Jack Christian thanked the receptionist who led him into Judge Dell's chambers.

"Wihelmina," Christian said warmly. "How have you been?"

"Wonderful, Jack, and you?"

"Equally as fine, thanks for asking. Listen, I know you're in the middle of the Giavonni murder trial, so I won't keep you long. This is actually a strange thing. I," Christian paused for effect, "I am a bit concerned about my partner Mr. Clifton. He's been a bit off-kilter lately. I haven't been at trial. How has he been? Has he done anything out of the ordinary?"

Judge Dell sat back in her chair and wrinkled her nose as she gave the matter some thought. "I'm trying to remember if anything happened during jury selection. Nothing happened out of the ordinary yesterday. The Parker woman testified, and Clifton crossed. No, nothing I can think of."

"Good. I am a bit concerned though. I can't put my finger on it, but I feel like he's getting desperate. Do me a favor, Willie, keep him on a short leash, please. Don't let him do anything that he'll later regret. I don't want him to bring disrepute to the firm. We've worked so hard to build our reputation."

"I hear you, Jack. I'll try to keep an eye on him for you. But so far, there's been nothing to worry about."

"Thanks, Willie, you're a gem."

Chapter Fifty

Gary Schofield pushed his way past the throng of workingmen, and knocked on general manager McGee's door. He could tell by the look on McGee's face that the overseer of the circus was about to fire him. But Gary decided not to make it easy on the little, ruddy-faced Irishman. Besides, Gary was just dying to know what the offense was.

"Gary," McGee greeted him, "please come into the trailer and shut the door." He motioned to a chair. "Please sit down."

It was obvious that McGee had done this, oh, a few thousand times or so before. He began speaking again even before Gary had settled into the metal chair with the frozen wheels. "Gary, I'm afraid I'm going to have to let you go." McGee opened his desk drawer as he spoke, and pulled out an envelope which he handed to Gary. "Here's your pay including today. You'll need to get your stuff, and clear out of the train this morning. Sorry."

"Listen, Mr. McGee," Gary began with a mix of sarcasm and respect. "It's not the end of my life. I'll find gainful employment somewhere. But I'd like to know why you're letting me go."

McGee looked a bit embarrassed. He leaned over and spoke in a hushed tone. "You know how offices have politics? Well so do circus units. Big time. Mora is the queen. She told me that there have been complaints that you've been, I dunno, sorta skulking around near the trailers. Just sorta hanging out a bit too much."

Gary nodded his head, accepted the envelope, thanked McGee, and headed back to the train to get his belongings. He threw his stuff into his duffle bag, and headed out the door, and toward the exit to the arena.

The Charlotte Civic Arena was modern and clean. It had very few nooks and crannies in which to hide. Gary headed out.

The disgusted private investigator got himself a cup of coffee and a danish at the local Denny's, and pondered his next move. Without a clue, he got back in his rented Ford, and headed back towards the arena.

As Gary approached the arena he saw two busloads of people pulling up. He checked his watch. It was almost noon, fully ninety minutes before the day's first show. The people seemed too early to be your typical patrons. Gary drove in for a closer look. As he glanced through the windows of the bus, he saw that many of the riders were carrying placards, though he couldn't see what was written on them. Many of the people had long hair, and their faces looked stern and purposeful. Gary doubted the placards read, "Go Team!"

The buses rolled to a halt near the front entrance to the building. The people, mostly in their teens and twenties, with a smattering of older folks, made their way onto the parking lot, signs in tow. Gary inched closer. It was an animal rights protest. Gary saw the first sign up close. It read, "World's Cruelest Show, Stone the Circus." The next one said, "Mora is Immoral." There were dozens more like the first two, some more crudely made than others, but the message was the same in each case.

Gary shook his head. Don't these people have anything better to do? Gary was no liberal. Far from it. But hell, he thought, people are starving in Africa, homeless in our cities, and killing each other in record number, and all these people can worry about is the way the circus might or might not treat its animals.

Gary got out of the car. He sauntered over to the group. He introduced himself as a reporter for the local newspaper, and asked if he could join the march. Needless to say, he was warmly greeted by the publicity hounds.

The activists were a ragtag group from a small, local offshoot of a national organization. Of the dozen or so demonstrators, three stood out. The leader was a gangly looking guy in his young thirties with a zeal in his eyes that Gary felt to be way too strong, too real to be safe. And then there was the guy with a limp. Why the hell would someone who couldn't even walk risk hurting themselves for something as inane as this? Finally, there was the babe. My God, she was gorgeous. Five seven or eight, curly brown hair, huge green eyes, and absolutely stuffed into a short sleeve sweater that most certainly did justice to her healthy chest.

The group was poorly organized, and, to hear them tell it, underfunded. Gary kept up a steady banter, glancing at the babe, whose name was Rikki, between his surveillance of the gates for any sign of Moran.

After a little while, patrons began to arrive. Some of the activists marched and chanted, while others tried to hand out leaflets. The majority of people ignored them, though Gary watched with bemusement as the more patient parents tried to explain to their toddlers exactly what it was the activists were protesting.

Gary saw McGee peek through the front doors of the

arena. Thinking it would be best to avoid an unpleasant scene, Gary swung behind the group and hid his face.

Before long the customers for the day's first show had passed the picket line and all was quiet. Gary momentarily forgot his little newspaper reporter's ruse, and lost his focus. The tall, rabid, so-called leader began pestering Gary about getting some favorable coverage. Gary was just about to tell him to go screw himself when he remembered what was going on. Gary made some vague promises about talking to his editors, but said it would have to get a bit more exciting to arouse anything more than a passing interest from them. Nevertheless, he agreed to stay on for a little while longer, maybe one or two more shows, to see what materialized. He needed some excuse to hang around, but this was pretty lame.

Gary took his leave for a short while, but sat in his rental car at the end of the main entrance to the arena. As he watched the demonstrators, his eyes came unglued from Rikki long enough to note that the limper was gone. Good thing, Gary thought. If that guy needed medical attention, the circus folks would have come out and I would have been running again.

Chapter Fifty-One

Donald Lubins wasn't surprised. Not really. McFerrin had been really spooked when he first saw Lubins, but Lubins knew the old man would help.

Lubins had quickly realized he had to get into the arena, his stint as an animal rights activist doing little to help him find Moran. So the former roustabout snuck into the Civic Arena through a side door where the concessionaires were unloading their wares. Lubins made his way out back and waited between the building and the train until he had spotted McFerrin. After nearly turning white, McFerrin had recovered and hugged Lubins, an act that so embarrassed Lubins that he fell silent. Eventually, Lubins brought McFerrin up-to-date on what needed to be done, and the old man agreed, albeit reluctantly, to help.

Once enlisted, McFerrin attacked his responsibilities. He found Lubins leaning against a tree, and began excitedly explaining how he had snuck right up to Mora's trailer and put his ear against the side. He could hear Moran speaking and guessed he was on the phone because Mora wasn't in the trailer.

Lubins tried to be patient. It was shortly after 10:30 and the performers would soon be returning from the evening performance. Lubins knew he needed to scoot but he wanted to learn what McFerrin had overheard.

It turned out to be worthless. The old man said Moran

was saying things like "just you wait, I'll show you I'm better than he was," and "I make the rules." Nothing that McFerrin overheard made any sense to Lubins. Maybe it would make sense to Mark, though.

Trying not to look too let down, Lubins thanked McFerrin, and headed away from the train. It was time to head for a fast-food joint, or an all-night eatery, to get a cup of coffee and think in private.

Lubins walked into the Denny's near the arena and sat at the counter. He ordered a cup of coffee and a piece of pound cake. He rubbed his temples gently and thought about whether to call Mark. He knew the lawyer was in the middle of the trial. He also knew that the lawyer probably thought that he was dead. Finally, he knew that the information he had to pass on about Moran's phone conversation was likely not to be of much help.

There were two issues. First, Lubins didn't want to do anything to throw Mark off or upset his preparation. True, the lawyer would probably be happy to learn that Lubins was alive if he had given Lubins' apparent death a second thought, which Lubins doubted, but in any event it would disrupt the lawyer's focus. Second, Lubins wasn't sure he was ready to give up his opportunity for a fresh start, McFerrin notwithstanding.

As Lubins pondered his options, some guy with a little ponytail pulled up the stool next to Lubins and sat down. Now why the hell did he have to do that, thought Lubins. There are plenty of empty stools in the place, what's so special about the one next to me?

"You Donald Lubins?" the guy asked.

Lubins tried to remain calm. The guy didn't seem too menacing. "Who wants to know?"

"Seems to me, that's an irrelevant question. Either you are or you're not. But don't worry, I'm a friend."

The guy knew who he was, so it was an irrelevant question. "Yeah," replied Lubins, "that's me."

"Gary Schofield. Mark Clifton's P.I. I saw you with the animal rights folks," Gary extended his hand.

Lubins shook hands with Gary. "Nice to meet you. And, by the way, thanks for finding my ex-wife."

Gary waved him off. "It was nothing. Listen," he continued, "it's late, and we don't have much time. Look, I mean no disrespect, and I think what you're trying to do to help Mark is very cool, but you're in way over your head. I think you should leave."

"I understand your concerns, Mr. Schofield, and I'll stay out of your way. But I can't leave. I've gotta try to finish this out."

Gary shifted in his seat and stuck his tongue into his cheek real hard, causing it to look momentarily deformed. Then he sighed deeply, releasing his tongue and beginning to speak all at the same time. The result was something like a steam engine hissing, and it caught Lubins' attention.

"Listen, Donald, this isn't a request, it's a demand. And it don't come from me. It comes from Mark. I'm sorry, but he wants you out of here."

Lubins sat at the counter for nearly four-and-a-half hours after Gary left. First he thought about returning to Dayton, but where would that get him? Then, he thought about ignoring Gary's obnoxious "demand" and staying on, but that was going to prove fruitless pretty soon anyway. So he did what was becoming increasingly natural. He decided to travel.

Connie Parker was at the center of this whole crazy mess. Lubins had never met her. No better time than the present.

Time was becoming more and more critical. Lubins

bit his lower lip as he thought. Finally, he decided he had no choice. For the first time in years, he rented a car.

It was late in the afternoon, and the streets of Capitol Hill were crowded with the ultra self-important daytime residents of Washington, D.C. as Donald Lubins made his way up to Connie Parker's office. As it turned out, it wasn't particularly difficult to find Connie's office, even for a novice investigator like Lubins. The phone number and the address were listed.

As Lubins loitered in the hallway of the glass, marble, and chrome, four-story building, office workers streamed out like lemmings heading for the cliff. No one gave him a moment's notice. He ambled up to the hall just outside the reception area, afraid to walk in and ask for Connie, but not wanting to miss her just the same. As he stood, eyes downcast, picking at the dry skin at the corner of his mouth, the double glass door to the consulting office opened. Two women strode out confidently, sharing a laugh, as the receptionist called after them, "goodnight, Connie." Both women said "goodnight" in reply.

Lubins followed the women, trying his damnedest not to limp too noticeably. They entered a small, but noisy, Chinese restaurant three blocks away. Once during the walk one of the women whirled around and Lubins stiffened, afraid he had been discovered, but she swung forward again just as quickly and the two kept walking. Lubins stumbled, his stump throbbing, as the hostess asked him how many were in his party, but the minor *faux pas* proved to be fortuitous since it gave the women a chance to be seated. Lubins managed to get himself seated two tables away.

The table between Lubins and his quarry was inhabitated by an elderly couple oblivious to Lubins' constant leaning, so he was able to pick up snippets from the conversation. The one item he couldn't pick up, was which of the two women was Connie.

After a dinner of mediocre shrimp lo mein, Lubins limped after the women as they departed the restaurant. He watched in horror as they each hailed separate cabs. Then his job got easy. The tall slender one, the more attractive of the two, got in a cab first, and there were no other taxis in sight. Nothing he could do. As the second woman hailed a taxi for herself, Lubins spotted a cruising cab which he waved down.

"Please follow that cab. I need to speak to that woman. She was just having dinner with my ex-girlfriend."

"Whatever you say, Mac."

Lubins' driver followed at a respectable distance stopping three townhouses away from the immense townhouse off Connecticut Avenue where the first cabbie stopped.

Lubins waited until the woman was safely in her house. Then he began to make his way over toward her window. The night was cool and crystal clear. The moon was bright. So bright in fact, that Lubins cast a shadow as he tried to steal over toward the appropriate townhouse. Another problem facing Lubins was that the humidity was unusually low for Washington and sound was carrying crisply through the still, night air.

Lubins scratched his head and let out a brief snort. Townhouses were a pain to try to spy into. No sides. Lubins tiptoed in his odd, slightly crippled way to the end of the block, counting the homes as he went. The one he was interested in was all brick, with dark grey shutters. There were four other townhouses between it and the end of the block.

Lubins made his way into the backyard of the first home. He grimaced as he momentarily lost his footing on a tiny chip broken off from a piece of flagstone. Righting himself, Lubins slithered into the second backyard. There, he was faced with a quandary. A six-foot-high dark brown, wooden fence separated houses number two and number three. Lubins thought about scaling the fence, then realized that it had probably been erected by the owner of the third house, therefore, it probably separated backyard number three from number four as well.

Making his way to the back end of the fence, Lubins held his breath as he peered around the obstacle. There was an alley way that separated the backyards from unattached garages that apparently belonged to each home. The ill lit passageway appeared to give Lubins an unimpeded shot straight through to the fifth backyard, the one to which he needed to gain access.

Lubins dragged his left foot as fast as he could into the alley and past the third and fourth yards. Once behind the house he was looking for, Lubins stopped momentarily to catch his breath and get his coordinates straight in his mind.

As he approached the back window, Lubins halted his movement every few steps to make certain that all was quiet, and that he hadn't been discovered. Finally, he was able to stand on his tiptoes, all eight of them, and peer in through the back window. His view was of the family room, or den. The room was cast in an eerie red light from a bulb which looked vaguely like it was composed of some type of liquid gel, and which was enclosed in a jagged-edged, modern glass fixture.

The woman whom Lubins had followed sat alone in the room, stretched out on a black leather sofa, her feet propped up on a matching black leather ottoman. The furniture was in stark contrast to a plush white area rug which covered two-thirds of the floor space in the room. The woman wore no shoes, and from the look of the rug, neither did any of her guests when they were in this room.

Lubins glanced toward the walls and could barely make out the photographs hanging in the room. He could tell that the framed pictures were in black and white, and that they seemed to be business pictures, not personal in nature.

Lubins stiffened as the woman picked up the phone. He pressed closer to the window which was shut tight to block out the cool evening. When she completed the task of dialing the number, the woman leaned over, picked up what appeared to be a small tape recorder, depressed a button, and then, in rapid sequence, put her ear to the receiver, and then released her finger and placed the recorder next to the mouthpiece.

Squinting and straining to see and hear, Lubins could barely make out what sounded like music. At first, it seemed to be a show tune of some sort. Then Lubins saw the woman fiddle with a knob on the recorder and the music got louder. Lubins hadn't watched television for a long time, but the music was unmistakably the theme song from *Jeopardy*.

Lubins shook his head, clueless about the bizarre solo being performed in the equally bizarre crimson setting. As the music ended, the woman ever so gently placed the receiver back in the cradle, jumped up from the sofa, pumped her fist in the air and began chanting, like she was a fan at a college football game: "I'm number one! I'm number one!"

Pushing away from the window, Lubins dragged his crippled foot behind him as he zigzagged out of the backyard and into the alley. He forced himself to run in his own, odd gait until he was back on the street where he allowed himself to slow to a fast walk, his cadence all wrong. Catching his breath, Lubins headed back toward Connecticut Avenue. He needed to catch a cab.

Chapter Fifty-Two

Mark Clifton sat at the counsel's table listening to the morning's testimony. He fidgeted, tugged at the corner of his mouth, and ran his fingers through his hair. He was shifting about in his seat so much that Peter finally told him to sit still. He tried to conjure up an appropriate Beatles' song to mollify himself with while he waited but not even John, Paul, George, and Ringo could help him now.

After he got over his shock at seeing Donald Lubins standing at his door at two in the morning, Mark had listened intently to his former house guest's story. None of it made sense, however, and it wasn't until Carol fished out the old *Gazette* story that the three of them began piecing it together.

Connie Parker was even less happy than Mark about being woken up in the middle of the night. And even more skeptical about what she was hearing. Hell, it was four a.m., and the defense lawyer was trying to get her to believe some outlandish tale.

Somehow, Mark got Connie to agree to show up in court at nine and to make certain Jayne was with her. She had agreed, but until Mark actually saw the two women walk through the door together at ten after nine, he wasn't at all certain if Connie had said okay because she meant it, or because she wanted to go back to sleep.

Whatever, there they sat. And Mark had not a single clue as to what he intended to do with them.

Nothing of major consequence occurred during the remainder of the prosecution's case. A toxicologist testified, as did two other witnesses who placed Katcavage and Giavonni at the party together toasting the holiday season. Finally, two of Stuart's closest friends and associates, both of whom were also former customers of Joseppe's, testified as to the investigation which Stuart had launched, and the rancor between Stuart and the defendant.

Evans had succeeded in planting a motive, and he painted the victim in an incredibly positive and sympathetic light. The jury seemed to be looking favorably upon the prosecution's case as Judge Dell indicated that the lunch recess was forthcoming.

Evans told the judge that the prosecution had two more witnesses to call in the afternoon, both of whom would be on the stand a short time. Then it would be time for the defense to present its case. As Judge Dell cleared up a few procedural items with Evans, Mark glanced through his notes, his foot tapping furiously all the while.

Mark, Peter Long, and Joseppe grabbed a sandwich and some coffee at a lunch shop two blocks from the courthouse. The walk felt good. They discussed the morning's testimony in detail. Mark assured Joseppe that nothing of consequence had occurred.

The afternoon session began much as the morning had concluded, with the jury struggling to stay awake, but clearly clinging to the belief that there was no other explanation than that Joseppe had panicked and done in Stuart Katcavage.

At 2:45 Evans rested for the prosecution. He wore a smug grin as he headed for the counsel's table, but Mark couldn't tell if it was a special one stored up for moments like this, or if it was the usual one the asshole wore when he was feeling particularly good about his loathsome self.

Mark tried to remember if he'd been like Evans when he was on the other side of the table. He doubted it, though he'd never really thought about it before. He promised himself that when the trial was over, he'd look up some of his old adversaries and ask them. He wasn't totally sure he wanted the answer.

Mark slowly rose. He looked first at the jury then at Judge Dell. "Ladies and gentleman of the jury, you've heard testimony for the better part of two days aimed at proving that my client, Joseppe Giavonni, is a murderer. However well-intentioned the prosecution is in this case—and I believe they are well-intentioned—the fact remains that they have a flimsy case, built on conjecture, innuendo, and guesswork. There is a so-so motive, no direct evidence, and a veritable patchwork quilt of ideas thrown together in a certain light to make things look bleak for Mr. Giavonni. But when a house is built of cards it can easily fall apart. The prosecution's house is an example of that. But in their case, it's even more extreme because we just found out about a wild card that will bring the rest of the house tumbling down. I doubt the prosecution is aware of what we learned in the last twenty-four hours.

"At least I, that is, we, the defendant's team, are certain that if the prosecution knew about this they would have brought it to our attention, since it is not only probative of the issue of the defendant's lack of guilt, but, quite likely, dispositive of that issue." Mark studied the jury, making eye contact with as many of them as possible as he spoke. He knew he was living on borrowed time. Dell was usually pretty lenient in allowing lawyers to pontificate, but this was pushing it.

Mark continued, "Mr. Evans will likely object to the admissibility of what we are about to—"

"Actually, your honor," Evans said, as he got to his feet, "I object to Mr. Clifton being given a second chance to give an opening statement, and I object to his characterization of what I might object to when it's so obviously nothing more than mere speculation on his part."

"Sustained. Mr. Clifton, get to the point and bring on your witness. We can hardly wait."

"Thank you, your Honor. The defense calls Ms. Jayne Procter."

"May we approach, your Honor," Evans wailed, jumping to his feet.

Judge Dell nodded and motioned the lawyers forward. Evans began to speak before they even reached the bench. "She's not on the witness list, your Honor, this is an unfair surprise. He didn't even tell me about her this morning."

"Your Honor, with all due respect, Mr. Evans is right that I didn't tell him about Ms. Procter this morning, but that is because I didn't know until about an hour ago that she would be testifying. One of my investigators came up with some new evidence last night and this morning and we've been trying to piece it together even as the trial has progressed."

"Mr. Clifton," the judge said, as she narrowed her eyes, "what is the nature of Ms. Procter's testimony?"

"Your Honor, that's just it, I'm not exactly sure myself."

"Let me get this straight, Mr. Clifton. You just called a

surprise witness based on newly discovered evidence, and you have no idea as to what she is testifying about?"

"I didn't say I had no idea. I said I wasn't exactly sure. Look, your Honor, I can assure you, I'm no happier than you are about this, but this woman is involved in this case and I'm just now beginning to sort out how. If you let me move forward, I assure you, I'll go slowly, and you can keep me on a tight rein, okay?"

"Very well. This should be quite interesting. Let's get on with it."

Mark began to elicit the usual testimony from Jayne concerning her name and background. All the while, visions of Professor Andersen, Trial Practice 101, kept flashing through his brain. "Remember future trial lawyers of America, the cardinal rule: Never ask a question that you don't know the answer to!"

Mark flexed his knees slightly and put his hands together. Never ask a question . . .

He took a short breath, "Ms. Procter, how long have you known Connie Parker?"

"Seven, maybe eight years."

"You consider her a good friend?"

"We've gotten closer since Stuart died."

"Why is that?"

"She needed a friend, that's all."

"And you were there for her?"

"I'd like to think so."

Mark turned around and faced the gallery. Connie was sitting impassively in the second row, directly behind Carol. Neither face registered an emotion as the lawyer spun around, hands clasped tightly together.

"Do you know why I called you to the stand?"

"I assume to talk about the letter."

Mark blanched. Professor Andersen, he thought, I'll always listen in the future, just get me out of this!

"What letter might that be, Ms. Procter?"

"The one which Connie dropped at dinner one night which I gave to your partner, Mr. Christian."

"And what was the essence of that letter? Why did you give it to Mr. Christian?" Mark wanted to add, "that asshole," but held back.

"I object, your Honor. Best evidence rule requires the letter if it exists so we can see it. Also, there's a hearsay problem setting up."

"I'll wait on the hearsay till we get to it. Mr. Clifton, under the best evidence rule, if the defense plans to rely on the letter which is so clearly within your possession, you need to produce it."

"Thank you, your Honor. We don't have the letter. I will stay away from the actual contents of the document itself."

Judge Dell shook her head and made a nasty face at Mark, one the jury was sure to see.

"Was this a personal letter?"

"Yes."

"Did Connie share many of her personal secrets or concerns with you?"

"Some, sure. I told you, we've gotten to be quite close."

"Did the letter upset her?"

Evans stood, thought about objecting, and then took his seat.

"Yes, though not enough to go to the cops about it."

"Did she tell you why she didn't want to go to the cops?"

"Yes. Connie told me that her life was already too much a part of the public eye. The *Gazette* article really blew her privacy, and it touched off a feud with her father. So she just didn't want anyone butting into her private life, even if it meant putting up with the letters and the calls."

"What calls?"

"The ones from Moran, the ones from Buell, and the ones from the nut who keeps playing the *Jeopardy* music."

"Would it surprise you to know, Ms. Procter," Mark said with a wicked grin, "that Ms. Parker specifically told me this morning that she never told you or anyone else about the *Jeopardy* calls?"

"She's under a lot of pressure, Mr. Clifton, she obviously forgot."

"The pressure didn't work on Stuart Katcavage did it, Ms. Procter?"

"Excuse me?"

"Strike that, please. Ms. Procter, who is Allan McQuade?"

"Allan is a dear friend who is a lobbyist for the banking industry."

"Good lobbyist?"

"Far as I know."

"Where did the *Gazette* rank him this year?"

"He didn't make it into the listing."

"How about last year?"

"I can't remember."

"He was third, Ms. Procter, just ahead of you. What happened to Mr. McQuade?"

"He had a nervous breakdown."

"Lot of pressure on him?"

"Could be, how would I know?"

Mark turned toward the jury, smiled and paused. Then he whirled around and faced the witness.

"Last year's article in *The Gazette* said McQuade was a veteran of the Vietnam conflict. He told me that one of his problems over the past year was that someone kept calling him and playing a tape of a helicopter hovering, or landing. Said it reminded him of Vietnam, and it started to cause him to have flashbacks. Seems eerily coincidental doesn't it, Ms. Procter?"

"I have no idea."

"What was your major, Ms. Procter?"

"Excuse me?"

"Your major, you know your course of study in college?"

"Why is that any of your business?"

"Getting a bit testy?"

"Mr. Clifton," cut in Judge Dell, "stop badgering the witness."

"Yes, your Honor." Then, turning to the witness, "What about Mr. Katcavage?"

"What about him?"

"Stuart was the toughest one to crack wasn't he?"

"You said something about that before, but I haven't the slightest idea of what you are talking about."

"You knew Stuart had a drinking problem, didn't you?"

"It was no secret."

"So you called him and played public service announcements for alcohol rehab programs, right?"

Jayne started to respond, then stopped. She smiled just slightly, threw her head back, and then snapped to attention. Her eyes bore through Mark's, burning holes right into his brain. She set her jaw, placed her hands on her thighs, and spoke in a tight, but sure, voice.

"Mr. Clifton, you have an overactive imagination."

"To the contrary, Ms. Procter. If I had even a decent imagination I would have figured out your game a long time ago. Instead, I was fixated on all the wrong people, thinking all the wrong thoughts. All I had to do was think about poor little underappreciated you. You know, I never looked at the *Gazette* article for more than a second. Bad lawyering, don't you think?" Mark didn't wait for an answer. He strode purposefully over toward Jayne, leaned against the wooden divider which separated the witness from the rest of the courtroom, and glared into Jayne's eyes. "It must be difficult being underappreciated when you know you're the best, isn't it, Ms. Procter?"

"You'd have to ask somebody else, Mr. Clifton," Jayne answered, her eyes vacant.

"Why is that, Ms. Procter, don't you consider yourself number one, the best lobbyist in town?"

"What I consider myself is irrelevant."

"What is relevant, Ms. Procter?"

"What others say, the magazines, the clients."

"Well they'll have to rank you number one now, won't they, you've destroyed the competition, Ms. Procter. Three cheers for you!"

Jayne momentarily stared off toward the left side of the courtroom, then regained her focus and let her eyes come to rest directly on Mark. With a mixture of venom and downright pleasure she sneered and smiled all at the same time.

"Stuart Katcavage was ranked number one, but he was a drunk," she said measuring her words like they were ingredients for a cake. "It was a total farce. Connie was ranked number two, but she's such a slut." Jayne looked out at the gallery. "Sorry, hon," she shrugged. "And Allan, well he's a helluva nice guy, but he's not half the lobbyist I am. You see, I never had the personality trait, you know that one identifying feature that the yo-yo's at *The Gazette* are always looking for. So, I hired a P.R. person, but she was for shit. So, I had to start taking people down, it was as simple as that."

Mark backed away. Jayne seemed quite pleased with herself, almost smug. Two of the women on the jury appeared stunned, one seemed embarrassed. The foreman grimaced.

Mark slowly ran his hand through his hair, pausing at the back to scratch momentarily and buy himself some time to think. Jayne had certainly confessed to something, although Mark wasn't quite sure what. She hadn't come right out and said she had killed Stuart, but the implication was clear. Should he press her, and try to go in for the kill? Or would he be providing her with a chance for rehabilitation? What would Evans do?

Mark crossed in front of the jury and glanced up at Jayne. She appeared feisty, ready to do battle.

"Tough when you do a standout job, yet don't get recognized, isn't it?"

"You asked me that already, Mr. Clifton," Jayne snapped. "The fact of the matter is it's okay if the others are deserving. It's only a problem if they aren't."

"Then you do whatever it takes to get them out of the way?"

"Well no, not whatever it takes. I mean trying to freak them with some tapes over the phone is hardly what I would consider a capital crime. Wrong perhaps, but not the end of the world."

"What about Stuart?"

"He was different," Jayne stared intently at Mark.

The lawyer stared back. "Oh, in what way?"

"Tough. Very tough. Wouldn't succumb. I mean, cyanide is not my favorite modus operandi, but he wouldn't give in, wouldn't break down. I had no other choice."

The courtroom was washed in silence. Jayne's last words hung in the air like humidity on an August afternoon. Mark did nothing for close to a minute, just stared blankly at the jury. Finally, he turned and looked at Judge Dell.

"No further questions, your Honor."

Evans didn't even bother to stand as he advised the court that he had no questions. Mark dispensed with his closing argument, and rested his case. Just like that, the murder trial of Joseppe Giavonni was over.

Chapter Fifty-Three

Donald Lubins picked at the styrofoam cup which, up until that moment, had housed his rather rancid-tasting coffee. He pawed at the ground with his damaged foot, gently so as not to cause pain, but firmly enough to remind himself that he still had feeling in the remaining toes.

To his left sat an Hispanic family, six kids with mom pregnant yet again. To his right sat an elderly black woman with a terribly worn denim suitcase bulging at the partially destroyed, rusted zipper.

Lubins stood quickly from the hard plastic seat when the announcement came that the bus to Cleveland had arrived in the station and was now taking passengers. He slung his crisp denim bag over his shoulder, dragged the mangled appendage which passed for his left foot behind him, and made his way over to the front of the gleaming Greyhound.

The driver nodded to Lubins, punched his ticket, and looked ahead to the next boarding passenger. Lubins shuffled toward the back where he found a totally unoccupied seat. Passing on the opportunity to hoist his bag into the overhead, Lubins plopped down on the seat with his denim companion firmly ensconced under his shoulder. He made a big production of appearing to be sifting through the bag each time a potential seat mate strode down the aisle until the doors were closed and he was left to sit alone. Knowing he stood the risk of someone joining him at any moment, Lubins kept the bag next to him as the bus pulled away.

The trip from D.C. to Cleveland was going to last fourteen hours. Lubins settled in and tried to sleep, but it was not to be.

As the sun set and the bus headed west on another sceneless highway polka-dotted with green destination signs, Lubins' mind began to wander. He thought about how it had all been sitting there for him to grab—the opportunity for a fresh start. No adoption, no divorce. No affair, no firing. It was when he got to the no kids part that he started having some trouble. That, and the thought of deserting Mark and Joseppe, two people who had helped him when they could just as easily have turned away.

Lubins smiled, and it was a grin that was full of irony. Irony for the way things sometimes work out in a life, for the chances that keep on appearing. Irony for the fact that his own clumsiness, something that had previously bothered him so, might well have saved his life by causing him to lose his footing.

It was ironic too that the trials, both of which had ended in acquittals, ended up having a positive impact on Joseppe's career. According to Mark, the barber had a two-week waiting list for appointments.

And Moran, well, the cops nailed him for assaulting Connie Parker. To hear the gossip columnists tell it, Moran had damn near strangled her before Schofield and three D.C. cops saved her. Mark said it was close, but not that close.

As for Mark, the news was good. He had told Donald that he and Carol left the firm and got engaged. But Mark was a bit freaked by the disappearance of his associate, Peter Long. The papers were full of the story, and how it had cast a pall over Jack Christian's awards dinner.

Lubins squirmed throughout the night. He hadn't spoken to Julie since leaving for the circus, thus the ticket to Cleveland. Lubins figured he would call his ex-wife from Cleveland, and if she was amenable, he could make it to Dayton in a heartbeat. If she wasn't available, or didn't want to let him stay, even for a night, he thought maybe he could try to establish something for himself in Cleveland. A base of operations so to speak.

With a job and a few bucks, Lubins figured he could truly get back on his feet again, maybe get a place not too far from the kids and maybe put together some semblance of a life. Dayton was too small for him to try to settle there, and Washington was simply too far from the kids. What the hell, Lubins thought, as he squinted at the brilliant glowing sun rising over the blacktop. Yeah, he smiled, what the hell. Cleveland was just as good a place as any, maybe better than most for his purposes. It was kind of nice too, but strange, to be looking at things so differently.

Lubins smiled and sat up in the seat, stretching his arms overhead and yawning. He took a deep breath, and didn't allow the stale mix of body odor and gasoline fumes to affect him. Cleveland was going to be okay, and the reason was clear and simple. For the first time in what seemed like forever, Lubins realized, he was looking for a place to live, not a place to hide.

About the Author

Bob Fleshner is the President of Incenter Strategies, a Washington, D.C. based consulting firm specializing in new business development. Previously, he spent nearly nine years as an executive with Ringling Bros. Barnum & Bailey Circus. He lives in Bethesda, Maryland with his wife, Phyllis, and their two children, Michelle and Daniel.

To order additional copies of *A Place to Hide*,
or for further information, please contact
O&W Publishing Co., Inc.
at 1-800-4WILBUR.